By Shari Low

The Story of Our Life
A Life Without You
The Other Wives' Club
With or Without You
This is Me

Winter Day series

One Day in Winter
Another Day in Winter
The Last Day of Winter

Non-Fiction

Because Mummy Said So

ONE DAY
IN
WINTER

Shari Low

HEAD
ZEUS

First published in the UK in 2019 by Head of Zeus Ltd

9 7 5 3 1 2 4 6 8

A catalogue record for this book is available from
the British Library.

ISBN (PBO): 9781789540574
ISBN (E): 9781786699008

Typeset by Divaddict Publishing Solutions Ltd

Printed and bound in Great Britain by
CPI Group (UK) Ltd, Croydon CR0 4YY

Head of Zeus Ltd
First Floor East
5–8 Hardwick Street
London EC1R 4RG

WWW.HEADOFZEUS.COM

To John, Callan & Brad
Everything, Always...

Once Upon A Time There Was...

Lila Anderson – 29, social media darling, selfie addict. Girlfriend of trendy menswear boutique owner Cammy Jones and mistress to heart surgeon Ken Manson.

Jack Anderson – 54, Lila's enigmatic father and cheque book.

Louise Anderson – 51, Lila's mother. Jack's patient, understanding and hopelessly devoted wife.

Caro Anderson – 32, teacher, single, on a mission to find the father who walked out on her and her mother and disappeared without a trace.

Yvonne Anderson – 54, Caro's mum, abandoned by Caro's father.

Todd Smith – 32, Caro's cousin, provider of moral

support, hair stylist extraordinaire, and son of Auntie Pearl and Uncle Bob now living in Spain.

Jared Bock – 29, Todd's Canadian fiancé.

Bernadette Manson – 50s, devoted nurse at Glasgow Central A & E, loving mum, Kenneth Manson's long-suffering wife.

Kenneth Manson – 52, eminent cardiac surgeon, controlling husband, cheating arse who has had a 7-year affair with Lila.

Nina and Stuart – 29 and 22, Kenneth and Bernadette's adult children.

Sarah Delaney – 50s, Bernadette's lifelong friend, found late-life love again with Piers on a Mediterranean cruise, now wants to help Bernadette find happiness.

Cammy Jones – 41, gym-god, owner of hipster menswear boutique, CAMDEN, Lila's boyfriend.

Josie Cairney – late 60s, Cammy's friend of many years, self-appointed surrogate aunt, proposal saboteur.

Val Murray – 50s, Josie's best pal and partner in crime.

A middle-aged Scottish mother with a huge heart and a sharp tongue.

Mel Cairney – the unrequited love of Cammy's life, now happily married to Josie's son Michael and living in Italy.

Digby Donnelly – assistant manager at Cammy's menswear store, CAMDEN.

Jen Collins – Cammy's friend and owner of the shop next door, Sun, Sea, Ski.

With Appearances From...

Marge – discreet PA to Dr Kenneth Manson.

Fred Johnson – Lila's boss.

Suze – owner of Pluckers, trendy hair and beauty salon, boss of Rod, Daisy and Kylie.

Jean-Pascal – incredibly handsome French football player.

Prologue

Saturday, 23rd December
One minute past midnight

It was nothing like a scene from Grey's Anatomy.

You know, when alarms sound, and pagers go off, and the model-esque doctor who was having sex with her unfeasibly gorgeous boss in the on-call room leaps to her feet, all tousled hair and bee-stung lips, pulls on her scrubs, and charges to the rescue, not even stopping to adjust her bra before she saves the day.

Nothing like that at all.

If this were a TV drama, the writers would be told to get back to the drawing board, add a bit of excitement, a touch of jeopardy, and perhaps some lascivious underwear, before bringing the scene back to the director.

Because this was... understated.

Just a person. Lying on a bed. In a hospital room. Breathing.

There was no time to say goodbye. No time for regrets or recriminations. No time to wait until the loved ones had gathered by the bed to bid them farewell.

They didn't know that somewhere out there a heart had just been crushed by the weight of broken promises. Or that someone else sighed with relief as they walked away from the past. Or that someone's plans for a new life had turned to dust. Or that a very unexpected love was pulling two people together.

They didn't know that the person they loved most in the world wouldn't make it in time. Maybe wouldn't make it at all.

They didn't know that a love had died, that when it came right down to it, the only love that mattered was the one that endured, that stuck, that was meant to be.

Just a person. Lying on a bed. In a hospital room. Breathing.

Just a heart, beating.

And then it stopped.

The day before…
Friday 22nd December
8 a.m. – 10 a.m.

I

Caro

'No, please, you go first.' The elderly man smiled gratefully, as the young blonde woman held the train door open for him. He'd read the *Daily Mail*. These... what was it they called them? *Millennials?* Anyway, according to the papers, the young ones these days were all supposed to be so entitled and self-centred that they didn't give a hoot for anyone else, but this young lady certainly didn't fall into that category. Actually, now that their faces were so close together, maybe not so young. Perhaps late twenties? Thirties? Pretty, and without all that make-up the young ones wear nowadays. Eyebrows like snails, some of them. But not this lovely woman.

Caro returned his smile and held the train door open until the gent had, painstakingly slowly, climbed the step on to the train. No hurry. She'd waited this long to make the journey south to Glasgow. Although, right now, there was a huge part of her that wanted to stay in the comforting cocoon of her home city.

Aberdeen train station was bustling with commuters arriving from less expensive postcodes. A city with the third largest population in Scotland, after Glasgow and Edinburgh, in the heyday of the oil industry this had been boomtown. The black gold that was pumped in from the oil rigs off the coast had seeped into every brick of the granite that lined the streets, bringing American oil companies, financial investment, big spenders and an air of confidence that it would last forever.

It didn't.

Only a couple of years ago, revenues suddenly plummeted, profits turned to losses, jobs disappeared, lives were ruined and the city was shaken to its grey stone foundations, a catastrophe made so much worse because they didn't see it coming.

That wasn't a mistake that Caro would make today. She had taken her time, thought this through, prepared herself for the juggernaut that she feared could come her way over the next twenty-four hours.

The irony was that today, 22nd December, should have been a day of chilled out relaxation after the bedlam of the last couple of weeks in school. It, and all the other school holidays, were marked on her phone diary with the 'party' emoji. Not that she didn't love her job, because she adored it. Even on the toughest days, she never regretted her career choice, but December in a primary school required more complex logistical planning than three wise men could muster without the aid of a team of helpers. There was the nativity show, the Christmas concert, the festive fayre, the end of term party, and of course, the added challenge of managing thirty eleven-year-old children who were overly excited about the prospect of a two-week holiday, and who only wanted to study the gift sections of the Argos catalogue.

When they'd charged out of school at home time yesterday, leaving her desk almost entirely obscured by tubs of chocolates, scented candles, and (from the more switched on parents) bottles of Prosecco, she'd been both sad to see them go, and relieved that it would be two weeks until she saw them again.

Today, she should be doing nothing more taxing than putting her feet up with a good book.

It wasn't too late to change her mind about going. She could get off the train now. Forget about the trip. Run for the hills – or at least for her sofa, with a Jilly Cooper and one of those bottles of Prosecco.

The thought was squashed by the sight of the old man struggling to put a leather holdall into the overhead rack. Caro stepped in. 'Shall I do that for you?'

He gratefully accepted.

One push and it was sorted.

Caro slid into one of the empty seats, put her leather satchel on the one beside her. She'd move it if anyone else needed the place. Couldn't stand those selfish gits that blocked off a seat with their bag so they didn't have to share a space with a stranger. Her new acquaintance, still standing in the aisle, removed his hat and scarf and gestured to the two empty seats facing her across a Formica table.

'Do you mind?' he asked.

'Not at all,' she replied, smiling.

He lowered his aching frame into the seat, placed his possessions – hat, scarf, paper – on the table between them. Normally, Caro would take out her Kindle, lose herself in a book, hope that no one would strike up a conversation, but not today. Today, she'd be grateful for any distraction, especially if it was the company of an elderly gent with a kind face.

'Going to Glasgow?' the old man asked, with a Doric lilt in a voice that was stronger than his physical appearance would suggest.

'Yes. And you?'

'Getting off at Perth. Going to stay with my daughter and grandchildren for Christmas.' His pride was evident.

'That'll be lovely,' Caro said, watching as he picked up his newspaper and laid it out in front of him. Going to see his daughter. A few years ago, she'd have automatically pictured her dad, Jack, there, a couple of decades down the line, saying the same thing to a stranger on a train. In fact, maybe even this train. It was the one he'd travelled on every month, for as long as she could remember, when his work took him down to Glasgow. It was all she'd ever been used to. When she was a kid, she always knew when he was about to leave. Her mum, Yvonne, would be just a little quieter, a little sadder, because he was leaving the next day. Off he'd go, all hugs and kisses, and Caro would look forward to him returning because Mum's face would light up again and she'd be truly happy, singing along to the radio in the mornings, brushing her hair and spraying perfume just before he was due to walk in the door.

It was all because Dad had a Very Important Job. A management consultant in the oil business. Caro had never been entirely sure what that meant. She'd asked a few times over the years and he'd given her spiels about development strategies, man-management, personnel restructures, performance optimisation. As far as Caro could grasp, what it all boiled down to was that his company worked with oil corporations to make the divisions within each organisation work as efficiently as possible. If they needed to expand, he helped them structure the new department, hire the best people and implement training programmes. If they needed to cut costs, he showed them where. He travelled a lot, sometimes faraway places like China, Abu Dhabi and Oman, but usually just down to the company office in Glasgow. He was a cavalier guy in a cavalier industry.

'Got to go where the money is,' he'd tell her, before the door banged behind him. In hindsight, Caro wondered where the money had gone. She and her mother had never seen much of it. There had never been any lavish holidays. No designer clothes. Yvonne didn't have a fancy car. They'd always lived in the house that her mum had been left by her parents, a perfectly nice semi-detached granite home on a perfectly nice street, that had been worth very little when Gran and Granda had bought it in the fifties, but had a couple more zeros added to the value by the arrival of the oil industry.

When Gran and Granda passed away, their house had been left jointly to Mum and her sister, Auntie Pearl. When Auntie Pearl married and moved out, they'd worked out a rental agreement and Mum had stayed behind, living on her own until she'd met Jack Anderson at college, got pregnant, married him and he'd carried her over the threshold into the home she'd already lived in for twenty-two years.

Not that Caro could ever remember him being there full-time. He probably was for the first few years, but he'd capitalised on the oil boom, and ever since he'd been gone more than he'd been home. Some months he'd be home for a few days, sometimes two weeks, rarely more. She'd never felt neglected or that she was losing out in any way. It was what she'd always been used to and, as Mum always said, just one of the sacrifices they had to make because Dad had a Very Important Job.

The payback for the sacrifice? A couple of years ago, just as her parents should have been starting to contemplate cruises and bucket lists for their early retirement, Jack Anderson had walked out of the door to go to his Very Important Job and he'd never come back.

Caro felt the familiar inner rage start to build now and she squashed it back down. He'd left them a week before her thirtieth birthday, so she was old enough to process her parents splitting up by some mutual consent. Yet she couldn't. Because it wasn't mutual and he'd bolted when her mother had needed him most, walked out to a new life and he hadn't looked back.

For a long time, Caro didn't understand why.

Only now did she realise that on the Importance scale, the job was up there with his Very Important Secret.

Maybe.

She still didn't believe it to be true.

She must be wrong.

Mistaken identity.

Surely?

Yet here she was, sitting on a train on a cold December morning on her way to Glasgow.

She pulled her iPad out of her satchel, logged on to the train's Wi-Fi, then flicked on to the Facebook page she'd looked at a thousand times in the last few weeks.

It was one of those coincidental flukes that had taken her to it in the first place.

It had been late at night and she'd been sitting beside her mum's bed in the hospital, feeling like she'd been battered by the storm that was raging outside. She shouldn't even have been there because it was outside of visiting time, but the nurses overlooked her presence because her mum was in a private room at the end of a corridor and they made exceptions when it came to patients at this stage in their lives. Yvonne's eyes were closed, her body still, but Caro wanted to stay, whether Yvonne knew she was there or not. It was the first night of the October school holiday, so she didn't have to get up early to be the responsible Miss Anderson for a class of eleven-year-olds the next morning.

Instead, she could just be Caro, sitting there passing the time catching up with Facebook. She only dipped in and out of it every few weeks, caught up with a Carpool Karaoke, the launch of a new book, or maybe a movie trailer.

A promotional link appeared for the new Simple Minds tour, twenty dates around the country, yet another band riding the nostalgic affection for the eighties and nineties.

Before she could stop it, the opening bars of Jim Kerr's voice belting out 'Don't You Forget About Me' flooded her head and she felt the bite of a sharp-toothed memory. Her dad had been a big fan, their music playing alongside Oasis and Blur on his CD player when he was home or in the car on the few mornings he was around to take her to school, and that had been his favourite song.

The irony in the title didn't escape her. 'Don't You Forget About Me'. If only she could forget he ever existed, then she wouldn't have to deal with the soul-sucking fury that he wasn't there.

Agitated, she started to scroll past the post when she noticed the first comment underneath, written by a complete stranger.

'OMG, *my dad will* FREAK *when he sees this. His fave band!*'

Mine too, she'd thought.

Then she noticed the surname of the person who'd posted. Anderson.

Mine too, she'd thought again.

Coincidence. The same surname. Maybe that was why she'd clicked on the photo of the person who'd posted. She didn't make a habit of snooping in other people's lives, but any diversion from reality was welcome and she'd come to realise that in the many long hours she had to fill, curiosity was one way to pass the time.

Click.

This was pointless. Didn't everyone have rigid privacy settings these days? Wasn't that what she taught her primary seven kids at school? Privacy. Protection. Common sense.

Apparently not.

Caro saw immediately that the need for privacy had bypassed the gorgeous woman with the expensive blonde highlights and the gleaming white teeth, her head turned so she was looking over her shoulder, pouting at the camera, her slender figure wrapped in a gorgeous white dress, her feet in shoes with red soles.

Click.

Caro was scrolling down the stranger's Facebook profile now, a vicarious spectator to her life.

Lila Anderson. In a relationship. Works at Radcal Pharmaceuticals. Went to Strathclyde University. A complete stranger, nothing to see here, time to move on... yet Caro couldn't seem to stop looking at the images and words on the screen.

The stranger at the gym. In a restaurant. In New York, kissing a very handsome man she called her 'Bae'. Caro knew from listening to the kids spouting today's slang that 'Bae' meant 'babe' or 'lover'. The stranger in a restaurant, with her arm around... her arm around...

Caro pinched two fingers together and then spread them to zoom in.

The stranger with her arm around a man that looked very familiar. Her eyes flicked to the status update at the top of the post. 'This guy! Happy birthday to my amazing dad! Jack Anderson, you've spoiled me for twenty-nine years and now it's my turn to spoil you. Love you so much!'

The sound of her mum's laboured breaths beside her made Caro realise that she hadn't exhaled for several seconds.

The resemblance was uncanny. Incredible. But of course, it wasn't him. This girl lived in... She checked the tag – The Rogano, Glasgow. Yep, Glasgow. The city that her dad had been working in for decades. A tiny, but persistent, seed of suspicion began to take hold.

Her eyes went back to the man in the photo, the one who bore a startling likeness to the guy she called 'Dad' too. But it couldn't be the same man. It was a ridiculous thought.

The facts and timescales didn't add up at all. This Lila person said she was twenty-nine. Caro was thirty-two. There was no way her dad could have another daughter of almost the same age. As far as she knew her mum and dad had never had any separations and there had never been a hint of an affair. Surely there was no way something like that could have been covered up for 29 years?

And anyway, her dad's birthday was... She scrolled back and looked at the date on the man's birthday post and the power to exhale was temporarily suspended yet again. November 1st. Same birthday as her father. They'd rarely managed to celebrate it on the actual day because he was invariably away working in... Glasgow.

No breath.

Her gaze went to the cake. Fifty-four. Same age as her dad.

Click. Photographs. A lifetime's worth. Retro pics of Girl With the Same Surname when she was five. Eight. Twelve. Sweet sixteen. Maybe 25. And countless others since then.

Loads of the early pics showed younger versions of the man who had been around when Caro was five, eight, twelve, sixteen, twenty-five. But not thirty. He'd left by then, a couple of years ago, right after her mum was diagnosed. He didn't come back.

He'd told her this was 'his time'.

In all honesty, there had never been a time that wasn't. Their lives had always orbited around his, fitted in with his schedule, sprang into action when he was around.

Click. Click. Click. This had to be him, but it couldn't be. This made no sense at all. None. It had to be one of those surreal coincidences. Had to be.

She went through them all again, lifted the phone to call him and then stopped. No point. Last time she'd tried, she'd got an automated message saying his number was no longer in service.

It was probably just as well. What would she say? Hey Dad, why are you on someone else's Facebook page? Why does someone else call you Dad? Where have you been going all these years? Where are you now? Why did you betray Mum, leave me, cut us off and walk out, you faithless, cold-hearted, arrogant, bastard?

It took a moment for her breathing to return to normal. Hate and fury, both emotions that rarely featured in her personality, had taken root on the day he left and they had grown branches that had wrapped around her and were now squeezing her ribcage.

She despised him. When he walked out, she'd thought she couldn't hate him more. Now, looking at these images, she realised there was a whole pool of hate she hadn't even dipped her toe in yet. Her mum, here without the man who had promised to love her in sickness and health. Him, away somewhere playing happy bloody families.

She didn't want to believe it was true.

It wasn't.

But if it was, then he'd spent a lifetime lying to her.

Now, for the cost of a seventy-quid ticket, she was going to find out.

This train was taking her to Glasgow, though she had absolutely no idea what she was going to do when she got there. Thanks to Facebook, and the fact that Stranger With The Same Surname – Lila Anderson – had no privacy settings on her account, she knew what company she worked for. She knew the bars she liked to drink in. It wasn't much to go on, but maybe it was enough.

She always warned the kids that any weirdo could track them down through their social network posts if they disclosed too much information. Now she'd become the weirdo, following the clues, desperate to find out if her whole life had been a lie, if her father had been in a family-share situation that she'd been blissfully unaware of.

It felt so, so wrong.

She still had time to back out, to forget all of this and just go back to her life, her mother. She could get off at Perth, change tracks, get the first train home.

As if the universe was sensing her hesitation, her phone beeped, bringing the cavalry storming to her aid.

A text message from Todd. Her mum's sister, Auntie Pearl's son, so technically her cousin but the closest thing she had to a brother. Caro knew that everything she'd been through would have been even more devastating if he hadn't been there to make her laugh and hold her when she cried. They were the same age, but while she'd chosen teaching, he'd gone into hairdressing, got engaged twice to beautiful women, then surprised everyone by falling in love with Jared, a Canadian colourist, at a styling convention. Five years later, they were still together. Jared was a lucky guy.

She read the text.

Are you on train? Have you lost the plot yet? Shall I arrange for Davina McCall to meet you to discuss long-lost father?

Smiling, she replied.

Yes. No. Tell Davina to be on standby.

She was doing this. No backing out. No turning around.

The next beep came a few seconds later.

Had to promise her my body, but she agreed to help. Will call you when coffee has restored power of speech. Love you.

Love you back.

She'd just put her phone down when the snack trolley stopped at her side. She bought two cups of tea and two mini packets of shortbread, pushing one towards her travel companion, accepting his thanks with a friendly, 'You're very welcome.'

Lovely girl, he thought again. The kind that any dad would be proud to call his daughter.

Lovely man, Caro thought. The kind that any daughter would be proud to call her dad.

The kind of man *she* would be proud to call her dad.

Because Caro hadn't had a father for a couple of years now – and she was terrifyingly aware that she might discover she'd never truly had one at all.

2

Cammy

He listened as the familiar chain of morning sounds permeated through from Lila's dressing room to the bedroom. The patter of the shower. The buzz of the electric toothbrush. The gurgle of the coffee maker that she'd put there so she didn't have to go the whole twenty feet to the kitchen to make her morning cuppa. The hum of the hairdryer. The ping of her straighteners. The clang as she dropped item after item of make-up on to the mirrored surface of the dressing table. The rustle of the clothes as she picked out an outfit. The thud as she pulled out a box of shoes and let it fall to the floor so she could step into them.

Cammy pushed himself up in bed, groaning inwardly as an ache spread across the back of his shoulders. He'd gone too hard in the gym last night. He'd got lost in thoughts of today before he realised he'd done ten extra reps on the bench press.

He reached over to the mirrored bedside table and grabbed the remote control. This was Lila's place, bought and decorated before he'd met her, thus the over-excess of reflective surfaces. It wasn't his thing. He owned a hipster gents' menswear shop called CAMDEN, in the Merchant City area of Glasgow, and – much as most of his regular customers were great – working there exposed him to enough vanity, posing and borderline narcissism for any lifetime.

'I only keep you around because you look like that in the morning.' The voice from the door.

He shrugged, grinning as he went for his usual retort. 'I only keep you around because I'm partial to people who share my shallowness,' he replied, rewarded with a flash of her smile, the one that he'd fallen in love with the first time he saw her six months ago. It was a June afternoon, just a few months after he'd opened the shop, and she'd come in with her dad to pick out a new suit. Her dad had left with a pretty cool Ted Baker number and Lila had left with his phone number. She'd called later that night, they'd met up, and he'd moved out of his rented flat and in with her a week later. He had no regrets. Although, her morning routine could definitely do with a volume control. He put it down to the fact that she was ten years younger than him so she woke up with far more energy.

'Right, I'm away,' she said, distracted, and he knew she'd be thinking about the location of her phone, her keys, her make-up bag – all the things that she lost on an hourly basis. When it came to her job, a pharmaceutical rep for a big blue-chip company, she raked in a substantial salary because she was religiously organised and highly efficient. When it came to everything else, she was borderline chaotic. It was one of the dichotomies in her personality that he adored.

She was already out of the door, teetering on heels that made indentations in the thick pile carpet, before he realised there'd been no kiss, no hug, no promise to call. That had happened a few times lately, but he wasn't worried. Didn't everyone fall into familiar patterns after they'd been together for a while? Anyway, if it was an injection of romance that was required, today was going to be the day for it. Or rather, tonight was going to be the night.

He slid out of bed and headed to the shower, still wet, with the aroma of her Dior shower gel hanging in the air.

Digby, his assistant manager was opening up the shop for him today. First time for everything, but he had total faith in him. And besides, he'd asked Jen, who owned the holiday shop next door, to keep an eye out and make sure it was all okay. If there were any issues she'd call him.

He sang along with the song on Clyde radio – 'Don't

You Forget About Me'. A retro classic from Simple Minds. He had no idea when he'd first heard it, couldn't remember learning the lyrics, yet he knew every word of it. It was one of those songs that was just there, in the West of Scotland DNA.

His shower routine and the song finished at the same time, and he climbed out, pulled a towel around his waist and shaved, something that he only did on weekends and special occasions.

Today was definitely the latter.

The most special occasion of all, if it all went to plan. And he had no doubt it would, because the people in charge would make sure of...

The doorbell. There they were. Half an hour early. He should have expected it. They'd probably been parked outside since sunrise waiting for Lila to leave.

Dropping the razor in the sink, he wiped the last of the shaving foam off his face and headed to the door, delivering an exaggerated bow as it swung open.

Two women. Perhaps, other than Lila and his lovely mum up in Perth, his favourite two women in the world. Josie and Val.

Actually, there had been two others. Stacy, his best friend in L. A., and Mel, his former boss, were the only other women he'd ever truly loved, but those chapters were closed now.

Even now, years later, thinking of Mel caused a tightening in his throat so he was thankful for the bedlam brought about by the loud and forceful entry of the new arrivals.

Josie was blissfully unaware that she was heading for seventy, the spiky-haired love-granny of Annie Lennox and Billy Idol. Cammy had worked with Josie and Mel in another lifetime, when they'd been employed in the His and Hers departments of Mel's lingerie boutique, a store that had been in the same premises as the one he owned now. They'd spent every day together for many years, become family, before he left and headed over to LA for a few years. He'd had a great time there, but it was all surface stuff. More and more, he'd realised that he missed his old life and wanted more than casual dating and wheatgrass smoothies. So he'd come home. Not to Perth, the city he'd grown up in, much as he adored his parents who still lived there in his childhood home.

No, he'd come back to Glasgow. Mel was long gone. The killer was that she'd married Josie's son and went off to live abroad. But at least he still had a circle of friends that included Josie and her best friend, Val, a fifty-something Glaswegian with a perfect blonde bob and pink pencilled lips. Her heart and personality were far larger than her five-foot frame and she collected waifs and strays, Cammy included, like other people collected shoes.

Val ruffled his hair as she teetered past in the wake of Josie's steel stiletto heels, the Ant to Josie's sexagenarian Dec.

'For the love of God, Cammy, put a top on. My libido hasn't been stirred since about 1996, and you don't want to waken the beast,' Josie barked, in a voice that came courtesy of a love of laughter and twenty cigs a day.

They barged ahead of him, into the kitchen and, without waiting to be asked, set about making a pot of tea, to go with the packet of caramel wafers that Josie produced from her handbag.

By the time Cammy joined them, only a few moments later, he was fully dressed in jeans and a black T-shirt, the table was set, the tea was steaming and the wrappers had been discarded. Cammy thought, not for the first time, that if the country ever considered invading a nation, they should send these two in first to clear a path using the mighty power of tea and chocolate-covered biscuits.

'Right then, love,' Val started, opening a notebook and getting out a pen. 'Let's go over today's schedule.'

'Hang on, I wish to interject,' Josie, well, *interjected*.

'Cammy, are you sure about this, my darling? Because you know, and I say this from a place of love, you could do better.'

He came close to spitting out his tea.

'Josie! That's enough. For God's sake, this is an anxious day for the poor boy and you're only going to make it worse. Don't be ridiculous. Of course he's sure.' Val turned to him. 'You are sure, aren't you son?'

'I'm sure, Val,' he said, 'and Josie, I'm past forty. I'm not some crazy kid rushing into this. I know for sure it's right. I wouldn't be doing it otherwise.'

'You thought that last time and look how that worked out,' Josie said, not unkindly, but making the point.

Cammy wasn't going there, refused to pick at that scab.

'I'm sure,' he repeated.

Josie pursed her lips, unconvinced. 'Fine. I suppose. I mean, I could test your resolve by listing all her bad points again. Only, I'm not sure if we've got time if we want to stick to the schedule.'

Val interjected on his behalf for the second time. 'Josie, insert that caramel log in yer gob and don't remove it until you have something civil to say.'

Josie rolled her eyes and chewed in silence, her discomfort at the unnatural state clearly killing her. Josie didn't do silence. She didn't do restraint. And she definitely didn't do withholding of her opinions.

To outsiders, it probably seemed like a strange friendship, the successful, good-looking man-about-town entrepreneur and the ageing punk rocker with a mouth like a sewer, but she'd forcefully adopted him the minute they'd met a decade or so before – some might call it more of a hostage situation – and he'd loved her ever since. People of all ages graduated to Josie and Val. They had an extended family that spanned the generations, and they were always happy to welcome newcomers into the fold, especially guys like Cammy, who had little family of their own.

They'd been the first people he'd shared his decision with, the first ones to know what he'd planned, the cohorts that were here now, helping him with his plan, even if they weren't entirely on board.

'Right, what's first then?' Val said, looking at the checklist in front of her. 'Okay, just so you know, we drove past the restaurant on the way here and it's looking gorgeous. All the Christmas lights are up in the square outside. It's going to be perfect.'

Cammy nodded. Despite Josie's antagonism and blatant disapproval, this was why he'd agreed to her offer of help. Now that she and Val had both semi-retired, they had time on their hands, and they were the type of women who let nothing stand in the way of a good party. There was no obstacle they couldn't climb over, no issue they couldn't solve.

Josie harrumphed and Cammy feigned exasperation. 'Why didn't you leave me to do this on my own if you disapprove so much?' he teased her. 'You know why? Because you're so bloody nosy.'

Josie shook her head. 'Nope, I just decided that there was more chance of me talking you out of it if I came along for the ride. It's a tactic of war. You just don't know when the ambush will come.'

There was no point in even trying to act offended, so Cammy laughed instead. Josie was all talk. Okay, so she didn't love Lila, but she'd come round eventually, and in the meantime, although his ears would probably be bleeding by the end of the day, there was no one else he would rather do this with.

He was sure about marrying Lila. Absolutely sure. Wasn't he?

Of course he was. The six months they'd been together had been the best of his life. He'd only just moved back to Glasgow after years in the States, and although he'd rekindled his old friendships, opened up the shop and found somewhere to live, it was Lila that had convinced him that coming back to Glasgow had been the right decision. They'd totally fitted from their first night together, even though it wasn't a typical first date. She'd called him from a hotel bar after a fight with her boyfriend and he'd picked her up, taken her for a late night drink, kissed her, and that had been it for both of them. At first he'd worried that it was a rebound from the boyfriend she'd left that night, but it wasn't long before that didn't even cross his mind. She never mentioned the guy again. Cammy didn't ask. It was inconsequential. All that mattered was that he wanted to be with her and she wanted to be with him.

And now he was going to make it official, not because he had a burning desire to be married, but because he knew Lila wanted it.

Hadn't she dropped enough hints? How many times had she said she wanted to be married by the time she was thirty? How many jewellery windows had they stopped at? How many wedding magazines had she left lying around? How many times had she mentioned the fact that marriage was definitely something on the horizon? He knew this was why she'd been a bit off for the last couple of months. She was starting to get frustrated, beginning to wonder if he really was serious about her or if this was just a passing romance, a waste of her time that could rob her of the future she had planned.

After tonight, she'd know that wasn't the case. The whole institution of marriage wasn't something he desperately wanted – he'd have been happy just living together forever. What difference did a piece of paper and a walk down an aisle really make? However, it hadn't taken him long to realise that it was important to her, and he was more than willing to make it happen.

At first he'd thought of using one of those proposal agencies, the companies that planned everything and took care of all the details to make it special, but when he'd told Josie and Val, they'd been outraged. 'Och, why would you be wasting your money on that when we could do it for you?' Josie had exclaimed, while Val had looked at her, mouth agape. 'You can't stand her,' she'd pointed out the obvious. Cammy took no offence. In fact, as Josie had said, he knew it came from a place of love. Josie treated him like a son and she'd never think any woman was good enough for him. He could turn up with a supermodel astronaut who spent her life improving the living conditions of the poor and brokering world peace, and Josie would still find fault.

He picked up a caramel wafer, dunked it in his tea, and took a bite, as he listened to Val running through the plans.

Whether Josie approved or not, Cammy knew with absolute certainty that by the end of the day he was going to be engaged to Lila.

3

Bernadette

Bernadette stared at the table to make sure it was just the way he liked it. Cup and saucer on the right-hand top corner of the white, freshly laundered and pressed place mat. Bowl of muesli in the centre, jug of milk beside it. Prunes in a dish to the left. Vitamins in a ramekin, next to the cafetière filled to a centimetre from the top with Jamaican Blue Mountain Roast. The coffee took a fair chunk out of her housekeeping budget every month, but, as he reminded her often, at this stage in life he'd worked hard enough to get the best.

He'd worked.

He made it sound like she had never lifted a finger in her life. Thirty years in nursing, part-time during the kids' first ten years, when she juggled night shifts with bringing them up, while he worked days and slept peacefully through the night. Thank God, she'd had her mother then to help out, because there was no way Kenneth would disturb his beauty sleep to rouse himself for a restless child.

Oh no. He'd always insisted on uninterrupted sleep because, as he regularly pointed out, his job was life or death. He conveniently overlooked the fact that hers was too, sneering that she was just a nurse in A & E, while he was a cardiac surgeon who required sufficient rest to operate successfully. And one thing that drove Kenneth Manson was success. He had one of the most lauded practices in the country, based in a prestigious private hospital near their home in the West End of the city. Kenneth Manson was a renowned expert when it came to matters of the heart. The irony didn't escape her.

She flinched as he walked into the room, his eyes barely registering her presence as he sat down and gave a murmured, 'Morning.' So it was going to be one of those days in the Manson household then. It was impossible to predict. Sometimes, she got a smile, perhaps even a peck on the cheek as he passed her. If they'd had sex the night before, he might even reach for the belt on her robe and pull her towards him. That happened less now. In fact, it had been months. Thank God. It meant she didn't have to pretend to respond, or hate herself when she did. Mornings like this were preferable. She'd rather he ignored her or even blatantly abhorred her, than have to put up with his touch.

She saw that he was already in his cycling gear, like something straight out of mid-life crisis central. What was it they called them? MAMILs. Middle-Aged Men In Lycra. Of course, she'd never say that out loud. Nor would she tell him that he looked ridiculous in the full regalia. That was one of those happy little thoughts that she kept to herself. As was the fact that there was every chance he'd freeze his bollocks off, cycling through Glasgow streets in December.

The cycling had been a new development over the last couple of years. He'd always taken care of himself – well, in his line of work it was advisable – but he'd taken it to a whole other level when the big 5-0 began to loom on the horizon. A natural inclination to vanity had ramped up many notches. It went one way or another, didn't it? He'd been such a good-looking man in his twenties and thirties, and when the choice came to relax and accept the passing of time, or to fight the ageing process with every fibre of his being, he'd chosen the latter. Now, he cycled the five miles to work every morning, then got showered and changed there, before fitting in a lunchtime training session at the gym and then cycling home at night. Sometimes he even went back out later for another workout, and she'd lost count of the cycling weekends, the active breaks and marathons he'd gone off to do in cities all over Europe. She didn't mind. Not in the least. Every day that he was away was a day less that she had to look at him over the top of his newspaper and silently hate him. Kenneth Manson. A fine, upstanding pillar of the community, saviour of many, much loved father, vile bastard of a husband.

His face flickered with annoyance as her mobile phone buzzed to signal an incoming message. He didn't approve of phones at the table, but he could hardly ground her, could he? She wasn't one of the kids – though even the kids weren't children now. Nina was twenty-nine and Stuart was seven years behind her. Who was she kidding? She knew good and well that the fact she was his wife wouldn't stop him doling out a punishment. Maybe a day-long sulk. Perhaps a barbed insult. A criticism of her appearance.

She didn't look at the text, aware that it could set him off, yet hating herself for succumbing to that fear and allowing him to control her actions. It would be Sarah, her friend, and lately, her co-conspirator. Nothing actually illegal. At least, not yet.

Because everything was about to change.

Today was D-Day. Operation Freedom. They'd been building up to this day for months and she still wasn't sure that she was going to go through with it, that she had the strength to take the steps and make it happen. But she had to believe that she had the courage to do it.

The fact that she had stayed with Kenneth for so long wouldn't make sense to most people. In the beginning she'd stayed because she loved him. For the first couple of years, she'd truly adored him and couldn't believe her luck that he'd loved her back. When that began to dim, and then finally die, she stayed for the kids, to give them the security of growing up in a stable home. God knows, he'd reminded her so many times that if she left him, he'd get custody. A man of his reputation? He was sure of it. Maybe he would, maybe he wouldn't, but she wasn't going to put it to the test and subject the kids to that kind of trauma.

When Stuart left home a couple of years ago, that should have been her moment. Nina was long gone by then, married and living a few miles away, while Stuart moved into a flat in the city centre with a friend, Connor, from university. By then though, her mum and dad were both poorly, and her marriage was the least of her worries, as she nursed them, visiting every day, co-ordinating with the care team and the nursing staff, spending every possible hour with them until the end.

She'd buried her dad in the spring, and then her mum in the autumn, so now there was no one who was still relying on her, no one to focus on, to take her mind away from the hell of this existence with a man she no longer loved. In some profound way, their deaths had convinced her that she had to start living. Now was her time. She just had to have the nerve to see it through.

'How hard?'

She barely made out what he said. 'What?'

'How hard is it to get this fucking right?' he said, and she realised he was staring at the assortment of vitamins in the tiny receptacle.

Her heart sank. She'd been distracted when she'd counted them out, too busy thinking about the rest of the day and everything that she had to do to make it work.

'Sorry, I…'

'Don't be fucking sorry,' he hissed, through gritted teeth, his words delivering a vicious slap. She'd almost have preferred it if he shouted. At least then, she could switch it off, like a thunderstorm, knowing it would blow itself out. But when he was like this… this was the worst. The most dangerous. This was when the insults started, the criticisms, the long list of her inadequacies.

Her eyes flicked to the clock. He had to leave in five minutes and he was never late. Just hold on. Five minutes. Three hundred seconds. Surely there was nothing that couldn't be endured for three hundred seconds. The last three hundred seconds she'd ever spend looking at his face, contorted into disgust and fury.

Her phone buzzed again and it was all she could do not to get up and run, not stopping until she was free of him.

He snatched it up, threw it at the wall. 'What have I told you about that phone?'

Bernadette heard the crack as the glass met with the corner of the picture that hung there. She'd always hated it. It had been inherited from his family home. A hunting scene. Apt, given that she'd been trapped for years.

Once upon a time, she'd chased him. He'd been so suave, so dashing, she'd gone out of her way to bump in to him, had hung on his every word. He still had that effect on people now. She saw it all the time, at social events or work gatherings, especially in some of the single (and married!) women. Oh, how they thought he was a catch, a debonair, charismatic alpha male with a twinkle in his eye and a reputation for brilliance.

She knew that's what they thought, because she once did too.

For those women, the fact that he was married didn't even factor into it. He didn't wear a ring, so many didn't know and the ones that did didn't seem to care. The only thing that made her feel worse than seeing him admired by others, was when someone with their eye on him realised who he was married to.

Bernadette had seen it many times, read their minds as they went through the steps of realisation. The incomprehension as they took in her appearance, her demeanour, her forgettable presence. *He* was married to *her*? Really? She must have some personality because she didn't get him on looks.

In the early years the physical chasm between them hadn't been so wide, and anyway, she consoled herself with the fact that he came home to her every night.

When the sheen of adoration wore off and she realised who he really was, it had stopped hurting altogether.

She was sure people wondered why he stayed. She did too. But then, thirty years was a long relationship to walk away from and he was from a family that stayed. Wasn't that what his mother, the evil old cow, used to say? *We're fighters, us Mansons. We don't walk away.*

Sometimes, Bernadette wished to God he had, then she wouldn't have to face him every morning and listen to yet another poisonous attack.

'Why do you always have to do this to me? Can't I even have my bloody breakfast in peace and quiet, and have it the way that I want it? Is it really too much to ask? Is it?'

No, it wasn't. It wasn't too much to ask at all. He'd have plenty of peace and quiet from now on and his breakfast would be bloody perfect, because he'd have to make it himself. She had to stop herself smiling at that thought. He'd have been sure to take that as a sign of defiance and that would rile him up even more.

A few more minutes. She just had to hold her nerve for a few more minutes. Sod him and sod his bloody prunes.

A phone ringing, this time his, not hers. He swore again, kicked the table leg like a petulant child as he got up, reached for his backpack and pulled it out of the front pocket. So it was OK for him to look at his phone, but not for her. A little voice of sarcasm in her mind pointed out that must be because he was a very important surgeon who lived by a whole different set of rules from lowly mortals.

He pressed a button as he put it to his ear.

'Yes? Okay, prep O.R. three and tell them I'm on my way in. I'll be about fifteen minutes,' he said, his furious hiss replaced with a matter-of-fact calm, the public side of him that everyone else saw and admired. 'No, no worries at all, you didn't disturb me, I was just leaving anyway. That's fine. Okay, I'll be right there.'

Yes, there was Dr Manson, cardiac surgeon. A man of medicine, of healing. Someone who had chosen to dedicate his life to making others better.

By the time that thought reached her brain the wave of hate was so violent she could taste it.

A dozen times in the last few months she'd resolved to go and backed out every time. Spineless, she knew.

If she could just go through with it, if she could actually take the step she'd been dreaming of for more years than she could count...

It had to be done properly, the ties had to be split before he even knew it was coming. That meant she had... she looked at the clock again... Twelve hours. If his surgeries went to plan today, that's how long she would have until he walked back in the door. A whole lifetime to unravel in half a day. It was the only way. She couldn't risk him getting wind of it and freezing their money. Of course, it was all in his name. She couldn't let him tell the kids before she could explain, lest he spin a story that wasn't true. She had to get all the things she loved out of the house, otherwise he'd never let her have them. She had to get settled somewhere else and make sure she was absolutely confident in her decision. No loose ends. Nothing that could force her to come back.

After thirty years, many of them spent looking at that face and hating the sight of it, listening to his criticisms spat out in a voice that made her teeth grind, feeling her skin crawl under his touch, being controlled and constantly on edge because she never knew if she would be dealing with Jekyll or Hyde, it was time.

Bernadette Manson made a promise to herself that by the end of the day, she would have walked away from her husband forever.

4

Lila

As decisions went, starting the day off with a tough choice between white, silk and virginal, and black, slutty and crotchless, hadn't been the worst one in the world. The anticipation had turned her on so much she'd almost made a mess of her eyeliner. Almost. Lila wasn't that kind of rookie.

Cammy was already sitting up in bed when she left her dressing room, so she'd distracted him with a joke about keeping him because he looked so great. There was some truth in that. His light brown hair, usually swept back, was falling over his eyes. His tan was still a honeyed, caramel colour, thanks to a weekend in Marbella last month, and that torso... It was the kind of six-pack that came from great genes and a dedicated gym regime.

Her phone rang and she tapped a button on the steering wheel of her Evoque. One of the perks of the job. When she'd started with Radcal Pharmaceuticals at twenty-two, as a junior rep straight out of university, she'd been given a Mondeo. Oh, the indignity of a standard rep's car. Since then, she'd worked her way up, courtesy of record-breaking sales and no-nonsense demands, until she got this baby. Red. Black roof. Sexy as hell.

'Good morning gorgeous, how are you doing?'

Her smile was instant. 'Morning Mum, I'm great. What are you up to?'

'I'm just about to leave for the golf club with your father. We've booked a double session on the simulator and we're teeing off at eleven.'

Lila frowned. 'Hang on – *you're* going to the golf club. To actually play on some computerised machine?'

'Yes. You know, if you can't beat them…'

'Join them on the fake golf course?' she finished for her, with a sigh.

'Honestly, you'd almost swear it was real. We're playing St Andrews today. We did Pebble Beach and Mar-a-Lago earlier in the week.'

Lila was no longer listening.

Bugger. She'd been planning to pop in on Mum later, but since Dad had taken early retirement, he'd been totally monopolising her. It had always been her and her mum, Louise, just the two of them, with Dad coming back maybe a week or so in every month. It was the sacrifice they'd had to make for a dad that supported them by working away, in his big shot consultancy role in the oil industry. Mum always said they shouldn't complain because it was so much harder for him being parted from them. And besides, he made it up to them. There had always been a couple of incredible holidays every year: the Maldives, California, Hawaii. Mum traded her BMW in for a new model whenever she felt like a change of colour. And when Lila had turned seventeen, her brand-new convertible Mini had been wrapped in a huge ribbon, waiting outside the door.

When Dad was away, she definitely enjoyed the rewards, and she didn't even care that he didn't seem to particularly notice her when he was home. Her mum had more than made up for his distance, in all respects, by lavishing Lila with love and affection. If anything, they were more like sisters or best friends than mother and daughter.

However, a couple of years ago, he'd come back here full-time, and now that he'd taken early retirement, Mum had undergone a personality transplant, embraced an outdoor sport, and was so busy with Dad that there was no time left for Lila.

Lila didn't understand it. Louise didn't do golf. She did girlie lunches on Lila's expense account on a Friday, sometimes a mani-pedi if Lila could finish early. She didn't do bloody golf with a husband who had suddenly become a full-time presence in their life and who was now monopolising his very willing wife. What was her mum thinking? Traitor.

'Look, I have to go, another call coming in.' She hung up before her mum had a chance to reply, determined not to let Louise's desertion kill her buzz.

She pressed the touchscreen on the dashboard a couple of times, until it took her to her call list. There he was. His name. Right at the top.

Ken Manson. Press.

'Yes?'

'Dr Manson, this is your favourite rep, on her way to meet you. I went for black and slutty.'

She knew he'd be trying desperately to keep his tone steady. His wife was probably right there in front of him. Poor cow. The thought actually added to the thrill.

'Okay, prep O.R. three and tell them I'm on my way in. I'll be about fifteen minutes.'

'I might have to start without you if you're going to be that long. A mistress has needs.'

'No, no worries at all, you didn't disturb me, I was just leaving anyway.'

'Well leave quicker. You don't want the party to be over before you get there.'

'That's fine. Okay, I'll be right there.'

Her grin lasted all the way to the Starbucks drive through – a cappuccino for her and a skinny macchiato for Ken.

She turned up Clyde on the radio, and sang along to a throwback song from Simple Minds. It was her dad's favourite song, and Ken liked it too – a bit weird but not entirely surprising given that they were almost the same age. Not that they'd ever met. Lila had never told her parents she was seeing a married man. What was the point of admitting that someone wouldn't leave his wife to be with her? At least, not yet.

If this were a Greek tragedy, she had no doubt that there would be some profound theory that she was attracted to older men because she'd missed her dad so much as a child and never really felt his closeness or approval. But what did the Greeks know? All that mattered was that she loved Ken, and when they'd been apart, she missed their meetings. Missed feeling like this. Missed him.

She'd met him on her first month on the job, bumped into him a few weeks later at a medical conference, and been in bed with him by midnight. Since then, it had been an excruciating seven years of secrets, promises, pleasure and pain. They only ever met in hotels, at quiet meeting points in remote locations or in his office. The closest they'd come to anything resembling a normal relationship was when he travelled to compete in marathons, or to medical conferences. She'd go with him, and there, out of sight, they could eat, and drink, and hold hands and be like every other loved-up couple. That was the pleasure. The pain kicked in when the jealousy crept up on her, when he broke another promise to leave his wife, or when she just desperately wanted to tell the world that she was his girl. She wanted to be Mrs Kenneth Manson. It was like an addiction that she just could not break, no matter how many times he let her down or how hard she tried.

When they'd split the last time, she'd been sure it had been for good, had tried to convince herself that was the case. They'd been in a gorgeous suite at the Blythswood Square Hotel, courtesy, once again, of her company expense account. They were well into their second bottle of wine when she'd pushed him to leave his wife, pressed him for a time frame for them to be together, accused him of keeping her dangling on a string for years, reminded him that she wanted to be married by the time she was thirty next year.

He'd refused. Given her the same old line. He'd leave his marriage when the time was right and only he would decide when that would be. She'd cried. She'd raged. But he didn't budge, so she'd stormed out of the hotel room, gone to the bar, and when she was pulling out her key card to charge her drink to the room, she'd come across the business card that cute guy in the menswear shop had given her that afternoon. On impulse, she'd called, he'd come and picked her up, and she'd cut Ken out of her life.

For a while.

The truth was, much as she tried to make it work with Cammy, he wasn't her guy. Gorgeous, yes. Funny too. But he didn't have a shred of Ken's maturity or come close to his intellect. That's what turned her on. His brains. His presence. What a cliché. The beautiful young blonde and the distinguished older doctor. She was a trophy wife waiting to happen, if only Ken would bloody hurry up and realise it.

When they'd met up again at the convention in London a few weeks ago, she'd immediately sussed that he'd missed her as much as she'd been lost without him.

She'd worn the red dress he loved in the hope that he'd be there and it didn't let her down. By midnight, it had been discarded on the floor of a room at The Dorchester – God bless the company credit card – and by dawn, he was promising her they'd make it work.

It was going to happen. She knew it. She hadn't gambled seven years of her life to walk away with nothing.

In the meantime, she hadn't had the heart to tell Cammy it was over yet. What was the point? So she could lie alone every night, thinking about what Ken was doing, visualising him sleeping with his wife? Cammy was fun, easy on the eye, and good enough in bed that she didn't think of Ken every time she orgasmed, so she'd been happy to hang on to him.

Now, it was time for that to change. It had to. Time to move on and seal the deal on the next stage of her life.

She pulled into the parking space outside the hospital and made her way through the complex maze of corridors and lifts to Ken's office on the fifth floor. Private hospital of course. Ken had given up working for the NHS years before, although that wife of his was still nursing over at Glasgow Central.

His secretary, Marge, was already parked at her desk, her face a mask of efficiency and disapproval. Over the years, Lila had given up trying to win her over. Thankfully, she was screwing Ken, not Marge, so what did it matter what the old boot thought of her? She'd soon change her tune when she was Mrs Lila Manson, wife of the esteemed cardiac surgeon. Then, metaphorically, Marge could kiss her slutty black-knickered arse.

Lila chirped a cheery 'Good morning' to the bitter crone as she passed, long having established that she didn't have to wait to be announced.

The noise of the shower in the office en suite told her that Ken had probably only just arrived before her, no doubt having cycled in. She loved that he kept himself in such good shape. He was over twenty years older than her, but his body – while it didn't compare to Cammy – was that of a man ten years younger. The age difference didn't even factor for her though. She'd always had a thing for older men, as her sixth year biology teacher had found out, when she bumped into him a year or two later on a visit to her uni to give a guest lecture to the science students. They'd spent the next two nights in his South Side flat doing things that they'd probably once covered in human anatomy.

The sound of the shower stopped, followed a few moments later by the click of the door. Ken smiled when he saw her sitting on his desk.

'Calling me this morning? Naughty,' he told her, but she could see he wasn't annoyed. He liked her boldness, just as long as it didn't actually go as far as getting them caught.

A familiar thought ran through Lila's mind. Surely Bernadette must know? She must. How could she not have guessed, not have questioned all those nights when he was with Lila instead of going home to her? Surely, for her own dignity, she should walk away and allow Ken to be with someone who was a perfect match for him?

Lila pushed the question aside, deciding to address the more pressing matters in front of her right now. She held up the coffee.

'Room service,' she announced, flashing a smile that came from the best cosmetic dentist in the city and had set her dad back ten grand. Not that her father had come and held her hand, but a BACS transfer was the second best thing.

Ken took the lid off, dipped his finger in, then trailed a slick of warm coffee from the middle of her neck down to the space between her breasts. She gasped as he leant down and followed the caffeinated path with his tongue. Lila threw her head back, lost in the double pleasure of his hand moving up her thigh.

She opened her legs wider to allow...

The buzz of the phone interrupted the crescendo of ecstasy that was working its way from the toes of her Louboutins upwards.

'Don't answer it,' she whispered, biting his earlobe, holding him there.

'You know I have to,' he said, yanking his head away, all business again now.

The ecstasy was immediately swept away by a tsunami of irritation. That bitch Madge. She'd probably timed that, waiting for what she reckoned would be just the right moment to disturb them.

Ken picked up the phone, slipped it under his ear and pulled his tie on while he spoke.

'Yes? Okay, I'm on my way. Tell them to go ahead and get him into pre-op.'

When he put the phone down, Lila looked at him quizzically.

'So you do actually have a surgery this morning? I thought you were just saying that as an excuse to leave home early. Didn't you only have an afternoon surgery scheduled today?'

'An angiogram. Came in late last night.'

She couldn't hide her disappointment. She'd booked out an hour slot for him this morning on her work schedule – her bosses didn't need to know that the wealth of orders that came from Ken's department required five minutes of conversation and fifty-five minutes of the kind of demonstration that hadn't come from her company presentation manual. So far today was turning out to be a complete bust. Unless…

'Will you be finished for noon? I was supposed to meet my mum for lunch but she got a better offer. We could…'

'River Hotel,' he said briskly, pulling his jacket on and making for the door, already in fully fledged 'doctor' mode. Lila got a flutter of a thrill just from watching him.

God, he was sexy. She felt no guilt about their affair, but even if she had, this feeling of desperate attraction would have been enough to muffle it to death.

'I'll have a couple of hours before afternoon surgery.'

'That's all?' Lila asked, exaggerating the petulance.

He smiled – that gorgeous, square-jawed smile that made him look like the doctor in an American soap.

'That's all,' he repeated, running a tantalising finger down the side of her cheek. 'But I promise we'll make it count.'

That was the moment. The moment that she decided that she wasn't going to wait any longer, couldn't bear not to have him. Enough of playing to his timescale. A plan had been forming in her mind for a long, long time, one that took bottle and a bit of subterfuge, and sure it risked backfiring in a major way, but Lila just had to have confidence that it wouldn't. She wasn't prepared to spend another Christmas hoping he'd get away to call her. She definitely didn't want to spend it pretending to Cammy that they were love's young dream.

She wanted Ken. And her. Together. Waking up on Christmas morning, swapping the kind of gifts that involved nudity.

No more procrastination. Ken would thank her when it was done and they were together.

By the end of the day, she decided, Ken Manson would be all hers. He just didn't know it yet.

10 a.m. – Noon

5

Caro

The old man was snoozing now and it reminded her of a photo she'd found in a box of old pictures of her grandad, fast asleep in a chair, still wearing his party hat after his Christmas lunch. Her granddad on her mother's side. Caro couldn't ever remember being curious about her grandparents on her father's side. There was no conversation that she could recall, no big discussion, only the knowledge, for as far back as she could remember, that her dad's parents had also died before she was born.

A memory, from a long time ago, surfaced into her consciousness. Her mum, Yvonne, brushing Caro's hair before bedtime. She'd been about five, maybe six. Her dad sleeping on the sofa. There had been something wrong with him, but Caro hadn't understood it at the time. He'd been ill and before he came back they'd gone to visit him somewhere. In hospital perhaps? Her forehead crumpled as she tried to pull out more details from the dusty recesses of her childhood. Nothing. Just a feeling that she'd been afraid, and that her mother, Yvonne, had been too.

'We're all he's got,' her mum had said, almost wistfully, as she ran a huge paddle brush through Caro's hair. 'That's why we have to take such good care of him.'

Her mind turned the volume up on another conversation from long ago. This time she'd been eight or nine. It was in the summer holidays, and her dad was home for a few days, before heading off somewhere else with his Very Important Job.

She didn't often get bored – there were always more books to read, more stories to write – but on this day she was missing the company of her school friends.

'I wish I wasn't an only child,' she'd announced over a banana sandwich lunch.

'What are you talking about?' Dad had responded, in what she could see now was feigned shock. 'That's the best way to be! Can you imagine sharing your Christmas presents with someone else?'

She'd thought about it and immediately decided that being an only child maybe wasn't so bad after all. Dad was okay and he had no brothers or sisters either.

Except... perhaps now she did.

Lila Anderson.

Her name floated on the tip of her tongue.

Lila Anderson. My sister.

Hi, I'm Lila's sister.

Nothing felt right about it.

Anderson was a pretty common name. Although, the fact that Lila Anderson had a dad called Jack, who just happened to share a birthday with her own father, and look exactly like him, was stretching the powers of coincidence way too far.

She'd searched the blonde's face for any similarities, but if they were there, she couldn't see them. Sure, they were both blonde, but even then, they were at opposite ends of the fair-haired spectrum. Lila was a light, baby blonde, tumbling in waves that fell halfway down her back. Caro was naturally dark blonde, cut in a long bob that just passed her shoulders. Usually, she wore it tied back in a ponytail, so it didn't get in the way when she was writing on the chalkboard, or marking jotters. Low maintenance, that was how she would describe her look. Not a trait that was shared by the woman, sister or not, in the photos. This was obviously someone who loved to be the centre of attention, who was the star attraction of any occasion. Caro couldn't think of anything worse. Not that she was a shy wallflower, but she definitely preferred to be more low-key than the extrovert in the Facebook photos.

Her phone buzzed and she picked it up quickly, before the noise woke her travel companion. 'Hey,' she whispered, desperately trying not to be one of those people who shared their whole life with every other passenger on a train journey.

Todd dispensed with the fripperies. 'Are you there yet and have you been arrested for stalking? Only, I haven't had a chance to set up a Crowdfunding page for the bail money.'

'Not there yet, no arrest and you've still got plenty of time. We got held up for a while somewhere around Dundee – leaves on the line, they said – so we're just coming into Perth now,' she told him, trying to keep her tone light because this whole thing was so ludicrous it couldn't possibly happen. Could it? She changed the subject. 'Is everything ok?' she asked him, 'Have you called?'

'I've called and everything is fine,' he promised her. It had been her one request, that he call the hospital and check on Mum for her every couple of hours. Actually, it wasn't so much her request as his order. He'd decided she had enough on her plate with one stressful parental situation, so had insisted he help with the other one. Caro knew he felt better because he was doing something productive, so she let him win that one.

'Thank you. So... what are you up to today?'

It was one of those questions that usually made Caro think she had to make more of an effort to enjoy life. Todd never stood still, never had an off day, and he and Jared were on a mission to make the most of their lives.

They went rock climbing. They took spontaneous trips. They went clubbing on a work night. They jet-skied on sunny days. They worked hard and played hard, though the two of them worked in different salons, having decided that they could get too much of a good thing. Todd was tall, athletic, and totally confident in his own skin. He'd always been that easy-going, non-stressy kind of kid, and now he balanced out Jared's boundless enthusiasm and fondness for drama by being an easy-going, non-stressy kind of adult. Caro loved him. Loved them both.

'Took the day off for a rugby tournament this morning. Travelling team from New Zealand. We'll get hammered, I'll get hypothermia, and I'm fairly sure some of my internal organs will be moved to a new location.'

'Ouch.'

'Yep... oh, and Jason will no doubt ask about you.'

Jason was Todd's best friend, and until two months ago, her boyfriend of three years. They'd split – her decision – after her mum's health deteriorated and she found Lila's Facebook post. She couldn't explain why. Something shifted. She didn't have the energy to give anything to him, when every waking moment was about caring for Mum and doing the best job she could as a teacher.

'You didn't tell him where I was going today, did you?'

'Are you kidding? He already thinks you're certifiable for ditching him, so this would only add weight to the theory.'

'Thanks. I think,' she smiled again.

'Right, I need to go. Are you sure you don't want me to jump on a train and head down? I've got the rest of the day off and I could be there this afternoon.'

'Thanks, but honestly I'm fine. Nothing's even going to happen. I just want to see... well, you know. I'm not planning on doing anything drastic. There's every chance I'll be back up on the last train tonight and none the wiser.'

She wasn't being glib. There *was* every chance. In fact, it would probably be the most sensible thing to do. Confrontation wasn't her thing. She just wanted to try to find a way to subtly suss out what was going on.

'You know, messaging her would have saved the train fare and made this all so much easier.'

Todd was convinced it was all a big misunderstanding. Or her dad had a doppelgänger. Or...

'I'm still going with the evil twin, separated at birth theory,' he added.

'Me too,' she agreed. Although, she absolutely didn't. Because, in a completely contradictory, nonsensical way, much of this actually made sense.

Dad had been spending most of his time in Glasgow for as long as she could remember. As far as she knew, he'd stayed in hotels there, but he could easily have been staying with someone else, living with another woman, spawning more kids. Her mum had never gone with him, put off by his protestations that he was swamped with work when he was there.

Mum couldn't protest any more.

The only blessing was that she was too ill to realise he'd gone.

Since Jack had walked away, Caro hadn't heard from him. A few days after he'd left, in a moment of fury and rage at the injustice of his behaviour, she'd called his mobile and discovered it had been disconnected. Not surprising, really. Her whole life, she couldn't remember him calling her a single time. It was always Mum. Mum made the arrangements. Mum visited after she'd moved out. Mum. Not Dad. They'd never been close, never had that emotional bond that she saw between her friends and their fathers. So now, she had to know if this Lila Anderson was the reason why.

'Well, look, if you change your mind, call me back. If the train times don't work, I can always jump in the car.'

'Thanks Todd, but honestly, I'll be fine. And besides, you'll be busy with that Crowdfunding page.'

He was still laughing when he hung up, just as the tempo of the train changed enough to rouse the gentleman sitting opposite her from his sleep. He leaned forward and peered out of the window.

'Ah, almost there.' All traces of sleep on his face were immediately cast aside by excitement. What a lovely man.

There was a screeching of brakes as the train slowed even further, the end of the platform coming into sight now.

Caro got up, steadying herself by leaning against the side of the seat, and pulled down his bag. The train chuntered to a stop.

'Thank you, my dear. It was an absolute pleasure.'

'Merry Christmas. Enjoy your stay with your family.'

'And you my dear,' he replied.

Caro didn't contradict him. Her family wasn't in Glasgow. Her family was Todd, his parents, and a few distant relations that she only ever saw at weddings and funerals. Even Todd's mum and dad, Auntie Pearl and Uncle Bob, had gone off to live in Spain. And there was Mum...

Slipping back into her seat, she glanced out of the window and saw a woman, maybe the same age as her, standing at the end of the platform with a couple of kids of maybe ten or eleven. They started running as soon as they saw the gent she'd shared the journey with. In seconds, they reached him, threw their arms around him, in a group hug. For a moment, Caro's heart ached.

Her children would never do that.

They'd never run and throw their arms around their grandfather, because he'd never been that kind of guy.

He'd never shown much of an interest in Caro, never mind any children she might have. No, he wouldn't be that lovely old man, thrilled to pieces to see his descendants, to know them and pass on his wisdom and the stories of his life.

And they'd never be able to throw their arms around their gran because she was lying in a hospital bed, clinging on to a broken life.

Caro blocked her mind from going there, closed her eyes to stop the tears from falling, then concentrated on her breathing to make her pulse slow back down. In. Out. Inhale. Exhale.

She couldn't think about it now. Over the last couple of months she'd become so practised at keeping it together, acting strong. Not that she'd had a choice. It almost came naturally to her now.

In. Out. Inhale. Exhale. It took a few moments, but she got the emotions under control and the combination of closing her eyes and the late morning winter sun that was shining through the window made her drop off into a welcome sleep.

The next thing she knew, the train was changing tempo once again, the movement and raised noise level in the carriage alerting her to the fact that they were near a station. Maybe Stirling? Falkirk.

She glanced at her watch. No, it couldn't be. Only a few minutes before they'd been in Perth, hadn't they? But no. Her fellow passengers were all on their feet now, the deathly slow movement of the train allowing them to yank down their bags, lift their children, pull on their coats, call loved ones to let them know they had arrived.

Caro stretched up, trying to kick-start both body and brain into action. She wasn't ready for this. She wanted a while longer in the safe cocoon of oblivion before she took any more steps towards finding out if everything she believed to be true was a total sham.

The train was crawling now, nearly stopped, alongside a platform that was almost deserted, making the sign that greeted her impossible to miss.

Glasgow.

She was here.

The truth was out there. All she had to do was walk towards it.

6

Cammy

'Right, action stations,' Val announced. 'Places to go, people to see…'

'… Unsuitable women to get engaged to,' Josie added, with a pointed glare at Cammy.

He grinned in return. 'Josie, I'm not rising to you.'

'Quite right, son – she's the root of all marital evil. Just ignore her,' Val concurred.

'That's not true!' Josie defended herself. 'I love a good romance. But what kind of friend would I be if I didn't warn the boy…'

'I'm past forty…' Cammy said, yet again, aware that when they were locked in debate, neither woman would hear him.

'… that he's about to marry the Glasgow equivalent of the Bride of Chucky.'

Even Val could no longer maintain the argument and hooted with laughter at that one.

'Bet you wish you'd just kept driving that day, ma love,' Josie told him, softening the blow with a grin of affection as she said it. Cammy couldn't remember the exact date, but he knew exactly what day she was referring to.

3 p.m. Glasgow City Centre. Many years before...

Two more drops on his run, then he was done.

Stopped at the traffic lights, he looked at the list on the clipboard next to him. La Femme, L'Homme. He'd delivered stuff there last week too. A new underwear shop that was opening in the Merchant City. Lovely girl, Mel, owned it... She sometimes made him a coffee while he waited for her to check the contents of the box he'd delivered. Forty pairs of Boss boxers, thirty Armani briefs, and a selection of bras that he was fairly sure had something to do with Kylie Minogue. Or perhaps he was making that last detail up in his head.

Anyway, it had been one bright spot in a day doing a job that only served the purpose of paying the bills while he figured out what he really wanted to do.

The traffic lights changed to green and he put his foot down and headed up Ingram Street. He needed to get finished early today if he was going to make it to the gym, before his usual crowd hit a new bar that was opening on Buchanan Street.

As he put the hazards on outside the shop, he noticed the sign, 'Opening tonight', in the window. They were cutting it fine. When he was in last week he'd have said they were nowhere near ready. Going by the crowd of workies he could see inside, they still weren't even close. He offloaded the box from the back of the van, ran up the steps, opened the door and...

'Yer a no-good wanker!'

The shout made his head swivel to the side, and the combination of shock, disorientation and the large box he was carrying conspired to distract him so much that he didn't notice the half-built bra rack on the floor, tripped, flew forward, and ended up in a seriously convoluted position involving a metal frame, a dozen G-strings, a pile of double Ds, and a naked mannequin.

And the owner, Mel, looking down at him, panic-stricken.

Their eyes locked, and he decided that, pain aside, the fall had been worth it.

'Oh, I'm so sorry. I'm so, so sorry,' Mel apologised, before turning to the source of the shout that had started it all.

'For God's sake, Josie, you're going to kill someone.'

'Was she shouting at me?' Cammy asked, confused, injured, dazed.

'No! She was shouting at that vacuum cleaner. It just cut out on her.'

'No good piece of crap,' Josie added, giving it a kick with a Doc Marten.

It was the first time Cammy had laughed all day. The sight of a woman who looked like she was in maybe her late fifties, cigarette hanging out of her mouth, in a profanity-laden, full-body combat dispute with a vacuum cleaner took his mind off the pain he was feeling from the knees down.

'I'm so, so sorry,' Mel said again. 'I don't blame you if you sue. I'll take it out of Josie's wages until the end of time.'

He'd climbed on to a nearby chair and waited until the pain in his legs had dropped from 'definite fracture' to 'perhaps just a strain' and had more amusement in that half hour than he'd done in weeks. Mel. Josie. Their band of friends and family. The banter and bickering between them all had been hilarious. Before he'd stopped to question his motives, he'd told them they were the last call of the day (they weren't), pitched in to help (with a slight limp) and informed Mel that he had retail experience (he didn't). Whether it was out of sympathy, gratitude, or the fervent hope that he didn't know a good lawyer, she'd offered him a job then and there. And that was it. What started as a temporary post in the blokes' section, led to a couple of promotions, until he claimed his *self-penned accolade, Manager of Sack and Crack Support Services.*

Mel and Josie had become his family from that day onwards. His hand-picked, wonderfully dysfunctional, endlessly dramatic family. Josie was the spiky-haired, chain-smoking, gloriously inappropriate aunt he'd never had. And Mel... Mel was his boss, his best-friend, his...

'Are you okay?' Val asked him, cutting into his thoughts. 'Only you look like...'

'...you're having second thoughts?' Josie asked, hopefully.

'Nope, just revisiting the past for a moment. The early days, you, Mel, and me in the shop. They were great times, Josie.'

'They were, right up until you hotfooted it off to LA and deserted us,' she agreed, her tone mellowing, showing the soft side that she generally kept disguised under a veneer of sarcasm and brutal honesty.

'How's Mel doing?' he asked, confident that he'd made the question sound nonchalant and casual.

Josie's response said otherwise. 'She's doing great.' That was all. No elaboration. No details. Just, perhaps, a tiny hint of sorrow. Or maybe it was sympathy.

He shook it off. No point in dragging all that back up now. And anyway, today wasn't the day for looking backwards. From the moment several years before that he'd said goodbye to Mel, he'd been all about moving forwards, keeping going, cutting losses.

Since he'd returned from LA, he'd used the cash he'd earned to fund the new shop, taking the vacant lease on the premises that had once been La Femme, L'Homme, now closed down and long gone.

His new venture had been a success from day one.

To the outside world, Cammy was a man about town, an irrepressibly handsome, successful businessman and – until Lila – one of the most eligible bachelors in the city.

It had all gone to plan so far. Career established? Tick. Financial security? Tick. Love? Tick. Now it was time to focus on the next stage in his life and after getting used to the idea for the last few weeks, he knew he wanted to marry Lila. He wanted to have kids. Enough of being the perennial bachelor. He'd had a couple of decades of partying hard, with no responsibilities or commitments, but lately, it hadn't been enough. Making this step was the right move, he was sure of it. This was the first time he'd felt this way since...

He stopped himself. Damn, it still hurt. He'd been in love before and he'd messed it up, not told her, let someone else have the life that he wanted. He wasn't going to make the same mistake again. And so what if he'd only known Lila for a few months? It felt right. That was all that mattered.

'Right let's go, ladies.'

'Under protest,' Josie muttered.

Val and Cammy ignored her.

As they pulled out of the underground car park, Val stopped for a moment and checked a page on her notepad. 'Right, first stop, the arcade. Today is going to go exactly to plan. I can feel it in my water.'

The traffic was heavy all the way into the city centre, to the busy streets surrounding the pedestrianised area, but eventually they slipped into one of the few parking spaces still available in the multistorey in Mitchell Street. Cammy was surprised there were any left. This was the last Friday before Christmas and the streets were heaving.

From there, they walked down Mitchell Lane, and onto Buchanan Street, crossed through the throng of festive shoppers, workers and buskers, then into the Argyle arcade, home to most of Glasgow's fine jewellery stores. He'd taken ages picking the ring. Who knew there were so many choices? A solitaire. A trilogy. Diamond. Precious stones. In the end, he'd gone for a square emerald, with a diamond baguette on either side. He'd no idea what a baguette was, other than something that could be filled with tuna and eaten at lunch, but the manager of the shop had won him over to it, said it was similar to the one that he'd bought his wife and they'd been married for thirty years. Cammy took that as a good omen. Not that he believed in omens, but still...

The trio hadn't even reached the shop when he realised something was amiss. The shutters were still down and there were a few people loitering outside.

'Someone must have slept in,' Val commented. 'I just hope they had a wild night and it was worth it.'

Cammy didn't hear the end of the sentence, too focussed on the sign that had now come into his field of vision, the one that was stuck to the barred window, in front of an empty display area and right next to the iron grate that was blocking the door.

CLOSED UNTIL FURTHER NOTICE.

'Cammy... tell me that's not the...' Val couldn't get the words out.

'It is,' he answered.

'The ring, you've already paid for it?'

Of course he had. Not all of it. But a hefty deposit, almost a grand, to secure the sale. He hadn't wanted to take it home in case Lila found it, so he'd decided it would be far better to leave it here and pick it up on the morning of the proposal.

They were at the door now, next to a woman who was being comforted by a man as she sobbed, a couple of elderly bystanders and a security guard.

'What's going on here, mate?' Cammy asked the guard, hoping that it was something minor that had delayed the opening. A puncture. A hangover. A lottery win.

'Shut down. Manager did a midnight flit with the

cash, the stock and the owner's wife. Don't fancy his chances if that guy finds him before the cops do.'

This couldn't be happening. For a moment, he hoped it was all an elaborate ruse dreamt up by Josie to derail the nuptials, but she looked as shocked as him and, God love her, was offering to sacrifice herself to fix it.

'Want me to break in and see if it's still there?' Josie hissed. 'At my age, they'd never convict me.'

That was all he needed – the intervention of Glasgow's finest CID. 'Thanks for the offer, but we're good.'

Except, this wasn't good. It wasn't good at all.

A grand. Gone. His ring. Gone. His plan for the day. Seriously gone awry.

Just as well he didn't believe in omens.

Because if he did...

7

Bernadette

'Bernie, what happened to your phone?' Sarah asked, clocking the screen as she placed a large box down on the table next to it.

'Dropped it when I was coming down the stairs earlier,' Bernadette replied, her face flushing as she realised she was still lying for him. Why? Habit of a lifetime.

One that she had to break now.

'Okay...' Sarah answered, failing to hide her scepticism.

Bernadette cut her off. 'What's in the box?'

'A cake. The order got cancelled last night after I'd already made it. Not sure what happened. They just left a message on my answering machine to let me know. Anyway, it's already paid for, so thought we could use it to comfort eat our way through any flashpoints of stress today.'

With a flourish, Sarah lifted off the lid to expose a perfect cake in the shape of a push-up bra. Bernadette reckoned it was probably around a 44D.

Despite the tornado of apprehension that was twisting her guts, she couldn't help but smile. Sarah had been her friend since high school, bonded over a mutual adoration for Martin Kemp from Spandau Ballet, and shoulder pads so wide they had to turn sideways to get through a door.

Sarah had recovered from her Martin Kemp crush and gone on to marry a journalist, Drew, who – oh the cliché – had left her for a younger woman when their youngest was only months old. Sarah had spent the next fifteen years working away at her home-based cake business, avoiding any kind of relationship, until she went on a cruise last year and met Piers, the man of her dreams. If Bernadette was being honest with herself, it was one of the events that had contributed to her final decision to leave Kenneth. Sarah was so happy now with Piers. At fifty, she had finally found the man she was meant to be with and it had given her a second lease of life. She radiated happiness, loved every day, and went to sleep beside a man who adored her and wanted to make her happy.

Bernadette had always thought the chance of that had passed her by. Sarah's joy convinced her otherwise.

Not that she wanted another relationship. No way. Not for a long, long time. Maybe ever. She'd be happy just going to sleep at night, content and relaxed, not on tenterhooks or seething with unspoken disgust for the man lying next to her.

'How are you feeling?' Sarah asked her gently.

'Like I want to forget the whole thing,' Bernadette answered truthfully, 'but don't worry, I won't.'

Listening, Sarah reached over for a spoon from the draining board and took a chunk of the cake, saying nothing because it had all been said. Bernadette had shared everything with her friend over the years. Sarah had never judged her for staying, but always made it clear that she would do anything she could to help her leave. Bernadette could sense that she was delighted that day had finally come.

'Want some?' Sarah asked, pointing to the sponge.

Bernadette would normally be first in the queue to join her, but not today. Didn't have the stomach for it.

'So what do we do first?' Sarah asked.

'That's the problem, I don't know. Any of the things could tip him off, so I don't know where to start. I need to tell the kids, but either of them could tell him. I need to take my share of our savings – I've set up my own account that he knows nothing about – but if he looks at the online banking he'll notice. And I need to move everything I love out of the house, but what if he comes home at lunchtime and there I am, trying to manoeuvre my mother's standard lamp into the back of your van?'

'Your mother's standard lamp will stick out the back window, but we'll get it in somehow,' Sarah retorted, trying to diffuse Bernadette's rising panic with humour. It wasn't working. 'Okay, breathe. Just breathe. Let's think about this rationally. Let's pack up the stuff from your wardrobes and anything else that isn't in plain sight, and take it to my house first.'

Sarah had convinced her to go stay with her and Piers at first. Bernadette was fairly sure it was so that she wouldn't crumble and return to Kenneth, but her friend's fears were unfounded. Once she got out of there, nothing would ever bring her back. This was the house that she'd brought the kids up in, that she'd lived in for thirty years, but she wouldn't miss it for a second. It was tainted. Every shade of paint, every carpet, every painting on a wall chosen by Kenneth, whether she wanted it or not. He'd controlled everything and she would be happy if she never saw any of it again. In fact, she was counting on today being the last day she had to look at it.

Sarah was still planning. 'Then we can come back later, once he's in afternoon surgery, and get anything he might notice.'

Bernadette nodded her agreement. Made sense. Jesus, she was a charge nurse, a woman who organised and ran a busy ward like clockwork, who commanded the respect of her peers and managed healthcare plans, traumas, tragedy, and – worse – patients' relatives, but this whole situation had completely paralysed her coping skills and initiative. He wasn't even here right now and still he was having an effect on her. Come on, Bernie, time to get moving, she told herself.

'And I think we should go speak to Nina first,' Sarah added. Just the very thought of it made Bernadette want to vomit. Kenneth had always presented the best of himself to the kids, so they only ever knew the public Kenneth, the funny, charming, successful, perfect dad they'd grown up with. How could she tell her daughter that she was walking out on her father after thirty years of marriage? Nina was a mother, with kids of her own, but still… no one wanted to deal with that kind of news.

Sarah didn't give her time to ponder the devastation she was about to wreak. 'Right, come on then, let's get started, before I eat any more of this cake and my hips explode.'

She forced her legs to move and follow Sarah. Upstairs, Bernadette pulled every one of their suitcases out of the hall cupboard and within an hour each one was full. Over the last few weeks, on the pretence of having a clear-out, she'd already sorted out everything she was taking with her. The jewellery her mum left her? Taking. The keepsake box from every one of the kids' milestones? Taking. Her uniforms and everyday clothes? Taking. The outfits she'd bought for yet another one of Kenneth's interminable work functions? Leaving. Her wedding dress? Leaving. Preferably on a pyre in the back garden before nightfall.

They humped the cases downstairs, Bernadette rejecting Sarah's offer to have Piers come over and help them. Her closest friend she could handle, but – much as she'd grown hugely fond of Piers in the short time she'd known him – she didn't want any other witnesses to the most traumatising, nerve-wracking episode of her life.

It was only when they were loaded and leaving that Bernadette's heart began to slightly decrease from a speed that would set off a monitor in her husband's ward. That was all she needed – to leave her husband and then end up on his operating table. Breathe. Breathe. Breathe. If she made it through this day it would be a miracle.

The traffic was light all the way to Sarah's home, only a couple of streets away in the West End of the city. Sarah backed the van into the garage and they unloaded in five minutes of pulling, pushing and exertion.

'Am I the only one wishing I'd taken up some of that boxercise nonsense?' Sarah asked, panting, leaning against the side of her van, hands on knees. 'Bernie, I love you,' she spluttered between breaths, 'but we're too old for this.'

Bernadette grinned, then realised that her emotional barometer had swung the other way, and felt tears falling down her face. She had no idea why. Bugger. 'Sorry, honey,' she immediately apologised. 'This is supposed to be a Thelma and Louise moment and I'm turning it into Sleeping with the Fecking Enemy.'

'Don't you dare apologise,' Sarah chided, summoning all her strength to push herself up and fold her arms around her friend.

Bernadette rested her cheek on Sarah's shoulder. 'I just feel... feel... like I've been totally spineless. And I still am. I'm bloody terrified. How pathetic is that? I keep thinking what if he's right. What if I'm hopeless, if I can't manage on my own, if I'll fall apart without him? I know I won't – but I can't stop the conversation in my head, that niggling bloody voice of his, the one that's always doubting me, telling me I can't do anything right.'

'Honey, you've listened to that for thirty years – it's not going to turn off overnight. But you're here, you're doing this, and it's going to be okay. It really is. I promise you.'

Bernadette lifted her head so they were face to face. 'And what am I going to say when he turns up here, or at my work?' Another two fat tears exploded from her eyes. That was it. That was the crux of it, the biggest bloody terror of all. What was he going to do when he found out? He'd never laid a finger on her, but somehow that didn't matter. How many times had she told patients that emotional abuse could be as damaging as physical abuse? When she was on general wards, before she moved to A & E, how many times had she watched a woman flinch at visiting time when her husband walked in the door, all flowers and proclamations of care. Bernadette had learned to spot them a mile off. The men who acted like the Billy Big Bollocks, the charmers who could win anyone over with the right words and a bit of charisma, while the pupils of the women's eyes darted from face to face, shadowed with the fear of knowing that it could change in a heartbeat, or that they'd pay for it later.

Sometimes she felt being married to Kenneth had made her a far better nurse. She understood. Saw the truth that others might overlook. If her thoughts were welcome, she'd gently caution those women to build a support network, to make plans, to find ways of building their confidence in the hope that they'd find it in themselves to make the break.

Now it was time to take her own advice.

'I can do this,' she said, to herself more than to Sarah.

Sarah's hug was warm and it was crushing to the chest area. 'You can, my love. Let's keep going. That's what we need to do today. One thing off the list, now on to the next. But I need to go to the loo first because I'm at that age.'

She nipped in through the side door from the garage to the toilet off the utility room, then reappeared a few moments later.

Bernadette was already waiting in the car, anxiety over telling her daughter rising with every second.

After the shortest fifteen minutes of her life, they pulled into the driveway of Nina's home in a new estate on the outskirts of Bearsden.

'I'm going to wait here.' Sarah told her, producing a Kindle from her handbag. 'Just shout if you need me.'

'Thanks. I mean it, Sarah. Thanks so much for this.'

Hands shaking, Bernadette pulled the handle on the door and climbed out. This was it. Everything that had been done already this morning could be undone. She could take her stuff back, unpack it again, put it where it had been and he would be none the wiser. But once the words she was about to say next were out, there was never going to be a way to take them back. After a lifetime of thinking about it, of planning how she'd break the news, of rumination over the sentences and coming up with arguments to counter the objections, the time had come. And her mind was totally blank.

She rang the doorbell.

Don't be in. Don't be in. Please don't be in.

The thudding of little Casey's footsteps down the wooden floor of the hall told her otherwise.

It took a few seconds for Nina to catch up, and another few for her to unlock the multitude of contraptions, designed to stop an inquisitive toddler, with a flair for the Houdini, from escaping.

Eventually the door swung open and there was her daughter, her three-year-old grandson Casey at her knee, eighteen-month-old Milo on her hip.

For a moment, Nina's likeness to Kenneth jarred her. The same tall, athletic frame. His blue eyes. The dark hair that he'd raged against when it began to turn grey. There was no denying that physically, she came from her father's side of the gene pool. Thankfully, emotionally, she had more of Bernadette's DNA.

'Mum! What are you doing here? Come on in! You should have phoned and I'd have made something for lunch and...' She stopped. Her gaze went to the van in the driveway, to her Auntie Sarah, as she'd always called her, sitting in the driver's seat. And then back to her mum, standing on the doorstep, her face grey, her eyes bloodshot with tears. 'Oh God,' she whispered. 'What is it? Has something happened to Dad?'

8

Lila

At the traffic lights, Lila fixed her lipstick, pouted, took a selfie, and posted it to her Instagram. No hashtags required. She'd have a hundred likes within minutes. That's what happened when you made a bit of an effort with your appearance. It was all marketing, wasn't it? Everything was just fodder for Facebook, for Twitter, for Instagram. Of course, she posted simultaneously on all of them. A gorgeous meal? It went on there. A great night out? A gym session where she was looking seriously cute? All of it snapped and posted.

Her boss at work had once questioned her level of social activity and she'd pointed out that she worked far longer hours than her job spec required, so she was more than entitled to a few minutes of online action throughout the day. He'd never mentioned it since and it was just as well, because she had no intention of stopping.

It didn't matter how she was feeling, whether she was up, down, pissed off or frustrated, the image that she put out there would convince anyone who looked at her pages that she had the most glamorous, perfect life.

And most of the time – okay, some of the time – she did. Her mother had taught her that. If they had a family crest, it would say 'hair done, lipstick on, face the world.'

According to her social media, every day was a good day. She didn't have stresses because she was *'too blessed to be stressed'*. She didn't have casual friends, she had *'brilliant times with people who loved her'*. Some might call it fake, but she preferred to think of it as spreading positivity.

Obviously, there couldn't be any photos of Ken on her pages, but that would change soon, when their relationship was out in the open and they were together. Telling Cammy would be a drag, because she was pretty sure he wouldn't see it coming and he'd no doubt be devastated at losing her, but it was just one of those things. He'd get over it. It wasn't as if they were married or had kids. They'd had a good time, and yes, when she'd split with Ken she might have led Cammy to believe she wanted more, might have been a bit vulnerable and emotional, but she was over it. Normal service resumed. Thank God. Now to take it to the next level. And she would. Just as soon as she felt one hundred per cent ready to make her move.

Before she could do anything, her phone rang. The office number flashed up, so she flicked it to answering machine. The last thing she needed was someone on her case today. Probably some paperwork query. Why did they get so hung up on that kind of stuff? Especially on the Friday before Christmas? She smashed her target every week – surely that should be enough for them to get someone else to take care of the menial grunt work?

She'd been working this territory since she started with the company straight out of university almost eight years ago, so she knew the best contacts and how to make them work for her. A bottle of whisky here. A spa voucher there. She had one doctor who insisted on an overnight stay at Gleneagles every time he placed an order – completely unethical and very expensive, but it was a small price to pay for the amount of business he put her way.

But enough about work. Time to get more important things sorted out.

She checked her watch. Ten forty-five. She'd made it just in time. She hopped out of the car and into the clubhouse. In the summer, it was packed with golfers sporting trousers that were crimes against fashion. In the winter, the die-hards still gathered to socialise, hit a few balls on the under-cover driving range or use the high-tech simulators to improve their game before the start of the next season. Mum had said that she was teeing off on that stupid machine with Dad, but if Lila made her a better offer there was no way she would resist.

Coffee and a gossip versus four hours of hitting a ball against a screen? No contest.

There were a few raised eyebrows of appreciation as she crossed the bar area, making a beeline for her parents, who were sitting at a table by the window.

Her mum spotted her first. 'Darling, what are you doing here?'

'Coming to save you from wrecking a perfectly good morning by spending it hitting a ball with a stick,' she said, punctuating her words with two cheek kisses for each parent.

Her dad didn't look thrilled to see her and that irked her. It always had. Even as a little girl, she could remember desperately wanting his approval, yet never quite feeling like she had it. In some ways, he and Ken had similar personalities. Both strong alpha males, leaders, not followers. Single-minded, driven, successful men who knew exactly what they wanted in life and made no apology for claiming it. Lila admired that kind of focus – unless it was, like this morning, hampering her social life.

'We're just about to get started. You're welcome to join us if you have shoes that are a bit easier on the feet. Or I could pick you up a pair in the golf shop,' he offered.

'Thanks Dad, I'd take you up on that… but I'd rather poke my eyes out with a fork.'

Her mum's laughter made several of the old guys at the bar smile their way. Of course they did. Her mum – hair done and lipstick on as always.

'I can't believe you're going over to the dark side, Mum. Can't one of those guys do this with you, Dad, and then my mother and I can sit here and drink coffee like civilised people do?' she quipped.

'But, darling, I want to do it. Your dad is going to help me with my swing.'

'Mum, you hate golf!'

'Well, sometimes it just takes you a while to appreciate something and now I'm learning to appreciate golf.'

If there was some loaded meaning in there, Lila didn't want to think about it. Nor did she want to think about the fact that her parents were holding hands and her mother was looking at her dad like they were fifteen and he'd just felt her up at the youth club disco.

Urgh, this was nauseating.

'And anyway, you know this is good for your dad's health. The doctor said so.'

Dad nodded, almost smugly. There it was. Dad's health. She had absolutely no recollection of it, but apparently Dad had had a heart attack when he was in his early thirties, and then a few scares since then, the last one just before he'd moved home full time. After the heart attack, his doctors had assured him that he'd live a long, normal life as long as he took care of himself and Jack had taken them at their word. He ate well, exercised religiously, and, as soon as he'd paid off their mortgage, stored up a considerable pension, and banked enough for a long, carefree retirement. It had been a well worn mantra over the years. 'Your poor dad, having to live with a heart condition.' To be honest, Lila sometimes wondered if it was just an excuse to give him an easy life and have everything revolve around him. It was after his last scare – thankfully nothing serious – he'd decided to take an early pension deal at work and come home full-time.

Lila had hoped that it would bring them closer together, but so far he hadn't shown a great amount of interest in her life. Not that she'd ever admit it or say it out loud, but deep down she knew that she wasn't a priority in Jack Anderson's world. She reckoned the pecking order was golf, Mum, holidays, and she perhaps scraped fourth place. Maybe that would change now. Or not.

'Never mind darling, pop over at the weekend and we'll have lunch,' her dad offered. 'Call first though, because we haven't made plans yet.'

With that, and a couple of guilt-free hugs, they were off out the door, still holding hands like they were in the first flush of rampant attraction. It was enough to put her off her lunch.

Back out in the car, she sat for a moment and quietly seethed. She and her mum had been a gang of two her whole life. She knew it was ridiculous, but just for a moment, she felt... envious. What was this? Make Lila jealous day?

She checked her watch. Eleven fifteen. She didn't feel like trying to squeeze in a couple of cold calls today – wasn't in the mood – so she should probably just head back across to the hotel to meet Ken. It was one of those faceless chain hotels, overlooking the Clyde, near the exhibition centres and concert halls. Not exactly The Dorchester, but she guessed that since he'd suggested it, he was planning to pay. Cash, no doubt. Didn't want to lay a paper trail that could make the wife suspicious. Lila totally understood that, just as she understood that he couldn't lavish her with gifts or take her to exotic places, and she'd been prepared to put up with it because she knew the endgame. It would all be worth it when she was Mrs Kenneth Manson.

But she was sick of being second choice. Sick of it. What was it they always said on those psychobabble training courses her company sent the reps on every year? Nothing changes unless you make it happen. If you want to be a winner, you have to see obstructions as opportunities. And a dozen more tosh-like phrases that everyone forgot the minute they left the Holiday Inn conference hall.

They had a point, though.

She wanted to be with Ken. But there were obstacles. All she had to do was remove them.

Before she could change her mind, she scrolled through her phone, found the number she was looking for and pressed the green button to connect.

'Central Hospital, Glasgow, can I help you?'

'Ward 34 please.'

She knew where Ken's wife worked. It was one of those details she'd sussed years ago. She'd even seen her once, when she'd persuaded a locum to give her a tour of the ward on the premise of a marketing survey. Short. Dark auburn hair, swept back in a bun. No make-up. Completely forgettable. It blew her mind that Ken could be with a woman like this.

'Ward 34, can I help you?'

It took her a split second to realise that the thudding sound was her heart beating out of her chest. Was she really going to do this? Was she going to be that cliché – the mistress that told the wife what was going on so she could have the guy all to herself?

'Yes, can I speak to Sister Manson, please? Bernadette Manson.'

Apparently she was.

'Sorry, Sister Manson isn't on duty today. Can I take a message?'

There was a pause as Lila fought to control an explosion of emotions. Disappointment. Annoyance. Despair. Impatience. And yes, perhaps a small tad of relief.

'No, that's okay, I'll call back tomorrow.'

Would she? Would she really?

She hung up, a sheen of sweat popping out above her Revlon red lipstick.

No, she wouldn't call back tomorrow. This had to happen today. Right now. Winners remove obstacles. Sure, Ken might be pissed off initially, but the last six months they'd spent apart had shown him that he couldn't live without her. They were meant to be together, so what was the point in waiting any longer? He'd thank her when she was riding on top of him in a bungalow suite at Sandy Lane on their honeymoon.

She picked up her phone and stared at it for a few seconds, waiting for her heartbeat to return to normal. That last call had been rash. Impulsive. This time, she wanted to think it through, be prepared for what was going to come back on the other end.

Be sympathetic, caring even, but firm.

'Bernadette? My name is Lila Anderson. I'm afraid I have some news that you might find disturbing, so I'll come straight to the point.'

Too direct? Too harsh? Too alarming?

'Bernadette, my name is Lila Anderson. I'm calling to talk to you about your husband, Ken…'

That made it sound like she was about to tell her he'd been run over by a bus. Or that he needed a top-up on his travel insurance.

'Bernadette, this is Lila Anderson, your husband's mistress. Yes, he's a great shag, isn't he?'

At least that one made her smile and took the heart rate down a notch or two. Maybe she should wait. Yes, that's what she should do. Go, have glorious, earth-trembling sex with Ken, then see how she felt after that. Only, she knew the answer already. She'd feel cheated. Sad when he left. Immediately followed by irritation that he wouldn't make the move he'd been promising for years.

She snatched the phone up before she could change her mind, then scrolled down to the number that had been sitting there, like an unexploded landmine, since about a month after she met the dashing doctor for the first time. She'd got it from his phone, stored it, knowing there would be a day she might want to use it.

That day was today.

Time to win the end game.

She blocked her caller ID just to be cautious, then pressed the phone call button next to 'Ken, home'.

It rang.

'Hello, Bernadette, my name is Lila Anderson. I'm a friend of Ken's. I wonder if we could meet and talk?'

Yes, that was it.

Still ringing.

Face to face. It would be uncomfortable, but that way Bernadette could see the competition, realise that she didn't have any chance of winning and she'd walk away. Job done. Obstacle removed.

Still ringing.

'Hi…'

The shock almost made Lila drop the phone. Ken. His voice.

'This is the Manson home. Leave a message and we'll return your call.'

An answering machine. Lila broke the connection and leaned her head back against the leather of the seat.

Fuck. Adrenalin coursed through her veins, closely followed by another dose of that earlier mix of disappointment and relief.

She put the phone down and switched on the engine.

Time to go get laid by her boyfriend.

She could deal with the wife later.

Noon – 2 p.m.

9

Caro

So now what? She was here. In Glasgow. A city she'd only visited twice – once when Todd begged her to go with him to a Beyoncé concert, and the second time when she and Jason were flying to New York and the direct flight from Glasgow was the cheapest way to go. Now she was here with no plan whatsoever, on a trip that could only be described as borderline deranged.

Great.

The buzz of her phone made her pause at the end of the platform. A message. Jason. The coincidence jarred her.

Hey, how's things? Drinks sometime over Christmas?

Her thumb returned the message.

All good thanks.

It wasn't.

Will call you re: drinks.

She wouldn't.

He was a nice guy. They'd been together a long time. But the truth was that she didn't love him and there was no point in keeping it going on false hope and delusion. Wasn't that what her dad had done to her mum? Mum had spent her whole life loving a guy, believing that he loved her back. Maybe he did. Or maybe he was just a vile, arrogant bastard who enjoyed her devotion and the adoration she lavished on him. Maybe he just needed a place to stay when he was in Aberdeen. Or perhaps he was keeping his options open by maintaining two completely separate lives, and now he'd chosen his preferred option?

She needed to find out for sure.

The streets were packed with shoppers as she left Queen Street Station, thick jackets on, hats pulled down against the chill, scarves around their necks, bags dangling from gloved hands. Over to her left she could see a beautiful building she recognised as the City Chambers, while George Square, directly across the street, was a Christmas wonderland of lights and stalls, an ice rink in the middle, filled with people getting into the festive spirit. The smell of food from the stalls and a tightness in her stomach reminded her that, other than the packet of shortbread on the train, she hadn't eaten since... since... God, was it really yesterday lunchtime? Todd had appeared at her house, bringing a sandwich and a last-minute plea for her to change her mind about this trip. She'd accepted the sandwich.

Something to eat. But where? She crossed the road and began to walk, taking the natural route along the edge of the square, going right, then left, along the other side, until she was standing on the opposite side to the station. This road was even busier, bustling with people, heads down, striding in every direction. It was the smell she registered first, her eyes followed a few seconds later. Tapas. A Spanish restaurant sat just a few yards away and her feet were already taking her there.

'Table for two?' the waiter asked, assuming she'd be meeting someone. Caro almost wished she were. Why hadn't she let Todd come? He thought it was because she was brave and stoic, but the opposite was true. She hadn't wanted anyone here with her in case she backed out, couldn't face it and hotfooted it home without an answer. 'Just for one,' she replied, then followed him to a cosy little table in the corner.

She scanned the menu, making up her mind to go for the easiest option. A set lunch. Three tapas.

'A tortilla, garlic mushrooms, and chicken croquettes please. And a black coffee.'

The waiter took the menu from her with a smile and went off to make it happen. On any other day, she'd enjoy this. Spain had been her holiday destination of choice for years, Mum's favourite too. Unexpected tears filled the tracks behind her lower lids, before a jarring memory beat them back down.

Spain. Mallorca. She would have been about fifteen. They had adjoining rooms in a hotel about ten minutes away from the beach in Puerto Pollensa. They didn't get away every year, but when they did, it was always to the same place. The hotel wasn't flash but it was nice, maybe a three star, with a buffet restaurant and a swimming pool big enough to do laps if you could avoid the families playing on their lilos. Not her parents. They would lie on adjacent sunloungers, holding hands across the gap, pretty much inseparable the whole time. Mum didn't exactly neglect her – they'd still have the odd swim and eat together – but she made it clear she wanted to spend as much time as possible with Dad. Caro always made a point of trying to find another single child on the first day, otherwise she knew it would be a lonely fortnight.

On this morning, though, she knew immediately that something was wrong when she woke up. There were voices already in the other room. That was odd. She was always first to wake, would read a few chapters of her book, before creeping about, getting dressed in silence so she didn't wake her parents.

She wandered through and saw Mum, face pale, the frown of desolation causing two deep lines between her eyebrows.

A glance to her right told her why. Dad was packing, throwing things in a suitcase. Again.

What was that? The third time? Maybe the fourth?

They'd be on holiday, supposedly for two weeks, and halfway through, Dad would have to leave because of some crisis with his Very Important Job.

Off he'd go, leaving just Caro and her mum to spend the second week alone. If Caro was being honest, she preferred it. At least then she felt like she had some company, albeit Mum would function like she was shrouded in a cloak of... not misery. Pointlessness. It was like there was no point being there, enjoying the holiday, making an effort, if Dad wasn't there with her, and even Caro's cajoling couldn't quite make her smile reach her eyes.

Dad's absence was a recurring theme that she hadn't even acknowledged at the time. Her teachers thought she lived with just her mum, because Dad never once went to a parents' night. Or a school show. Or a sports day. His Very Important Job didn't allow it.

How many birthdays had he missed? How many bank holidays was he gone? And Christmas...

Another flashback. She was perhaps nine or ten. The house was decorated, the tree was up, Mum was singing along to the Christmas songs that were playing on the music channel on the TV. Dad was on his way back from… somewhere. She couldn't remember where, but he was going to be home soon. They were going to have a fabulous Christmas together, just the three of them tonight, and then Mum's family were all coming tomorrow for lunch. Auntie Pearl and Uncle Bob. Todd. It was going to be great.

The song changed to that one by Chris Rea, but Mum knew the words to that too, still singing along as she chopped the vegetables for tomorrow's soup. Then the phone rang. It was before they had a mobile phone – just a house phone, with big push buttons to make a call, sitting on a side table by the couch.

'Will you get that, Caro? It'll be Auntie Pearl. She's probably just remembered she's to bring pudding tomorrow.'

Caro lifted the big red handset. 'Hello?'

'Caro, it's Dad. Can I speak to your mum?'

The recollection jarred with Caro now. He never spoke to her like he was in the least bit interested. There was no, 'Hello, darling, how are you? How's school? What are you up to?' Nothing. She hadn't even registered it at the time – it was all she was used to – but looking back as an adult, she could see that it was strange. Cold.

'Sure, Dad.' She took the phone away from her ear. 'Mum, it's Dad!'

The expression on her mum's face changed instantly.

Her eyes shot to the starburst clock on the wall, then, like a stone statue crumbling, her features began to fold in on each other, her shoulders slumped, her whole demeanour deflated. A few moments ago, she was singing and laughing. Now she was dead woman walking.

She took the phone and Caro could only hear her side of the conversation.

'Oh, Jack, no. But we've got everyone coming and we were so looking forward to...' Pause, then all her annoyance evaporated, changed to sympathy. 'No, I know it's worse for you. I know. I'm sorry. Yes. I understand. I'll just... miss you. No, we'll be fine. Really. It's fine. I love you. Yes, that would be great, even if you can only get five minutes on Boxing Day...'

And then the conversation ended and Caro knew what it meant. He wasn't going to make it back. Something had happened in his Very Important Job that was going to keep him away for Christmas. Again.

Mum slouched on to the couch. No more singing, now there was just Mum, staring into space, looking like her world had fallen apart. Caro got up and went over to the kitchen area, took over chopping the vegetables for the soup. Mum wouldn't get anything else done tonight. She'd just stay there, miserable, wishing that he would walk in the door and make it all better. It was only hours later that Caro realised he hadn't asked to speak to her again to explain he wasn't coming home, maybe even wish her a merry Christmas. Of course he hadn't.

The waiter appeared back, took her dishes and coffee off a huge circular tray and placed them down in front of her with a flourish.

When he'd retreated, Caro realised that she'd lost her appetite.

That Christmas, like many more of the same, had come with a complete façade of merriment. Auntie Pearl and Uncle Bob and Todd had joined them as planned, and they'd had lunch, sang carols, played board games, sat down together between the main course and the pudding to watch *Top of the Pops*, but although mum's mouth was arranged into a smile, she oozed unhappiness. It was like someone flicked off the buttons marked happy, joyous and engaged in life whenever Dad walked out of the door, and only flicked them back on when he came home. And no matter how much Mum tried to pretend, she wasn't convincing anyone.

Had it all been a sham? Had that phone conversation been a lie, had everything he'd said and done for the last thirty years been an act to an unwitting audience of two?

It couldn't be. This was the kind of thing you read about in those magazines that came with lurid headlines. *'My double life!' 'My husband was a bigamist!' 'One man, two wives!'*

That kind of stuff wasn't in her life. Was it?

And if it was, how was she going to find out? This was madness. Complete madness.

All thoughts of eating now gone, she pushed the plates back and pulled her iPad out of her satchel. The Wi-Fi password was on a blackboard on the wall, so she was logged in within seconds.

Facebook. Lila Anderson. She clicked on to her profile and immediately saw a new pic, only added a couple of hours ago. Lila, her platinum hair falling in a sheet of glossy perfection, her lips bright red, looking like a forties movie star, or that American pop star... what was her name... Gwen Stefani! That was it.

Anyway, there she was, pouting at the camera, announcing to the world that she was having a fantastic day.

Caro contemplated giving her own version of reality.

In a tapas restaurant. Alone. Can't eat. Shit day. Might be about to find out my dad has lived a lifetime of lies. Oh and I may have a sister that looks like Gwen Stefani.

She picked up her phone, but not to boost her social network profile.

'Am I mad?' she said, before Todd even had a chance to say hello.

'Absolutely,' he answered, without hesitation.

'Okay, so I was hoping for something a little more consoling than that. It was one of those instances that required you to humour me.'

'Ah, right.' He coughed, then went on, 'No, you're not mad at all. I completely understand, I'd do the same thing, as would any sane, rational, human being with a free day and a train ticket.' He paused. 'How was that?'

'Perfect. I feel so much better now.'

'Then my job is done.'

Caro could see him in her head, laughing as he prattled on, and felt a definite loosening of the vice that was gripping her shoulders. And actually, the smell of the food was making her stomach grumble now. Maybe she could manage a few bites.

'So, you got a plan yet?' he asked, not stopping for an answer. 'I saw that woman's update on Facebook. I've been keeping an eye on it too. She's gorgeous. Looks nothing like you.'

Caro laughed, causing a few people at surrounding tables to stare. 'Again, thank you. My ego would thank you too but it's too busy being kicked to death by your kind words.'

'You know I didn't mean that,' he said, laughing. 'She is gorgeous though. Although, keeping tabs on her does make me feel slightly stalker-like.'

'Don't worry about it. Going by the number of posts she puts up of her perfect life, and the fact that she has no privacy settings, I'm thinking she enjoys the attention. God, was I just bitchy about a half-sister I may or may not have, on the basis of the fact that she is gorgeous, glamorous, and leads a far more exciting life than me?'

'You were. It's a whole new side of you, but I quite like it. Anyway, you didn't answer me. Have you got a plan yet?'

'I have...'

'And it is?'

'Two-pronged.'

'Oh, get you – a double strategy, Nancy Drew.'

'I'm going to look at the places she normally goes to, find out which ones are near here, and then go check them out in the hope that she's there...'

'Okay, I can see the sense in that.'

'At the same time, I'll keep an eye on her Facebook and see if she checks in anywhere. If she does, I'll follow the trail.'

'And if you find her?'

'I have absolutely no idea... but I guess we'll soon find out.'

10

Cammy

It wasn't the money. Sure, he'd lost a grand, but in the big scheme of things, that wasn't the end of the world. It was the fact that he had been sure that was the right ring and that Lila would love it and he could picture it on her finger until the end of time. Now, three shops later, he still hadn't found another one that made him feel the same way.

'I swear to God, Cammy, if you don't pick one soon, I'm telling them to gift-wrap the biggest piece of tat they have and then we're dragging you out of here,' Josie warned.

'And I'll help her. Although, I lost the feeling in my feet ten minutes ago,' Val added.

'Sorry, it's just…' Cammy ran his fingers through his hair, a sure sign that he was stressing, '…which one?'

He stared at the ring tray again, then looked beseechingly at the very attentive assistant, the one who'd put up with an hour of deliberation in the hope that the good-looking guy with the two stroppy older women would actually bloody buy something.

Josie stepped in again. 'Right, what's the bottom end of your budget?'

'Ten grand.' Cammy replied, forcing Josie into a non-Benson and Hedges choke.

'Sweet Jesus – ten grand? I don't even want to know what kind of talents that girl has to warrant a ten-grand ring.'

The assistant tried not to sigh at the negativity. If this sale happened, the commission would be enough for the flights to New York that were on sale in Thomas Cook's window. It had to happen. Fifth Avenue beckoned.

'I could show you something else…'

Josie pretended to faint.

Thankfully, Val attempted to steer the situation in a more positive direction. 'Look, Cammy, you don't make a massive purchase like this in a hurry. There's nothing here that's close enough to the one that you originally picked. So why don't we go home, look online, think it through.'

The assistant had a mental image of the plane taking her to New York screeching to a halt on the runway.

'No. I need to get it now. I can't propose to her tonight without a bloody ring.'

'Then maybe you could wait a while, postpone the proposal… Give you time to think about it a lot, lot more,' Josie mumbled. 'Just saying.'

Val took up the mantle again. 'Maybe you should buy a "holding" ring.'

'What's that?' Cammy asked.

'Just a lower-priced ring. A temporary measure. Something gorgeous to pop the question with – and then you can bring her along here afterwards to pick the perfect ring of her dreams. It means there's less risk of making a monumental mistake because you're being pushed into a panic buy.'

Cammy could see the sense in that and his mood slipped a few notches down the tension scale. 'Okay, let's go with that.'

Val took charge of adjusting the plan. 'Let's go with something under the £300 mark, maximum. Cubics are fine.'

The sales assistant tried not to grimace. Goodbye New York, hello day trip to Millport.

A tray of sparkly rings arrived and Cammy scanned them, hoping one would jump out. Nothing. A second scan. This time, one caught his eye. It was a plain, white gold band, one diamond (okay, a cubic) inset into the metal. He'd seen a similar one before and the thought made him sigh.

Mel. That looked exactly like the ring she wore on the third finger of her left hand. Her wedding ring though, not an engagement ring. She'd never been one for elaborate gestures and blinged up statement pieces. A thought struck him – she'd have hated the huge rock he'd been planning to buy for Lila. She'd have been embarrassed by it. Thought it too flash. Working with her for all those years, he knew everything about her. Loving her for all those years, there was not a single thing he'd have changed. Apart from the fact that she was married to someone else.

When he'd fallen in love with her, about ten seconds after he'd fallen flat on his face in the shop, she'd been married to her first husband, Joe. The fool had cheated and Cammy trod easy, waiting for the right time, trying not to blow it. It hadn't worked. After he left for LA, Mel had married Josie's son Michael and now they'd built a family together. It had taken him a long, long, time to stop wishing that he'd been the guy to make her happy. The only time he'd ever heard Josie's voice crack with emotion was when she called him a year after he'd left to tell him that Mel and Michael had fallen in love, and had decided to marry.

'I'm so sorry, son. I know how much you loved her.'

'Is she happy?' he'd asked.

'She is,' Josie replied softly.

It took Cammy a moment to speak. 'Then I'm happy for her.'

He meant it. Most of the time. Since then, he and Josie had never discussed it with anything other than a casual 'how are they?' and 'fine.' It was all he needed to know and he was just glad it hadn't affected his friendship with Josie in any way. He loved her. He'd loved Mel. The second one was past tense.

He pushed the thought back into his memory bank. Why was he thinking about Mel again now? On the day he was planning to propose to Lila, it should be all about her, shouldn't it? His stress levels slid back up the pressure scale.

Why was this happening? Mel was over, a closed chapter in his history. He'd blown it with her, because even when he did have the chance, he'd made a huge mistake that had meant they could never make it work. End of story. Now, years later, it was time to move on. It had taken him until now to realise that he wasn't going to find someone else exactly like her. That's why it worked with Lila. She and Mel couldn't be more different. Mel hated a fuss, hated to be centre of attention, wasn't bothered by stuff like designer labels and flash cars. Stacey, the only other woman he'd loved, had embraced the trapping of the L.A. lifestyle, but she saw it for what it was and didn't get too carried away with the pursuit for material things. Lila was the opposite and he loved that about her – she was entirely unapologetic about liking the finer things in life and going after them. Nothing wrong with that. And yet...

'I'll take that one,' he said, pointing to the white gold band.

'Hallelujah!' Josie threw her arms up like she was singing the chorus in a gospel choir. 'Okay, let me try it on.'

'Isn't there an old wives' tale about that being bad luck?' Val mused.

'He's planning to marry Lila. His luck doesn't get much worse than that,' Josie said, deadpan.

At least that made Cammy laugh, relieving the anxiety on several counts. First of all, it reminded him how much he loved her brutal honesty. Although, there was no denying that he preferred it when it was aimed in someone else's direction. Secondly, he had the ring, so panic averted. Thirdly, he could now go about the rest of the day, back on schedule, knowing that a hitch like this hadn't derailed them.

It was all good. Lila would love the ring. Okay, maybe not love it, but as Val said, it was only a temporary measure. Disaster averted.

'Why do I feel like I've seen this ring before?' Josie mused, slipping it on. 'Argh, the ageing process is bollocks. I think every time I pee I lose brain cells. My memory is shot.'

'No idea,' Cammy shrugged. 'Anyway, let's get this and get out of here. We've still got loads to do.'

Don't remember. Don't. Please don't.

Josie, hand out in front of her, was still staring at it. 'I have definitely seen it. Val, do you recognise it?'

Val shook her head. 'Don't think so. I'm more of a

yellow gold person. If I was a young one nowadays I'd be drowning in gold chains and rapping out my shopping list down at ASDA.'

Save me. Cammy looked heavenward to the Gods of romance and age-related forgetfulness.

'Mel!' Josie exclaimed, channelling Angela Lansbury, solving a mystery at the end of every episode ever of *Murder, She Wrote*. 'Mel had a ring just like this when she was married to Joe and… oh.' She finished on a low point, was looking at Cammy now with genuine concern.

'Josie, it means nothing. I just liked the ring. I didn't even remember that it was similar to Mel's. Look, this is for Lila. End of story.'

Was it though? If he was entirely truthful with himself, he wasn't even sure that Lila would like it. It definitely wasn't the kind of ring that would make her exclaim with delight, throw her arms around him while feeling like the luckiest girl in the world. But it was fine. She'd love what it stood for and she'd be thrilled when he explained it was a two-part operation and she could come and choose her own afterwards.

The events of today were seriously killing his buzz. This morning he'd woken up so sure of what was ahead, excited about how it was all going to play out, and now… Maybe he just needed something to eat. It had been hours since breakfast. Yes, that was it. Once he'd eaten he'd be thinking straight again and Mel would stop popping into his head. A bit of lunch would sort that out and then he could just get on with making everything perfect for Mel. Oh bugger – he meant Lila.

After he handed over his credit card, the assistant went off to box up the ring.

'So what's next on the agenda?' he asked Val, ignoring Josie's raised eyebrow of inquisitive disapproval. It was nothing he hadn't seen before. Ignoring it wouldn't make it go away, but he could only hope she got distracted and moved on to some other outrage or point of interest.

'We're going to the restaurant to check everything is ready for the proposal tonight. Do you think Lila has any idea what you're up to? What does she think you're doing this evening?'

Cammy shrugged. 'I've told her we're going out for dinner with you two.'

'Och, Cammy, could you not have come up with something a little more appealing than that? I bet you my last pair of support kecks that she'll cancel. She's never exactly taken to us, has she?' Val was looking worried now – and if Val was worried, then there was something to panic about because the woman could cope with just about anything. 'Maybe you should make the offer a bit more appealing. Is there no one else you could ask?'

She had a point though. He'd thought it had been a clever move, because it didn't involve anyone that could let the secret slip, but now he could see that it may be slightly flawed. Lila had never really engaged with Josie and Val. He knew why – they were, as far as she was concerned, part of his old life, a life that she wasn't connected to. On top of that, Josie and Val, and their extended circle of family and friends, were a tight group to penetrate. It made total sense that Lila felt a little out of place and would rather spend time in the company of people she knew and loved. He got that.

Perhaps he should have invited her parents along.

'You're right. I'll call her mum.' He pulled out his phone and called Louise.

'Louise? Hi, it's Cammy. I'm good thanks, how are you? You're where? Oh. I didn't realise you golfed. I won't keep you then. I just wondered if you and Jack were up to anything tonight or if you'd like to join Lila and me for dinner? You did? And is she still with you? Didn't think so – don't think she's got the shoes for it. Yes, sure, I'll hold...'

Strange, Cammy thought, Lila hadn't mentioned anything about popping over to meet her parents this morning. She'd said she had a completely jam-packed day of appointments and presentations. There was a muffled sound at the other end of the line.

'Hi, yes, I'm still here. Ah, no worries. Another night then. Nope, completely understand. I'll see you soon.'

He hung up to four raised eyebrows of inquisition.

'She said no?' Val asked, blatantly unimpressed. Cammy knew she was all about her family and nothing would stop her joining them for dinner. Only a couple of years ago, she'd lost her daughter, Dee, in a car accident just before her thirtieth birthday, and it had brought the rest of her family closer than ever.

'Yeah, Lila's dad had already made plans to take her mum out to dinner, so they're doing that instead.'

'But that's…'

Josie was cut off by the ring of Cammy's phone.

'Louise! No of course not – that would be great. I'm glad you changed your mind. Yes, Grilled, on Royal Exchange Square, at eight. The table is booked. Look forward to it.'

He hung up; pleased he'd claimed a small victory against the doubters in front of him.

'Guilt,' Josie sneered. 'That's what changed their minds. Pure guilt. But at least if Lila thinks she's having dinner with Ma and Pa, she'll show up. Yer support pants are safe, Val.'

'Here you go, see you again soon,' the sales assistant said hopefully, handing over a navy and gold gift bag.

Outside, Cammy paused, looked around him, adjusted the game plan.

'Okay, restaurant next, but I'm starving and I don't want to eat there twice in one day. What about stopping off somewhere on the way?'

Josie and Val both nodded, before Val, mission leader, synchronised her watch. 'What about that tapas place just off George Square? Service is always really quick in there.'

11

Bernadette

'He's fine. Your dad's fine, so don't worry,' Bernadette blurted, reassuring her daughter, just as little Casey threw his arms around Bernadette's leg, like the koala bear he'd seen at Edinburgh Zoo the weekend before. He refused to be prised off, so she had to walk to the kitchen, dragging one leg behind her. 'Remind me how cute he is when I'm in getting my hip replacement,' she said, so grateful for the light moment that she could have let him stay there, hugging her all day, delaying the inevitable.

Eventually Nina tempted him off using the persuasive powers of strawberry yogurt, while scrutinising her mother's face for a hint as to what had warranted the unexpected visit.

'Right Tiger, why don't we give you a treat and let you

watch SpongeBob,' Nina said, evoking a riotous cheer from her son, who then darted over to the family area of the kitchen and parked himself in front of the TV. 'Yet another thing I said I'd never do,' Nina mused. 'It's up there with feeding them anything that isn't organic and bribing them to go to bed at night.'

'I was guilty on all those counts too,' Bernadette said, with a wry smile. Her daughter was a great mum to Casey and Milo. Compassionate. Thoughtful. Focussed. It was what had made her a great nurse. Bernadette had been surprised when Nina had followed her into the job, albeit in a very different field.

'The kettle's just boiled, Mum. I'll just be a sec, if you want to get the mugs out.'

Bernadette busied herself making tea while Nina sorted the TV out for Casey, trying to steady her hands as she poured the water into the mugs.

Nina had married a lovely guy, Gerry, an electrician for a local house-building company. They'd got a good discount on this house because Gerry worked for the company and finished it himself. They didn't have a great deal of money, now that Nina was only working part-time, but they were happy. At least, Bernadette thought they were. Who really knew what went on behind closed doors? She was pretty sure anyone who looked at her life with Kenneth would think they'd had a great marriage. If only it had felt that way from the inside.

Casey settled and engrossed in the cartoon, Milo gurgling happy in a playpen next to them, Nina finally sat down.

'Ok Mum, you're going to have to tell me really quickly what's wrong because my imagination is running riot here and my heart is thudding like a train. So whatever it is, you need to blurt it out. Are you sick? Is Dad sick? That's it, isn't it? Oh God, Mum, I'm so…'

'I'm leaving your dad, Nina.'

That hadn't come out the way she'd planned at all. What had happened to breaking it gently, pre-empting it with reassurances and explanations to soften the blow? Nina had always been a daddy's girl, adored her father, hung on his every word. And now she was staring at her, chin dropped, eyes wide, completely speechless.

Bernadette reacted to the silence by going into panic mode, a state that sent a direct message to her gob to ramble like a woman possessed. 'Nina, I'm sorry, love, I didn't mean to blurt it out like that. I know this will be shocking to you, but I promise it won't change anything. I'll still be here. I just can't stay and there are a million reasons, but I won't go into them, because…'

'It's about time.' Nina had finally found her voice.

'…What?' Bernadette wasn't sure she'd heard right.

Nina sighed, then took a sip of her tea. 'It's about

time,' she repeated. 'Mum, I don't know how you've stuck it so long.'

Bernadette sagged back in her chair, completely flabbergasted. 'I don't understand. I thought you'd be upset, devastated even.'

Nina sighed, clearly neither upset nor devastated at all.

'Mum, you've been unhappy for years.'

'I have. Oh God knows, I have. But I thought... I didn't realise I'd let it show. Or that you'd picked up on it.'

The corners of Nina's mouth turned up as she leaned over and put her hand over her mother's. 'Mum, I'm a psychiatric nurse. I'd be pretty shite at my job if I hadn't noticed.'

Bernadette was finding it hard to absorb this un-expected turn of events. 'But you never said.'

'Because you didn't either. Look, Mum, I get it. I love Dad, but I see how you live. I know that there's no warmth, no real affection. I wasn't aware of it when I was growing up, but I think as I got older, maybe when I started my training, that I began to notice it. Not to mention the fact that you have nothing in common except us.'

'I wish you'd said something.'

Nina shrugged. 'Mum, some people go through their whole lives like that because it's what works for them. I'm not going to take sides in this, and to be honest, I don't want to know the details – I think that's between you and Dad – but I understand and I'll support you. I just want you both to be happy.'

A lump formed in Bernadette's throat. 'How did you get so wise?'

'Ah, that's Dad's genes,' she joked. 'I'm kidding! Look, he's a great surgeon but he has the emotional intelligence of a plant. Oh, God…'

'What?'

'Have you met someone else?'

'No, of course not!'

'Sorry. I knew the answer to that before I asked it.'

A silence while both of them recalibrated.

Nina's energy dropped a little. 'So what did he say when you told him?'

'I haven't.'

This time Nina's reaction came with a very definite edge of shock. 'You haven't told him?'

Bernadette shook her head. 'No. Look, Nina, I'm not going to bad-mouth your father to you, or put you in the middle of us, and there's no way to make you understand without doing that.' She didn't need to know that he was controlling, that he was short-tempered, aggressive, cold, cruel. He'd never shown any of those traits to the kids – if he had she'd have left him years ago. Only her. Her daughter still had a lifelong relationship with her father ahead of her, so Bernadette didn't want to do anything to taint that.

And yes, the irony was there. Even now she was still defending him, making sure people only saw him in the best light. 'You're just going to have to trust me on why I'm doing it this way, but the reality is that if I tried to tell him in advance, he wouldn't accept it, Nina,' she said, desperately hoping her daughter would accept her reasoning without question. 'So I'm going to move out today, and I'll tell him when he gets home tonight. It'll be a done deal. There's no other way – I just wanted to make sure you knew because I didn't want to spring that on you, my love.'

Nina leaned over into the playpen to give Milo back the baby elephant that he'd tossed out of his reach. 'But, Mum, surely you could discuss it with him and do this properly? I mean, for God's sake, it's not like he'll go nuts and wreck the place.' She finished with a laugh, finding the thought preposterous.

Bernadette didn't react.

'Mum…?' She took Bernadette's silence, analysed it, interpreted it, and went to the conclusion supported by perception skills honed over years of pulling information out of people who were reluctant to volunteer it. 'Mum, is Dad violent?' Every word in the question was seeped in horror. 'Oh God, Mum, don't tell me he's been…'

Bernadette shook her head. 'No, not violent. He's never laid a finger on me, I promise, love.'

Nina visibly sagged with relief and Bernadette

struggled with how to give her just enough to explain, but not enough to damage.

'Let's just say, he hasn't decided this is to happen, so he's not going to take it well.'

'He's controlling,' Nina said. It was a realisation, not a question, so Bernadette didn't reply. This was the nurse talking now, not the daughter. 'I should have seen that.'

'Nina, you couldn't…'

'I did see it.'

'What?'

'Not with you, Mum. With me. When I said I was marrying Gerry. Dad ordered me not to, said he wasn't good enough, didn't earn enough, that I could do better. He said there was no way he was letting me marry an electrician, or any other kind of tradesman.'

Now it was Bernadette who was shocked. 'When? I had no idea! I'm so sorry, pet, I would have said something if I'd known. Oh bollocks – I said I wouldn't bad-mouth your father to you, but what a pompous arse he is. Gerry's a great husband and dad – that's a good man you've got there. To be honest, I knew your father wasn't impressed, but I didn't think for a minute that he'd share that with you. What did you say?'

Nina shrugged. 'I told him it was none of his business and I was marrying Gerry whether he liked it or not. That's why Gerry doesn't come over so much…'

'I thought it was because he was always on overtime.'

'It's that as well. But Dad has just never made an effort with him. Tolerates him. I thought he was just being overprotective – being a dad – and that he'd chill out eventually. I didn't realise that it was a sign of something more. I'm sorry, Mum. I should've seen it. Do you want me to come over tonight, to be there when you tell him? Gerry is working late but I can get someone to come look after the kids and be with you.'

'No, love. This is between your father and me and I don't want you involved. Besides, you shouldn't have to deal with my dramas.' A pause. 'Feels strange saying that. My dramas. I've spent my whole life keeping the peace.'

Nina refilled their cups, then sat back down. 'So where are you going to go? You know you can always come here. There's an extra bed in Milo's room…'

For the first time since she got there, Bernadette's eyes filled with tears. It was the kindness that did it. She could handle aggression, and disdain, and anxiety and unpleasant truths, because that was what she was used to, but the kindness made her soul melt. The gods had been on her side when they'd helped her create this incredible woman in front of her.

'Thanks, but I'm going to go to Auntie Sarah's for a while until I find somewhere just for me.' That thought pushed the tears back. Her own place. Hers. No one looking over her shoulder, no demands, no tension. Just hers. That was the picture she was going to hang on to today until it was all over, the mental image that was going to get her through. That, and the fact that Nina had been so supportive.

Bernadette felt a niggle of guilt. She'd known nothing about Kenneth warning Nina off Gerry. What an arse. Why hadn't Nina mentioned it? Why hadn't she known? Had she been so busy keeping the peace and walking on eggshells that she hadn't noticed what was going on under her nose? Kenneth was forever telling her what a terrible wife she was. She just prayed her kids didn't think she'd been a crap mum too.

Nina spoke up. 'Do me a favour then – if it suits, make it near here, Mum. We'd love to have you closer. The boys would love to see you even more. And then when you meet someone else…'

'Trust me, I'm never going to meet someone else. I've had enough of men for a lifetime.'

It was meant as a joke, but there was no hiding the grain of truth in there.

'Do you think Dad will?'

'What? Meet someone else? I don't know. I suppose he will.' It wasn't a scenario she'd contemplated, hadn't thought that far ahead. Over the years, she'd thought he might have played the field at those conventions he went to – heaven knows he was good enough with the charm – but she'd long since ceased to care. God help the poor woman who fell for Kenneth Anderson. Bernadette could see how it could happen. The distinguished, attractive looks, the greying hair that worked just fine for George Clooney. Add in a shade of Piers Brosnan, Sean Connery's accent and the prestigious medical career, and there was no denying that on the surface, he was a catch. There was every chance that some other woman out there would step into her shoes. Whoever it was, she was welcome to them – but she just hoped that the deluded soul wouldn't regret it as Bernadette had done.

Nina leaned over and hugged her. 'As long as you're okay, Mum. We love you.'

'I love you too, pet. I can't tell you how much or how proud I am of you. And thank you. I was dreading telling you all this. I'm so grateful you took it so well.'

'So what are you going to do now?' Nina asked, as they both stood up.

Bernadette leaned into the playpen to lift Milo out and give him a hug goodbye.

'I'm going to tell your brother. I don't mind telling you I'm not looking forward to it.'

The look of concern on Nina's face said it all. 'Yeah, that one might not go quite so smoothly.'

12

Lila

The receptionist at the hotel didn't bat an eyelid when Lila checked in with no luggage, nor when she paid with the company credit card. It was a bit naughty, but her organisation had so many employees that she knew they didn't go through the credit card statements and query the transactions. It wasn't like she was charging them for a fortnight in Barbados or a new pair of Jimmy Choos.

These were just little perks of the job.

She could have waited for Ken and let him foot the bill as she'd planned earlier, but she wanted to get in and think about what she was going to do. And anyway, it was already noon and he clearly wasn't here yet. Occupational hazard. Surgeries always ran late. It was something she'd need to get used to when they were married.

When she got to the room, she realised her heart was

still beating a little faster than usual but she wasn't sure if that was the double espresso she'd picked up from Starbucks on the way here, or the phone calls she'd made. She paused, did a quick assessment – nope, no regret about making them. Although, she still wasn't sure what the hell she'd have said if the wife had picked up. Bernadette. She preferred to just call her 'the wife'. More impersonal. It wasn't like they were ever going to be friends, although, no doubt their paths would cross at Ken's family functions in the future. That was fine. Lila was prepared to be civil and show them all exactly why Ken had moved on and chosen to leave his marriage for her.

Her plans to slip into the bath were shelved when she realised that would be a waste of the black slutty knickers and curve-enhancing bra that he'd asked her to wear. Actually that wasn't true – he'd just suggested two outfits and told her to wear one of them. She loved that he knew what he wanted and didn't care that he made demands. It just showed how much he loved her. She'd grown up with her father calling the shots and her mother hanging on his every word and look how happy they were now.

Not that this was anything like her parents. Urgh, she didn't want to think about them sneaking to hotels in the middle of the day. No, what she and Ken had was incredible, passionate, dangerous.

Instead, she peeled off her clothes, leaving on just her

underwear, stockings and stilettos. Ken could take the rest off when he got there and then he could...

A knock at the door.

This had better not be housekeeping or they were going to have a story to tell their pals down the pub tonight.

She opened the door and there he was, her gorgeous doctor. In his suit and with his grey hair swept back, he looked like he'd just walked off the set of *Grey's Anatomy*. Strolling in, his sexy grin lit up his face when he saw her outfit.

'You.' Kiss. 'Are.' Kiss. 'Bloody.' Kiss. 'Irresistible.'

Then another kiss, one that lasted a long time, spread to many parts of her body, until he'd claimed every inch of her. It was his routine, and he rarely veered from it. She wasn't complaining. He liked things a certain way and the thrill of his commands turned her on like no other guy ever had.

'Get on top, right now,' he ordered, and she was happy to oblige. She pushed him back and rode him until they both came, in a shudder of ecstasy that probably contravened the PLEASE RESPECT THE OTHER GUESTS BY KEEPING THE NOISE DOWN signs in the hall.

Only when they were done, did she realise that he was still fully clothed, only a slightly squinty tie and a lowered zip giving a hint of what had just happened. Not that she cared. It just showed how desperate he'd been to have her that he didn't even stop to undress.

She slowly dismounted, then kneeled beside him, stroking his face while he played with one of her nipples.

'You're amazing,' he told her. 'And far too skilled at that for your own good.'

'It's a talent,' she replied, teasing.

'Do you do that to your other guy?' His face darkened as he said it and Lila had to stop herself from smiling. He was jealous. Irritated. Good. It was another reason she wouldn't leave Cammy until Ken was hers – she knew how much he couldn't stand thinking of her with another man.

She'd told him about Cammy when they met up again after the split and he made it clear that he wasn't happy about it at all. He'd told her he wanted her to end it, but, for once, she'd refused him. There was no way she wanted to be on her own, like a complete sad case, before Ken made his move and they could be together. At least with Cammy around she went out for nice dinners and had a bit of a life. The fact that he was leverage that might nudge Kenneth along a tad quicker was just an extra bonus.

Besides, there was one way for him to make sure that she never slept with anyone but him ever again...

'Ken, I...'

His eye caught the time on his watch and he immediately unhanded her nipple. 'I need to go. I've got another surgery in an hour.'

He registered the disappointment that fell over her

beautiful face and stopped, halfway up, to kiss her, his manner softening as it always did when she pouted. 'I'll make it up to you, I promise.'

Hadn't she heard that so many times before? And how many more times was she going to pretend she believed it?

'Baby,' she said, in the breathy voice she knew turned him on, 'I know we said we wouldn't talk about it again for a while, but I can't stand this. I can't stand not being with you when I want to, I can't stand sharing you with someone else, I can't…'

His mood changed instantly. 'Oh, for Christ's sake, Lila, you know there's nothing I can bloody do about…' He stopped, paused, regrouped. 'I'm sorry.' He leaned over, kissed her again. 'You know I'm working on it. You know I want it every bit as much as you do. But I can't leave yet. Bernadette… isn't ready.'

Lila felt a ferocious urge to argue, but bit it back. What was the point? He would only get pissed off and besides, he was saying yet again how much he wanted to be with her too. That's why he got so frustrated. It was hard for him, living in a house with a woman he didn't love. What was Bernadette's bloody problem? Surely she could see that she wasn't enough for Ken? Would she ever be woman enough to have the dignity to let him go?

He wanted Lila. She wanted him. This should be so simple. Seven years, she'd waited and her time for waiting was over. It had to be done.

Removing obstacles. Seeing challenges as opportunities. She was going to do this.

He kissed her slowly, passionately before he left. 'I'm going to make it happen,' he told her, 'it just needs to be the right time.'

'I think that's now,' she said, trying not to sound petulant. She decided to play the one card that she knew irked him more than any other. 'I can't stand lying next to someone every night that isn't you.' It wasn't strictly true, but she saw the shadow of jealousy cross his face once again. Direct hit.

'Soon,' he said, through slightly gritted teeth. 'When the time is right.'

He kissed her again, then he was gone and it was just Lila, in a faceless hotel, in lingerie that cost more than a week in one of these rooms.

Fucking depressing, she decided. How had her life come to this? If she needed confirmation that action was required, this was it.

Sighing, she pushed herself up, peeled off the underwear and jumped in the shower, only leaving the soothing jets of the water when her phone rang. She stepped out and grabbed it from the vanity unit.

Cammy's name flashed on the screen. She thought about answering it, then decided to ignore it, then changed her mind again. If it were important, he'd only keep trying until he got her, and if it wasn't, then she'd get him off the phone quickly.

'Hi babe,' she said, doing her very best 'good girl-friend' act. No point in stirring things up with him until she had to. She didn't need two dramas on her hands.

She dried herself off while she spoke.

'Hey honey, how's your day going? Busy?'

'Rushed right off my feet,' she said, phone under her chin now while she pulled on one of her stockings. 'I just... finished a really promising call with a cardiac surgeon.'

'Sounds like you're killing it out there,' he said, encouraging as always. She'd miss that about him.

She pulled on a second stocking. 'Yep, I think good things will come of it.'

'Great. Listen, I'm just calling to say there's a change of plan for tonight.'

Lila almost punched the air. Thank God. She didn't have to pitch up for dinner and pretend to like those bloody women that Cammy was friends with. What was all that about? A forty-one-year-old guy hanging out with two ancient old dears. She didn't get the dynamic at all. And all of that stuff about Josie being a second mother to him went right over her head. What was up with the mother he had? Apart from the fact that she lived in Perth and he only saw her a few times a year when he went back for a visit. That seemed more than reasonable to Lila. But none of that mattered right now because this call had saved her faking illness and calling off later. Result.

'That's fine, babe. I quite fancied going to the gym anyway. Maybe a spin class.' Maybe turning up at my boyfriend's house and telling his wife it's time to let him go. She didn't say that last option out loud.

'No, dinner's still on.'

Her heart sank.

'But your mum and dad are going to join us now instead of Josie and Val.'

Oh. That made it better then. Strange Mum and Dad didn't mention it at the golf course earlier. Must have slipped their minds, or maybe Cammy had only just invited them. No matter. It was a better option than the original plan. And she could always cancel if events this afternoon got in the way.

'That sounds good. Where are we going?'

He hesitated.

Damn. If it was somewhere she didn't love, she was definitely cancelling.

'Thought we'd go to Grilled. I know you love it there.'

Okay, so that was another result. It was her favourite restaurant and she always got some fab pics there, so at least it wouldn't be a total washout. And with her mum and dad, it would be even better. Unless of course, she got a better offer – but no point showing that hand just yet.

Instead, she used her entire childhood and teenage experience of weekly drama classes to project enthusiasm and glee. 'That sounds great. Can't wait. Oops, have to go, another call coming in. Love you babe.' She rang off, and looked at the other call flashing in front of her. The office again. Jeez, they were persistent today. And she was just as persistently ignoring them. Probably the area manager, wanting to make sure she was on target for this month. Of course, she was. It was only the fact that she was so bloody good at her job that gave her the luxury of being able to take the odd easy shift like today.

Some people found the life of a rep hard to adjust to because it was a pretty solitary existence, especially if, as in her case, the head office was down south. Lila's job was to represent the company in the west of Scotland and central belt, so she spent four days a week out on the road visiting clients and one day a week working from home, doing admin and planning the following week's appointments. She'd been doing it for so long it was an absolute breeze. Along the way, she'd picked up a few habits that made it all so much easier – like scheduling Glasgow meetings on a Friday so that she was close to home and could get away with pretty much taking the day off. The call sheet she would submit to the office would have her meeting with Dr Kenneth Manson, a few fabricated conversations with other doctors in the same hospital, a couple of fake cold calls and a some other manufactured stops that would make it look like she'd had a busy day. Of course, she couldn't get away with that all the time. The first week back after the Christmas break she'd work her ass off in Stirling, Edinburgh, and a few other smaller territories to make up for it. Balance. It was all about balance and making the system and circumstances bend to her best advantage.

Talking of which... She dressed, brushed her hair, reapplied her lipstick and headed out to the car. On the way past reception she dropped the key in the slot and registered a flash of judgement on the receptionist's face.

'My husband,' Lila wittered, with a smile and a dramatic shudder. 'He can't get enough of me.' She strutted on past, adding just a shade of an extra wiggle to her walk.

In the car, she checked the time. Two p.m.. There was a hospital just a mile or so from here – maybe she could fit in a couple of spec calls after all. Or she could completely fabricate this afternoon's appointment sheet and take the rest of the day off. Maybe go get her nails done. Nip into House of Fraser for some new Clarins.

Or she could phone his wife again.

Or...

Maybe his wife would be home now. Perhaps she shouldn't call. What if she just went over there and knocked on her door? What if she just calmly and honestly told his wife what was going on. She must know anyway. She must. Ken had fallen out of love with her so long ago she was probably desperate for him to move on and find happiness elsewhere. They could discuss it calmly, rationally, and make a plan for going forward.

Ken's house was only about fifteen minutes from here. It wouldn't be a stretch at all to get there, speak to her, get this done. And then... Cammy. He'd be home from work at six, so she could let him know, break it to him gently, and they could all just get on with their lives, be with the people they were meant to be with.

What was the alternative? Wait another seven years? She'd be heading for forty by then, and much as she didn't ever see herself with children, if she changed her mind she might be too late.

That wasn't what bothered her most though. It was spending more years without Ken in her bed every night, going on holiday without him, enduring special days without him there. It reminded her too much of her childhood. Dad's job took him away so much that half the time he didn't even make it back for Christmas. Mum tried to hide the fact that she missed him – hair done, lipstick on, face the world – but Lila knew. There was one year, the best year ever, when he'd walked in the door unexpectedly late on Christmas Eve and Mum had been so happy she'd danced for hours.

The circumstances were obviously very different, but Mum had her husband with her all the time now. Wasn't it time that Lila had that too? It would work out so much better for all of them. She'd be happy. Ken would be happy. And she'd get to spend more time with Mum again because Dad would have a new golfing buddy. And even better, he was a heart surgeon, so they'd already have stuff to talk about. What were the chances? Her dad had a heart condition and she was marrying a cardiac surgeon. It was fate. Serendipity. Yep, this was the best outcome for all of them and it was up to her to make it happen.

She indicated left, and turned on to the expressway that headed out to the West End, to the house that she'd driven past so many times over the years, wondering what he was doing inside. In the early days, sometimes she'd just go and sit there, with a coffee and her favourite songs on the CD player, just watching the curtains, feeling close to him because he was a few feet away, but trying not to think about the wife that was in there with him.

This was her time to get the life she wanted.

She deserved it. So did Ken.

And if she wanted those obstacles and challenges gone, she was more than prepared to make that happen.

2 p.m. – 4 p.m.

13

Caro

It took Caro a while to decide where to start. In the end, geography made the decision. Of all the places that Lila visited, the beauty salon on Ingram Street was one of the more regular and it was only a five-minute walk from the tapas restaurant, a bonus given that it was a freezing cold day.

She left her table, fought her way through the piles of Christmas shopping bags hanging on the edges of chairs and piled beside tables. That was what normal people were doing this week, yet Caro had no notion to celebrate. This year, it would be just a day like every other now, where she'd sit by her mum's side and hope for a miracle.

On the way out the door, she stepped aside to let a tall guy and two older women come in. He was past her before she got a chance to get a look at his face, but from the back she could see that he was probably in his twenties or thirties, so she guessed one of them was probably his mum. Pretty cool way to spend a Friday afternoon, out with mother, doing a bit of lunch and shopping. She'd give everything she had to be doing the same thing.

The sadness never got any easier, but she shrugged it off and kept walking, using the map on her iPhone to guide her. Straight along, right, left, a few hundred metres, past a holiday-wear shop – Sun, Sea, Ski – and what looked like a trendy guys' boutique, CAMDEN, and there it was, on the left-hand side: Pluckers.

There was a moment of hesitation, before she shrugged off the fear, pushed open the door and was met by a wall of music and chat. There were three nail bars, with about six seats at each one, all of them full, and behind them, ten leather chairs, facing into a circular mirrored console, hairdressers working away at every station.

Caro had been in one of these places exactly zero times in her life. Much to Todd's considerable frustration, she never visited his salon, preferring to just have him pop round to her flat and trim the bottom of her hair every few months, before she stuck it up in a ponytail and forgot about it until the next time.

'I could do so much more with this,' he'd moan.

'And it would be wasted on me,' she'd reply, every time.

Nails fell into the same category. They'd occasionally get a quick coat of clear varnish on school days, and something that matched her outfit for special events, but that was as far as her beauty regime went.

This was another world to her, an alien landscape, one that – she scanned the room – showed no sign of Lila. What to do. Go or stay? Go or stay? Go or…

'Hi, can I help you?' A stunning woman behind the counter had looked up from the computer and was smiling at her expectantly. Rabbit. Headlights. Suddenly, she felt slightly intimidated by the trendy surroundings, a ridiculous reaction, really, given that every day of her life she stood in front of thirty eleven-year-olds. That was a far tougher crowd, yet she handled it with cool ease. Right, what was the plan? Walk out now or wait and hope Lila turned up? She knew from Facebook that this was her regular Friday haunt, so it was her best option. She could do this. She could.

'I'd like an appointment please.'

'First time here?' the receptionist asked.

Caro nodded. See, her out-of-depth-ness was written all over her face.

'No worries. I'm Suze, and this is my salon, so let me know if you don't enjoy your first experience and I'll fire whoever is responsible.'

A few of the nail technicians at the nearest nail bar overheard and laughed. Suddenly, Caro felt a bit more comfortable. There was a really good vibe in here. It might look flash, but the atmosphere was chilled out and relaxed, thanks – she suspected – to the woman behind the counter.

'Okay, so would you like beauty, hair or both?'

Caro hesitated. 'I'm not sure. Nails? Yes, nails.'

'No problem. There will be a space in about half an hour, would that be okay?'

Hopefully that would keep her here long enough for Lila to appear. 'Perfect.'

Just at that moment a hair stylist, a spiky-haired guy who was dressed like the lead singer in a punk band, popped his head around Suze's shoulder. 'Suze, I'm on a roll of magnificence today – who's next?'

'No one. Your two-thirty just cancelled.'

Hair! A hair appointment would stretch her time here even longer.

'I'll take it!' Caro blurted, then immediately backpedalled. 'I mean, if that's okay?'

Suze's grin became a cackle. 'Are you sure? His last customer left looking like Cindy Lauper from 1984.'

The stylist feigned outrage. '1986! Man, I'm working with amateurs here.'

'I'm sure,' Caro said, feeling a wave of gratitude that, for at least the next hour or so, her mind would be on something other than the purpose of today and

A few of the nail technicians at the nearest nail bar
erheard and laughed. Suddenly, Caro felt a bit more
mfortable. There was a really good vibe in here. It
ight look flash, but the atmosphere was chilled out
d relaxed, thanks – she suspected – to the woman
hind the counter.

'Okay, so would you like beauty, hair or both?'

Caro hesitated. 'I'm not sure. Nails? Yes, nails.'

'No problem. There will be a space in about half an
our, would that be okay?'

Hopefully that would keep her here long enough for
ila to appear. 'Perfect.'

Just at that moment a hair stylist, a spiky-haired guy
ho was dressed like the lead singer in a punk band,
opped his head around Suze's shoulder. 'Suze, I'm on a
oll of magnificence today – who's next?'

'No one. Your two-thirty just cancelled.'

Hair! A hair appointment would stretch her time
ere even longer.

'I'll take it!' Caro blurted, then immediately
ackpedalled. 'I mean, if that's okay?'

Suze's grin became a cackle. 'Are you sure? His last
ustomer left looking like Cindy Lauper from 1984.'

The stylist feigned outrage. '1986! Man, I'm working
ith amateurs here.'

'I'm sure,' Caro said, feeling a wave of gratitude
hat, for at least the next hour or so, her mind would
e on something other than the purpose of today and

13

Caro

It took Caro a while to decide where to start. In the
end, geography made the decision. Of all the places that
Lila visited, the beauty salon on Ingram Street was one
of the more regular and it was only a five-minute walk
from the tapas restaurant, a bonus given that it was a
freezing cold day.

She left her table, fought her way through the piles
of Christmas shopping bags hanging on the edges of
chairs and piled beside tables. That was what normal
people were doing this week, yet Caro had no notion
to celebrate. This year, it would be just a day like every
other now, where she'd sit by her mum's side and hope
for a miracle.

On the way out the door, she stepped aside to let a
tall guy and two older women come in. He was past

her before she got a chance to get a look at his face, but from the back she could see that he was probably in his twenties or thirties, so she guessed one of them was probably his mum. Pretty cool way to spend a Friday afternoon, out with mother, doing a bit of lunch and shopping. She'd give everything she had to be doing the same thing.

The sadness never got any easier, but she shrugged it off and kept walking, using the map on her iPhone to guide her. Straight along, right, left, a few hundred metres, past a holiday-wear shop – Sun, Sea, Ski – and what looked like a trendy guys' boutique, CAMDEN, and there it was, on the left-hand side: Pluckers.

There was a moment of hesitation, before she shrugged off the fear, pushed open the door and was met by a wall of music and chat. There were three nail bars, with about six seats at each one, all of them full, and behind them, ten leather chairs, facing into a circular mirrored console, hairdressers working away at every station.

Caro had been in one of these places exactly zero times in her life. Much to Todd's considerable frustration, she never visited his salon, preferring to just have him pop round to her flat and trim the bottom of her hair every few months, before she stuck it up in a ponytail and forgot about it until the next time.

'I could do so much more with this,' he'd moan.

'And it would be wasted on me,' she ⌐ time.

Nails fell into the same category. They' get a quick coat of clear varnish on sch something that matched her outfit for s but that was as far as her beauty regime w

This was another world to her, an alie one that – she scanned the room – showe Lila. What to do. Go or stay? Go or stay? (

'Hi, can I help you?' A stunning wor the counter had looked up from the cor was smiling at her expectantly. Rabbit. Suddenly, she felt slightly intimidated by surroundings, a ridiculous reaction, re that every day of her life she stood in fror eleven-year-olds. That was a far tougher cro handled it with cool ease. Right, what wa: Walk out now or wait and hope Lila turn knew from Facebook that this was her reg haunt, so it was her best option. She cou She could.

'I'd like an appointment please.'

'First time here?' the receptionist asked.

Caro nodded. See, her out-of-depth-ness all over her face.

'No worries. I'm Suze, and this is my sal know if you don't enjoy your first experie fire whoever is responsible.'

anxiety over whether or not she'd succeed in getting answers.

'Excellent. I'll get a nail technician to come over to Rod's station and do your nails while he's massacring your head. Don't say I didn't warn you.'

'Ignore her. She's bitter and twisted,' Rod said, eliciting another cackle from Suze, as he came around to the front of the desk. 'So what can I do for you today?'

Caro shrugged. 'Maybe just a trim? I don't know. Coming in was… spontaneous.'

He was right next to her now, touching her hair, moving it around, thinking, serious for the first time. 'How about you let me give it a bit of a cut, put in a few layers, nothing drastic? And I'd love to see how you'd look with a bit of brightness around your face. We've got some brush-in colour that would just lift it and it washes out. What do you think?'

He started walking backwards, and Caro automatically followed him. Talking and walking now, talking and walking. 'That sounds fine. Whatever you think…'

'Ace, let's get cracking.'

At the back of the salon, she was handed over to a junior to wash her hair, then taken forward to one of the seats in the circle.

A woman in a black T-shirt that announced she was in the NAIL TEAM strolled over, pulling a small trolley behind her, packed with nail paraphernalia.

'Hi, I'm Daisy. What colour would you like?' she asked, with a sweeping hand towards the vast array of varnishes on the top of the trolley.

Caro pondered for a moment. What would Lila choose? From her Facebook pics, she knew it would be a dramatic red or a bright cerise. Caro checked them out and plumped for a pale pink. Nothing too dramatic or over the top. Surely there was no way they were related.

Rod reappeared behind her, sat on a wheeled stool, and pushed himself around her, from side to side, studying his canvas. 'Okay, you sure I can go for it?' he asked.

'I'm sure.' This would normally be terrifying, but compared to everything else that was going on today, this didn't even register as a blip of fear.

Rod stopped talking and got to work, lifting hair, cutting, combing, sometimes just flicking the hair up and cutting it while it was in the air, scissors tapping at an almighty speed. Todd would kill her for letting anyone else near her locks, but right now Caro was so grateful for the safe haven that she didn't care.

Without moving her head, or doing anything with her hands that could smudge Daisy's work, she glanced around the other customers in the circle. Still no Lila. However, she was surprised at the wide spectrum of clients. There were a couple of young women she suspected were models, long, elegant limbs, and cheekbones like spring rolls. There were two elderly ladies in rollers. A teenage boy with the biggest quiff she'd ever seen. And four women in a group conversation, their ages suggesting they were two mums and their adult daughters.

A pang. She'd never done this with mum. Never would now. Mum had gone to the hairdressers religiously the day before Dad came back from a trip, so sometimes it was once a fortnight, sometimes a month, sometimes a couple of months. She was a bit more adventurous than Caro. Their hair was the same colour, but twice a year mum would have blonde highlights to brighten up her natural waves. She was pretty, without trying, striking but in a completely manageable way.

Caro clenched her jaw to try to keep herself together. Now wasn't the time. There had been enough regret and recrimination since her mum got sick, and nothing new would come from revisiting it all now. She'd rather just, for a while at least, forget.

But, no. That thought came with the wrong choice of words.

A flashback. Mum. Caro. That first time. About four years ago. Caro had already been living on her own for many years, since she left university and started work, but she still popped over to see Mum a couple of times a week. That Sunday, she'd found the house empty, the cooker on, a chicken burnt in the oven. She'd waited an hour. More. Called her mum's mobile. No answer. She wasn't one to panic, but she still breathed a huge sigh of relief when her mum walked in the door.

Caro gave her a hug. 'Mum! I was getting worried!'

'Why darling? I'm absolutely fine.'

'Tell that to the chicken in the oven.'

'The…?' Yvonne stopped, a look of concentration coming over her, as if she was searching for something in her mind but just couldn't quite grasp it.

The chicken. That's how it had started. The first thing she'd forgotten. Old age, she'd joked. The menopause. Too much on her mind. Caro had gone along with it, unconcerned at first. After a while, that changed.

Her mum would make plans and not show up. Drive to the shops, then come home on the bus, completely forgetting where the car was parked or that she'd even taken it in the first place. Every time, she'd laugh it off, blame being dippy, or being too busy, or stressed.

Caro researched Yvonne's behaviour on the Internet and came up with many possible reasons, but there was one suggestion that stood out – forgetfulness could be a symptom of depression. It wouldn't have been a surprise. Her mum had always had highs and lows, so perhaps this was something in the same vein. That must be it. She tried to persuade Mum to see a doctor, but she wouldn't agree, so she'd left it for a while, visited as often as possible, hoping that it would get better.

It didn't. And now…

'Okay, so what do we think?' Rod asked her, snapping her back to the present.

Caro checked out her reflection – her damp hair still looked a similar length to when he'd started, but it seemed fuller, with choppy layers, some of which fell to just under the curve of her chin. There was definitely a touch of relief that she didn't look like Cindy Lauper, circa 1984 or 1986. She loved it. She looked the same, but different. Better. Healthier. 'It's a triumph, thanks,' she told Rod, laughing as he gave her a low bow in return.

Out of the corner of her eye, she saw Suze come towards her with a young girl, maybe about sixteen or seventeen, dressed in the salon colours of black trousers, her black T-shirt emblazoned with the words FACE TEAM.

'Since you're a new customer, and we like to throw as much emotional blackmail as possible at you so that you'll leave a great review online and then come back, we're wondering if Kylie here can give you a facial and make-up? On the house. She's still training, so she needs as much practice as she can get. And don't worry, if it's a complete balls up, there's always wet wipes.'

The young girl looked so hopeful that Caro didn't have the heart to argue.

Before she could respond, the door pinged and Caro almost jumped, then craned her neck to see the new arrival. Nope, not Lila.

She sighed and then realised Suze and Kylie were waiting for an answer. 'Sure, that would be good, actually.'

Rod took advantage of the moment to attend to his next appointment.

'I'll be back in a sec. I'll just go sort out my next client then I'll be back to give an even more triumphant blow dry.'

Off he went, while the newest addition to her glamour team grabbed a cotton wool pad and a cleanser.

'What kind of look do you normally go for?' Kylie asked, beaming at the opportunity to flex her talents.

'Erm, I'm not sure. I don't usually wear make-up, so something really natural would be great,' Caro suggested.

The teenager's nod and look of determination told her she was up for the challenge. Rod returned and picked up a hairdryer and a huge brush.

Slotting in on the opposite side of Daisy, Kylie got to work, and suddenly a whole host of images popped up in Caro's mind – photographs that Lila had posted of very similar situations. In this salon, hair being done, make-up, nails too, surrounded by stylists and technicians. So this was what it felt like to be Lila. This was part of her life. Part of what made her who she was. Caro took a moment to think about how it felt and came up with... nice. That was it. Not amazing, or wonderful or special. Not boring or annoying. She appreciated their work but this wasn't her. If anything, all the attention was a bit embarrassing. Give her Todd and his hairdressing scissors in her kitchen any day of the week.

Another ding as the door opened again. Anxiety. Apprehension. Then… Disappointment – and a touch of admiration – as an elderly lady with a bright purple bouffant bustled in.

If the bell went again over the next half hour or so, Caro didn't hear it over the noise of Rod's hairdryer.

Daisy finished first and Caro thanked her for her flawless pink nails. Kylie finished at exactly the same time as Rod switched off the hairdryer and reached for a tube that looked like a large mascara.

'What do you think?' Kylie asked. 'And please don't worry about saying if you don't like it. Suze won't really fire us.'

Caro looked in the mirror and for the first time saw herself… and someone else. Kylie had done exactly as she'd been asked. The make-up was barely noticeable. The perfect shade of foundation. Subtle blusher. A nude lip. Beautifully blended contouring. Two coats of black mascara that widened her eyes in a natural way. She looked like herself, but she also, more than ever before, looked like her mum. The shock and sadness must have fleetingly registered on her face.

'Oh God, you hate it. I'm so sorry. Is it too much? Not enough? Wet wipes coming right up!'

'No, no!' Caro blurted. 'I love it! I really do. Sorry, I just don't wear a lot of make-up so it took me a moment. But I honestly love it. Thank you so much. I'll tell Suze you're wonderful.'

'Yes!' Kylie fist-pumped the air, then did a dance that involved intensive shaking of her arse. The two mothers and daughters in the adjacent seats gave her a round of applause and she bowed her way back to reception to a high five from an amused Suze.

Rod unscrewed the tube, releasing a gold-tinged brush about an inch long. He lifted a few thin sections around her face and slid the brush along them, instantly lightening the colour several shades. Then he picked up some contraption from the counter, and started to roll tendrils of her hair around it, working his way around her head until it was a mass of loose, wavy tendrils.

The door went again. Her heart thudded. She looked. No Lila.

Rod wafted hairspray over her new style to hold the waves and then stood back.

'I can tell by your smile that you love it,' he said, clearly one for appreciating his own brilliance. He was right, though. If she'd known this was possible she'd have done it years ago. She looked younger, brighter, more polished. On any other day, she'd be thrilled by the result, even if she'd downplay it to anyone who complimented her, because she hadn't actually done it herself.

'I do,' Caro agreed, thinking that, much as this was the most unexpected turn of events, she was glad she'd come in.

It was only when she stood and Rod took her robe off and insisted she check out the side view that she saw yet another image in her mind. Not her. Not her mother. But a Facebook photo of Lila, a few weeks ago, after a ten-mile jog on a Sunday morning, no make-up – or at least, not as much as she wore in every other photo – her hair loose and wavy instead of her normal sleek shine.

Perhaps it was the fumes from the hairspray, or just the emotion of the day, but Caro was just a little bit sure she saw a resemblance.

Very faint. Nothing obvious. But maybe it was there. She shook the thought off and headed to the front of the salon, where Suze greeted her at the desk. 'Well, you look great,' she said, chuckling. 'I'm so glad. I hate firing anyone on a Friday.'

She put the bill on the top of the reception counter.

A hundred quid. Holy crap. Who spent a hundred quid on a Friday afternoon just to look good? Caro got her credit card out. Apparently she did, and she didn't regret a single minute of it, or of the twenty quid she added on as a tip. If today wasn't one of the most terrifying of her life she'd actually have been enjoying it. A nice lunch. An out-of-the-ordinary trip to a salon. Meeting some people that made her laugh. At least if she headed back on the train tonight completely empty-handed, she had some positive experiences to show for it, and she could retreat, undamaged, while she came up with another plan.

But she wasn't finished trying yet.

She tried to sound as nonchalant as possible as she spoke to Suze. 'While I'm here, can I ask… a friend of mine comes in here all the time and I was wondering if she was due in today.' She could have led with this at the start, but then if Lila had come in, Suze would have pointed her in Caro's direction, giving no way out for Caro. Now, she was leaving anyway so there was nothing to lose.

'Really? Who's that and I'll check the book.'

'Lila. Lila Anderson.'

There was something in Suze's reaction that piqued Caro's interest. A flicker of something. She saw it in her kids when one of their classmates irritated them, but they didn't want to show it. If she had to guess, she'd say Lila wasn't Suze's favourite person. Suze covered it well though. With a few clicks of a mouse, she checked the screen in front of her.

'Ah, no, Lila isn't due in today.'

Caro's spirits crashed. She really felt she'd got close and now she was back at square one.

'But you should pop in next door,' Suze said, while organising the receipt.

'Why?' Caro asked, then realised that next door must have some significance and if her story that she was

Lila's friend had any truth, she should probably know what it was. She decided to bluster her way through it. 'I haven't seen Lila for a while so I'm a bit out of touch with things.'

Please don't call the police. Please don't. How did undercover investigators pull this sort of stuff off? One small lie and she was already in danger of sweating off Kylie's finest work.

Thankfully, Suze didn't seem suspicious. Or if she was, she didn't care. 'Well, the menswear shop next door – CAMDEN – is owned by Lila's boyfriend Cammy.'

Caro felt her knees weaken as she took in this information. Next door. Right next door. Lila could be there right now and if she wasn't, then there was a man who could tell her where she was.

Oh crap, she couldn't do it. She couldn't just walk in there and ask for her.

Could she?

14

Cammy

The potato tortillas, chicken croquettes, albondigas, pintxos and large carafe of sangria had barely hit the table when Josie morphed into Agatha Christie on an inquisitive day.

'So what do we really know about her though?' she pondered, doing her best Poirot.

Val laughed and Cammy tried not to. 'Christ Almighty, Josie, you need to give it a rest.'

'I can't,' she wittered, digging a fork into one of the meatballs. 'Since they banned smoking in public places, and I cut down to one pack a day, I need to keep my mind distracted and my mouth busy. Anyway, Cameron...' she sometimes liked to use his full name when she was attempting to take the moral high ground, 'all this comes from a place of love. And a burning desire to keep you out of the divorce courts in a year's time.'

'Josie, she's great. Her mum and dad are nice.'

'What about her friends? Who are they? Do we know any of them?'

It wasn't such an outlandish question. Josie had worked in La Femme, L'Homme for over a decade and built up relationships with just about everyone who shopped there and in the beauty salon next door. Val worked part time in Sun, Sea, Ski, the shop on the other side of CAMDEN, and struck up friendships with loads of the regulars. In the grand scheme of city centre life, it wouldn't have been particularly unusual for them to know someone, who knew someone, who knew someone, who knew Lila. In fact, given their interrogation skills and a gossip database that rivalled the amount of information held by Interpol, it was pretty surprising that they didn't.

Cammy shrugged. 'She doesn't actually have a lot of mates…'

Josie's head flew up like a meerkat in heat. 'What? Why? What's wrong with her?'

Cammy had refused the sangria – determined to keep a clear mind for the day ahead, but he lifted Val's glass and took one sip, for medicinal purposes. As much as he adored her, Josie was giving him a headache and a growing pain in the arse.

'Nothing. You know what it's like. Her mum says

girls have always been jealous of her, so she's never really built up a big circle of pals.'

He saw Josie and Val ponder that one for a minute, but he refused to admit that it was strange. No girlfriends popping in for a cuppa, no late night calls to a pal to chat about her day, no group outings or weekend trips. Okay maybe it was a tad... unusual, and even before she spoke, he knew Val, a woman who constantly surrounded herself with friends and family, would pick up on it.

'That might be the case, my love,' Val said, always a bit more reasonable than Special Agent Josie, 'but to be honest, it's a bit strange. No pals at all?'

He went for a white lie to divert her concern. 'I'm sure she has, but we've been a bit wrapped up in each other since we met.' There was some truth in that. In the six months they'd been together, they spent most nights going out for dinner, or chilling at home with a movie – at least, that was on the nights that Lila didn't have spin, or boxercise, or personal training sessions. She'd had loads of those lately – said it was because she wanted to look great in a bikini if they went off somewhere tropical in the post-Christmas lull in January.

That's why the friends thing had never really fazed him. He just thought they were doing that thing a couple does when they first fall in love, where they want to spend all their time together. Usually naked. Nothing wrong with that. Understandable, actually.

Before he'd gone over to LA, he'd been a die-hard founding member of the party scene in the city – out every night with an ever-evolving group of party people. He'd gone back to that for a few weeks when he first got home and he just felt... past it. Out of place. He'd soon realised he was getting too old for all that carry-on, so after twelve hours a day in the shop, six days a week, chilling out with Lila suited him just fine. In fact, he felt really lucky to have found someone who felt the same way he did.

'She's just so busy being madly in love with me that she's let her friends slip a little over the last few months,' he added for good measure.

Josie snorted. 'She's not too busy to post twenty photographs a day on that Facegram.'

'Instagram. Or Facebook. I'll explain it to you again later,' Val said, sagely, sounding like she was so up on these things she had Zuckerberg on her friends and family list.

'Well, whatever. I've never known a grown woman who needs that many photos of herself.'

Okay, so she had a point. And yes, he'd thought it strange at first that she detailed every aspect of her life online, but so what? She enjoyed it. It was a hobby, and she got a buzz from the interaction. He had zero interest in Facebook or Instagram or any of the social media sites, but if Lila enjoyed them, where was the harm?

Cammy was about to issue an irritated rebuttal when Josie followed the criticism up with... 'Although... wouldn't have minded that in my day. It would be good to have photographic evidence of how I looked before I went grey, developed wrinkles and my baps headed south.'

A woman at the next table froze, unsure if she really had just overheard that correctly. Couldn't have. Not from that elderly lady.

'Val, please change the subject and get her off my case,' Cammy pleaded, still laughing. 'World politics. Religion. Brexit. Wrestling. Anything at all. I beg you.'

Val knocked back the last of her vino before she spoke. 'I'd love to help, but you know it would take a bigger force than me to make it stop.'

Josie ignored them, filling up her glass, then Val's. Cammy stuck to water, fearful that they would deploy a back-up plan to get him so pissed he'd crash out before he could propose.

'Previous boyfriends, then?' Josie continued the interrogation.

'Erm.... Well... ah... No one serious.' He immediately realised he should have known better than to try to bluff that one out in front of women with lie detection sensors that went off like car alarms at the first hint of a fib. He immediately cracked and surrendered the truth. 'Right, so you're not going to like it and don't judge her...'

'Of course we won't, love' said Val, as she and Josie pursed their lips, judgemental heads on, ready and waiting.

'She had a long-term relationship before she met me. Over six years.'

He tried to leave it at that. Stop there. He even picked up his fork and dug it into the last chunk of tortilla, before the heat of their steely stares forced him to abandon the idea.

'Okay, so the guy she was seeing was married.'

Josie practically started a Mexican wave. 'I knew it. I knew there was something. Sometimes you just need to dig deep, don't you Val?'

Val, in fairness, was looking more concerned than outraged.

'But I'm not judging, son,' Josie added, serious again.

'And neither am I,' Cammy said pointedly. 'Would be a bit hypocritical, wouldn't it?'

They all knew what he was referring to. Years ago, when Mel's first marriage broke up and he told her he was in love with her, they both acknowledged that there was a connection between them that went further than friendship. But then, before they could take it much further than a kiss, she'd found out he'd been having an affair with a married woman all along and backed off.

That kind of stuff didn't fly with Mel. After everything she'd been through with her husband, she hated cheats and she hated liars. Especially when she discovered that he was the liar who'd been sleeping with Suze, the woman who'd been Mel's sister in law and best friend for years, and they'd both been covering it up. Yep, he'd been having a long term, meaningless fling with a member of Mel's family. There was no coming back from that. Instead, devastated that he'd blown it, he'd taken off to LA and put it all behind him. Some might find it weird that he now owned a shop next door to Suze's salon, and they were still good friends, neither of them ever mentioning their misguided affair, but that was just life. They were all adults and it was a long time ago. Although… the tortilla got stuck somewhere above his stomach as he acknowledged that, even now Mel was nothing more than a memory, he still missed everything about her. Most of all he missed her friendship. The same went for Stacey. She had been his best mate in L.A., before he'd developed deeper feelings for her. Those emotions had long returned to something platonic, but the deep bonds they'd formed as friends for ten years still remained.

A thought struck him – did he have that kind of friendship with Lila?

He immediately realised the comparison was unfair. He'd known Lila for six months. She was beautiful, they'd fallen madly in love, had a great time together, and she'd made coming back to Scotland and starting all over again so much better than he'd ever thought it could be. Okay, so they didn't have that deep friendship bond, but they had so much more.

Jesus, why was he even thinking this stuff? Bloody Josie! She was getting into his head and it was driving him nuts.

He dived back into the conversation. 'So… Lila had an affair, I had an affair, now we've both learned from our mistakes. Maybe we are pretty well suited after all, eh Josie?'

Josie didn't answer, just topped up her sangria glass again.

He'd been looking forward to tonight so much, but the sheen was definitely starting to wear off. Lila had sounded a bit subdued on the phone too. She was usually well up for a night out and a nice dinner somewhere flash, but she'd been more than a bit reluctant, even now that her mum and dad were coming. Or maybe he was just reading too much into it because Josie was deploying her mind-warping tactics on him.

He checked his watch. After three p.m.

'Right ladies, let's head to the restaurant and make sure everything is set up there, and then we just need to nip over to the shop and pick up my suit.'

Val nodded. 'That would be great – I'll pop in and see Jen while we're there.' Jen was Val's adopted daughter, who owned Sun, Sea, Ski.

Cammy paid the bill and they headed off to tonight's venue, Cammy modifying his stride so that the click of Josie and Val's high heels could keep up with him. Josie and Val were unusually quiet as they walked – no doubt hatching a new derailment strategy. He was relieved when they finally got there, with no mention of abduction or protest marches.

The restaurant, Grilled, was one of the most beautiful in the city, a throwback to a more glamorous era, with chandeliers and intimate booths. Dinner for two cost about as much as a flight to Majorca, dinner for four would cover the return journey, but hey, it was going to be worth it for the romance, the tranquillity, the perfect ambience of it all. Besides, it was Lila's favourite restaurant, mainly because it was frequented by celebrities and she could take surreptitious selfies and post them on social media.

Hang on, that made her sound really shallow. Although, he supposed, sometimes she could be. But then, so could he. There was a reason that he never left the house without stopping at a mirror to check he looked good. There was a reason that he enjoyed the finer things in life. There was a reason that *Fake Bake* profits in Glasgow had increased since he'd moved back to the city. And there was a reason that he was planning to propose to his beautiful girlfriend in the flashiest restaurant in town. Did it make him a bad person? No. Did it make him perfectly suited to Lila? Hell yes.

'Cammy, mate, how are you? Good to see you.' Neil, the restaurant manager, was a regular customer at the shop and straight out of the Cammy school of suave élan. He spotted Josie and Val and immediately opened his arms, giving them hugs and double kisses. Neither refused.

'Och, son, if I was twenty years younger and single,' Val told him.

Josie shook her head. 'Och no, Val. They're all into filming it these days – sex tapes. I'd rather watch *Emmerdale*.'

Cammy looked at Neil with an expression of desperation. 'Save me. Please. I'll give you anything you want.'

'Not enough money in the world, pal,' he said, laughing, earning a nudge of rebuke from Val.

'Anyway, so listen, I was going to call you just to let you know we've had to tweak a couple of things tonight,' Neil said, with a definite hint of apology.

Cammy's face fell. What the fuck was going on today? Was this one of those shows where a hidden camera follows someone and throws all sorts of crap in their way just to get a reaction out of them?

'What's happened?' he asked, fearful of the answer.

'The French football team are over here, playing Scotland at Hampden on Sunday.'

'Yeah, I've had a couple of them in the shop. Spent a fortune.'

'They're coming here for dinner tonight,' Neil added, then let that sink in for a moment.

Grilled was romantic. It was intimate. It was exclusive. It was the perfect place for a proposal. Not, however, if two dozen bloody French football players were taking up the rest of the fricking restaurant. For Christ's sake, this was a nightmare. And now he was torn between a rock and a French bloody hard place.

This was Lila's favourite restaurant, so he knew it was where she would want her engagement to happen. But on the other hand, it could be completely ruined by a crowd of blokes discussing their tactics for World Cup qualification.

Bollocks. This wasn't going well.

'But look, I said I'd take care of you and I will,' Neil promised hurriedly, trying to salvage the situation. 'I've allocated them one section of the restaurant, and I've booked you Lila's favourite table in the window. With any luck, you won't even notice they're there.'

He sounded more optimistic than confident. The restaurant was small, maybe 100 covers at most. Cammy reckoned the chances of not noticing an influx of international sportsmen were slim to none – approximately the same as the chances of anything going right today.

But what choice did he have? If he swapped restaurants at this late stage, there was every bit as much of a chance that it could all go wrong because he hadn't had time to prepare it properly. At least here he'd already picked the champagne, the table decorations, and organised for the ring to be brought out with dessert.

The ring.

That jogged his memory and made the decision for him. He was just going to stick to the plan and hope for the best.

'Look, let's just go with the original plan,' he announced to Neil, noticing that even Josie and Val weren't commenting on the latest twist of doom. Maybe it was those two that were causing this with their subliminal vibes. Jinx One and Jinx Two. 'Man, first the ring disaster and now this...'

'What happened with the ring?' Neil asked, curious.

'Shop shut down. Owner did a runner,' Val announced, like a *Crimewatch* presenter delivering the facts of an open case.

'Had to buy another one instead,' Cammy added.

'Unlucky, mate,' Neil whistled. 'Not going well, is it?'

'Had better days,' Cammy agreed. 'But hey, it can only pick up from here.' He was crossing his fingers as he said it, while deciding that all facts from here on would be double-checked. 'Right, so we'll come in for dinner. The table will have her favourite white flowers. The champagne will be on ice. Oh, and her parents will be joining us, so we need the table to be set for four.'

Neil looked like he was about to object, then clearly decided not to kick a man when he was down and adjusted his response. 'No worries, I'll make that happen.'

Cammy carried on. 'I'll bring the ring with me and give it to you. Then, after the meal, when the waiter or waitress brings out dessert, they will also deliver a silver tray and the ring will be on it.'

To their credit, neither Josie or Val came out with a single sarcastic comment at that point. Perhaps they were mellowing. Or coming down with a dose of romance. Or lockjaw.

'And then I'll ask her to marry me and she'll say yes, and we'll live happily ever after, while doing our damnedest...' he pointed to Josie and Val, 'to avoid these two.'

Neil nodded thoughtfully. 'I think that about covers it. Don't worry about a thing. I've got this and I'll make sure it's everything you hoped it would be.'

'Mate, at this stage I just want it to happen without any more disasters.'

Neil held out his hand and Cammy shook it. 'It'll all be good. Like I said, don't worry. Everything is going to be perfect and it'll absolutely be a night you'll never forget.'

Cammy didn't doubt that. He just wanted to remember it for all the right reasons.

As they went back out into the afternoon chill, Cammy pulled out his mobile to call Lila again. He wasn't surprised when it went to voicemail.

In the beginning they'd speak a dozen times a day on the phone. Now it was just a couple of actual conversations and a few chats with her answering machine, but that was understandable – she was packing in the clients to make sure she smashed her targets every month.

'Hi, this is Lila. Leave a message…' He hung up. He'd try her again later.

'Right, mission command, what do we still have to do?' he asked Val.

'Just pick up your suit from the shop and that's it,' Val answered.

Josie interjected, her words dripping sarcasm. 'Still think you should have organised a Red Arrow flyover. If I were Lila, I'd feel a bit short-changed to be honest.'

He laughed, despairing. 'Josie, it's at night. We wouldn't be able to see a thing.'

'Well I've got a pal in the ambulance helicopter. I could get him to fly past the window and flash his lights a couple of times.'

Cammy turned left and led the way. 'Thanks, but we're good. I'm beginning to wish I'd gone to work today and just asked her in the kitchen tonight with the ring pull off a can of Fosters.'

Val tried to console him. 'I know it's not going to plan, but nothing is irretrievably broken. And let's face it, you've had enough disasters for the day, so that's all the drama over and out of the way now. So let's nip into the shop for ten minutes, get a cuppa and we'll all be laughing about this in no time. From here on in, there will be no surprises or drama.'

'What makes you so sure about that?' Cammy asked, waiting for profound words, sincere reassurances, witters of wisdom.

'I told you already – I can feel it in my water. You've got to be positive.'

Not exactly the deep, philosophical reply he'd hoped for. So far, the only thing he was positive about was that the day could only get better.

15

Bernadette

Sarah pulled out of Nina's driveway, tooted the horn, waved, then as soon as they were out of sight, pulled over, parked and turned to Bernadette in the passenger seat.

'I'm scared to ask, but you're not a weeping mess, so I'm risking it. How did it go?'

'She said she's surprised I didn't leave him years ago.'

'You're kidding!'

'Nope. I always thought she worshipped the ground her dad walked on. I had no idea she saw the flaws in him. Turns out Kenneth told her Gerry wasn't good enough for her.'

Sarah didn't hide her outrage. 'No way! Gerry is a lovely bloke! Och, yet another piece of evidence that you – no disrespect – married an arse. This isn't a split, Bernie, it's an escape from a dictatorship.'

Bernadette didn't answer. Even now, she still found it difficult to criticise him to anyone, even her friend of many years.

How had she not known how Nina felt? Had she been in such a cloud of misery and fakery for all these years that she'd been totally unaware of what was really going on around her?

She checked the time. Just after 2 p.m. Stuart finished at lunchtime on a Friday and headed to the Mitchell Library to study and tie up all his assignments for the week – said that way he could relax and enjoy the weekend. He was a man of habit, like his father, but she hoped – today at least – that was where the similarities ended. He'd spent a lifetime trying to follow in his dad's footsteps and now he was training to be a doctor, just like him.

'How do you think Stuart will take it?' Sarah asked, as if she was reading her mind.

Bernadette sighed. 'I honestly don't know. He respects his dad so much, and you know Stuart – he doesn't like change or drama. Maybe I should have told him first and if he was too upset by it I could have changed my mind before I told Nina and...'

'Stop,' Sarah said, firmly but not unkindly. 'Bernie, you've lived your whole life for other people – for the kids, for your mum and dad, for the cretin...' They both let that hang, although it did lighten the moment. '...And now you need to live it for yourself. It doesn't really matter if Stuart doesn't approve, because he's a grown man and he'll get over it.'

'But look at the future I'm taking from them. I'm sure they expected to bring over the grandkids to our home, to have years of big family Christmases and celebrations. I'm tearing that whole picture to shreds.'

'Because it never existed. What they would actually have had was years of visiting, with gran spending the whole time a nervous wreck in case anyone did anything that would upset granddad.'

'He never let them see that side of him,' Bernadette argued. 'He has always been the big shot, the total charmer. At least, I thought he was. After what Nina just told me, I was obviously wrong about that.'

Sarah slipped the van into drive. 'Okay, let's get it over with. What time will Kenneth be back tonight?'

'I'm not sure. I don't even know if he went back to the house at lunchtime. Lord, I hope not. What if he noticed that stuff is gone?'

'He wouldn't have and if he did, he'd have phoned,' Sarah said, perfectly calmly.

'You're right but... Bugger it, I need to check.'

She pulled her mobile phone out of the blue navy bag Nina had got her last Christmas. Marks and Spencer. She'd spotted it when they were in doing their Christmas shopping and Nina had bought it there and then. That had been a lovely day, but Kenneth had been furious because she wasn't there when he got home. The thought made her stomach clench. If that upset him, what was he going to do when he discovered that this Christmas she wouldn't be there at all?

Marge's voice on the other end of the phone was a welcome interruption. 'Dr Manson's office, can I help you?'

'Afternoon Marge, it's Bernadette.'

'Oh, hello there. How are you?' she chirped happily. That was Marge. Always so warm and happy. She'd been Kenneth's secretary forever and... a sudden thought... she'd miss her. Wow. She hadn't even considered that she'd have no need to talk to Marge any more. How many other things had she not thought through?

'Marge, is Kenneth still in surgery?'

'No, his morning one finished just before twelve.'

Oh, shit. Buggering shit. He'd have gone home for lunch. He already knew. He was probably still sitting there, staring at the empty cupboard in the upstairs hall where she'd stashed all the stuff she was taking and then removed it this morning.

She stuttered over her words. 'Oh. Eh, I didn't realise. I would have made him lunch if I'd known he...'

'Ah, no, he had a lunch appointment today so he didn't go home. He's already back and he's doing afternoon rounds before he goes back to theatre,' Marge said. She didn't go into detail, but Bernadette was so busy being relieved that she didn't probe any further.

'Do you need to speak to him? I can try to get hold of him...'

'No, no, it's absolutely fine. Can you give me an idea of what time he'll be done though?'

There was a pause as Marge checked his schedule. 'I think around seven. But you know how these things go – could be sooner or later. Shall I leave a message for him to call you?'

'No, no, it's fine. It's nothing that can't wait. I'll see him when he gets home. Thanks Marge. You have a good weekend.'

And a good month. Year. Life.

She hung up, the relief now tinged with sadness. Marge had been a lovely constant in her life for a long time. Not as close as a friend, mainly due to the fact that Kenneth didn't like to mix professional and personal life, but someone she would miss chatting to.

'I've always loved this building,' Sarah said, almost to herself, as they drew into a parking space at the side of the Mitchell Library.

'Me too,' Bernadette answered. It was indeed glorious. Opened in its Charing Cross location in 1911, it was an architectural marvel constructed of blond sandstone, with a stunning dome on the roof. At night it was illuminated, its beauty breathtaking.

Bernadette loved the interior even more. When the kids were small there had been none of those soft play areas or baby yoga, or all that other stuff they had now, so this was where she had brought them, at least once a week. They'd sit in the children's section and read, then have a juice and a treat in the café. It had been their favourite thing. Such a shame kids had so many other distractions these days.

'Oh God, you've gone all misty-eyed. Are you getting sentimental and nostalgic? Do I have to break out the tissues?'

Bernadette sniffed, smiled and steeled herself. 'Nope, all good.'

'Great, let's go then. I'll wander around the Scottish crime section while you talk to Stuart – see if I can come up with a back-up plan involving murder and mayhem in case Kenneth kicks off.'

Sarah slipped her arm through Bernadette's as they walked around to the back entrance, the one that led into the café area. All the while, Bernadette was listening to an internal battle in her mind.

Don't be there. Be there. Don't be there. Be there. Don't be there. Aaaaargh.

She cast her glance across the sea of heads in the bright, airy café, past pensioners, students, mums and kids, people in suits, some young teenagers, a gaggle of elderly ladies hooting with laughter, a guy sitting alone... Stuart. There he was. She felt a moment of pure misery that she was about to wreck his day and perhaps part of his future. She paused, steeled herself, then forced her legs to walk towards him.

If Nina had taken after her father's side of the gene pool, Stuart came from hers. The auburn hair, natural, not out of a bottle like hers had been for the last few years since the grey started coming in. The same green eyes. He'd never quite reached the height of his father. At least in inches. In Bernadette's eyes, he was already a greater man than his dad had ever been.

He was so engrossed in his books; he didn't even see her coming until she was almost at his table.

'Mum! Auntie Sarah! What are you two doing here?'

'We've come to tell you that we're running away together. We're lesbians,' Sarah replied, deadpan, making Bernadette splutter.

Stuart's eyes widened so much she worried that he'd do himself a permanent injury.

'I'm kidding! Although, she does have great legs,' Sarah added, grinning.

'Sarah!' Bernadette chided, although she was thankful for the intervention.

Stuart shook his head. 'I love you two, I really do.' He got up to hug them both. 'Good to see you, Ma. You too, Auntie Sarah. To be honest, I kinda wish it was true. It would be a great story.'

After Sarah had released him, she made her excuses and headed over to mingle with Chris Brookmyre, Val

McDermid, Denise Mina, Tony Black, Anna Smith and the other voices in the crime section.

'Can I get you a coffee? Tea?' Stuart asked his mother.

Bernadette slid into a chair and hung her handbag on the back of it. 'No, thanks. I've just had one with your sister.'

For the first time, there was a hint of concern in Stuart's expression and Bernadette felt her stomach flip yet again. Lord, this was hard. Stuart had always been the far more sensitive child. Nina would be climbing trees and rounding up a gang of neighbourhood kids to play in the garden – as long as Kenneth wasn't home, of course – while Stuart would be quite happily ensconced on the big chair in the corner of the kitchen, reading a book. He liked calm. Predictable. Still waters. And now Bernadette was coming along with a tsunami of change.

'What's happened? Is something wrong?'

For the second time, Bernadette decided to go straight to the truth. 'Stuart, I'm so sorry to tell you this, but I'm leaving your dad. There's no other way to say it. I've been unhappy for a long time and I've decided that I need to make some changes...'

'With Auntie Sarah?' he blurted, incredulous.

'No! She really was just joking about that.'

He didn't respond and she could see there were a million conflicting thoughts running through his mind. That was Stuart. Pensive. Thoughtful. That was why he'd make a great doctor.

'Look, I know it's a big shock, and I'm so sorry, but I'm leaving today, so I had to tell you. I'm moving in with Auntie Sarah for a while – separate rooms – until I can find a place of my own. And no, I haven't told your dad yet. I wanted you to know first. I understand if you're upset with me and I'm so sorry to be changing things and I know you'll need some time to process it all and get used to the idea...' Bernadette knew she was rambling, but she couldn't stop. '... But I'll be here for you, just like before. And if there's anything I can do to make this better for you, you know I'll do whatever I can. I hope you can forgive me and...'

Elbows on the table, his head went into his hands and Bernadette went straight to apology mode.

'Oh God, son, I'm so sorry,' she repeated, reaching over to put her hand on his trembling shoulder. 'I know this must be terrible for you...'

'It is,' he murmured.

'Stuart, you know I'd never hurt you intentionally, it's just...'

He raised his head, sighed, closed his eyes for a second then opened them again, his response more positive now. 'Mum, it's fine.'

'I know it isn't. You don't need to say that just to make me feel better. No one wants to hear their parents are separating and I can see how hard this is for you...'

'Mum, honestly, it's fine,' he repeated, his hand taking hers from his shoulder and hanging on to it. He'd always been the far more tactile child as well. 'I get it. And I'll always want you to do what makes you happy.'

Bernadette welled up again. The universe may have given her a shit husband, but by God, she'd managed to get two great kids.

'Thank you. I can see how much this has upset you and I know you hate it when things are on an uneven keel.'

He took a sip from the bottle of fresh orange juice that was in front of him on the table. 'It's not that, Mum. Since we're baring souls here, the thing is…' He stopped, stuck for words.

Bernadette's heart went out to him. He'd always found it difficult to share how he felt, unlike his sister who wore her feelings on the outside.

He had another try. 'I kind of wish the thing with you and Auntie Sarah was true, it would make this so much easier.'

Bernadette wasn't following at all.

'Right. So. The thing is…' He was struggling and she had no idea how to help him. 'The thing is,' he repeated, 'I was going to come and speak to you and Dad sometime soon… I was working up to it… because I wanted to tell you that… that… Mum, I'm gay. Connor, that I share the flat with – not just a housemate.'

This was astonishing. Surprising. Right out of left field. Yet, she suddenly realised that it made perfect sense. She'd never seen him so happy, so content, so relaxed, than he'd been over the last few months. Without giving a second thought to what anyone else in the café would think, she threw her arms around him. 'Oh, Stuart, I'm so glad for you, I really am. I'm thrilled that you've found someone that makes you happy. You know that's all I've ever wanted for you.'

His shaking shoulders told her he was either laughing or suffocating so she eventually released him. 'I know, Mum.'

Sitting back, she could see the relief. 'I wish you'd told me before. I don't understand why you didn't.' It was true. They'd always had a close relationship; she'd thought they'd been able to share anything. He hadn't had a lot of girlfriends in his life, but there had been a few – were those just attempts to fit in?

Had she failed to make him understand that she'd love him unconditionally and accept him no matter who he was? Did he not realise that she wouldn't give a hoot about his sexuality, as long as he was with someone who was good to him and loved him the way he deserved to be loved? Had staying with Kenneth all these years actually given her children the wrong message?

'I didn't know myself. I mean, I wondered. Kind of. But I wasn't sure. Some people know from when they're kids, but it's only been in the last couple of years that I've realised, and I only knew for sure when I moved in with Connor. It was just a flat-share at the beginning, although I knew he was gay. Didn't take me long to realise I definitely was too.'

'Are you together now?'

He nodded. 'Yeah. I don't know if it's going to be the everlasting love of my life, but we're good. He's a great guy.'

'I'm so, so happy for you.'

Now it was his turn to squeeze her hand. 'And I'm happy for you too, Mum. I mean, it'll take a bit of adjustment, but we'll get there. If the last few months have taught me anything it's that you just have to go with what you feel. When are you going to tell dad?'

'Tonight.'

'Ah. He won't be happy.'

'That might be an understatement.'

Stuart thought about that for a moment. 'He'll be fine, Mum. So will you. We all will.'

Dear Lord, so far, today wasn't playing out how she thought it would at all. And that could only be a good thing. On what should have been the hardest day of her life, she was actually, right there and then, feeling pretty over the moon. Her kids accepted her decision. That was the single biggest fear and worry that she'd had since she decided to leave – actually, longer than that. It was the single biggest fear and worry for the last thirty years. She could handle anything that Kenneth threw at her from here on in. She could cope with every issue and difficulty that would come her way. But she couldn't have functioned if her children had been devastated by this or, worse, rejected her. They hadn't and her gratitude was immense.

Still holding Stuart's hands, she sat back slightly in her chair, something niggling her. 'Now that you know for sure, why would you have to work up to telling us?' It didn't make sense. Kenneth was many things, but he wasn't homophobic. At least, she'd never seen any signs of that. Sure, it might be a shock to him, but she didn't think he'd react badly to it. 'Your dad wouldn't have been disappointed or upset about your sexuality.' At least she hoped he wouldn't be, but after his reaction to Nina's decision to marry Gerry, who knew? He'd never shown any sign of it, but maybe there was a part of Kenneth that wanted to control the kids' lives too.

'No, I know... but, er... he would have been pretty pissed off when I told him I'm also dropping out of medicine,' he confessed sheepishly.

It took her a moment. 'Seriously? Why?'

There was no anger, no judgement – she was in no position to dole out either, given her bombshell of the day. Although, *she* might be off the hook on telling Kenneth, because if Stuart got in there first with this revelation, the shock would probably kill him.

Stuart took another drink before he spoke. 'Because I was doing that for him. Because it was what he expected. Because it was what I'd always thought I'd do. But it's not me, Mum. I've realised so much about myself in the last few months. I know exactly who I want to be and what I want to do, so I'm switching to something that interests me far more.'

'What?'

'Law. I want to be a lawyer. Financial law, I think, not criminal. Although, obviously there's some crossover there.'

The gale of amusement swept Bernadette away before she even saw it coming. The stress. The relief. Everything about this crazy day. It all tipped over from the surreal to the absolutely bizarre, and for some reason she couldn't comprehend at all – probably the menopause – she suddenly couldn't stop the hilarity taking hold. People were turning to stare at the laughing woman now, curious and faintly amused at the tears of merriment that were streaming down her face.

'Mum?' Stuart joined in, chuckling too, but clearly not quite understanding her reaction. 'Are you okay?'

'I am, my darling, but it's just…' Off she went again, huge guffaws now, a sound so contagious that the spectators, trying their best to pretend they weren't aware of her, were having to mask their smiles and suppress their urge to giggle. It was like one of those viral videos, where someone on a train started to laugh and within seconds the whole carriage was in an uproar.

'… It's just…' Another chuckle. 'Law!' she said, collapsing again with the hilarity of it.

Much as he was enjoying his mum's reaction, the reason for her hysteria still wasn't clear to her son. 'Why is that so funny?'

It took every iota of effort Bernadette possessed to pull it together. She fought to stop laughing. She wiped her eyes. She took a deep breath. She cleared her throat. 'Because I'm about to take half our savings and there's a fair chance your dad will have me arrested.'

16

Lila

At the traffic lights on Crow Road, Lila checked out her reflection in the rear-view mirror. Her new Prada aviators looked fabulous, especially now that her hair was a bit beach-wave-casual after her lunchtime interlude with Ken. The very thought of it turned her on. The prospect of being able to have sex with him every day just fuelled the determination to make it happen.

Shaking off the memory of him, she whipped out her phone, pouted, took a quick selfie, then uploaded it to all her social media sites, with the hashtags #fridayfeeling #fabulous #wintershades #pradarocks #eveninDecember.

An irate woman in a Skoda behind her beeped the horn to let her know that the lights had changed. How rude. Did nobody have any patience these days?

She gave her the finger, removed the glasses, then accelerated off. Probably just some jealous cow going home to four brats and a husband that only shagged her when his football team won on a Saturday.

She turned right, then wound her way around the maze of Victorian crescents and terraces that made up this part of the city. This was one of the finer areas, populated by wealthy professionals, academics and a fair share of the glitterati. House prices were among the highest in the city, there were fabulous bars and restaurants and she could absolutely see herself living here instead of at her waterfront flat. Okay, so her place was on the river, but that's where the glamour ended. Here, however, she could pop to one of the bijou little delis for lunch and have one of the gorgeous florists deliver her weekly flowers, all white, for the hallway in the house. Actually, maybe they'd move. Perhaps Ken wouldn't want to stay in the home he'd shared with Bernadette. Fine with her. It would be fabulous to find their own place, and work with a designer to make it absolutely perfect.

Her stomach started to rumble and she realised she'd had nothing to eat all day. One of those bijou little delis was coming up on her left and there was a space right outside it, so she pulled in and jumped out, noting the head turns of a couple of guys who were walking past. Her ego took a bow, then pretended not to notice.

She picked up a goat's cheese salad from the display and a bottle of Perrier. The cheesecake in the fridge area looked delicious, but she didn't maintain a size six figure by giving in to temptation, so she ignored it.

Back in the car, she tossed her purchases on to the passenger seat and set off again.

The traffic was slowing down with the mums in their estate cars and jeeps starting to mobilise on the school run, so it was ten minutes later that she finally turned off Great Western Road and into Ken's street, a gorgeous, curving, tree-lined road of detached villas and townhouse terraces, all of them built some time near the end of the nineteenth century. Lila didn't give a toss about architecture, but even she could see that they were impressive buildings.

She crawled along, some weird sensation making her skin prickle. Nerves? Excitement? Maybe a combination of both.

There it was, on the right. Not the grandest house on the street, but still striking by anyone's standards. Constructed from stone, it had double bay windows downstairs, and three windows on the front upstairs. Lila knew the centre one and the one on the right-hand side formed Ken's bedroom and en suite. One night, a few years before, she'd been sitting out here, when she'd seen him pull the curtains, then watched as the bathroom light went on. At the same time a text from him had pinged on her phone saying goodnight. She'd realised he must be sending it from the bathroom before joining Bernadette in bed. She'd responded with a suggestion of what they could be doing if he was with her, before adding two kisses and sending. The return text came with a promise to take her up on her suggestion next time they met. Always in the future, she thought. Never now. That was going to change.

Her hands tightened around the steering wheel as she spotted the side of a vehicle in the driveway. It couldn't be Ken's. He drove his sleek red Mercedes to work on a Monday, then left it there all week as he cycled to and from the hospital. It was a peculiar habit that she didn't fully understand, but she was sure there was some really smart reason for it.

Closer now, she realised the car in the double driveway belonged to Bernadette. A Fiat something or other. Lila sighed. Bernadette was the wife of an eminent surgeon – what the hell was she doing in a Fiat? Where was the Merc? The Lexus? Ken was wasted on her.

Wasted.

She pulled up on the opposite side of the road, and – much as she was desperate to march over and ring the doorbell – she decided there were a few other necessities to take care of first. Food. Make-up. Hair. All of which would give her a chance to scope out the situation.

Without taking her eyes off the house, the garage, the front path, she lifted her phone and dialled the house number again. Still no answer. How could that be? Her car was parked right there, so she was almost definitely in. She didn't strike Lila as the type of woman who would go for an afternoon jog, so she was probably in there lying on the couch watching daytime TV while scoffing a six-pack of prawn cocktail crisps.

Okay, time to prepare. Food first – but after a few mouthfuls of the salad, she put it back to the side. Couldn't eat. She was too busy strategizing to take incoming nutrition. Instead, she gulped back some water and got on with touching up her make-up. Her foundation was almost flawless, just a couple of slightly shiny patches – that was what happened after Botox – so she damped them down with her Elizabeth Arden sponge and powder.

Hair next. The perfect, poker-straight sheet from this morning had been ruffled by her antics with Ken, so she pulled her battery-operated tongs out of the glove compartment and flicked them on. Less than a minute later, they pinged and she got to work, adding to the waves so at least they looked deliberate, and not the result of a wild, lunchtime shagging session. Only when she had restored a gorgeous mane of baby blonde – all her own, no extensions required – did she switch the tongs off and toss them on the floor to cool down.

Lipstick. Should she go with her favourite Revlon red again? Or go with a softer pink that would be more flattering at this time of day? Daylight was beginning to fade outside, so she flicked on the car's interior light, and took a selfie. Caption: Red or pink pout? Posted. Her phone immediately started pinging with responses, but she ignored them all. Red. Definitely red. She needed every bit of vampish confidence she could garner.

Butterflies well and truly stirring, she slid out of the car, locked it and crossed the road. Actually, strutted was a more apt description.

The gate squeaked as it opened and she checked out the car to her left. The driveway was big enough for two vehicles, one directly in front of the garage and one to the left of it. That's where the Fiat sat now.

Surreptitiously, she peered in the front room windows – no sign of life. Bernadette must be in the back of the house. Time to do this.

Only when her Revlon red nail polish was pressing the doorbell, did Lila notice that her hands were shaking. No time for weakness now.

Remove obstacles. Conquer challenges. Remove obstacles. Conquer challenges.

She still jumped when the bell rang.

Five seconds. Ten seconds. Fifteen seconds. Nothing.

Come on, how long does it take to answer a door? Was daytime TV really that engrossing?

She rang it again.

Five seconds. Ten seconds. Fifteen seconds. Nothing.

Maybe she was out in the garden at the back. Lila looked to each side of the house, but there were fences at both, stopping anyone from getting to the rear of the home. Fuck. Irritation mounting, she pulled her phone from her Mulberry Bayswater and dialled the number once again. Ring ring.

She could hear the chirp of the phone inside the house. Five seconds. Ten seconds. Fifteen seconds. Then Ken's voice cut in again, asking her to leave a message. Nothing. Again, fuck.

She strutted back to the car, threw her bag across to the passenger side and then climbed in, making a conscious effort to think about this rationally. The house was empty. The car was there. So chances were that Bernadette hadn't gone far. Go or wait? Wait. She hadn't come all this way to have wasted her time. Throwing lipstick caution to the wind, she picked up the salad and finished it, eating slowly, chewing every mouthful twenty times as her mother had always told her. That passed fifteen minutes or so. Still nothing.

She finished the water. Still nothing. And now, she was beginning to feel the need to pee. Damn it.

Another five minutes. Still nothing.

She just about needed to be peeled from the roof of the car when the ring of her mobile phone cut into the silence.

She checked the screen. Head office again. What was it with them today? They were driving her nuts. She flicked it straight to voicemail. There was no way she wanted to get into a conversation about orders, or travel, or team-building bloody sessions, in case Bernadette came back and she lost her window of opportunity. And now she definitely needed to pee.

Trying to take her mind off it, she picked up her phone and flicked on to her Facebook – 206 likes for her last post, and they were about fifty – fifty as to red or pink.

She scanned the comments. One said, *Stunning either way, hunni!* Lila checked the name of the person who'd posted – nope, no idea. She'd never met them in her life.

Another one. *Wow, looking great as always! #beautygoals #princess #babe.*

She'd never actually met the person who wrote that one either, although they made it sound like they hung out every night after work.

She had over 2000 Facebook friends and she actually only knew about fifty of them. As for true friends? Well, none of them really. She'd never needed friends. The girls at school and university had all been so jealous, she'd never bothered keeping up with them, and then she'd met Ken, and landed this job, and – before her dad moved back here full time – she did loads of things with her mum, so her life just seemed to roll on without the need for anyone else. Some people might think it was a bit strange but it suited her just fine.

The buzz of the adoration gave her enough of a high to dilute the annoyance that she was wasting her time here.

But she really, really, needed to pee.

Sod it, she couldn't wait any longer. She was furious. Bloody Bernadette wrecking her plans again. Today was proving to be an absolute bust and she had to redeem at least some of it. She checked the clock. Three-forty.

She'd hoped that she would have a long, lazy afternoon with her mum, or an even longer, sexy afternoon with Ken if his surgery schedule changed, so she hadn't made her usual Friday afternoon appointment at the salon. Still, Suze would definitely find a way to fit her in for something. Anything.

Horns blared as she did a swift U-turn then sped back in the direction she'd come from. Salon, it was. She could take care of everything else later.

Friday rush hour traffic was really building up now, so what should have been a fifteen-minute journey took twenty-five. And oh, she now needed to pee so badly. She practically abandoned the car outside the salon – one of the junior staff could come and move it – before dashing in, straight past a surprised Suze at reception and rushing into the loo.

An exhalation of relief later, she checked her reflection in the mirror, washed her hands and then returned to the desk.

'Hey Suze!' she chirped breezily. Just because she was having – lunchtime quickie aside – a completely shit day, didn't mean the rest of the world had to know about it. 'Do you have a slot for a blow-dry? Maybe an updo? I know I don't have an appointment, but I just feel the need to be pampered.'

Suze greeted her with a smile that didn't quite reach the eyes. She'd always suspected Suze wasn't her greatest fan, but she got a thirty per cent discount in here because Suze and Cammy had been friends for, like, ever. Although, like his friendships with Josie and Val, Lila didn't get it. It wasn't like they were particularly interesting. And why did he need female friends when he had her?

'That's so spooky, you walking in right now. Someone was in here, just a few minutes ago, and asked for you.'

'Really, who?'

Suze shrugged. 'I didn't get her name. Really pretty. Maybe thirty. Blonde. She had an accent – sounded like Inverness or Aberdeen. I always get the two of them mixed up. Anyway, she said she was a friend.'

Lila quickly flicked through her mental Rolodex for a clue but there was nothing. 'A "friend" friend, or a Facebook friend?'

Suze shrugged again, her attention already back on the computer at the desk. 'No idea. I prefer to wait until the second appointment before I hold them down and grill them for every detail of their lives.'

Lila fought the urge to bite back with a bitchy retort.

As for the 'friend' who had asked for her? It could be anyone. A few of the nurses and a couple of the doctors she'd interacted with in hospitals or at conventions were from up north, so it could be one of them. Or perhaps it was someone who had come across her on Facebook and liked her page – one of those strangers who acted like her very best friend.

'Anyway, I told her to pop in next door and speak to Cammy, so you might want to talk to him. It was only about ten minutes ago, so she's probably still there.'

4 p.m. – 6 p.m.

17

Caro

Buying time to pluck up the courage to go in, Caro stopped to look in the window of the menswear shop. It took a moment to realise that the wavy-haired reflection in the window was her. She never wore her hair like this but maybe she would in the future. The thought came back into her mind that she had come down here looking for answers and all she was going to go home with was a new appreciation for the occasional beauty treatment and a shaggy hairstyle.

Perhaps that wouldn't be such a bad thing. New starts.

She reached for her phone to call the hospital, then stopped. Todd was taking care of that today. He had it. A pang of longing took her by surprise. She wanted her mum to be here with her right now. She wanted to wander around the city, arm in arm, strolling through Christmas markets and sampling mulled wine and hot pies from the stalls she'd seen in George Square when she arrived. She wanted to be planning their dinner on Christmas Day, a feast like the old days, with Auntie Pearl, Uncle Bob, Todd and the more recent addition of the lovely Jared.

And Mum. She just wanted to be with her mum.

In reality, she would be – even if it was just lying on her bed in the hospital, listening to her breathe.

For the gazillionth time that day she wondered what she was doing here.

Really, what the hell was going on? This wasn't her. She didn't do this kind of stuff. She was a teacher, a responsible adult. Her only defence was that everything that had happened in the last few months – hell, the last couple of years – had brought her to this point. Yep, that's what her lawyer, paid for by Todd's Crowdfunding, would tell the jury when she was arrested for stalking. She'd lose her job, of course. And then she'd be skint and have to resort to selling her story to *Take A Break*. It was a dark future that was ahead of her if she didn't cut out this nonsense and go home.

It would have been so much easier just to send Lila a message on Facebook, but she just couldn't bring herself to do it. If it was a mistake, she didn't want to give some poor girl the shock of her life. If it was true, she didn't want to alert her dad to the fact that she'd discovered his second family, and have her half-sister find out that way. Basically, messaging on Facebook was a lose–lose situation for Lila and Caro couldn't do that to someone she didn't know, no matter how happy and carefree she seemed.

So she should go home. And she would.

But first…

Okay, you can do this, Caro. Get it together. You've got this.

She pushed open the door, immediately coming into the eyeline of a hipster, bearded guy behind the counter to her right, chatting to a young woman whose back was to her. Caro just about fainted before she realised that it couldn't be Lila. This girl had brown hair, swept up in a messy bun on the top of her head. The guy wasn't Lila's boyfriend either. Thanks to Lila's Facebook, Caro knew he was clean-shaven, tanned, insanely good-looking, usually topless (with finely carved six-pack on show) or fully dressed in incredibly stylish clothes, while presenting her with gifts and calling her 'babe'.

Honestly, Lila's life was like a reality show, one in which everyone adored her and showered her with love, affection and jewellery.

'Hi, can I help you?' It came from the hipster dude.

'No thanks, I'm just… looking,' she answered, immediately making a show of browsing through the nearest rail, although why she would be wanting a three-pack of men's Calvin Klein boxer shorts she wasn't entirely sure.

Hipster dude carried on talking to the woman, a friendly conversation, so probably not a customer then. Okay, two choices. Ask for Lila, or leave. Actually there was a preferable third, but she knew that taking up residence here and hoping for a cloak of invisibility to keep her presence secret probably wasn't the most feasible option.

She picked a packet of boxer shorts off the rail and carried them to the till area. That was Todd's Christmas present sorted.

The guy behind the counter took them with a smile, while the girl asked, 'Is there anything else you'd like? Actually, I'm not sure why I said that – I work next door, not here. Force of habit.'

Hipster dude feigned exasperation. 'She tries to steal our customers all the time. Tempts them in with the smell of coconut suntan lotion.'

'Ah, the holiday shop,' Caro said, going for pleasant and jocular. 'I noticed that. If I'm ever looking for coconut suntan lotion I now know where to find it.'

'Excellent. My work here is done then,' the interloper declared. 'Right, Digby, I'm going to shoot off now. If you get a rush just shout and I'll storm in to the rescue.'

'No worries, Jen – thanks for the help today.'

'Pleasure,' she replied, then turned to Caro. 'Coconut. We never run out.'

'Good to know,' Caro said, laughing now.

The doorbell pinged as she pulled it open and left.

'Actually, while I'm here… The girl who owns the salon next door…'

'Suze?' he said.

'Yes. Well, I was looking for an old friend and she said that you might be able to help. Lila Anderson?'

Digby nodded. 'Yeah, that's the boss's girlfriend.'

'Is she here today?'

'Nah, she doesn't come in so much.' He must have sensed her disappointment. 'But the boss, Cammy – he might be able to help.'

Caro's heart was thudding out of her chest again and she was fairly sure that very unattractive beads of sweat were forming on her upper lip. This was it. She was about to take that defining step, because as soon as she'd spoken to Lila's boyfriend she'd have to tell the whole truth and then there'd be no going back.

Do it? Don't. Do it? Don't…

'Is he around?'

Digby shook his head. 'Sorry – he's got the day off today. And he *never* takes the day off so you've just been unlucky.'

She bit back something trivial, like, 'story of my life', and replaced it with a more casual, 'Ah, no worries.'

'Do you want me to leave a message? Ask him to pass it on?'

Caro shook her head as she lifted the bag containing

the boxers. 'No, it's fine – thanks. I'll just drop her a note on Facebook.'

'You'll definitely get her on there – she's never off it.'

'That sounds like a plan then. Thanks for this,' she held up the bag and then wondered if he noticed the sweat beads. He probably had that down as guilt, and irrevocable proof that she had another four boxes of Calvin Klein's up the front of her jacket.

This was ridiculous. She was actually losing the plot altogether.

The door pinged again as she left, her attention immediately grabbed by an Evoque that was practically abandoned in the middle of the road. That was some crazy parking right there. The thought momentarily distracted her from the realisation that she had absolutely no idea where to go. Ok, focus. She was still only a couple of streets away from the station, so she could head back there. Actually, not could – she *should* head back there. This had gone far enough. There was no progress to report, but maybe that was fine. After all, she had nothing to gain here. Nothing. If it *was* her dad cosying up to his other daughter, Lila, in those photos, was he going to come rushing back to her, arms open wide, begging to take care of her? No. So finding out the truth had absolutely no upside, yet the downside was a whole big hot mess with the potential to create havoc.

Walk away.

Once again, she decided that the best thing to do was to stroll back to the station and get on the next train north. Definitely this time. That was what she should do.

She retraced her steps back to George Square, which was still heaving with revellers. The afternoon daylight had already almost turned to nightfall, so the brightness of the Christmas lights was stunning. On any other year, it would fill her with Christmas spirit and joy, make her want to drink mulled wine, and pick up gorgeous little presents for everyone that she loved. Not this year.

The station was directly ahead now, across the square, all she had to do was walk there. Two minutes max. That was it. Her feet kept on going. One minute. *Keep on striding*. Thirty seconds. That's when she noticed it – the hotel to the right-hand side of the station, a beautiful old white building with a glass frontage that looked directly on to the square. Inside she could see people sitting, drinking, chatting, and suddenly she wanted to be in there. To be one of them. Not a care in the world other than the wait for the next French Martini. She wanted to shrug the weight and worry of the day off her shoulders and just be another tourist, sitting in a bar, gazing in awe at the Christmas spectacle through the window. The train could wait.

Before she'd even made a conscious decision to do so, she'd changed course. She went inside, reaching the glass frontage just as a couple were leaving a corner table. Perfect timing. The waiter appeared almost instantly.

'I'll have a gin and tonic, please.' This felt so strange. She could honestly say that she had never, ever sat in a bar and drank on her own before. Another first.

He came back with the G&T and deposited it with a small bowl of nuts on the table. Caro asked for the Wi-Fi code before he went, then typed it into her iPad.

Click. Facebook. Search. Lila Anderson.

Lila had posted two, no, hang on, *three* photos that afternoon so far. Didn't she do anything without turning it into an attention-seeking expedition? How did she even have time to take so many photos?

There was a ridiculous one in the car, wearing sunglasses in flipping December. The next one asked for a poll on her lipstick and the last one, in the car again, declared it was champagne and pamper time.

Caro was already halfway into an eye roll when she realised she had no right to judge, given that so far her afternoon consisted of a grooming session, a lovely lunch, and a large gin and tonic.

She went back to Facebook and realised with a jolt that Lila was in a salon.

Hang on, had she missed her in Pluckers? Was she there now? Definitely not. Suze had been sure she wasn't coming in today. But then, a girl like Lila probably frequented many beauty venues, so there was nothing to say that she was definitely referring to Pluckers. Time to accept that finding Lila in a city the size of Glasgow was highly unlikely. Right now she could be absolutely anywhere.

She pulled out her phone and called Todd again.

'How do you feel about Calvin Klein?' she asked when he answered.

'You mean, personally? I don't think we've ever met. I'm fairly partial to his underwear though. In a manner of speaking.'

'Excellent, because you just got a lovely box of kecks, thanks to my hopeless undercover skills. I discovered Lila's boyfriend owns a shop. Went in, but he wasn't there. So I flaked and bought you boxer shorts.'

Todd's cackling laughter sounded like interference on the line. 'I like your style. And I hope you got them in large, but skinny round the hips.'

'Eeew, too much information.'

'Sorry. Any chance you can go back in and flake again? I could do with a six-pack of socks and some fleecy pyjamas.'

'Don't mock the afflicted,' Caro chided, seeing the humour in it. A pang of wishing he was here made her take a very large sip of her gin. 'Anyway, this sad reflection of my limitations has persuaded me to come home. I'm not sure what I thought I'd achieve, but this isn't it.'

'Where are you now?'

'In a hotel bar next to the train station. I'm just having a drink and then I'll get the next train. Will you pick me up from the station?'

'Of course I will.'

Another sip of gin. 'Thanks. You're the best cousin anyone could ever want. Actually, scrap that. You're a terrible cousin for not talking me out of coming here.'

'I tried but there are limits to my superpowers,' he joked.

There was a pause. That happened a lot – it was like a natural interlude between happy normal life and serious sad life.

'Have you spoken to the hospital?' she asked, desperate for news, or reassurance.

'Twice and she's absolutely fine. I'm just about to go by there. If there are any problems, I'll call you.'

Her vocal chords took a minute to respond, caught by a wave of guilt. This was the first day in two years that she hadn't gone to see her mum, either at home, or in hospital. Yet, she couldn't remember the last day that her mum recognised she was there. Not that it mattered. She would carry on going until...

'Caro?'

'Sorry,' she cleared her throat. Getting emotional while sitting alone, drinking gin, in the middle of a crowd of strangers in a hotel wasn't going to happen. Not to her. The thought of anyone looking at her with curiosity, of attracting that kind of attention, filled her with absolute horror.

No. Woman up. Get a grip. Keep it together.

The waiter appeared again in her peripheral vision and signalled to her almost-empty glass.

What the hell. One more drink. She could get the train after the next one. What was she rushing home to do anyway?

Today she was being… normal. She wasn't being a teacher in front of a classroom full of kids. They would all be counting down the hours to Santa's arrival, wrapping gifts, visiting family, or heading off on ski trips, or making some other plans for the Christmas break. She wasn't being a girlfriend, now that she'd split with Jason. She wasn't being a daughter, because she was down here. She was just being… normal. Just a normal person, doing the kind of normal things that other normal people did on a normal Friday in December.

Even the coolness of the last sip of gin couldn't numb the lump of pain that had formed in her throat.

Normal. How could any of this be normal? Did normal people wonder if the dad that had walked away from them had actually been living a double life? Or have a mum that couldn't remember her family?

That was how she'd known for sure that something was wrong.

It was a couple of years ago. A sunny day, the first of the school summer holidays. She'd taken her mum some lunch and planned to spend the day with her. Yvonne was in the garden, looking happy, fresh-eyed, wearing a huge floppy hat to keep the sun off her face. She could have walked right off the set of one of those health insurance adverts, or perhaps an M&S commercial. Younger than her years, vibrant, pretty. Caro's spirits had soared to see her so healthy and happy. Perhaps the strange behaviour and erratic events of the previous months had been the result of depression after all. Nothing more sinister to worry about.

They'd chatted. Laughed. Caro had told her all about her plans to go travelling for the summer. 'When's Dad home again?' she'd asked, hoping to see him before she went.

'Not for a couple of weeks yet,' her mum had answered.

Caro had gone in to unpack the lunch and that's when her dad had called to say he was on the train home and wanted to be picked up from the station.

'But Mum said you're not due home for a while,' Caro said, confused.

'What? We spoke yesterday. She knew I was coming back today,' he replied, irritated.

That was it. Right there. The woman who had waited with bated breath for her husband to walk through the door every single time he returned, had forgotten he was on his way.

Todd's voice at her ear snapped her back to the present. 'Caro?'

'Sorry, I think it's a bad signal. I just... miss her.'

'I know you do.' She could hear the sadness in his voice and Caro knew that he missed her too. Yes, physically her mum was still there, but the truth was that the woman she'd been was long gone.

'Anyway, so I've just ordered another drink – that's two gin and tonics in the same day. I haven't done that since university. I may keel over and wake up tomorrow morning in a gutter.'

Todd laughed. 'About time. I'm sick of that only being my party trick.'

'You're right. Somewhere there's a gutter with my name on it. Anyway, I'll be home later tonight. I'll...'

Her eyes drifted to the notification on the iPad in front of her.

Lila Anderson has updated her status.

'Hang on...'

'Yep, your colleague at Stalkers Anonymous has just had a notification too,' Todd replied. 'God, I hate being a weirdo.'

A photo – Lila with her boyfriend, taken on a beach somewhere. He was, as always, topless, and she was in a bikini that looked like three pom poms tied together.

Can't wait for dinner tonight at Grilled with this gorgeous man! #spoiled #luckyme.

'Urgh, is it wrong that I'm really jealous of your might-be-half-sister? I mean, seriously, there should be a law against being that happy.'

Caro was too busy thinking the development through in her mind. So she knew exactly where Lila would be. No question. She could go to the restaurant and speak to her and clear this up once and for all. Not that there was anything sensible about striding over to a stranger who was enjoying a romantic date with her boyfriend and announcing that they may share a dad. With a bit of luck she could do it subtly, in such a way that didn't cause too much drama. Unless, of course, Lila was actually her half-sister, in which case the drama would be unavoidable. But at least she'd know. No more wondering.

'Okay, change of plan. I'm just going to check into this hotel tonight – I don't even care if it costs a fortune. And I'll go to the restaurant and see what happens.'

'Are you sure?'

'No,' Caro said, with a wry chuckle.

'I know I keep saying this, but you don't have to do it, especially if you don't feel ready.'

'I don't think I'll ever be ready. But what's the point of coming home with nothing?'

'I get that. Ok, well, if you're doing it, you might need to take a couple more of those gin and tonics for bravery purposes,' Todd suggested. 'And call me back the minute you get to the restaurant. I wish I was there with you.'

'Me too. But I'd rather you were there so you're close in case Mum needs you.'

'Don't worry about it, Caro – I've got this. And so do you. You'll go there, you'll meet her, you'll sort this out. You can do it. You can. You're the strongest person I know. But just, promise me one thing…'

'What?'

'That you won't get so pissed you lose my Calvins.'

'I promise I'll bring them home to you,' she vowed. 'But right now I'm going to go. Will buzz you later. Let me know how Mum is, will you? And Todd… thank you.'

'You're welcome. You can repay me in designer boxers.'

It was impossible not to smile as she hung up. She might just go in and buy another set in the morning as an extra gift. Services rendered for moral support.

Another sip of gin and tonic, then she went on to the website for the restaurant that Lila mentioned. Wow. The images on the home page showed a decidedly upmarket venue, with deep-stuffed, crushed velvet booths, exquisitely set tables, and a huge, dramatic chandelier dropping in a myriad of glass beads from the high ceiling to the centre of the room. It was breathtaking. She deliberately avoided looking at the menu prices. Instead, she cast a glance over her jeans and

Converse. Not exactly the outfit of choice for this kind of place.

It would be crazy to go there. Mad. Why would she put herself through that?

But… maybe, if she timed it right, she could go speak to Lila in the toilets, casually, and somehow engage her in a conversation that would absolutely prove that wasn't her dad in the pic. Maybe that guy was English. Or French. Maybe he had lived with her and her mum every day of their lives. Maybe he was a distant cousin who just happened to look like her dad. Maybe it was her dad's twin, separated at birth and kept secret all this time. Maybe she'd had way too much gin.

Picking up her phone again, she dialled the number at the top of the screen.

There was only one way to get answers to her questions.

'Hi, can I make a reservation for tonight please?'

18

Cammy

The ping of the doorbell at CAMDEN set off yet another twang of nostalgia. It was the same bell that had been there when the shop was La Femme, L'Homme and he, Josie and Mel had worked there. Every morning, it would start his day, and every evening, it would mark the end of another shift in the company of the woman he'd loved... and lost.

He shook the thought off. What the hell was going on today? He'd realised long ago that he couldn't change what happened with Mel, couldn't do anything about the fact she didn't love him, couldn't alter the reality that she was now happily married to someone else, so he'd put her out of his mind. Closed chapter. Done deal. Yet today she was round every corner and in the ping of every bloody door. Enough.

'Hey man, how's it going?' Digby's laid-back drawl greeted him.

'So the place didn't collapse without me then?' Cammy asked, feigning disbelief.

Digby did a theatrical scan of the room. 'Nope, still standing. Guess you're dispensable after all.'

Cammy laughed. 'I never doubted it for a moment.'

Digby nodded to Josie and Val as they spoke. 'Have these two beat your romantic intentions out of you yet?'

'Nope, but I'm a shell of the man that I was when I woke up this morning.' It was meant to be a joke but there was definitely an element of truth in there.

Digby nodded conspiratorially to the two women. 'Disappointed in you two. Thought for sure you'd have persuaded him against all that oppressive marriage stuff. You've let me down.'

'Day isn't over yet, son,' Josie said, defiantly. 'I've still to deploy firm persuasion, and if that fails I'm just going to take him hostage and keep him in my hut.'

Cammy had stopped listening. While Josie and Val parked themselves on the two leather chairs outside the changing rooms, he headed into the back office, reappearing a few moments later. 'Digby, did my suit arrive from the tailor?'

Digby stopped polishing the counter top and thought for a moment. 'It did not. He called. Said there had been some issue and it wouldn't be back until Monday.'

He started polishing again, then froze, as he realised that three astonished faces were looking back at him.

'What? What did I say?'

Josie and Val now swivelled their heads, in perfect synchronisation, to face Cammy, their expressions incredulous.

Josie was the first to speak. 'Val, did you or did you not say this morning, and again this afternoon, that you could feel it in your water that everything was going to come good today?'

'I did,' she admitted solemnly. 'But I was lying through my teeth to make Romeo feel better.' Josie switched her gaze to Cammy. 'Starting to feel like someone's trying to tell you something yet?'

Cammy began to resist the notion, then just slumped against the door frame.

'What's up?' Digby asked. 'It's only a suit. And I hate to point out the obvious,' he said, his hand sweeping the room, 'but you own a clothes store. You have options.'

Cammy knew he was right but still… He'd picked that suit especially, had it tailored, and yes, he could wear something else but that wasn't the point. He wanted everything about the night to be special. And – for fuck's sake – so far he had a substitute ring, an audience of French football players, nothing lined up to wear and Josie and Val were looking more self-righteous by the minute.

Nothing was going right.

The door dinged again and Lila walked in. What the hell…?

Actually, maybe something was going right after all. He had no idea why she was here, but whatever it was, it was lucky timing. He'd told her he'd be at the shop all day, so if he hadn't popped in to pick up the invisible suit, he'd have been rumbled.

He did his best to act natural. Nothing to see here. Just an ordinary day. Nothing special at all.

'Why are you wearing a jacket? Are you going out?' she asked.

Bollocks.

'No, I er, just popped out for… milk. Yeah, we were running low. Because, you know, er, Josie and Val came in for a coffee.'

'We did,' Val told him with a wink. 'Only, I don't know what happened to the coffee, because my hands are still empty. How are yours, Josie?'

Josie looked at her lap. 'It would seem that mine are empty too, since you ask.'

Digby chuckled and took pity on Cammy. 'Two coffees coming up,' he said, finishing off whatever he was doing at the till.

Lila, meanwhile, gave Cammy a kiss and then pretended to be pleased to see Josie and Val, who were watching his panic with barely disguised amusement. Life would be so much easier if Lila's relationship with everyone else was a bit more amenable. Cammy knew they'd grow on her eventually, and vice versa. No other choice. He was marrying Lila and that was it.

Cammy cleared his throat, desperate to act nonchalant. 'Didn't realise you were coming in,' he told her, thinking how gorgeous she looked. Her hair was messier than usual, almost the way it was when she woke in the morning and she was, in his opinion, at her most beautiful.

She didn't need the make-up and all the other stuff – she was beautiful just the way she was.

Lila sighed and pulled herself up to sit on the mahogany counter. 'I wasn't but I just went in next door and Suze told me someone had been in there to see me and she'd sent them in here. A woman.'

'Oh, it er… must have been when I was out for the milk.'

'You know you have staff to do that, don't you?' Lila remarked.

Over in the chairs, Josie had a coughing fit.

Cammy knew exactly what she was doing. 'Slap her back, Val. If she chokes in here, the crime scene team will be here for a week and we'll lose a fortune,' he said dryly.

Josie made an instant recovery, just as Digby reappeared clutching two mugs of milky white coffee from the instant machine in the staffroom.

'Mate, was someone in here looking for Lila?'

Digby nodded. 'Yeah, forgot to say. Just before you got here...' He froze... 'Eh, *got back* with the milk.'

Cammy sagged with relief that he hadn't blown the story.

'Blonde. Pretty. Said she was a friend and asked for you,' Digby told Lila, as he handed over the hot drinks to the spectators in the comfy seats. 'She'll be on the CCTV if you want to have a look?'

'Yeah, sure,' Lila said, then added to Cammy, 'Baby, will you show me?'

'Right this way,' Cammy answered, heading back into the office.

Lila followed him in and waited as he rewound the CCTV footage back to just before he arrived. If she wondered why he came in at the same time as Val and Josie, she didn't ask.

'You okay?' he said, pausing the footage and reaching over to hug her. She returned the gesture, but he could sense something was off. She'd usually have her arms around him by now, be kissing him, and... okay, so yes, they'd had a couple of quickies in the staffroom over the months. There was a lock on the door and they kept the noise down. It was allowed, wasn't it? He loved that about her – that free, sexy, adventurous side. But today and, actually, over the last few weeks, she'd just seemed a bit... flat.

A thought. Did she know? Had she guessed? That was it. Bugger, he must have left some clue to what was going on and she'd sussed it. Although, if that was the case it was a definite worry that she didn't sound too excited about it. No. She was probably just tired. Yeah, that must be it. She'd been working way too hard lately and she was just knackered and a bit burnt out. Hopefully, she'd feel a whole lot better after tonight.

After a few seconds wrapped in his arms, she pulled back. 'I'm fine,' she assured him. 'Just tired.'

Okay, so he'd got that right. He kissed the top of her head. 'Then how about I take this weekend off, and we just chill out and spend two whole days in bed, just me and you?'

Was it his imagination, or did she just flinch when he said that? Imagination. Must be. Jesus, all this engagement subterfuge was making him paranoid and oversensitive.

'Yeah, babe, maybe. Got a few things I need to do though, so we'll see.'

Like stay in bed, looking at your engagement ring. Or going out to pick a new one. Or making plans and talking about just how happy they were going to be. A bubble of excitement caught him off guard and he cleared his throat. Enough of the doubt. She was going to be thrilled that they were engaged and they were going to live happily ever after. The end.

He pushed a stray lock of her hair off her face and kissed her, then turned back to the screen, before opening the door a few inches and popping his head out.

'Digby, was she wearing jeans and Converse?'

'She was indeed.'

Cammy refocussed on the screen. There she was. Blonde. Jeans. White Converse.

Looking at the clock at the top of the screen, he could see she'd been here just a few moments before he'd waltzed in with Val and Josie.

'That's her there,' he told Lila. He played, rewound, played, rewound. The CCTV covered the till area, although it also caught the rest of the room, but the black and white image was a little grainy. It was the same system that Mel had fitted when she opened La Femme, L'Homme over ten years ago. If nothing else, this was a reminder that he should probably update it.

He paused on the best image, and both he and Lila strained forward to see it closer up.

'Do you know her?' Cammy asked, studying the image.

Lila shook her head. 'Don't recognise her at all. I thought maybe it was someone I'd met through work, but... no, never seen her before,' she declared, her tone unquestioning. 'What about you?'

Cammy was still staring at it. 'I don't know. There's something... familiar about her.' He was flicking back through scenes in his mind. Was she someone from the glory days when he was out in Glasgow clubs every night of the week? Or someone that used to come into the shop? He had such a feeling it was more recent. 'Could it be someone you're friends with on Facebook?'

Lila shrugged. 'Don't think so, but I've got over two thousand friends and I've never met most of them, so it's possible.'

That whole concept never failed to bemuse Cammy. Over two thousand friends online, and she couldn't pick most of them out in a line-up.

'It could be one of the nurses or doctors from hospitals I've dealt with. I've told loads of people this is your shop...'

'Thanks for the plug,' Cammy interjected.

'You're welcome. Anyway, people always look different out of uniform so that could be it.'

Cammy stared at the screen again. There was definitely something about the woman that struck a chord. 'I'm sure it'll be something like that. But look, just keep an eye out. There are all sorts of weirdos around these days. Crazy stalkers on every corner,' he said flippantly, then realised that Lila wasn't in on the joke. 'Hey, I was only kidding.' He pulled her towards him, kissed her, long and slow, his hands gently tracing a line down the side of her face. 'It'll be fine. There will be a perfectly innocent explanation. In the meantime, why don't I get Digby to lock up and we can go home, and I'll pour you a drink, and do filthy things to you to take your mind off all this.'

Usually her shoulders would relax, her breath would deepen and her hands would start to wander at that very suggestion, but not today.

'I'd love to, baby,' she said, and she looked so sexy that, for a moment, he was sure she was going to agree, 'but I'm not finished work yet. I've got one more appointment.'

His arms still around her, Cammy's face was one big question mark. For fuck's sake, this was all he needed. Hadn't enough things gone wrong today? And now she had to work late.

'At this time on a Friday?'

His irritation dissolved when he saw how mournful Lila was.

'Sorry, babe, but it's a meeting that got postponed from earlier. A cardiac surgeon. He got called into theatre. I'm just going to pop into Pluckers for a quick something, then go back to see him.'

'Can't it wait until after Christmas?'

She was already disentangling herself from his arms. 'It can't. I just need to get an order from him and if I don't get it today I'll miss my target. You know how it is – these guys work all kinds of hours and sometimes I just need to be flexible and fit around their schedules. It'll be worth it.'

Cammy didn't have much of a clue how her

commission structure worked, but it had to be a big deal or there was no way she'd be going there instead of knocking off early.

She stretched up on to her tiptoes and kissed him on the cheek – the cheek.

'I'll be back in time for dinner though. What time are we going?'

'We're meeting your mum and dad there at eight o'clock.'

'Okay, well I'll try to make it home for sixish. That'll give me time to beautify myself even more,' she added with a giggle.

Leaning down, he kissed her again. 'I love you, Lila Anderson. Don't be late,' he said softly, wondering if she could tell his heart was banging at the prospect of the unlimited list of things that could still go wrong – attempting to propose to a girlfriend who was working late and couldn't make it being top of that list.

'I won't,' she promised. 'Love ya.'

And then she was gone, her heels clicking all the way through the shop, only stopping when the ping of the front door told him she'd exited the building.

He wandered out of the staffroom after her, trying not to pay any attention to Josie and Val's beady, inquisitive stares. He cracked in seconds.

'Oh for Christ's sake,' he said, laughing. 'I'm no match for you two. Okay, so she has to go back to work and it's no biggie – she'll definitely be home in time to get ready for dinner. We're still on for tonight. All systems go. Houston, we do not have a problem.'

Their silence told him that neither of them were impressed by this news.

'So you have two choices,' he continued. 'Go spread your evil cynicism elsewhere… or stay here while I try on a few suits and help me choose one.'

They thought about it for a moment.

'Will there be partial nudity involved?' Josie asked suspiciously.

'Almost definitely,' Cammy answered.

Josie pondered that for a moment, then, 'I don't have anywhere to be, do you Val?'

Val shook her blonde bob. 'I don't, now that you mention it. Digby, son, I'll have another coffee, if you don't mind.'

Cammy shook his head, ruefully. 'You two are a complete nightmare, you know that don't you?'

'We do,' Val said solemnly. 'It's part of our winning charm.'

'Can we ban them from the premises?' Digby asked, joining in. He'd only known Val and Josie for a few months, but he could see why everyone loved them – they could dish out banter and take it back in equal measure.

Cammy sighed. 'They'll just keep coming back. We're better putting them to good use.' He rubbed his hands together. 'Right ladies, we're game on. I have about an hour to find the perfect outfit in which to ask the woman I love to marry me.'

'No problem, son,' Josie replied. 'Digby, have you got any straitjackets in stock? Size 42 long.'

19

Bernadette

Bernadette's pulse was racing as she opened the door, even though she knew he wouldn't be home yet. Marge had said seven o'clock, but experience told her that meant nothing. The simplest operation could take double the usual time if they hit complications, while the most complex of surgeries could go smoothly and finish in less time than estimated. Seven was a guideline, not a fact.

'So what's first?' Sarah asked. 'After switching on the kettle, making tea and finding some kind of high carbohydrate snack in your cupboards. I swear your life is making me gain ten pounds a week.'

'Nothing to do with the cake you were shovelling down your gob earlier then?' Bernadette asked.

'Nope, absolutely not,' Sarah said with an act of pure

innocence while she set about grabbing cups, teabags, getting the milk from the fridge.

Bernadette paused, slipping back into that sentimentality that kept creeping up on her today. 'You know, Sarah, I'm so grateful you're here. I'd be a blubbering mess if I was doing this on my own.'

Sarah stopped, sugar spoon in air. 'No you wouldn't, Bernie. You've lived with that man for thirty years. That takes balls of steel.'

'Or cowardice.'

'We both know it wasn't, and don't say that again,' Sarah chided. 'If I wasn't here you'd have got on with this, you'd have done it all yourself and you'd have walked out that door. This is your time now, Bernie. You know that.'

Bernadette sniffed. 'Don't make me cry. I don't think I'd be able to stop.'

Sarah could see how vulnerable she was, how close to melting, and deployed diversionary tactics. 'You know what has been clinically proven to help with that?' she asked.

'Prozac?' Bernadette joked.

'Nope, cake. Why do you think I've got an arse the size of a small island? When Drew left me I cried for a decade.'

Sarah's ex-husband, Drew, had just divorced his third wife, each one going down a decade in age. Consistency or middle-aged women obviously weren't his strong points.

'But you? You've got this, Bernie. And now you know the kids are fine, it'll give you the strength to stand up to him. Anyway, when you're standing in front of him, just lead with the fact that Stuart has quit medicine – nothing you say after that will register.' Laughing, Sarah put the cups down on the coasters on the table.

Bernadette lifted them one after the other, took the coaster from underneath and flicked them, frisbee-style, into the sink. 'I fucking hate coasters,' she said, swearing coming naturally to her for perhaps the first time in her life. She did. She fucking hated them. Almost as much as she fucking hated him. She could do this. She could.

But first, a check… She made a quick call to Marge. 'Hi Marge, twice in one day! I know – just like buses. I just wondered if you had an update on how the surgery is going and when Kenneth would be done? Right. Yes, of course. Okay thanks.'

Sarah waited expectantly.

'She doesn't have an update. As far as she's aware it's still due to finish around seven. She's just about to leave so I won't be able to ask her again, so we're going to have to get a move on.'

'What's first?' Sarah asked, pulling out the chair next to her at the kitchen table.

'Cash,' Bernadette explained, embarrassed. 'I know it shouldn't be about money, but he'll cancel all my access to our accounts the minute I tell him I'm leaving, and I didn't want to take any money out before now, just in case I changed my mind after speaking to the kids. We need to do it now, because he might walk through that door in half an hour. My clothes and stuff I can leave behind, but I need some of our savings to start again.'

The very thought made her heart beat even faster. At this rate she was going to be a patient on Kenneth's operating table by the end of the night.

She reached into the drawer underneath the table and pulled out her laptop. It was Stuart's old one, long replaced with the shiny new MacBook she'd bought him when he moved out. However, all she really needed it for was Internet and email, so it was perfectly adequate.

She switched it on and entered her password, realising that her hands were actually shaking. What if Kenneth was already out of theatre? What if he was online right now, on the banking website? He'd see the funds start to move and he'd be furious, getting angrier and angrier as he watched their money disappear.

She ordered herself to take a deep breath. He was still in surgery. It would be fine. She could do this. How many times had she told herself that today?

She signed in to the banking website, typing the username and password from memory. He thought she didn't know them. Had no idea that she'd watched him, time after time, over the years, and sussed out both. Username: Doctor Manson. Password: Violet1966. His mother's name and the year he was born. Didn't take a rocket scientist to work it out, but still he would have been astonished that she knew – and more so that she knew that it was the same password for two other accounts in their names. They'd originally opened one for each child when they were born, but they'd cleared them out and given the kids all the cash when they were twenty-one. He'd told her he'd closed them down, but she'd discovered that he'd been lying and regularly transferring money into them. Bernadette suspected either a tax dodge or some messed-up power game, but if she'd asked, she'd have had to confess that she'd accessed them. The pretence of ignorance had been the path of least resistance.

With shaking fingers, she keyed in the details and then waited until the account flashed up on the screen. The first time she'd seen it she'd been astonished how much was in it. Quite a pretty penny. Although the account was, in theory, a joint one, and both their salaries went into it, Kenneth had set up a standing order to another account that was in her name only and he transferred money into it for her every month. That was all she got. Her housekeeping account he told her, like they were some kind of fifties relics. She didn't care. It was in her name only and that was all that mattered.

With trembling fingers, she waited for the screen to fully download the details of the joint account that only Kenneth was supposed to have access to. Over sixty grand in savings in that account alone. As well as the accounts in the kid's names, he had more tucked away in other accounts, family ones that he already had when they met, but she wouldn't touch those. On screen, she could see the figures showing her salary going in every month, and then the paltry amount he transferred to her as an allowance. Rage bubbled. Anger with herself, not Ken. Why had she permitted this? The truth was that she had allowed him to set it up this way thirty years ago, and never cared enough, or had the bravery, to challenge it.

She did now.

She clicked 'transfer' then wrote £9999 in the box. Next 'recipient'. There her name was, ready to accept another measly cash payment for taking care of the house. This payment was going to be the biggest one yet. A quick call to the bank a couple of weeks ago had informed her that the maximum online transfer was £10000. With trembling figures, she re-entered the password, then pressed 'confirm'. Please work. Please work. Please…

'Payment completed.'

She said it out loud and Sarah punched the air. 'Yes!'

She repeated it twice more. The same amount out of the old kids' accounts he'd told her he'd closed, putting all the cash into the account that was in her name only. He'd controlled almost every pound she'd ever spent – now, he couldn't control what he didn't know about. Three pounds short of thirty grand in total. It was far less than half their assets, but it was all she needed. He could have the house, the stocks, the shares, the rest of the cash. Thirty grand would get her set up in a rented house, until she found somewhere to buy, and then it would be a deposit on her own home. She had her nursing salary to live off. She'd never be wealthy, but if it was a choice between being comfortable and waking up next to him every morning, or being alone, skint and free, she'd chose the latter.

'Done?' Sarah asked.

Bernadette nodded. 'Done.'

Sarah came round to her chair and wrapped her in a hug. 'You're doing the right thing and it's going to be great. Keep telling yourself that. Just keep reminding yourself.'

'I'm fine, Sarah, honestly. It's just all a bit... terrifying, if I'm honest.'

'But you did it,' Sarah reassured her, then drained the last of her tea. 'Okay, what now?'

Bernadette gestured upwards. 'Clothes, jewellery, some things that have sentimental value. There's still some more stuff in the garage, but I couldn't pack too much in case he realised anything was out of place.'

Sarah followed her diligently, a large roll of black plastic bags in hand. They could use a couple of the suitcases that were in the loft, but after that they were out of carriage options, so black plastic sacks it would have to be. All her worldly goods in bin bags – and she didn't care.

In her bedroom, she opened one of the sets of double doors, then gave a bag to Sarah. 'Okay, so let's start here,' she said, pointing to the clothes inside.

They spent the next hour filling them, then dragged everything downstairs, piling it up in the hallway. Nerves and adrenaline compelled her to pick up the pace because if he came home now they were stuffed.

'I'll take these downstairs,' Sarah announced, passing her with an armful of coats on hangers.

The wardrobe was bare now. The chest of drawers the same. Only one place still to empty and she'd been putting it off until last.

She sat at the beautiful walnut burr dressing table and opened the long drawer in the middle of it. As she did, she caught sight of herself in the mirror. When Kenneth's mother had given them this dressing table as a wedding present, she'd been a young woman. Hopeful. In love. Beyond happy. Thrilled that she'd found this incredible man. And she'd been – yes, with the passing of time she could admit it – beautiful. Not pageant queen stunning, but beautiful in that young, healthy way, before time and the ageing process takes hold.

What had happened to that woman? Why had she locked herself away, not physically, but emotionally? When had she decided that her needs didn't matter, that she had to accept the hand that she'd been dealt? And why hadn't she fought harder against it?

It didn't matter. All that was important now was that she was going, and that she could spend the next few decades of her life making up for the unhappiness she'd lived with since the day she'd made her bed and lay in it.

She looked in the drawer and saw the blue velvet box sitting in the same place it had been since her mum handed it to her on the night she passed away.

How shocking was it that she was a nurse, yet she hadn't seen the end coming? Her mum had been ill for so long, lung cancer, bed-bound for the last few months, but she'd insisted on staying in her own home. Often she could barely speak, her words lost in the black swamp of her contaminated lungs. But not that night. Bernadette had been sitting on the edge of the bed, wittering away, telling her stories about the cases that had come through the doors of A & E that day, sharing the staffroom gossip, the latest news about Nina and the kids, about Stuart's flat and how happy he was at University, when her mum had suddenly taken her hand.

'Bernadette, you don't need to stay,' she'd said, her voice coming in raspy gasps that chipped Bernadette's heart with every strangled sound.

'Mum, of course I'm staying. I'm not leaving you, don't you worry about that. I'll always be here.' It wasn't a hardship. In fact, the few weeks that she'd spent in her old bedroom, using the very real excuse that she had to be there to look after her mum, had been both the most heart-breaking and at the same time most relieved she'd felt in years. She didn't have to see him every day, to look at him, to breathe the same air.

'No,' her mum had said, before a racking cough had sent her body into spasms. 'You don't have to stay with him. Leave him, Bernadette. Be happy.'

The words shocked her. Her mum and dad had been married for over fifty years, and they were old-school. Staunch Catholics, they disapproved of divorce. Just get on with it. Make it work. Everyone had their ups and downs. It helped that there was rarely a cross word between them and they'd co-existed in mutual contentment for their entire lives. When Dad had died a few months before, Mum had been crushed. Ever since, she'd refused to take off the gold locket she wore around her neck, the one with old, black and white, faded photos, one of her mum, Cathy, one of her dad, Arthur, taken on their wedding day.

'Mum, I...'

'Ssssh,' her mum had said, her frail hand pointing upwards. 'I don't want your dad to hear. He wouldn't approve.'

Bernadette could see how much effort it took her mum to smile and she leant down, kissed her forehead. 'Thank you Mum,' she whispered.

Cathy had passed away that night, off to meet up with Arthur again.

It was a few weeks later, after the funeral, after the house had been cleared out and handed back to the council, that Bernadette finally got time to think about her mum's words.

Leave him, Bernadette. Be happy.

Bernadette opened the navy blue box, took out the locket and fastened it around her neck.

I'm doing it mum. Just help me get there.

'Are you okay?' Sarah asked, making her jump. She hadn't heard her coming back upstairs.

'I'm fine,' Bernadette replied. 'Let's just get the rest of this stuff and get out of here before he comes back.'

20

Lila

It was getting harder and harder to act normal in front of Cammy. And why should she? Yes, she'd figured that it made life a bit more enjoyable to keep him around until she could be with Ken, but perhaps it just wasn't worth it. She no longer wanted to be held by him, didn't want to kiss him, and definitely didn't want to have sex with him, when every part of her just cried out to be with Ken.

The pretence with Cammy in the shop had firmed her resolve that she had to bring things to a head today. Right now. The sooner the better.

And if this was going to be one of the most important nights – cancel that, *the* most important night of her life, then she wanted to look her best.

Detouring slightly from her original plan, she crossed

the road and popped into the dry-cleaners she used to launder all her clothes. Lila didn't do washing. She didn't do ironing. Cammy had been surprised at first, but he soon adopted her ways, and while he washed his gym clothes and casual stuff at home, he'd got into the habit of dropping all their stuff off here a couple of times a week, and then bringing it all back a few days later, freshly laundered.

The woman behind the counter – Lila could never remember her name – looked up and smiled. 'Hi there,' she said, with familiarity, but not friendly enough to use her name. Just as well. Overfamiliarity really got on her nerves. 'Can I help you?'

'Yes, my boyfriend dropped off some items a couple of days ago and I want to pick one of them up. A Cavalli dress. Pink.' It was small and it was strappy, and in this weather there was every possibility that she'd lose body parts to frostbite, but she didn't care.

'I'll need the ticket.'

Lila sighed, glad she'd remembered to pick it up off the hall table, but come on, how many pink Cavalli dresses was this place actually going to have?

She tried to stop the irritation pursing her lips. No point in getting wrinkles round the mouth just because some shop assistant was on a power trip. She rummaged through her bag, found the little pink ticket and grudgingly handed it over.

While she was waiting, she pulled her phone out of

her bag and called Ken's house. No answer. Where the bloody hell was the wife? Shouldn't she be there?

Lila waited until she'd listened to his voice on the answering machine before she hung up. God, she loved him. Even hearing him on a machine turned her on.

The assistant returned with the dress, and Lila paid and left, walking back across the road on her tiptoes so that the spike of her heels didn't get stuck in the cracks on the tarmac.

She hung the dress up on the hook above the back window of the car, then took a quick snap of it. *#tonightsoutfit #beautiful #designer #lilalovescavalli.* Post. Immediately the pings started and the number of likes increased by the nanosecond. People loved to see what she was wearing. The designers should really give her stuff for free.

She headed back into the salon, where Suze sat, like a stunning, slightly scary sentry at the door.

'Ah, you've returned. Did you track down your friend?' Suze asked.

Lila shrugged. 'Nope, no idea who it was. We had a look at Cammy's CCTV, but I didn't recognise her. Probably just someone that follows my fashion and lifestyle advice on social media.'

Suze immediately looked down at something on the desk in front of her – almost as if she was covering up some snide reaction. Another one that was jealous of her, Lila decided. Small talk dispensed with, she cut straight to the point.

'Cammy and I are going out tonight,' she chirped, 'So I'd like something done with my hair and I'm way too tired to do my own make-up. Do you have anyone free?'

Suze checked the screen. 'Okay, so Rod can do a blow-dry or styling, but I've only got Kylie free on make-up.'

'The young girl who's still training?' Lila sneered, as if she was saying 'the young girl who has fleas, nits, and a suspected case of the plague?'

'That's the one,' Suze confirmed, with the widest fake smile. Lila could spot it a mile away. Took one fake bitch to know another. Suze was still talking. 'She's actually great. She did the girl who was in here asking for you and she looked beautiful when she left. Don't think I've seen a more stunning face today.'

Ouch, insult with a sting. Lila would have fired back with an equally subtle but venomous barb if she wasn't quite aware that she held the worse hand here. If she pissed Suze off, she could quite easily end up going to dinner with hair that looked like she'd been caught in a wind tunnel and disastrous make-up. Although, that might happen anyway if she was getting palmed off to a junior, but at least Rod knew what he was doing. She needed these appointments so it was time to suck it up and play nice.

'Wow, I wish I'd met her. Anyway, Rod and Kylie would be great thanks.'

There was a hesitation, as if Suze was deliberating whether or not to mess up her day, but she clearly decided to take the business. 'No problem.' She turned to the shop floor. 'Kylie, we have another victim for you. Rod, you're up too. Make this woman beautiful.'

Ouch, another sting. Make her beautiful? She was already fricking beautiful. This time Lila couldn't resist the urge to purse her lips. Don't bite back. Do not rise.

Rod, the punkish weirdo who was, despite his awful taste in style and fashion, a genius with hair, appeared at her side and ushered her to a free seat at the centre console. Kylie pulled a tray of cosmetics over.

'Okay, so what are we doing today, gorgeous?' That was more like it. A man that recognised something special when he saw it.

'I'm thinking maybe big waves, side parting, Cindy Crawford eighties look. Something breathtaking that will make me impossible to resist.'

Rod thought the second part of that request was a little joke. If only he knew.

'And your make-up?' Kylie asked.

Lila swallowed her hesitation over letting someone who had only ever washed her hair loose on her face. If it was that bad she could fix it herself in the car.

Lila thought about it. She would be wearing pink, so red, vampish drama would clash. 'Dark, smoky eyes, nude lip,' she answered. She'd worn that look at a convention last year and Ken had loved it. He'd had her naked before dessert. Said she reminded him of Kim Basinger. Whoever that was.

The two of them got to work, Rod parting her hair and wrapping it, section by section, in huge rollers. Kylie got her cleaning pads out and started removing the make-up that Lila had been touching up all day. Lila held up her phone and snapped a selfie, careful not to get Rod or Kylie in the frame. There was no way she was giving this place free publicity. *#glamsquad #rockingthe8osvibe.*

She scrolled back up to the last post – over two hundred 'likes' already, and tons of comments.

'Gorgeous!'

'Sexy'.

'You'll be stunning, babe!'

The last one from someone she didn't know at all. There was that overfamiliarity right there. That thought jolted her back to the stranger that was looking for her.

'Suze said someone was in here asking for me earlier. A blonde woman. Maybe similar age to me. A north of Scotland accent.'

'Caro!' Kylie blurted. 'Oh, she was lovely. Is she a friend?'

Rod's firm grip on a large roller he was currently inserting prevented her from shaking her head. 'No, I've no idea who she is. She went next door to Cammy's shop to ask for me there too. Did she mention me?'

Kylie threw a quizzical look at Rod. 'I don't think so, did she?'

'Nope, not that I heard,' he said, while holding several grips between his teeth.

'Did she say anything at all?' Lila asked. The truth was, she didn't much care, but she was mildly curious and it passed the time to chat to these two. It wasn't like she was doing anything else or had anyone else to speak to.

Kylie thought about it for a moment. 'She said she was a teacher. Down for the day from Aberdeen. Don't think she's been to Glasgow much before. Fairly sure when she left here she was going for a train home. She was really nice. Lovely, in fact. My favourite customer today.'

That made Lila bristle again. So this stranger was, so far, one of the most beautiful faces Suze had seen, and Kylie's favourite customer of the day. Lila hated her already.

Her phone rang, interrupting her irritation, and the office number flashed up once again on her screen. She flicked it to voicemail. Technically, it was after five p.m., so she wasn't strictly at work, but she still didn't want to speak to someone at head office with the rumble of hairdryers and the cackle of chat in the background. She'd phone them on the first day back after Christmas. Whatever it was could wait.

Kylie was focussing on her eyes now, so Lila closed her eyelids, enjoying the excuse to drift off. This would be her life soon. Staying beautiful for her man, just as her mum had done for her whole life. Her dad had taken it for granted, but she'd seen how much effort her mother went to every time he was coming home. And every time, he'd walk into the house, throw a passing smile at his daughter, and then kiss his wife like she was the only woman in the world. That's what Lila wanted – to feel like she was the only woman in the world. Cammy tried, but he didn't have the presence, the maturity, to make her feel that way. She wanted a man she could look up to, somebody who really was a man to respect and admire. Her dad had been a management consultant, someone important. Ken was a surgeon. Neither of them ran a shop selling the latest in gents' thongs. It was a different circle altogether and it was the one that she wanted to live in. The one she belonged in.

She kept her eyes closed, enjoying the solitude of her thoughts, when another realisation dawned. If all went to plan and she left Cammy for Ken, she'd no longer be welcome here. Unfortunate. Suze's underhand and barely concealed dislike aside, the staff were great and the thirty per cent discount didn't hurt. On the bright side though, she'd never have to see any of Cammy's other friends again. No Josie. No Val. No Jen from the shop along the road. No hipster Digby. She wouldn't miss anything about them at all, especially the look on Cammy's face when anyone mentioned the girl he used to work with. Mel. Lila didn't know much about her – wasn't interested – and Cammy didn't like to talk about her. All she knew was that they had a brief thing, it didn't work out, and Cammy went off to Los Angeles. Mel lived in Italy now, or maybe France. And she was married to... something clicked. 'Rod how long have you worked here?' she asked.

'About eight years.'

'Did you know Mel who owned the shop next door?'

'Of course. Yeah. She lives in Italy now. Got married to Josie's son. The guy who used to be a partner in this place.'

Ah, that was it. Things hadn't worked out with Cammy and Mel, and she'd married Josie's son. If that wasn't weird and incestuous, Lila didn't know what was. Besides, worse than that, in the only photo Lila had ever seen of the famous 'Mel' she looked completely... plain. Unremarkable. She didn't even have any make-up on. Honestly, some people should learn to make an effort. Anyway, soon she'd be able to put this whole crowd behind her and she'd never have to think about them again. She couldn't wait.

The noise and heat of the standing dryer that Rod had put over her head must have made her drift off, because the next thing she heard was Rod's voice saying, 'Okay, how does that look?'

Lila opened her eyes and immediately scrutinised the image looking back at her. The hair was huge and fabulous. A side parting instead of her usual middle one, then tumbles of gigantic waves falling down over her shoulders, but backcombed at the sides so that they swept out to emphasise her cheekbones.

Grudgingly, she had to admit that Kylie had done a good job on the make-up too. The eyes were a medley of blacks and greys, with just a hint of silver on the upper and lower lids to bring out the blue of her eyes. She'd applied false eyelashes that looked like mascara brushes, thick and sweeping upwards, making her eyes appear even bigger than they were. The cheeks were beautifully contoured and the lips were a pale shade of pink gloss, but subtly outlined into the perfect pout. Not bad. Not bad at all.

In fact, she was ravishing. Ken wouldn't be able to resist her. Absolutely not. And his wife would see that she couldn't compete the moment she set eyes on her. She checked her watch. Just after six p.m. She didn't need to be at the restaurant until eight – that's if she even went. It would depend on what happened in the next hour.

She'd warned Cammy she had one more appointment, but of course she hadn't told him the whole truth.

She wasn't going to a hospital for a meeting with a cardiac surgeon.

She was on her way to deliver some bad news to the wife of the love of her life.

6 p.m. – 8 p.m.

21

Caro

The hotel she'd had a gin and tonic in had no rooms available that night, so she'd hit a hotel bookings website looking for a reasonable deal. City centre. Within walking distance of here and the restaurant. What was it called again? Grilled. Yep, walking distance to there.

There were a few hotels nearby, most of them well out of her price range. Then she hesitated. Wait a minute, what exactly was her price range? She had money in the bank, and this was, undoubtedly, an exceptional event in her life. The problem was that she just didn't go in for lavish hotels and expensive nights out, designer clothes or celebrity hangouts. Maybe tonight should be an exception.

This was potentially a seminal day in her life. Besides that, she'd had four gin and tonics and her decision-making skills had gone to crap, so she was giving herself a pass on the sensible choices front.

Before she had the wherewithal to stop herself, she booked a night in the Hilton, twenty minutes walking distance from her current location, twelve minutes walking distance from the restaurant. And because it was a same-day booking, she actually got a rate that wasn't going to give her sleepless nights when this was over.

After she'd made the booking, she checked out Lila's recent posts. A pink dress, Roberto Cavalli, for dinner tonight. Bugger. Once again, she was reminded that jeans and Converse were hardly going to match up to the occasion and now it was – dammit, six o'clock. Why hadn't she done something about it two gin and tonics ago? She already knew the answer. Third drink. Fourth drink. The time had just got away from her and now the shops would be shut. Clearly she hadn't thought this plan through. She'd brought down a change of clothes in case events had compelled her to stay the night but they consisted of a different top and fresh underwear. Not exactly a sequined cocktail dress that would make her blend in in a trendy restaurant.

She went to the concierge in the hotel to beg for help.

'I need to buy something to wear for a dinner tonight, but I think I've left it too late. Is there anywhere still open?'

The concierge checked his watch. 'Ah, you're lucky. Buchanan Galleries closes at nine o'clock – late opening for Christmas. You're bound to get something there.'

One more drink and she might have pointed out that her mother was in hospital, her father was potentially leading a double life, her suspected half-sister appeared to be a spoiled princess, and she was here on her own – luck clearly wasn't on her side.

Instead, she thanked him, accepted his directions and left, walking at a speed that was unwise after the consumption of alcohol.

There were crowds of people walking in and out of the Galleries when she got there. The first shop she spotted when she entered was Next. That would do. Hardly Roberto Cavalli, but she was a few hours and several hundred pounds short when it came to matching up to that.

Caro barrelled into the women's department, and immediately spotted a dress on a mannequin: off the shoulder, calf-length, black and scattered with flowers. It would be totally out of place in her wardrobe. She didn't do off the shoulder. She didn't do flowers. She didn't do tight. But apparently, four gin and tonics did all three, so she tracked down the relevant rail, picked out a size fourteen, then headed off to the shoe department. Ten minutes later she was clutching a pair of sexy high-heeled black suede boots. Nope, she didn't do those either. Tonight, it would seem, she did. Her final purchase was spotted on the way to the till, a thick black velour cross between a shawl and a cardigan, perfect for wearing over the dress and warm enough that she wouldn't die of hypothermia.

As she handed over her credit card, she realised that she'd just bought a full outfit in less than fifteen minutes. A record, even for her. Feeling like she could relax a little, she decided to walk to the hotel she would be staying in. She made her way through the hordes of people on Buchanan Street, then turned off as directed by Google Maps on her phone, into St Vincent Street, and then walked right along to the end, until she could see the M8 flyover ahead of her. The hotel was on her left, a tall, striking, modern building made of glass and pale stone.

At reception, she checked in, handed over her credit card and was allocated a room on the executive floor. An upgrade. The first time in her life she'd ever been upgraded and she was on her own with no one to share it with. Even if Todd was here, she could have giggled with him over the price of the pecan nuts in the minibar, and gasp at the incredible view over the city.

Instead, she flopped back on the bed and placed the call he'd told her not to make.

'Hi, it's Caro Anderson here, I'm just calling to check in on my mum.'

'Hi Caro, Gillian said you'd call. She's left a note to

say there's no change. Your mum has had a comfortable day and I've just looked in on her now and she's absolutely fine.'

She wasn't. Nothing about her mum was fine.

'Okay, thanks. I'll be back tomorrow, but if you need me please call me. I'm actually down in Glasgow, but I'll have my phone on all night. Could you do me a favour please? Could you tell her I won't be in tonight? I know she can't understand, but just in case... I'd hate to think of her waiting for me.'

The voice on the other end of the phone oozed professional compassion. 'Of course I will. We'll see you tomorrow, Caro. You enjoy your night.'

Caro sighed as she hung up. The nurse clearly thought she was out on the town, not on some absolutely insane wild goose chase that had so far led to not much more than the kind of makeover normally seen on a TV show featuring Gok Wan.

Everything that had happened in the last twelve hours had made her think about her life though. She'd always played it so safe, so sensible. If today had taught her nothing else, it had brought home that there was a big world out there and perhaps she needed to experience a little more of it.

Perhaps.

Right now she'd settle for exploring the identity of the bloke in Lila's photos. She still wasn't convinced it was her dad. Yes, they looked alike. Yes, they had the same name, but a double life? Surely that kind of thing couldn't happen in her world?

There was no denying, though, that it would explain a lot.

Caro pushed herself up, made her way over to the tea tray and flicked the kettle on. She was so rock and roll she was giving up the option of a gin and tonic from the minibar to have a cup of tea and a ginger biscuit. Maybe she was too set in her ways to change after all.

Tea made, she lounged back on the bed. Seven o'clock. She'd decided to get there for seven forty-five, figuring that if Lila was still in the salon, she'd probably show up later than that, and she wanted to get there before them. She had another half an hour or so and she just wanted to close her eyes and think about what was ahead.

Her mind, however, was still stuck in the past, revisiting the weekend that had been a foreshadow of the clouds ahead, when her mum had forgotten her dad was coming home.

He'd greeted them in the same way he always did. A smile for her, then a long kiss for her mother. Some things never changed. Disney movies were full of dads who crouched down, arms wide when they came home from a trip or from work, and all his picture-perfect children ran towards him, gleefully screaming his name.

Their house definitely wasn't Disney.

Her father had never been cruel, or nasty, or dismissive, he'd just been... detached. Distant. Like he was going through the motions with her, but never really engaged. He had no idea what her favourite colour was, what subjects she excelled in at school, what things she liked to do in her spare time or who her friends were. When he was there, he was perfectly civil, nice even. Like a friendly uncle. But one that was perfectly happy to walk away without looking back every time he left. If it wasn't for Uncle Bob and Auntie Pearl, and their crazy, loving marriage, Caro would have thought her mum and dad's dynamic was just the way every family behaved.

That day was no different.

'Hey Dad, how's things?' she'd said, after her mum had bustled off into the kitchen to make him a coffee.

'Good. You?' he'd asked, picking up a newspaper, clearly not waiting with rapt anticipation for the answer. Caro didn't expect hugs and boundless enthusiasm, but still, there was no 'hey, I've really missed you. Come here and tell me what's happened to you in the month I've been away.' There was barely a passing glance.

'Look Dad, while Mum's not here, can I ask you – have you noticed anything... different about her?'

The narrowing of his eyes told her that he had. 'Why, what are you thinking?' He was giving nothing away.

Caro had paused, finding it hard to say the words, as if that would make her fears real. 'I think there's something wrong,' she'd said candidly. There. It was out. 'Sometimes it's like she's in a world of her own. She's forgetting things. Last week she went out and left food in the oven again. Another day, she took the car to the shops and forgot about it, so she got the bus home. I just think… I think we need to persuade her to get checked.'

He'd nodded. 'Okay, whatever you think.'

That was it. Whatever Caro thought. Not, 'let me take care of this'. Or 'don't you worry, it's all going to be fine.' Just 'whatever you think.'

Over the next few months, Caro had to do all the thinking. Dad went off again, and every time he came back, Mum was a little worse. It took countless appointments and tests before they eventually got the diagnosis. Early onset dementia.

So now they knew.

Over the next couple of years, Mum declined, receding more and more into her own world. Caro moved in, paid for a nurse to cover for her when she wasn't there. Dad would come back less and less until one day Mum had no idea who he was.

Then he packed his bags.

'But how can you leave her like this? She's your wife!'

'Caro, she has absolutely no idea who I am.'

'That doesn't matter! What happened to "sickness and health"?'

'Don't be like that.'

'Like what?' Caro had yelled. 'Like a decent person? Like a loving family member? What the fuck am I being like, Dad?'

He'd walked out. Conversation over.

He never came back again.

No word.

No communication.

The bastard.

It was the last time she spoke to him. The mobile phone number he'd had was long since disconnected. He was just gone. Vanished. Time passed and she'd come to terms with the fact that he'd erased them from his life… until the moment she'd seen Lila's Facebook post.

She absolutely didn't want it to be him because it would open a new chapter in a book she'd come to terms with finishing. A book in which the villain walked away with no punishment for his crimes. To be honest, she figured he'd probably taken early retirement and was living in Thailand or somewhere else that the sun was hot, the beer was cold and he could live like a king on his earnings.

Sometimes she wondered if she should be furious, raging at the injustice of it, and a little part of her felt that way, but the bigger part of her refused to give him the opportunity to pick at a scab. They didn't need him. He wasn't worth it. In truth she wasn't surprised. He wasn't the guy who'd choose the hard path, who'd opt to live with someone who couldn't take care of him, who had no idea who he was, of who he had been to her.

That's exactly what Caro had done ever since and it was tough. Really tough. Especially since the accident. Yep, as if the fucked up gods of shit luck hadn't given them enough to deal with, they'd heaped on more. A couple of months ago, while the carer who stayed with her overnight had been dozing, Mum had – for some unknown reason and for the first time ever – found the house key, unlocked the door, and wandered out of the house during the night, onto a main road. The lorry didn't even have a chance of seeing her. So now it really was over. No hope of coming back from it. The guilt that Caro felt about allowing that to happen sat like a lead weight in her gut. She'd thought she was doing the best she could for her, making sure a trained carer was with her. But no. It hadn't been enough. Since that night, her mum had been in hospital. She knew she would lose her soon. The accident had left her with irreparable damage and in a deep coma. The brain that was failing her had now shut down altogether, the body still alive but in a hospital bed, being tended by kind strangers, while Caro and Todd sat by her bedside for an hour or two or longer if the nurses – as they often did – turned a blind eye.

She was happy to do it, but it was a devastating vigil that shredded her heart when she thought of the woman her mum used to be. Sometimes – and she'd not shared this thought with anyone – sometimes, she wondered if it was a blessing that she was asleep, that Caro didn't have to worry about her getting lost, getting hurt, or feel her heart break when Mum got upset or frustrated or scared or confused. Right before the accident, the dementia had been so advanced that Caro had lived in a permanent state of fear. Now, she knew exactly where mum was. Right there. In bed. Where Caro could hold her hand, tell her she loved her and brush her hair until it shone, even though her mum never responded. It didn't matter. She told herself that Yvonne knew she was there.

The combination of the come down from the gin and the thoughts of the past were bringing on the kind of melancholy that Caro did everything to avoid. What was the point? There were no choices when it came to her mum, nothing she could do to make it better. All she could do was be there.

But her dad? She had a choice here. She could put on her new Next boots and walk away, or she could go face this situation, work out a way to speak to Lila, find out the truth and deal with it.

Stretching up on the bed, she shook off the tiredness that was seeping into her bones. She was doing this. No choice. Nothing to lose. It wasn't as if he was going to be there and there was a potential for a scene. Ugh, the very thought of that made her shiver. If she didn't get a chance to speak to Lila, if there was no way of finding out the truth, then she'd come back here, get a good night's sleep on this lovely bed, and go home in the morning. If she did speak to her, then at least she'd know and she could come up with a new plan.

A quick check in the bathroom mirror told her that the hair and make-up were still looking great. Determined not to spoil them, she ran a bath, carefully tucked her hair into a shower cap, then soaked for fifteen minutes, loving the feeling of the warm water on her skin. She should do more of this. Item number one on the agenda after she got home – spend more time relaxing. Stop fretting. Stop filling the day so she didn't have to think. Stop thinking too much when the incessant activity didn't work. Just chill. Relax.

Reluctantly, she climbed out, dried off, and brushed her teeth. She'd thrown a toilet bag into her handbag this morning as an afterthought, and now she was glad of it. Toothpaste, toothbrush, deodorant, hairspray.

Her new dress was hanging in the wardrobe and she pulled it out, slipped it on, thinking it would probably have been wise to have tried it before now. She needn't have worried. It fitted like a glove. The boots and the thick opaque tights she'd picked up at the till matched it perfectly, and by the time she draped the shawl over her shoulders she was starting to feel a bit better until… damn, no bag. All she had was a huge bag that wasn't exactly evening attire. Bollocks. Her gaze fell on her toilet bag. It was red satin, a gift from Todd, and as long as no one looked too closely, it could pass as a clutch. Probably.

After dumping out her toiletries, she threw in her phone, purse and room key. No room for anything else.

She checked herself in the mirror. Was this a 'Hello, I might be your sister' outfit? Or an 'Oh, so sorry, I mistook you for the daughter of someone I once knew' ensemble?

She was about to find out.

Down in reception, the doorman greeted her with a smile. 'I'm going to a restaurant called Grilled,' she said. 'Can you tell me which direction I should head in?'

He looked down at her feet. 'It's probably not wise to walk in those heels or in this weather, madam,' he replied, with the air of a man who knew such things…

'In that case, taxi for one please.'

The cab took over ten minutes, almost as long as it would take to walk, because they had to negotiate the Glasgow one-way streets. She didn't mind. This was agony enough, without adding sore feet and shivers to the mix.

When the taxi stopped outside it was five minutes to eight.

Turn around. Go back. Flee.

No, don't.

She paid and got out before she could change her mind. Behind the smoked glass, decorated with hundreds of fairy lights, she could see a packed restaurant and it struck her that Lila could be in there right now, looking out, absolutely unaware that her half-sister was about to enter her world. Or she could be gazing out at the completely crazy person who had put two and two together and given Lila four million reasons for a restraining order.

She pulled her phone out of her bag and dialled. He answered on the first ring. 'Todd, where are you when I need you?'

'Oh my God, what's happened? WHAT'S HAP-PENED?'

'Nothing. I'm just about to go into the restaurant and called you for a bit of moral support.'

His deflation was obvious. 'Oh, for God's sake, I'm near hysterical with suspense here.'

It wasn't moral support, but it did make her laugh.

'Just calm down there, dear,' she giggled.

Todd sighed. 'I can't stand being out of the loop. If you can, put me on FaceTime when you get in there and then I can at least see what's happening.'

'I think that may be frowned upon in an establishment like this.' She was fairly sure that would be the case. Now that she was here and could see the restaurant in all its glory, it was even more upmarket than she'd anticipated.

'I don't care,' he exclaimed. 'What are they going to do – ban you? You're never going to be back there. And we've already covered the fact that I have bail money ready.'

'Okay, I'm going to hang up now. I'll see what I can do. Might be worth keeping an eye on Lila's Facebook though – no doubt whatever happens will get reported on there.'

'I'm on it. And Caro…'

'Yep?'

'I'm proud of you.'

She hung up before he said anything that would ruin her mascara.

The door of the restaurant opened as she approached it, and she nodded a thank you to the doorman.

The first thing that hit her was the noise. The second thing was that there were an inordinate number of men two huge tables in the middle of the room.

'Can I help you?' a beautiful young woman behind a desk asked her.

'Yes, I have a reservation under the name Anderson.'

The maître d' checked her tablet, then smiled in acceptance. 'For one?'

'Yes.' Caro caught the moment of scrutiny and realised this was probably an odd scenario – a woman, on her own, in a posh restaurant, on a Friday night. 'Hopefully my husband is joining me later – his flight has been delayed,' she blurted.

'Ah, that's absolutely fine,' came the reply.

Where the hell had that come from? Her husband? A late flight?

She decided to cut herself a break. The lie was unnecessary, but it was a toss-up between that and raising suspicion that she was a secret shopper, an undercover cop or a restaurant reviewer. She'd much rather just be the sad case in the corner that had been stood up by her husband; that way, they'd probably give her a wide berth and leave her to mope.

'If you'd just like to follow me...'

Caro did as requested, walking past the gorgeous circular booths that sat along the window, around the two tables of guys who were... Was that French? Yes, definitely French. Must be some sort of convention attendees or tour party.

'French football team,' the maître d' whispered, using the menu to shield her face so they wouldn't hear her saying it.

Ah, football team. That made sense. They looked like athletes. Way too many of them were seriously handsome, and all of them were impeccably groomed, with sharp haircuts and stylish suits. Not that she was paying attention. She was too busy looking for Lila in case she'd missed her slipping in.

Just past the sporting contingent, there was another row of tables at the back of the room on a raised area, separated from the body of the restaurant by a beautiful wrought-iron and mahogany banister. Caro's table was in the corner and she realised there wasn't a more ideal spot from which to scope out the other diners. She took the seat that was against the wall, semi-protected from the gaze of the other customers by the deep padded, grey velvet wing of the upholstered chair-back. However, if she leaned forward a few inches, she could see the whole room. It was perfect. Her fake husband could have the nice seat opposite her if his plane landed on time.

'A drink while you look at the menu?' the maître d' asked.

'I'll have a still water please.'

The bath, tea and journey here had definitely sobered her up. Now she was going for a beverage option that was both frugal and not likely to get her so drunk she propositioned a French athlete. Win–win.

Okay, deep breath. She could do this. Nothing to lose. If it didn't feel right, she could just walk away.

After all, Lila had no idea who she was... and it wasn't like her dad was about to walk in the door. Was it?

22

Cammy

Digby turned the sign on the front door of the shop to 'CLOSED'. 'Are you sure you don't want me to stay and lock up?' he asked.

Cammy was lounging on one of the leather chairs outside the changing rooms, one leg over the studded arm, the suit he'd eventually chosen hanging on the wall behind him.

Josie and Val were on the other two armchairs, both of them with their shoes off and feet up on the coffee table in the centre of the seating area.

'No, you're fine, mate – I'll do it,' Cammy answered. 'But if you come in tomorrow morning and something seems off, check the store cupboard in case I'm in there, hands and feet bound with duct tape.'

Josie leaned over to Val. 'Scrap that one off the list, Val – we no longer have the element of surprise.'

'Bye, ladies,' Digby said, as he kissed them in turn on the cheek. 'I think you're on to a lost cause there.'

'There's still time. And hope. And drugs that Josie got off the Internet that could make him unconscious.'

Digby hesitated, not quite sure whether Val was kidding, before realising that would be too far even for them. Possibly.

As Digby headed off, Josie leaned down to the side of the chair and brought up her bottle of beer, courtesy of the minibar in Cammy's office. It had been there since the old days, one of the fixtures that had been left behind when Mel sold up and moved on.

'What a day,' Cammy said, wearily. 'I'm knackered.'

Val tutted. 'Och, for God's sake, a young man like you shouldn't be knackered. I swear, Josie, energy is wasted on the young.'

Josie nodded. 'Yep, energy and good sex. Wasted.'

Cammy's laugh coincided with trying to swallow a mouthful of beer, and the result was a coughing fit that sprayed Miller Lite over his 7 For All Mankind jeans. He made a mental note to drop them into the dry-cleaners across the road first thing Monday morning.

'Okay, so I'm good to go,' he reflected, leaving the half-full bottle on the counter. 'Ring, venue, suit. Thanks for keeping me company today. And Josie, I know you don't approve, but you came along anyway and I appreciate that.'

'We never do agree on anything,' she said, with a twenty-cigarette-a-day cackle. It was true. Their whole relationship was built on a solid foundation of love, affection, bickering and disagreement.

'Nope, we do not. It's why I love you.'

Val tipped up her beer and finished it off. 'Right then, my loves. I could sit here all night but my Don will send out a search party if I'm not back, clutching a chicken chow mein, in time for *Strictly*. It's the little things in life...' she said, grinning. 'Since Josie has led me astray with alcohol, we'll jump in a cab and Don will bring me back in for the car in the morning.'

Cammy reached over and took her hand. 'Tell Don I said hello and I'll give him a shout during the week for a pint.'

'Will do. Maybe make it the same evening as our book club. What night is it this week, Josie?'

'Thursday.'

'Okay, will do. What are you reading this week then?'

The two of them gave him the pursed lips of warning. He'd discovered months ago that 'book club' was their euphemism for a 'drink gin and gossip with pals' club. Josie and Val had been going for years and they'd never discussed a classic novel yet.

'You ready to go now too?' Josie asked him as she

wandered over and deposited her beer bottle in the bin.

'I'll be five minutes. Just want to sort out a tie and quickly cash up today's takings.'

Josie leaned down and gave him a hug, then a kiss on the cheek. 'You know we love you, don't you?' she said affectionately.

'I do,' he replied truthfully.

'Right, I said I wasn't going to go there...' Josie announced mournfully.

'Don't, Josie,' Val warned.

'It's for his own good,' came the retort.

'Jesus, we were almost out the door,' Val sighed.

Josie, however, was unconcerned about the protest. She turned to face Cammy. 'Cammy, you know that, as always, this comes from a place of love...'

'Oh God,' Cammy groaned, knowing this wasn't going anywhere good.

Josie carried on, undeterred. 'I promise I'll butt out of your life and get on board with this wedding. I'll even wear a hat the size of a manhole cover. I'll do a jig. And I'll tell Lila that she's the best thing that ever happened to you despite the fact that she's down there on the list below chickenpox and the boot in the bollocks you got that time at five-a-side footie...'

Cammy turned to Val. 'The biggest "but" in history is just around the corner, isn't it?'

Val nodded sadly. 'Coming right at you.'

Josie took a moment to prepare the rest of the declaration. 'BUT only if you can absolutely 100 per cent without a doubt tell me honestly that you feel the same way about Lila as you did about Mel.'

'I do,' Cammy blurted.

'Honestly?' Josie asked sceptically.

'Is that why you don't want me to get engaged? Because you don't think I love her enough?'

Josie looked sheepish. 'No. It's because she's shallow, stand-offish, she'll bleed you dry and she couldn't find a sense of humour if it was gift-wrapped in tissue paper and backlit with a strobe light. But apart from that, you're right. I think you've come home and you want to settle down, make a new life, banish old ghosts, and that's what she's done for you. I worry that it's the idea of her that you love more than the real thing. I don't see her make you laugh, I don't see that you're best friends like you and M…'

Cammy interrupted her before she could finish the sentence. He didn't need to hear it. 'She does, and we are. I want to marry her, Josie.'

'Then I'll get shopping for a manhole cover,' Josie replied, beat. She'd given it her best shot. There was no more to be done.

Val moved in to hug him. 'Good luck tonight. If you're happy that's all that matters.'

'Thanks Val.'

And then they were gone, leaving him sitting in an

empty shop with an expensive suit waiting to go on, and an engagement ring burning a hole in his pocket. And Josie's words replaying in his mind.

'Tell me honestly that you feel the same way about Lila as you did about Mel.'

Why? Why did he have to feel the same? Wasn't it perfectly okay to feel differently when there was a different woman involved? Surely a guy was allowed to find love more than once in his life, and it would be a unique kind of love, depending on the other person.

'Tell me honestly that you feel the same way about Lila as you did about Mel.'

Of course he wouldn't feel the same. Absolutely not.

Because, he knew he didn't.

Mel had... He swallowed back an obstruction that seemed to have formed in his throat. For ten years, Mel had been the first thing he'd thought of when he got up in the morning, yet he'd kissed her only once. In a nightclub. They'd gone there, Mel, Josie and Cammy, to cheer her up after her marriage fell apart. They'd ate too much, drank too much, and then somehow, inadvertently, gatecrashed an Elvis tribute night in one of the function suites. Josie had been swept off her pop socks by some bloke called Ernie, in blue suede shoes... Christ, even the thought of it made his sides hurt. It was the funniest thing he'd ever seen. Meanwhile, he'd been dancing with Mel, her wild mane of red hair all messed up and falling down over her shoulders, both of them far too drunk to care that four Elvises and a Priscilla were questioning their right to be there, when the music had switched from an up-tempo number to 'One Night With You'.

They were dancing, laughing, and then suddenly he was kissing her, slowly, tenderly caressing her lips. She reciprocated, her tongue running softly, teasingly across his.

Their hips seemed to press even more tightly together, their arms came up higher and hands found their way on to faces that they'd never touched in that way before.

Suddenly, as if Mel's brain caught up with what was happening, she broke it off, panicked, and then she was gone.

That had been it. Their moment. All those years of quietly loving her and that was all it ever came to. A few weeks later, Mel had discovered that he'd been having an affair with Suze, her very married sister-in-law, and any chance they'd ever had blew off in the wind. Gone. Dream over. He couldn't bear to see her disappointment in him every day, so he'd left, moved to LA – and the next thing he'd heard, Josie's son, Michael, had come home after spending years working in Italy, he'd married Mel and they'd gone off back to live in Milan. Or Venice. Or somewhere else fricking romantic that would be perfect for living a life of bliss with the woman he'd adored.

Did he feel the same way about Lila? No. Theirs was a different kind of love. A 'can't keep your hands off each other' kind of love. There was a connection, a meeting of two similar souls. He couldn't explain it. All he knew was that when he came home to Scotland and decided he wanted to be with someone, there she was. Beautiful. Positive. Upbeat. Loving life. With a vulnerable side that he just saw a tiny hint of every now and then.

By some miracle, she'd fallen in love with him too.

And no, Mel had never done that.

He'd only had a few sips of the beer, and most of that he'd sprayed over his jeans, but it was starting to make his guts ache. Or maybe it was the step into the past that was turning his stomach. Either way, he was beginning to feel decidedly nauseous.

He got up, went into the office, to where Digby had left the till tray with today's takings. He quickly cashed it up and stored it in the safe, then grabbed his suit and headed out, setting the alarm, before locking the door and pulling down the shutters. Just as the beeps of the alarm stopped, a taxi came down the street. First lucky thing that had happened to him all day. He flagged it down and gave the driver the address for home, then gave himself a pep talk the whole way there.

Her late appointment was bound to be done by now and she should be in when he got back so he had to act natural. Do not act weird. Do not seem suspicious. Be cool. She doesn't know. You can pull this off. Yes you can.

Outside the door to the flat, he paused, took a moment, steeled himself to be casual and nonchalant, then opened the door.

'Hey babe,' he shouted out, the same way he did every other night when he got home.

Nothing.

'Lila?'

Still nothing. Maybe she was in the shower. He checked the en suite. Nothing.

Every other room. More nothing.

She wasn't home. He checked his watch. Almost 7.30 p.m. Lila was a woman who took at least an hour to get ready to go out. When she'd left the shop she'd said that she had one more appointment, but she should definitely be back by now.

He pulled his phone out and called her, relief soaring when she answered.

'Babe, is everything okay?' he asked.

'Of course it is, darling.' She sounded fine. Normal. Maybe a bit tired.

'I thought you'd be back home to change before we go out to dinner. I just got here and there's no sign of you.'

'I'm sorry, honey, I just got held up with this meeting. Anyway, I picked up my pink dress from the dry-cleaners this afternoon – you know, the Cavalli one – and it's in the back of the car. I'll just change and meet you there.'

Pros and cons.

Cons first. He'd been hoping to start the night with a glass of champagne at home, just to have a moment together before they went to the restaurant. If she was going straight there she was bound to be a bit harassed.

Also, she would absolutely, definitely, positively be late. It was only his constant prompting that got them anywhere even remotely close to being on time. Her parents were exactly the same so it was obviously a family trait.

Pros. He wouldn't have to act natural or pretend that this was just another ordinary Friday night.

'Ok, babe, try to get there as soon as you can.'

'Will do.' She rung off a bit abruptly – but then, so would he if he was still at work at 7.30 p.m. on a Friday night. She really needed to take her foot off the gas a little with that job. She was working herself into the ground, doing all sorts of crazy hours and sacrificing her personal time for overnight stays at exhibitions and conferences. It wasn't fair on her. Although, he did find her dedication to her job and her work ethic pretty sexy. Mel had been the same.

Argh, fricking Mel again. This had to stop before it made him crazy.

He took a quick five-minute shower, shaved, then ran some styling wax through his hair, dressed in his sharp new suit, and was ready to go twenty minutes later.

He was almost at the door, when he realised he hadn't picked up the most important item of the night. He retrieved it from the jacket he'd had on earlier, opened the box and watched as the one tiny diamond inset in the band caught the light. It was simple. Elegant. Beautiful. Even if she wanted to go pick something much more blinged out, she could always keep this one too. She deserved it.

Outside, he decided to walk to the restaurant. It would clear his head and give him a chance to think through what he wanted to say.

Lila, you've made me the happiest guy... Nope, too corny.

Lila, from the first moment I saw you I knew... Nope, not strictly factual. The only thing he knew in that first moment he saw her was that he was deeply in lust.

Lila, I love you and I want to spend the rest of my life showing you just how much. Bland. Uninspired. Fuck it, he'd just have to wing it.

As soon as the restaurant came into view in the distance, he forced himself to think positively. It was all going to work out. He was going to propose. She was going to say yes. They would live happily ever after, while avoiding Josie at all social gatherings. It would be perfect.

Enough had gone wrong today. From here on in, it was all going to go exactly to plan. As Val would say, he could feel it in his water.

He'd barely finished the thought when a passing car veered right through a puddle and soaked him.

23

Bernadette

The ring of her phone made her jump out of her skin, and it took a few moments after she saw the name 'Nina' flash up for her to compose herself enough to answer.

'Hello, love, is everything okay?' she asked, hoping she didn't sound like the stressed out wreck that she was.

'Mum, I'm calling to ask you exactly the same thing. How is it going? Honestly, I'm on tenterhooks. Can I help you? Is Dad home yet? Do you want me to come over? Gerry is back from work and he can look after the boys and it's really no problem at all.'

That was Nina, Bernadette thought fondly – always one to pitch in, but prone to going a hundred miles an hour in a crisis.

'Oh, love, I really appreciate it, I do. But I don't want you involved and I think this is something I have to do myself.'

'That's what I told Stuart,' she admitted. 'He says you went to speak to him and he told you everything.'

'You knew?'

'Of course, I'm his sister!' Nina exclaimed.

And I'm his mother, Bernadette thought regretfully. I should have known. He should have felt it was easy to tell me. Once again she beat herself up about the fact that over the last couple of years she'd been so wrapped up in taking care of her parents and dealing with Ken, that she hadn't spent as much time with her children and grandchildren as she should have. It was the thing she was most looking forward to changing.

'I'm so sorry that he felt he couldn't tell us, Nina,' she confessed.

'Mum, it wasn't you. He wanted to tell you a long time ago, but he just didn't want to put you in a position where you were keeping something from Dad, and he wasn't ready to tell him. He had to make sure he was happy with his choices, both of them, before he announced them.'

Bernadette understood that. She really did. It was scary taking that step into the unknown.

'That makes me feel a bit better, love, thank you. And I appreciate you and Stuart wanting to come over, but I'd be so worried about you both that I'd crumble, so I really think I need to do this on my own. And besides, Auntie Sarah is with me.'

'Stuart says you two are considering hooking up now,' Nina said, laughing for the first time.

'If I was up for a same-sex affair, she'd be just my type,' Bernadette joked. 'But I'm off romantic relationships for life. It's just me and my family from now on. That's all I need.'

Nina must have heard the crack of her voice as she said that. 'Mum, we're both going to be by our phones all night and you know you just need to call and we'll be there to support you. I know what Dad can be like but he wouldn't dare speak out of turn if we were there. What time is he due home?'

'In an hour or so. But honestly, there's no need to come over. I promise I'll be fine. I'll call you later and let you know all is okay.'

'Okay Mum. I'll be thinking about you and if you change your mind, just call. Love you.'

'I love you too, pet.'

She'd no sooner hung up than the phone rang again.

'Connor and I want to come help you, Mum.'

'Son, I've just had your sister on the phone and she said the same thing.'

'I figured that. I was trying to get through and it just kept going to voicemail. Mum, let us come help. There must be something we can lift. Or move. We're really useful for that kind of stuff.'

It broke Bernadette's heart to hear him trying to lighten the mood. How had she managed to end up with these two incredible adults?

'Stuart, I appreciate it, I really do, but there's nothing left to lift or move. Your Auntie Sarah and I have sorted it all. We've just got one final drop-off to do and then I'm going to come back and wait for your dad and break the news to him. Then, we're going to agree to part like the mature adults that we are...' She didn't believe a word of this, but it somehow helped to paint a positive picture. 'And then I'll go back to Auntie Sarah's and this will all be over with. You need to stay out of it, Stuart. I'd hate your dad to think you were picking sides...'

'But I wouldn't be. I just want to be there to make sure you're both okay.'

'I know, Stuart, but it wouldn't work out that way. He'd say something, or I'd say something... Look, I'm not kidding myself that it's going to be easy. Your dad and I have been together for over thirty years and that's a long time to unravel. But we'll get there – and I'll do everything I can to make sure that it all stays as amicable as possible. It's going to be fine, it really is.'

She had a flashback to every time her children had ever hurt themselves, every broken bone, every aching stomach. *It's going to be fine, she'd promise them. It's going to be fine.* As she hung up with more assurances and a promise to call later, she knew she was kidding herself if she thought it was all going to be fine this time.

Year after year she'd thought about this day, hoped that it would come, and now it was here and she was as scared as she'd been when she'd first contemplated it.

She remembered it well. A medical conference. Not long after Stuart was born. Bernadette had been feeling tired, frumpy, frazzled after spending months alone with a young child and a new baby. Kenneth had spent the whole night chatting up the attractive doctor who was sitting on the other side of him during dinner. He was so practised, so smooth, that Bernadette realised he'd done this before, and probably many times since. Somewhere along the line, she'd stopped wondering if he was unfaithful and accepted that he probably was.

Back then, that night, she could see that the woman thought he was attractive, charming, a real prize. It wasn't until after dessert, that Bernadette bumped into her in the toilets.

'I'm Georgina Wilson, Head of Gynaecology at Inverclyde,' this gorgeous lady had said.

'Bernadette Manson,' Bernadette had said, expecting to be swiftly brushed off.

'Which hospital are you from?'

'Oh. I'm not. Well, I am – I'm a nurse at Glasgow Central.'

Bernadette registered the confusion. The attendees at this function were senior doctors and consultants.

'I'm actually here with my husband. Kenneth Manson.'

'But I've been chatting…' the other woman broke off, immediately getting an understanding of the situation. 'I'm so sorry,' she went on. 'I've been hogging your husband's company all night. I didn't realise…'

'No, no it's fine,' Bernadette said, trying to brush it off. She hated to cause a scene. Besides, humiliation was nothing out of the ordinary. She'd learned over the years that it came with the territory.

'Are you coming back through?' Georgina had asked.

Bernadette nodded. 'Yes. I actually just popped in here to phone my mum and check on the kids.'

'What age are they?'

'Our daughter is seven and our son is ten weeks.'

The pity on the other woman's face nearly broke Bernie and she felt a wave of tears sweep up to her eyes. She blinked them back, desperate to avoid making a fool of herself in front of this beautiful creature.

Too late.

Georgina fished a tissue out of her bag and handed it over.

'Hormones,' Bernadette murmured gratefully.

The two women went back to their seats arm in arm, and Kenneth's face was a picture as he watched them. When they sat down on either side of him, she saw Georgina lean in towards him but was the only one close enough to hear what she said.

'You've flirted with me all night and your wife was sitting on the other side of you the whole time. You really are a dick.' With that, she toppled a glass of red wine into his lap.

It was all Bernadette could do not to give her a standing ovation.

But oh, how she paid for that moment.

Kenneth was seething, absolutely raging. The worst ever. When they got home, he waited for her mother to leave in a taxi, then he ranted and raged, he called her every name under the sun and a few more. Even Stuart waking for a feed didn't stop the torrent of abuse. She was worthless. Pathetic. A piece of crap that only had a place in this world because of him. Rant after rant, he delivered one cruel, snide comment after another. That was a turning point. The end of them. That night, something inside her broke. Never again had anyone challenged his insidious ways. Until now.

That thought made her realise that she was wasting time here. Why was she still waiting around, picking up things that were easily replaceable, when she could just go, drop everything off and be done with dragging out this stress?

She had to come back and tell him, that went without saying. Sure, she could leave a note, or phone him, or send him a bloody email, but that would only be delaying the inevitable and she would live in a perpetual state of anxiety waiting for it to happen.

No, she was going to do this and she was going to do it right.

She was going to face him, to look him in the eye, and she was going to stand up to him.

It was the only way she'd be able to sleep at night.

'You still on the phone?' Sarah's voice behind her.

Bernadette turned around and shook her head. 'No, it was just the kids, checking in. Stuart is deeply disappointed that we're not having an illicit affair.'

'We can if you want…' Sarah joked. 'I mean, I've never tried it, but at my age I'll try anything. I ate quinoa last week.'

Bernadette hooted with laughter. 'I don't necessarily think you can compare the two. Okay, that's it. Let's just get this lot into the van. There's honestly nothing else I care about enough to warrant the heart attack I'm about to have at the thought of him walking in that door. I've got enough clothes to keep me going, I've got all the kids' photos, I've got the jewellery my mum left me – nothing else matters.'

Sarah nodded. 'You're right. Let's fill her up.'

Downstairs, Bernadette opened the door cagily, checked there was no sign of him. Nope, nothing. The wall clock in the hall said 7 p.m. If the surgery finished on time, he'd be back within the next twenty minutes or so. The anxiety came flooding back. Bravery had its limits and it would appear it was intermittent. A tightness pulled her chest muscles together and she had to steady herself with an internal dialogue. Come on. You've got this. Keep going. Just keep on moving.

'Coast clear,' she announced, heading out of the door with two huge black bags, Sarah right behind her. They opened the back doors of the van and deposited their loot, then shuttled back and forwards until the last bag was pushed into the packed space. It took all the weight of both of them to squeeze the doors shut, an exertion that had tears streaming down Bernadette's face – she wasn't sure if they were of happiness, sadness, stress or relief. Sarah spotted it and held out her hand. Bernadette took it gratefully.

'You've got this, lovely,' she said.

Bernadette nodded. 'I've been telling myself that all day.'

'So what next?'

'We take all this stuff to your house and unpack it.'

Bernadette locked up, and they both jumped into the van, indicating left as they came out of the driveway.

As they passed a Range Rover Evoque on the other side of the road, it was Sarah who noticed the blonde behind the wheel.

'Wow. There's something you don't often see in December.'

'What?'

'In that car. The Evoque thingy. There's a blonde woman in the driver's seat wearing huge sunglasses.

Think we should tell her there'll be no sun until next June?'

'Maybe she's some kind of private investigator on a stake out, Miss Marple,' Bernadette teased, glad of the momentary break from the nervous dread.

'If she's there when we get back, I'm going to investigate,' Sarah announced. 'Just in case she's staking out the joint for a burglary crew to come in and ransack the street.'

'Good idea. You'll get a special commendation from Neighbourhood Watch.'

As they waited at the traffic lights at the end of the street, Sarah exhaled.

'Okay, Bernie, here goes. Final stage in Operation Freedom.'

'I wish it was,' Bernadette sighed, that choking anxiety right back and shooting to unsurpassed levels. 'But I still have to come back and tell him.'

24

Lila

Lila had left Pluckers, jumped back in the car, and retraced her earlier journey, so that less than twenty minutes later she was sitting back outside Ken's house. The Fiat was still in the driveway, and there was a white van there now too with a huge cupcake on the side. Probably the wife's weekly delivery of stodge to keep her going while she was gorging herself in front of the TV. If someone else was there, the confrontation would have to wait. She wasn't going to go charging in to a situation that came with an audience. This was between her and Bernadette. That was it.

She pulled out her phone and snapped a quick pic, a smiling one this time as opposed to a pout, then uploaded it to her Instagram and Facebook with the hashtags *#Fridayfeeling #cantwaitfortheweekend #blessed*.

Although, right now, she didn't feel very bloody blessed at all. Rod and Kylie had excelled themselves, and for what? Was she in a bar drinking cocktails? Was Ken licking champagne bubbles from every crevice of her body? Oh, that very thought made her shudder. Was she somewhere fabulous that she could show off the results of the last hour?

Nope. She was sitting in the seat of a car, shades on so no passers-by would realise she was staring at her lover's house, hoping – for the love of God – that she could get on with speaking to his wife and revealing all.

Ken wanted this. She knew he did. He just didn't want to break the news to Bernadette, but once it was done he'd be so grateful. There was no way a man could make love to her the way he did today and not want that every day of his life.

She turned the temperature down on the dashboard to the point that it was almost uncomfortable, so that her perfect face wouldn't begin to shine, then she sat back and stared at the doorway. And stared. And stared. The ringing of her phone was almost a welcome distraction. The office again. Jeez, didn't they know it was a Friday and she was finished for the day? Sighing, she realised now was as good a time as any to answer. It wasn't like she was doing anything else.

'Lila Anderson,' she said haughtily.

'Lila, it's Fred Johnston.' Her boss. The director of sales. In some ways, he reminded her of Ken – strong, direct, a powerful alpha male who exuded the kind of presence that absolutely appealed to her. She'd flirted with him on every occasion, but, unfortunately, like Ken, he had a wife – in his case, the very efficient, decidedly frosty head of HR. Lila absolutely couldn't imagine the two of them having sex. She probably asked him to fill out a form, complete an inventory and sign a disclaimer before she took her knickers off. Why did these men always choose women who were no match for them? Anyway, she'd never acted on any attraction to Fred because he didn't quite come close to what she already had.

'Fred! So lovely to hear from you,' she purred. 'What can I do for you?'

He cleared his throat. 'Lila, I've been trying to get hold of you all day…'

Damn, so it had been Fred who'd been calling. If she'd known that she'd have answered first time.

'Sorry, Fred, it's been hectic today. So many meetings. I don't know how I managed to cram it all in but it's worth it when I smash those targets every month.' No harm in reminding him of that not so insignificant fact.

'Erm, yes. Well, the thing is, we'd like you to come down to head office on your first day back after the Christmas holidays.'

Her smile widened. A visit to head office could only mean one thing. Actually two. When they were firing someone, they always asked them to come down, so they could retrieve the company car, but that wouldn't be the case here. What she was excited about was the other reason a rep got called to the mothership. Promotion. She was finally getting the step up she'd been lobbying for. Area manager for Scotland, Ireland and the North of England. A twenty-five per cent increase in salary, loads of travel, and an even better company car. This was the closest she'd been to delight since Ken made her come at lunchtime.

'Of course!' she said, excitement bubbling. 'What time would you like to see me?'

She could go down the night before, stay the night in a spa hotel, get a few treatments and a good night's sleep so she looked her best. This was it for her. New job. New man. New life. After years of waiting, it was all about to happen.

'Eleven o'clock. You'll be meeting myself, the head of finance and there will be a representative from HR.'

Of course his wife, Lady Frosty Tits would be there – it would be in her remit to action the promotion. And the finance director would be there to talk about her pay rise.

'Great!'

He cleared his throat again. 'Actually, Lila, just so we're on the same page, I have to inform you that this is the opening meeting in what may be a disciplinary situation.'

Not so great. 'Sorry? I don't understand.' A disciplinary? For what? She was their best fucking seller, trouncing every other amateur out there. What could they possibly be disciplining her for?

'There are several issues that we wish to discuss.'

Lila felt her stomach begin to clench. Several? What the hell...?

'An allegation has been made that there may have been an inappropriate relationship with a client.' He let that hang there.

Lila wasn't one for swearing – so unladylike – but again, fuck.

Who would report her? 'From who?' Too late she realised her first reaction should have been to deny the allegation.

From his tone, she immediately realised that Fred had picked up on that too.

'I'm afraid it's confidential, but as you know, it's in your terms and conditions of employment that there can be no inappropriate relationships that could be a detriment to our business, or could lead to accusations of... let's just say, we like to know for sure that we get orders based on the quality of our products and services.'

Oh. For. Fuck's. Sake. Now, if she was reading between the lines correctly, he was implying that she swapped sex for orders. She pulled her shades off as her head fell forward on to the steering wheel and, for once, she didn't give a toss that she would have to reapply her foundation.

He couldn't do this. This was ridiculous. Besides, if anything she should get a bonus for the affair with Ken because it had brought the company extra bloody sales.

'We'd also like you to bring down a full copy of your schedule for the last three months, together with receipts for all purchases made using the company credit card.'

Her fury and disbelief were now, slowly but surely, being frozen out by a deep chill that was working its way up from her feet, consuming everything in its path. 'Why?'

'Again, we have reason to believe there may have been some impropriety in your use of the card.'

No, no, no. This wasn't how it worked. She smashed targets, the company left her to her own devices. That was the way it had always been. Sure, she knew about the rules, but over the years she'd taken a few chances and nothing had ever been questioned Yes, she'd probably got a bit cavalier, but she hadn't taken anything she didn't deserve.

'I can assure you my card has only been used for legitimate company expenses,' she replied, going on the offensive. No way was she taking this crap from him.

'Indeed. So we would very much like to understand the breakdown of the payment to the...' There was a rustling of papers. 'The Dorchester, two months ago.

And perhaps also the Glasgow River Hotel, today at lunchtime.'

Holy shit, how did they know about that already? They must have full visibility of every transaction. Her mind flew back through everything she'd used the card for in recent times. Flowers for Mum. The new suit she bought for the sales conference. That red dress for the evening reception. Every hotel bill. Why were they questioning it now? Why?

There were thousands of employees in the company so there was very little micro-management, especially when it came to reps who worked their own territory. As long as they were performing well, they didn't attract any negative attention. However, someone had made an official complaint against her, and that had been enough for the bean counters to probe deeper into her actions.

Who? Who the hell...? She racked her brain. There was no one. She'd always made a point of being sweet to everyone that mattered so that she'd get more business. Another thought. Ken's wife? Had she found out and reported her? No way. Ken would have known about that and stopped it.

Sweet to everyone that mattered. The phrase repeated in her mind. *Everyone that mattered*. Suddenly, another image, Madge's disapproving but smug face this morning when Lila had left Ken's office. Madge knew. Of course she did. She'd known right from the start, and there had never been a shred of love lost between the two women.

Had she been the one who'd reported her? How dare she? Rage was now heating up the chill factor. That fat, evil bitch. She was so jealous, she couldn't stand it. Had probably been in love with Ken all along and now she'd decided to interfere and try to destroy their relationship. Well, the cow wouldn't win. No way. She might cost her this job, but there was absolutely no chance that she would wreck Lila and Ken's future. That was theirs and it was going to happen. But in the meantime…

'I can assure you that I have a perfectly good reason and solid evidence to support every expenditure,' Lila declared forcefully. She didn't, but now wasn't the time to cave. Her mum's motto. Hair done, lipstick on, face the world. She already had the first two covered, thanks to Rod and Kylie, so now it was up to her. She would buy time to come up with something, and if she didn't, well it wouldn't matter. This was the weekend that she was going to make the breakthrough with Ken, so she could go down to head office and tell them that, as the future Mrs Lila Manson, wife of cardiac surgeon Dr Kenneth Manson, they could stuff their job.

'I do hope so, Lila. You've been one of our best performing account managers for many years. I really hope this can all be explained and we can go on to develop your career with the company. I look forward to hearing what you have to say.'

He rang off and Lila stared straight ahead, unable to move. By the very implication in his last words, if she couldn't explain everything, there wasn't going to be a future with the company for her. Argh! The truth was, she realised in hindsight, that she'd crossed a line that she wouldn't be able to justify. So her job was gone. She was about to be out of work. And while the prospect of that terrified her, it made one thing clearer than ever: the stakes had just got higher. There was now absolutely no room for hesitation with Ken, because she was not going to be the woman with no job, no husband, no chance of gainful employment, because she'd just been fired for misconduct. She could lose everything here. Everything.

She blinked back the tears, determined not to spoil her lashes. Don't cry. It's all going to be fine. This was a blip in the road, but she hadn't crashed and burned yet. Although, petrol bombing that old witch Madge now seemed like a perfectly reasonable proposition.

Across the street, she saw the front door opening. Yes! The cake delivery person must be leaving. This was going to be her chance. A woman stepped out of the doorway carrying bin bags. That was odd, but what did it matter as long as she was going to piss off and let Lila make her move.

Another woman appeared behind her, also carrying black plastic bags. She gasped as she realised it was Bernadette. Okay, still strange, but at least things were moving. Both women then went back inside, only to reappear carrying more bulging black sacks. What the hell was going on?

For fifteen minutes, they carried out bag after bag, then came clothes on hangers, all of it shoved into the back of the van. Lila had a moment of clarity – they were packing for a car boot sale. That was it. Bernadette absolutely struck her as the kind of woman who went to those things, flogging worn jackets and cheap tat ornaments for a few pounds to put petrol in that bloody Fiat. The woman had not an ounce of class.

Still, she waited. The two women were leaning on the side of the van now, deep in conversation and… Oh for God's sake, they were holding hands. Were they related? Or was this some kind of secret affair? Wouldn't that be ironic – if Ken and Lila had been meeting in secret for the last seven years, while Bernadette was also sneaking around with an illicit lover. They looked like they could be a couple. Both the same age. Both the same shape. Both in unappealing, decidedly unflattering outfits. Yep, they could easily be a couple. That would be brilliant – a free pass for Ken. Before she even thought through what she was doing, she lifted her phone and shot a couple of pics of the two women embracing. Got you.

Okay, now get in the van and leave, lady. Go on. Clear off.

Lila actually thought the subliminal commands were working when the visitor jumped in the driver's seat, but her hopes were dashed a few moments later when Bernadette locked the front door and climbed into the van too. Argh! Fuck, fuck, fuck! Where was she going? When would she be back? And why was she completely wrecking Lila's plans?

Slipping the shades back on, Lila watched, fuming, as they drove past her, the driver staring intently at her. They stopped at the traffic lights behind her, then turned the corner, taking away her opportunity for confrontation with them.

Damn it. What to do? She could wait here for them to come back, but who knew when that would be? She could wait for Ken to get home, but again, that could be any time. His surgery could run hours late.

As if answering her dilemma, the phone rang again. Cammy. Much as the last thing she wanted to do was answer it, she did it anyway.

'Babe, is everything okay?' he asked and she could hear the concern in his voice.

No, it's not. My boyfriend's wife is being a royal pain in the arse by refusing to allow me to destroy their marriage, he's not taking the initiative and doing it for me, and now there's a fairly good chance I'm about to get fired. No, everything is not bloody okay.

'Of course it is, darling,' she assured him. Hair done, lipstick on, face the world.

'I thought you'd be back home to change before we

go out to dinner. I just got here and there's no sign of you.'

She looked at the clock. Shit, it was after 7.30 p.m. Her first instinct was to just blow this whole thing off, but her parents would already be on the way. Nothing else for it. She'd have to go. She could eat, make some pretence about not feeling well, then come back here as soon as possible. No point in wasting a perfectly good restaurant booking. Besides, she was looking smoking hot, there was always some celebrity or another there, and the pics would go down a storm on her Instagram.

'I'm sorry, honey, I just got held up with this meeting. Anyway, I picked up my pink dress from the dry cleaners this afternoon – you know, the Cavalli one, and it's in the back of the car. I'll just change and meet you there.'

She would just pop into the Hilton to get ready. It was the perfect work to party hack for someone with her social life. It was also another company perk she'd lose. Free membership of the gym in the basement of the Hilton. It was so close to the city centre that it came in handy for a quick swim, or a spa treatment, or getting dressed for a night out in a hurry.

Now wasn't the time to dwell on that. It was all going to work out. No question. Lila Anderson didn't do failure and she certainly wasn't going to back down from getting what she wanted.

'Ok, babe, try to get there as soon as you can.'

What was wrong with him? She'd get there when she bloody well got there. He was becoming entirely too high-maintenance. Just as well it was about to end because he was starting to seriously get on her nerves.

'Will do,' she said, managing to keep her voice light. The last thing she needed was an argument with him right now as well. What was the point? One more dinner, then back here, force the issue with Ken, and then they could just be together and none of this other stuff – Cammy, her job, the wife – would even matter.

She was so busy running the internal dialogue, that as she pulled out, did a U-turn and headed back towards the city centre, she didn't notice Ken's car coming from the other direction and slipping into the driveway in front of his empty house.

8 p.m. – 10 p.m.

25

Caro

Lila wasn't here.

Caro's eyes swept the room on a thirty-second repeat cycle. Nope, still not there – but she was getting slightly lecherous looks from one of the guys at the footballers' tables.

The waitress came to take her order, and she decided that since she needed to stretch this out, she would go for starter, main course and then she could order a dessert later too if she needed to buy more time. She went for brioche, salmon steak, and a large still water on the side.

She was taking a sip when the door opened and Caro's diaphragm flipped as a man entered. She knew him. It was Lila's boyfriend, he of the defined abs and unlimited capacity for gift-giving.

She was fairly sure she lost the ability to breathe for several seconds as she waited to see if Lila was there with him, but he let the door bang behind him.

Bugger.

But she must be coming, otherwise why would he be here?

Okay, time to calm down and regroup. The boyfriend – from Lila's pictures she knew his name was Cammy – was shown to a table in the window, a semicircular booth with a crisp pink table cover and a huge goldfish bowl full of lilies in the centre. It was the only table that had that adornment, so he must have requested it. What kind of guy thought about stuff like that?

Caro knew it would be on Lila's Facebook page the minute she walked in here. *#cheesyboyfriend #luckycow #imrollingmyeyes #eurgh*.

Time passed achingly slowly. Lila still wasn't here and the boyfriend was now on his second drink and looking a little agitated, his eyes flicking between his watch and the door. She had to admit, Lila had good taste. This guy could be on the cover of a magazine. He was even better looking than any of the football players, even if he didn't seem to have their laid-back confidence. Though that probably came from public adulation and having millions in the bank.

The door opened again. Heart started pounding. It was… Nope, a group of four – maybe two couples – all now standing chatting to the maître d.

Caro really, really wished she'd ordered a gin. This wasn't the kind of emotional stress that could be soothed with still water.

Her eyes caught a movement at the desk. The two couples were still there, but behind them, she could see the top of the door and it was opening. Yes! It was opening again and... Her eyes darted to Cammy. He'd spotted something, he was standing up, he was smiling, his arms beginning to open...

Why the bloody hell couldn't those people move and let her see who had just come in? It took every ounce of self-discipline not to yell right over the restaurant for them to get out of the bloody way.

It was like slow motion. Like the old episodes of *Baywatch*, where the lifeguard was running across the sands. Only in this case, it was Caro who was drowning and there was no one there to pull her out of the swirling riptide.

Cammy was stepping forward now. Eyes on the door. Someone small. A blonde. Yes it was...! No, it actually wasn't. This woman was blonde, beautiful, but older than Lila. She searched her mental hard drive for a recollection. Her mother! It was her mum. Lila had posted countless photographs of them on cosy lunches, pamper days for two, weekend breaks, side-by-side sunloungers on tropical beaches. Things Caro and her mum had never done... and never would do now.

She was so distracted by the sudden flood of tears that swamped her lower lids that she almost missed him. The man. Walking behind Lila's mum. It was the one in the pictures, the one Lila called dad, the one who looked, from this distance and through a mist of incredulity, a whole lot like the man who had walked out of Caro's life years before. But she couldn't be sure.

Turn this way. Turn this way. Let me see your full face, she begged, silently.

The waiter appeared out of nowhere with her starter, cutting off her view, blocking sight of him. She could see the boyfriend hugging the woman, then pulling out a chair for her.

By the time she had a clear view again, the older man was sitting down with his back to her. Nooooooo. Come on. Don't let this be happening. Her heart was beating like a drum now, so loud it must be drowning out the music, the chat, the tactics the French team were discussing with the aim of securing a win against Scotland. She slipped her phone out of her bag and made the call.

'WHAT IS HAPPENING?' Todd wailed again, definitely his catchphrase of the day. 'This is killing me. KILLING ME!'

'Not as much as it's killing me,' Caro murmured, trying desperately not to let any other diners hear her speaking. Using a phone in here was probably frowned upon. Besides, there was nothing worse than someone who broke the ambience of any environment by chattering on a phone. 'I think he might be here.'

'Who's there? Stop whispering. Did you mean Lila? Lila is there?'

'No, she's not here. *He's* here.'

'Who?'

Jesus, he didn't catch on quickly, did he?

'My dad!' There was an audible gasp on the other end of the line, before she went on. 'At least, it might be my dad. I honestly don't know. He's at the table with Lila's mum and boyfriend, but he's got his back to me so I can't see for sure. Oh, that's weird...'

'What's weird?'

'Lila's mum just jumped up and hugged the boyfriend. She looks delighted about something. The two men are now shaking hands. I've no idea what's going on. Oh, God, Todd what will I do?'

'Can you walk past him and get a closer look?'

'No, he's sitting at the front window. There would be no reason to go there unless I was leaving.'

'Then you have to just go over there and confront him.'

'I can't.'

'You can.'

'I can't.'

'What are we – six?' Todd teased, and she was grateful for the humour.

A woman at the next table but one didn't seem to share her feeling, and gave her a filthy look, presumably for using her phone. Caro smiled at her, then turned her attention back to the door.

'I can't stand this,' Todd groaned. 'Why am I not there?'

'Because we didn't know it would turn out this way.'

'It doesn't matter! I should have come. This is better than a double bill of *EastEnders*, and I'm having to hear about it second-hand through a phone.'

'Shhhhh,' Caro chided him. 'Hang on...' Her voice trailed off as her gaze fixed on the opening door. Wider. Wider. Then wider again. Then it seemed like everything and everyone else in the room faded away. It was just Caro, watching, as the spectacle that was Lila Anderson strutted into the restaurant. She wasn't exceptionally tall, perhaps five foot six, with two added inches for hair that was last seen on an eighties supermodel. Tumbling, gorgeous, big mane, swept back from a face that had cheekbones you could ski off. But it was the body... It was enough to make an entire table of French football gods turn, as one, like a cross-channel wave, and stare in her direction. That dress looked a whole lot different on her than it did when she had posted a picture of it on the hanger. It was a pale pink, almost nude colour, with spaghetti-thin straps that left her shoulders bare, high cleavage and a silhouette so tight the outlines of her hip bones were visible. She walked like she was striding down a catwalk, aware that she had suddenly become a focus of attention.

'Hang up, quick, hang up...' she hissed into the phone. She had no idea if Todd did as she asked, until she hit another button and immediately called him back on FaceTime. She surreptitiously aimed the camera at Lila, still standing, allowing her boyfriend to hug her, then working the table, kissing her mum on both cheeks, then her father. Caro tried once again to subliminally mind-warp him into turning around, but without success.

'Buggering bollocks.' That came from the speaker on her phone, thankfully only loud enough for Caro to hear. Although, Mrs Stern Face, at the next table but one, still wasn't looking best pleased.

After the gregarious greetings, Lila sat down, her smile wide and flawless as she launched into an animated discussion with the group. Caro decided right there and then that the guy over there couldn't be her dad, because even taking into account different mothers, there was no way she even had one foot in the same gene pool as that goddess.

Caro took the phone off speaker, hung up, and switched back to a voice call, so that she could hold the phone to her ear again. 'Listen, I don't have too much battery left because I didn't think to bring a charger. I need to hang up for now.'

'Don't you dare! Caro, don't even think...' Click.

She hadn't lied. Her battery was down to less than twenty per cent. But she had to get him off the phone because she wanted to focus on the group at the other table with no distractions, even loving ones. Also, she couldn't stand what was already unbearable anxiety being added to by the worry that Mrs Stern Face would have her papped out for using a mobile phone in a high-class restaurant.

It was almost ten o'clock by the time Caro had finished all three courses, dragging it out by chewing every mouthful multiple times, and then adding a coffee on to the end. The food here was supposed to be among the best in the city, but Caro had been so distracted, even her taste buds were switched off for the night.

The whole time, she'd watched as the party of four who may or may not be related to her ate, chatted, laughed like they didn't have a care in the world. The perfect happy family – even if the boyfriend seemed a bit on edge. And they all seemed to be absolutely fine with Lila's incessant selfies. There was an incredible moment, just after they'd finished their main courses, when Lila got up and went over to one of the players at the French team's table and whispered in his ear. Caro saw him nod, then watched, astonished, as Lila went around the entire table taking a photo with every player.

That's some level of confidence right there, she thought. *And more compelling evidence that we don't paddle in the same gene pool.*

There had yet to be an opportunity for intervention or clarification. Of course, Caro could walk over there right now and look that man in the face, and know if it was her dad, but she couldn't bring herself to do it. She would, but just not yet. Soon.

A text appeared on her screen.

If you don't call me I'm sending in a SWAT team.

Despite her stomach-clenching, agonising state of stress, she phoned Todd back.

'I've got nothing to report or I would have called. They've had dinner, they've chatted, and Lila hasn't gone to the toilet even once. The woman must have the bladder of a camel. She has, however, gone around the two tables of the French football team taking a selfie with every one of them.'

A pause on the other end of the line, then 'The French football team is there?'

'Yeah, didn't you see them when I FaceTime'd?'

'No, I was too busy being overcome by a dose of giddiness. Seriously? Are you sure it's *the* French football team and not a pub team of farmers from Marseilles?'

'Yes. The maître d' told me.'

She heard a loud, repetitive thud.

'Todd, are you banging your head off your table?'

'Maybe,' he admitted. 'I swear this is the worst night of my life.'

'It's not going too great for me either last time I checked,' she retorted.

'Sorry. You're right. But I mean, the French football team in the same restaurant. That's the equivalent of you getting stuck in a lift with Brad Pitt and Matt Damon.'

'Point taken. Todd, I think I'm going to go for it. I need to go speak to this guy. Rule him out. I've finished my meal, I've paid the bill, my fake story about my husband's flight being delayed is losing ground and it's starting to get a bit suspect that I'm loitering. So I'm just going to leave the restaurant and on the way past, I'm going to stop at the table and do it.'

'I take it you've planned this all out?'

'Not a single second of it,' she admitted, words tight with terror.

'Terrific. What could go wrong? Leave the phone on, I want to hear everything.'

'Okay, I'm going to do it.'

'You said that a minute ago.'

'I know! I'm working up to it. Give me a break! Right, I'm going…' Halfway to a standing position, Caro froze as she saw what was happening across the room, then plumped back down on her seat. 'Oh God, I can't.'

'Yes, you can. You've got this,' Todd said encouragingly.

'No, I mean I actually can't do it right at this minute.'

'Why? Why not? What's happened?'

'Lila's boyfriend just got down on one knee.'

26

Cammy

Nothing was going to plan.

For a start, he got there first, which – on the positive side – gave him enough time to sort out the ring. Neil, the manager, was nowhere to be seen so he gave it to the waiter who came to take his drinks order and introduced himself as Jude. 'Can you give this to Neil please? I'm proposing to my girlfriend tonight and Neil has it covered. The ring is to be brought out with dessert.'

'No problem at all,' Jude said, slipping it in his pocket and going off to get the requested bottle of bubbly. Not Cammy's drink of choice, but this was Lila's night. He'd stick to water until the deed was done. Slurring out a half-assed proposal probably wasn't the best way to seal the deal.

As he watched Jude depart, he did have a moment of hesitation. He'd just given over the most important component of tonight's events to a guy who didn't look old enough to legally marry let alone to oversee another person's proposal. Enough. He was just panicking, of course it would all be fine.

It would.

His phone buzzed with an incoming text, and he checked it anxiously, worried that Lila was cancelling.

It was Josie.

Not too late to change your mind. We're here for you. Can storm building and have you out of there in seconds.

His reply was succinct.

Go away.

At least keep us regularly updated? We're old, could die at any minute.

I'm switching my phone off.

Smiling, he flicked the handset to silent and put it back in his pocket.

Josie and Val coming tearing in here would be a nightmare.

He had plenty of time to ruminate over that, and

at least a dozen other disaster scenarios in the twenty minutes he spent sitting on his own before Lila's mum and dad came in. They were late, but at least they were there.

Okay, this was progress. Although, he would feel easier if Lila was here too.

He tried to engage as they chatted away about the round of golf they'd played that afternoon, but he'd be lying if he said he wasn't distracted. So much for the French bloody football team being at the other end of the restaurant. He'd thought they'd be right up the back on the raised area, separate from the rest of the diners, but no – they were smack bang in the middle and just a few feet away from their table.

Great.

It did somewhat blow the romantic ambience. He could see Neil, the manager, floating around in the room, but, probably wisely, he avoided coming within shouting distance of Cammy. Instead, he gave him a thumbs up from a distance, and then pretended to ignore Cammy's glare of annoyance. He'd be making sure he recommended trousers that were way too tight next time he was in the shop.

Lila's parents were still talking. Sometimes, he thought they were a strange couple. Lila's mum, Louise, looked just like her daughter, even shared her mannerisms, her voice, her opinions. They said if you wanted to know what your wife would be like in twenty years' time, look at her mother. Going with that theory, Lila wouldn't change much at all. Her dad though – Cammy had never quite clicked with him. Apparently he'd worked away most of Lila's life, and that would probably explain why he always seemed a little... detached? Once or twice, it had actually jarred with him to see how much Lila sought to get his attention, his approval even. That said, he was a nice enough bloke, good company, and Cammy knew he had to stay most definitely on his good side if he wanted to marry his daughter.

A thought struck him. Shit, should he have asked him first? He should have.

It wasn't too late. Lila wasn't here yet – now was his chance.

'Jack, Louise, you know I love your daughter very much...'

Crap, he'd gone with an adaptation of the corny line and now Louise was frozen, her glass halfway to her mouth.

'We do,' Jack replied, a shade of anticipation in his voice.

'Well, I'd like to ask her to marry me and I'd like your blessing.' There. That was okay, wasn't it?

Louise gasped, yelped, then threw her arms around him. He took that as a blessing delivered. Jack, on the other hand, merely nodded, as if he'd been asked if it was Friday or if he'd like a sauce with his steak.

After a pause, he seemed to muster up the right words, even if they weren't exactly delivered with overwhelming enthusiasm. 'That's fine with us, Cammy. Welcome to the family.' He shook his hand, and Cammy marvelled again at how cool he was, unruffled, like he was dealing with a situation that really didn't matter too much at all. Cammy decided never to play him at cards – that kind of poker face would be unbeatable.

'When are you going to ask her?' Louise chirped, unable to keep the beaming smile off her face or the pure excitement out of her voice.

'Tonight,' Cammy replied. 'I'm sorry I didn't ask you before now. It was a spur of the moment thing.'

'When you know, you just know,' Jack said, but he wasn't looking at Cammy, he was looking at his wife, his hand over hers, her grin now even wider, the two of them locked in their own moment.

The volume from the football tables lowered sharply, and as Cammy turned to investigate, he immediately saw why. Lila had just walked in the door and she was gliding towards them. She was poetry. Mesmerising, intoxicating poetry. Every second thought he'd never admitted to having, every doubt, every hesitation was squashed right there and then. She was the most breathtaking woman in any room and he wanted nothing more than to spend the rest of his life with her.

A response, it would seem, that was shared by the guys with the fancy footwork at the middle two tables. Almost all of them had eyes on her now, a few of them continuing conversations, but most of them having given up trying to speak and stare at the same time. Cammy saw Lila register their attention, and put just a little more hip action into her strut. She liked to be admired. Nothing wrong with that.

Jealousy had never been high on his radar. Years of loving Mel while she was married to her first husband had forced him to dampen any twinges of envy and it was a life lesson that had stayed with him. Damn, Mel again! Why did she keep creeping into his thoughts today? He fought to get back on message. Yep, he was thinking about how jealousy was a wasted emotion. Pointless. Anyway, while he knew Lila enjoyed the approval, she would never act on it. Not once had she ever given him a reason to doubt her fidelity and that was saying something given that she could absolutely have any guy she chose, including, it seemed, her pick of these French footballers.

As he stood to greet her, he felt like the luckiest guy in the room – which was saying something considering at least twenty of his dining companions earned more than ten million a year and were adored by an entire nation of almost 67 million people.

Lila kissed both her parents before sliding into the seat to the left of Cammy.

'Hey babe, tough day?' he asked her and watched as a shadow crossed her face.

'It wasn't great. You know one of those days when you know what you want to achieve and you just can't get there? That was today.'

'Did the last appointment not work out?' he asked, aware that he wasn't quite sure what he was talking about. Lila visited doctors, they then ordered her company's products. That was about as much as he'd picked up because she avoided talking about work at home. 'Way too boring – let's talk about something else,' she'd say when he tried to take an interest and ask her about it.

She clocked the bottle of champagne in the ice bucket at the side of the table. Cristal. Her favourite. 'Oooh, are we celebrating something?' she asked. There was an irrepressible chirp from her mother and Cammy thought for a moment that she'd given the game away, but then saw that Lila had already been distracted by the two rows of tables to her right.

'Is that the... the...' If she hadn't had Botox, her brow would have been frowning in puzzlement.

'French football team,' Cammy answered, while filling the glass in front of her with bubbly liquid. And, he saw, a couple of them were still casting glances in Lila's direction.

There was no avoiding her reaction. Back a little straighter, boobs a little higher, smile a little wider and a dramatic flick of her hair. He knew she probably had no idea she was doing it – it was a completely unconscious reaction.

Great. The night he's proposing to the woman he loves and he's in a packed, noisy restaurant, with other blokes ogling his intended fiancée.

This wasn't going well. Perhaps he should postpone, but he'd already told her parents and he definitely didn't trust Louise to be able to keep this one a secret – she was already sitting there with an expression of rapt anticipation that was hard to miss.

It was a relief when the waiter appeared in front of them with his tablet out, ready to take their order. No common pads and pens in this place.

Lila hadn't had a chance to look at the menu but he knew that wouldn't matter.

'A green salad, dressing on the side,' she said, repeating the same order that she placed in every restaurant they ever went to. No meat. No fish. Nothing other than green salad leaves, kale and spinach. As a rule, he avoided carbs and treated his body well, but Lila took discipline to a whole other level.

Except, it would seem, when she was responding to some casual interest from a nearby table. As he gave his order – steak, side salad – he noticed her flick her hair yet again. Okay, time to get this back on track. Small talk. Get control back with casual conversation.

'So, Jack, Louise, have you booked any holidays this year?' he asked. Great. He now sounded like a hairdresser making chitchat over the sound of a hair dryer.

'Actually, we just booked yesterday – we're going to Mauritius for two weeks over New Year,' Louise said, before turning to Lila. 'Your dad has always wanted to go there, but don't worry, darling, we'll still be here for Christmas.'

Cammy spotted Lila's fleeting shadow of disappointment. 'But you'll be away for New Year? We always spend New Year together...' There was no hiding the touch of petulance that had taken residence at the table. 'And especially this year...'

Had he heard that right? It was so damn busy in this restaurant that he could barely hear himself speak, never mind pick up everything the others said. Yet, he was sure he'd heard her say...

'Why?' Cammy blurted. 'Why "especially this year"?' Bollocks. Did she know? Had she sussed it out? Did she want her parents here to celebrate the end of the year that she'd got engaged?

She shrugged, stuttering, 'Oh, I don't know – I just meant it would be nice for us all to be together every New Year now that Dad's retired. We missed so many years when he was working away.'

Okay, phew. It was fine. Her head was in a different place altogether and she had absolutely no idea he was about to pop the question.

'We'll have lots of years ahead of us,' her dad said, dismissing her objections. Cammy felt a twinge of sympathy. For just an instant, she looked crushed, but then she immediately rallied, smile back on, and changed the subject. That was why he loved her, he thought again. She never let anything get her down.

Instead, true to form, she pulled out her phone. 'Let's get a picture!' she rearranged her position, so that she could capture the full scene, the gorgeous table, the champagne, her mum and dad, Cammy, and of course her, eyes wide, chin down, megawatt smile.

'I'll post it later – can't see in this light if it needs tweaking,' she said, and by that, Cammy knew she meant a touch of Photoshopping. A photo didn't go up unless it was a hundred per cent flattering. OK, so that might be a tad pretentious. Or maybe it was just the way things were done these days. Sometimes the ten years in age difference between them felt like nothing – he'd always prided himself on being hip, current and frequently immature – but sometimes it felt like they came from completely different generations.

Somehow, he managed to keep it together throughout their starters and main course. If Lila noticed that her mother was particularly smiley, she didn't comment, and for once, he was grateful that her dad kept the conversation going with endless talk about golf. He put on his best 'paying attention' face, he laughed when the others laughed, he asked questions when he thought they were relevant. By the time the plates were cleared away after the main course, he felt like he had a fairly good chance of acing the entire history of golf on *A Question of Sport*.

The dessert menus came out. 'Nothing for me, thanks,' Lila said, waving dismissively.

'Nor me,' said her mum, her gestures completely mirroring Lila's. 'And you shouldn't either, Jack. Remember what the doctor said about your cholesterol.'

Bugger. Cammy had forgotten that he was with the family that never bloody ate dessert. It was a stupid idea in the first place, one that he clearly hadn't thought through. This proposal planning stuff was way out of his league.

'Shall we just get the bill and go?' Lila asked. 'I'm already feeling completely full. I might actually pop out to the 24-hour gym later and work this off.'

Work off a green salad? Sometimes her dedication to her body went too far.

Lila turned to the waiter again. 'Can we just...'

Nooooooo. They couldn't wrap this up now. He had a ring to deliver, a proposal to make.

'Actually, I'd like a dessert,' Cammy blurted. The other three rounded on him in surprise.

'But you never eat dessert,' Louise said.

Cammy tried to give her a loaded look, but she wasn't grasping the significance. He should really have filled Jack and Louise in on the running order for the proposal before Lila got there.

Lila, meantime, was looking less than impressed. 'Can't you just get something at home? I'm, like, so tired, babe.'

Oh God, this was going to turn into an actual argument. Great. A fight, right before he asked her to marry him. This wasn't helping the case for an acceptance.

'I just fancy trying the new meringue dessert – Neil was raving about it when he popped into the shop this afternoon.' He was a terrible liar. Terrible. She was sure to pick up on it. Or maybe not…

Lila sighed, then shrugged her acquiescence, but the pouting expression made it clear she wasn't happy.

'Can you ask Neil for the dish we discussed earlier please?' he blurted before any more protest could be made, then he turned back to the others. 'And would you guys like coffee?'

Jack and Louise agreed immediately, and Lila reluctantly followed, sighing 'I suppose I could do with a shot of caffeine.'

The waiter nodded and went off to find his manager, looking more than a little flustered. Cammy had no way of knowing that this had something to do with the fact that Jude, twenty-one, working at Grilled to pay off his student loan, had suddenly realised that he had left the ring on an empty beer crate when he'd popped out for a cigarette earlier in the evening.

'It won't take long,' Cammy tried to console Lila. This wasn't going well. Flattery. That was what was needed here. 'By the way, you look incredible tonight...'

She'd already turned to look at the other diners and wasn't listening. 'Did you say that was the actual French football team there?' she asked.

'It is.'

'So which ones are the big stars. I mean, they're not all famous, are they?'

Cammy's knowledge of football was up there with his expertise on the schedule of the Dover to Calais ferry, so he shrugged. 'No idea. Jack?'

Lila's dad wasn't sure either. If it had been the French golf team, he'd have been able to give them their history, statistics, and inside leg measurements.

Lila stood up and tossed her napkin on the table. 'I'll just ask them all then.'

Cammy watched, horrified, as she marched over, and leaned down to whisper in the ear of a dark-haired guy who could give Ronaldo a run for his millions in the looks department. And yes, the only reason he knew anything about Ronaldo was because he had a fashion line.

Whatever Lila said to him, the man was in full agreement – well, of course he was going to be – and immediately put his head towards hers and grinned as she held up her phone and took a selfie.

'Oh, what's she like,' Louise chuckled. 'That girl and her photos. She's always been the same. Completely adorable.' Her mother's encouragement did, perhaps, give a clue as to why Lila had embraced the world of the selfie.

Her father said nothing, just sipped his champagne while checking his phone. Probably looking at golf scores from some tournament going on somewhere. If the guy was interested in anything that was going on around him, he hid it well.

The only good thing about Lila's distraction over at Le Selfie Central, was that it bought Cammy some more time to mentally prepare for what was about to happen. He could do this, he told himself yet again. His internal dialogue was like a stuck record today.

But he could do it. He definitely could.

'*Lila, you know you mean everything in the world to me...*' Nope, made him sound like an X-Factor contestant talking about why their only hope of a lifetime of happiness was to get enough votes to go through to judges' houses.

'*Lila, until I met you I had no idea how much I could love someone...*' Somewhere, in the truth halls of the universe, a lie detector test was wailing to signal a big fat porky.

'*Lila...*' He was interrupted by the arrival of the waiter, looking slightly harassed, and shiny around the edges. He was clutching a tall glass with some kind of meringue in it, resting on a silver tray. Cammy cast his eyes across, looking for the ring. It wasn't there.

Shit. No ring. It was supposed to be on the silver tray. This couldn't be happening.

Lila was still ten feet away, now on the second table of players. Cammy could feel the anxiety rising. No way. He hadn't spent the whole day sorting this out only for it to go horribly wrong yet again, this time at the most crucial part.

It couldn't be happening. It just couldn't.

'Eh, I think,' he said through gritted teeth, 'that Neil mentioned this dessert came with a *special* decoration?'

Blank looks from Jude, the waiter. Obviously subtlety was wasted here.

'The ring...' he hissed, causing Louise to gasp and clap a silent ovation of excitement. Thankfully Lila was too busy with les hommes to notice.

Jude was a picture of confusion. 'It's there,' he whispered, gesturing to the meringue. Thankfully, Cammy didn't realise that Jude had spent the last ten minutes going through the recycling bin to find the bloody ring, giving it a quick wipe over and burying it in the meringue.

Cammy followed his gaze and saw it, the thin band poking out of the top of the meringue. This wasn't what he'd planned at all. Neil was bloody dead when he got a hold of him. But maybe... maybe it wasn't so bad. Perhaps this could actually work out kinda cute. Louise had spotted the ring too now and her eyes were already glistening. Lila and her mum cried a lot. It was one of the first things he learned about them. Happy things. Sad things. Exciting things. Gorgeous things. Mostly any kind of things could bring on floods of tears that warranted careful, expert counteraction so that they didn't ruin make-up.

Okay, they were back on track. They just had to wait for Lila to return so they could get on with it. A few guys still left to get snaps with. Two now. One. And, oh for Christ's sake, she was chatting to him now. He saw her shake her head, adopt an expression of... what?... apology? Then she pointed over at Cammy and the other guy seemed to get the message, responding with a very Gallic shrug.

Ah, he must have been asking her out. That was his girl. Asked out by a handsome sports star, and still she rebuked him because she was with Cammy. It just went to prove how much she loved him and betrayal or infidelity just weren't in her make-up.

He was a lucky guy and he'd be even luckier when they were married.

It was another few moments before she got back to the table, and she sat down with a dramatic flourish. 'Oh my goodness, those guys are charmers. I'll go online when we get home and suss out who the big names are. I'm only posting pics with them. No point in putting up snaps of the nobodies.'

Cammy was barely listening. Right, new plan.

'Babe, try a bit of this, it's delicious,' he said, pushing the tall glass of meringue towards her. She'd look down, see the ring, understand the meaning, scream with delight, say yes, and he'd scoop her up, swing her round, hoping that her heels took out at least a couple of the footie guys. Either way, it was happening. She was about to realise this was one of those life-defining moments. It was going to change everything. Make them the happiest couple that...

'Cammy don't be disgusting. Meringues are loaded with sugar. I'm not putting that in my mouth,' she sneered.

He should have seen that one coming. Change of tactic required. 'But doesn't it *look* great? Isn't the presentation gorgeous?'

'Whatever,' she replied, and he saw her hand go towards her phone. He was about to lose her to Photoshop. Shit. There was nothing else for it. He delved into the sticky pudding, fished out the ring, and tried to overlook the fact that it was now adorned with a gooey substance. Then, he just went for it. Full traditional knee bend.

'Lila, I love you – and I want to love you every day of our lives...' No idea where that came from, but it was the best one yet. She seemed to think so too. She was staring at the ring, at him, back at the ring, then him... He could see she was shocked, astonished, couldn't quite believe what was happening.

Neither could he. After all the disasters and dramas today, it was finally working out just the way it was supposed to.

Meanwhile, around them, the head-splitting volume had descended to near silence. Every set of eyes in the room were now on him. Kneeling there. Expectantly. In trousers that definitely weren't meant to facilitate full movement of the knee joint. If she didn't say yes soon, he was a shoo-in for DVT. No doubt Josie would claim that was yet another sign from the gods.

Lila. Staring at the ring again. Still not answering his question.

It was only then he realised that he hadn't actually asked her.

'Lila Anderson, will you marry me?'

27

Bernadette

The whole way back from dropping off the last of her stuff at Sarah's house, Bernadette had been running the same mantra in her mind: *Please don't let him be home yet.*

She wanted to be there, be prepared, be in control of the situation, not walking into a confrontation because he'd already guessed what was happening.

Please don't let him be home yet.

It was well after eight, but it wouldn't be unusual at all for him to be delayed this late.

Please don't let him be home yet.

They stopped at the traffic lights around the corner from the end of her street.

Please don't let him be home yet.

They turned, her house was just up ahead on the right now.

Please don't let him be home yet.

Ken's car was in the driveway.

He was home.

As they drew to a stop outside the house, Sarah saw it too. 'Are you sure you don't want me to come in? Or to wait for you? You don't have to do this alone, Bernie.'

'I know,' Bernadette replied. 'But I do really, for me. This is between Ken and me. It's why I didn't want the kids here either. If anyone else was here, I'd be too worried about them to say the things that need to be said.'

Sarah tried again. 'You know you don't have to worry about keeping things from me, though, Bernie. I've seen everything that's happened. I know the truth of what you've been dealing with.'

'I know that, lovely, and thank you,' Bernadette replied gently, 'but part of walking away is knowing that I am finally standing up to him, taking responsibility for my future and having the strength to do it on my own. So I'm going to go in there,' Bernadette steeled herself to go on, 'I'm going to tell him I've left him and then I'm going to get in my car and drive away, and I won't look back. Not even once.' It sounded so easy when she said it like that, but her confident tone belied the butterflies in her stomach.

Sarah leaned over and hugged her, squeezing her tightly. 'You can do this. You're the strongest woman I've ever met.'

Bernadette knew it wasn't true. 'Strong would have been walking away from him years ago,' she argued, ruefully.

'Strong is staying in a crap situation because you feel it's what's best for your family,' Sarah countered.

Bernadette didn't carry on the debate. She'd often wondered how she'd have reacted if Kenneth had been openly abusive, or physically harmed her? Would she have left then? She was sure she would have. There was no way she'd have allowed her children to be brought up in that environment. Somehow, though, because she was the only one affected by his behaviour, she'd decided, somewhere along the line, that she could tolerate it in order to give her children a life with their father. Now, with the benefit of detachment and hindsight, she could see how ridiculous that was, how it was a shocking testimony to her feelings of low self-esteem, how he'd broken her down to the point where her own happiness didn't matter to her. How many times had she tended to victims of domestic abuse, and told them they deserved to be happy, to live their lives free of suppression or pain? Yet she was the one who had not been able to live by that advice.

It would always be a regret, but not one that she would dwell on. She had too much living to do.

She hugged Sarah again, then climbed out of the van and walked up her driveway. From the outside of the house she could see that the lights in the front rooms were not on, but there was a faint glow from the back of the house. He was in the kitchen then. With a heavy heart and a trembling hand, she put her key in the door and pushed it open.

Be strong, she told herself, repeating another line of the encouragement she'd given to so many other women, and a few men too, over the years.

She walked down the hall, through into the kitchen, and there he was, sitting at the table, typing something on his laptop.

Chest palpitations were thudding as he stopped, looked up at her.

'Where have you been?'

'With Sarah,' she replied, trying desperately to gauge his mood. Did he know? Had he been upstairs and noticed her stuff missing from the wardrobe? He was dressed in his suit, having driven his car back from the hospital instead of cycling, just like he did every Friday. On Monday morning, he'd drive in, with his bike attached to the back, and then cycle home, leaving his car at the hospital for the week, biking back and forth every day. Bernadette had never questioned why – quizzing Kenneth was something she preferred to avoid – but she had a sneaking suspicion it was so the car was always there, in his named space at the hospital door, serving two purposes – first, it would make him look like he was so dedicated that he was first in and last out every day. And secondly, it meant that Bernadette couldn't use it while he was at work. Not that she ever would. Flash cars like that just made a driver look desperate for attention, as far as she was concerned. She much preferred her Fiat – even more so because Ken hated the sight of it and went on and on about it lowering the tone of their driveway. Pretentious arse.

He was just staring at her now, telling her nothing. Of course, he'd be furious that he'd come home to an empty house. If she wasn't working, he expected her to be there, waiting for him when he walked in the door. It was Friday, so he liked to eat out, to go to one of the nicer restaurants in the city, where he'd smile and shake hands with acquaintances and show that he was a man of cosmopolitan habits, while the waiting staff gave impeccable service in return for a generous tip. The whole world thought this guy was something. Only Bernadette knew he was nothing.

She felt unsettled, unsure of her next move, unable to gauge where she was with this. She decided to go for it. Pull the Band Aid off.

'Kenneth, I need to talk to you,' she said calmly. Reasonably. For all he knew it could be about the weather or a blocked drain.

'Is it about the thirty grand you stole from me today?'

Her pulse went into overdrive. Oh dear God. He knew.

He turned his laptop around and she could see that he was on the online banking website. Hopefully that meant he'd just discovered it and hadn't had time to think things through.

Bernadette sat down at the table and took a deep breath, mustering every ounce of strength she possessed. 'I did not steal it from you, Kenneth. That was my money too. My salary goes into that account.'

He fixed her with a chilling stare. 'Did Nina or Stuart need it? Was it some kind of emergency?'

Oh Jesus, he was still deathly calm. This was the worst bit, right before the storm, when he would listen to her, as if taking symptoms from a patient, before delivering some brutal diagnosis.

'No, I took it for me.' Death knell about to be rung. 'Kenneth, I'm leaving. And the way that I see this, you have two choices:

You can let me go and accept the situation. I'm taking no more than that money. A fair deal after thirty years of marriage.

Or you can rant and rave and try to intimidate me into staying, but I won't, so you'll be wasting your breath.'

He did the last thing she expected. He laughed. 'Of course you're not fucking leaving,' he countered, as if she'd just said something completely preposterous.

Okay Bernadette, regroup. Be firm. Don't let yourself be cowed.

'Oh, I am, Kenneth – and there's no point in talking it through or giving reasons, or shouting and screaming, because it's happening and that's it. Let's end this peacefully.'

His top lip curled, a cruel gesture she'd seen way too many times before. 'Is there someone else? That's it. You're fucking someone else.' For a man who kept up the pretence of dignity and decorum, he wasn't above getting crude when it served his purposes. Bernadette knew if she challenged him, returned the attitude, it would escalate so much quicker, so she kept calm, absolutely still, like she was in the presence of a viper that was hissing, ready to bite.

'Trust me, Kenneth, the last thing I want in my life is another man, so let's focus on the reality. Like I said, I want nothing else from you. I've been miserable for years, and I can't do it any more so I'm going to go now. This conversation is over.'

She moved forward, about to push herself up, when his fist came down on the table so hard the whole structure shook.

'Sit down,' he roared. 'You're not going anywhere. Don't be so fucking ridiculous. Leave me? I'm all you've got. You've got nothing if you're not my wife. Don't think for a minute those kids will stand by you, because they'll turn their backs on you just like I should have done years ago. Years ago!'

Every single word stung like a hot poker on her seared flesh, but she remained standing.

'You need me more than I need you, you hopeless bitch. Now. Sit. The. Fuck. Back. Down.'

'No,' she said, quite simply. What was he going to do? Drag her back? Much as he was cruel, and vile and an unashamed bully, he'd never actually harmed her and she didn't fear him physically.

His eyes widened with rage. 'Don't you dare walk out that fucking door,' he roared again. It barely registered because she knew it didn't matter anymore. She was leaving him and his abuse behind. Enough.

She took her keys out of her pocket, threw them on the table, turned and began to walk, stopping only when he spoke again. 'Bernie…' That was more of a shock than anything else. The shouting, the intimidation, the abuse, she expected. But he hadn't called her 'Bernie' in over two decades. Now it was always Bernadette. Or bitch. What was even more astonishing than what he said, was how he said it. He'd flicked the anger off and now he was tender, convivial, trying to placate her.

'Don't leave,' he said. 'Bernie, we can talk about this, work something out.'

His change in tone was having no affect on her whatsoever, but she was curious to hear what angle he would come from next. 'Why?'

That caught him off guard and it took him a few moments to answer.

'Because we've got thirty years of history and two children, grandchildren, a future with our family.'

This was the kind of emotional manipulation he excelled at. The anger didn't work, the control was slipping, so he was going for any other route he could take to change her mind. She was trying not to rise to white hot fury and lay it all out for him – the abuse, the control, the rages – but that would be sinking to his level.

'But no love,' she said, then watched as he had a sudden moment of realisation that he should have led with that.

'Of course we have love!'

'No, we don't, Kenneth. For as long as I can remember, you've controlled me, bullied me, treated me with cruelty and disdain, and – God forgive me – I've let you. There's been no love between us for a long, long time. Sometimes I wondered why you stayed with me, because Lord knows, you had other options. But we both know the truth – this is how you get your kicks. You need to be the big guy. To be in control. To get a rush from dominating me. It's what gets you off, isn't it? No more. I'm out. I wish you well, Kenneth, I really do. I hope you have an excellent life. But it'll be one without me in it.'

Her pulse was still thumping, as once again, she started walking towards the door, the hairs on the back of her neck standing up in both fear and an overwhelming sense of relief. She was almost out. Almost.

'You get back here, you stupid bitch!' he growled, fury spitting from every word. 'Because trust me, I will destroy you. I will ruin your fucking life. I'll make sure the kids never want to have anything to do with you again. There is nothing, NOTHING, I won't do to make you see that this is the biggest mistake of your fucking, miserable, worthless life, until you come crawling back to me, begging me to take you back.'

'I don't think so, Dad.' The voice made Bernadette freeze, her focus going to the corner of the room, behind Kenneth. Stuart. He was there at the back door, Nina beside him, and from the expressions on their faces, she knew that they'd heard it all and that realisation destroyed her. Their whole lives she'd protected them from knowing this side of him, and now they'd just seen it in all its Technicolor glory.

'Wasn't sure if the back door would be open. Glad it was, otherwise we might have missed that little speech Dad.' Nina said dryly, clearly struggling to contain her anger. The kids had never used the front door – force of habit from the days they'd be in and out a dozen times.

This was a sight that had never greeted them before, and Nina was clearly bristling. She had always been a daddy's girl, strong, vocal, not one to let anyone mess her around. Now that was biting Kenneth on the arse.

'I'm sorry, you shouldn't have heard...' Bernadette started to apologise.

'But we did, Mum,' Nina replied.

Bernadette could see that it had hurt her to know that the man she'd looked up to her whole life could behave that way.

Like a trapped animal, desperate to find a way out, Kenneth immediately went on the defensive. 'You don't understand. Your mother, she... Look, she presses my buttons and I just said a couple of things I didn't mean. All couples do. Just one of those things. You don't get to be married for thirty years and not have spats like this.'

'Spats?' Stuart blurted, incredulous. 'You're an even bigger dick than I thought...'

'Who the hell do you think you are, you little jumped-up shit...?'

'Kenneth!' Bernadette spat, and this time the fury was all hers. 'Don't you dare speak to our son like that. Don't you bloody dare or I swear I will kill you myself.' The vehemence in her voice took every single person in the room by utter shock. Bernadette decided it was time to take the higher ground. 'I'm going to leave now. We're done.'

'Mum, wait,' Nina blurted, and Bernadette's heart sank. She'd thought during their chat this morning that Nina had accepted what was happening, but now it seemed she was going to have a go at persuading her otherwise. This was exactly why she hadn't wanted the kids to be a part of this. It wasn't their battle and they didn't know enough about the background to fully understand why there was no possibility that she would reconsider. However, Nina had asked her to stop, so she did, and now she was standing in the doorway, desperate to get this over with. Her gaze went to the clock on the cooker. Five minutes to ten. Five more minutes and she wanted, no *needed,* to be gone.

'Dad, I just wanted to say we heard how you just spoke to Mum. We will never choose you, we will never allow you to play us off against her, and I swear to God, if I ever hear you speaking that way about her, or to her, you'll never see either of us again. Do you understand?'

'Nina, you don't have to…' Bernadette tried to cut her off, still unwilling to put them in the middle of this.

'But I want to, Mum. It's been a long time in coming.' She turned back to her father. 'Both of us are beyond proud of what Mum's doing and we support her. That doesn't mean we're choosing her over you, but it does mean that we want her to be happy and we know that to do it she needs to leave you. I can't speak for Stuart, but I'd still like you to be in my life, in the kids' lives too, but only if you treat Mum with respect, because I don't want to be walking on eggshells every time you're both invited to a school show or a football match. Oh, and you'll give Mum half the value of the house. It's the least she deserves. That's the terms, Dad. Take it or leave it.'

Bernadette waited for the explosion. Kenneth hated to be told what to do, hated ultimatums even more. Surprisingly, he said nothing. Not a word. Just stared ahead, until he finally lifted his gaze to meet Bernadette's. 'There's nothing I can do to change your mind?'

'No.' As she said it, it felt like a physical weight was being lifted from her shoulders.

He shifted his gaze to Nina. 'I understand. You don't need to worry – I won't argue any further.'

'Good,' she said, with a forced air of positivity.

Stuart spoke now. 'Let's go, Mum – I'll walk you to your car.'

'Do you want me to stay, Dad?' Nina asked him, and Bernadette was grateful for that. She didn't want him sitting on his own, brooding, getting angry.

'No, it's fine.'

'Okay, well I'll call you tomorrow and check in, but you know where I am if you change your mind.'

How did these kids get to be so smart and mature? She had desperately wanted them to stay away tonight, but perhaps in hindsight it was good that they'd come. Now everyone knew where they stood. No more lies, no more covering up, everything out in the open.

Almost everything.

'Oh, and Dad, while we're on life-changing events, I've switched from medicine to law. I'm not going to discuss it with you. It's a done deal and I'm much happier. Right Mum, let's go.'

Bernadette had to suppress a smile. Good on him for getting it in there. She couldn't help wondering what Kenneth would be most upset about tonight after they'd all gone – the fact that Bernadette had left him or Stuart was dropping medicine. She suspected the latter.

'I'm coming too,' Nina said, and for the first time since Bernadette could recall, she didn't kiss her dad on the way out. Despite Nina's conciliatory words, there was no forgetting what she'd just seen. That was Kenneth's fence to mend. It was between them. She was officially absolving herself from any responsibility for Kenneth's relationships with his children or anyone else. Although, she would give Marge a call and thank her for all the years of friendly chat on the phone. She'd miss her.

But for now? Time to go. Her legs were weak, her shoulders heavy, yet she didn't think she had ever felt the kind of euphoria that was surging through her veins right now. Stuart put his arm around her shoulders as they walked down the hall.

No more drama. No more pain. No more stress.

Bernadette wasn't even looking outwards when she opened the door, so it took her a moment to register the scene in front of her. A young woman. Blonde. Beautiful. Maybe a friend of Nina's? How would she know Nina was there tonight? Must be someone at the wrong house. That happened sometimes on this road.

'Can I help you?' Bernadette asked.

'You're Kenneth Manson's wife,' the young woman said in a tone that was more of a statement than a question.

Bernadette nodded. 'I am. Sorry, who are you?'

'I'm Lila Anderson.'

28

Lila

The call had come just after eight o'clock, seconds before Lila walked into the restaurant. Ken.

'Hey baby, were you missing me?' she teased playfully.

'Were you at my house?'

'What?'

'Were. You. At. My. House?'

'No, of course not! I wouldn't...'

'You're lying.'

How did he know? Had someone seen her? Reported her car? Did he have a CCTV camera that she hadn't spotted? Oh God, he sounded so angry, so absolutely furious that she kept waiting for him to come out with a punchline and tell her he was joking. She'd never heard him like this before.

'Baby, I...' she stuttered, playing for time, realising that she had to come up with something fast. Maybe he'd just nipped home and spotted her car driving past him. Yes, that must be it. 'I think I may have driven down your street,' she said hesitantly. 'I'd... I'd...' She needed an excuse. Any excuse. Something convincing. 'I was picking some things up for my mum at a gorgeous little deli not far from there. And... Oh, wait a minute, I pulled over to take a call. The office needed some figures, so I had to get my laptop out...' She was warming to her story now, 'That might have been in your street. I can't quite remember. But I certainly wasn't at your house. Why would I be there?'

It was lame, not an entirely waterproof story, but it was all she could do in the circumstances. He didn't reply immediately so Lila could sense he was thinking about it. That told her he didn't have actual proof she was at his house, knocking on his door, determined to throw his whole life into chaos. She decided to probe further, but go with teasing and cajoling in the hope of de-escalating things.

'Anyway, my gorgeous grump, how did you know where I was? Are you missing me so much you're having me followed?' She added a giggle for effect.

Another pause. 'Your Facebook post about fucking lipstick. You, in the car. I recognised the street in the background.' Her stomach lurched just a little. Shit!

Number one, she hadn't thought of that. And number two, even if she had, she wouldn't have thought there was enough of the background in the shot for someone to identify it. But then, he was the smartest guy that she'd ever met. Wasn't that one of the things that turned her on most?

'Baby, I'm sorry if I gave you a shock, but I promise it was all perfectly innocent.' It wasn't. And no, her plans hadn't changed, but if she was going to reveal all to that frump he'd married, she didn't want to give him advance warning.

'Look, Lila,' he didn't sound angry now, maybe just a bit weary. Well, she could certainly make him feel better. In fact she could... 'Maybe we should take a break from this for a moment.'

'What?'

'I just think that we need a break.'

What was he saying? The words were floating out there but she couldn't quite grab them and make sense of them. A break. They'd just got back together again a couple of months ago after the last break. That's not what they needed – what they needed was for him to leave his wife so they could be together.

He was the first to fill the silence. 'It's a really busy time for me at work, and my son and daughter need my time...'

'I need your time,' she blurted.

'Lila, I know, and I want to give it to you. I do. But

my schedule is just so intense. You deserve someone who can be with you all the time, and until I'm free to be with you, that can't happen.'

Now it was her turn to get angry. She'd heard all this before, last time he'd called it off, and the previous time too. He loved her – the fact that he kept coming back proved that. 'Make it happen! For god's sake, Ken, it's not difficult. People leave their wives all the time, marriages break up, it's no big deal.'

'It would be a big deal to my children. Look, you know I don't love Bernadette. It's always been you. But I can't just walk out – the consequences right now are unacceptable. My children would be devastated…'

'They're adults, living their own lives! Nina is almost the same age as me! I really don't think her world will stop if her parents divorce now.'

The urge to scream was almost too strong to ignore. This wasn't happening. Not now. She wasn't giving him the chance to push her aside yet again. For seven years she'd waited for him to make good on his promises, and yes, she knew it all came from a place of decency. He just didn't want to be the bad guy who left his millstone of a wife. Well too bad. Time had come. After this stupid meal with Cammy was over she was ending Ken's marriage for good. He'd thank her for it in the end. In the meantime, she wasn't going to give him a chance to finish what he'd been trying to say.

'Listen, darling, I'm just about to walk into a restaurant now... and by the way, I'm wearing that dress that drove you wild in London. I'll call you later. Kiss kiss. Love you.'

She disconnected the call and threw her phone into her clutch, trying desperately to steady her breathing. She wasn't prone to violence, but she had such an urge to kick something, anything. The huge window at the front of Grilled would do. Although, nothing was worth scuffing her Louboutins. And nothing was worth spoiling this make-up, hair and dress. The only way to deal with this was to focus on the big picture. Ken would be hers, tonight – just as soon as she managed to put herself in front of Bernadette. End of story. Getting angry would only make her Botox work harder, so there was no point. Instead, she paused for a moment, inhaled, exhaled, put a huge smile on her face and entered the restaurant.

The difference in the energy was obvious the minute she walked in. Usually, the restaurant was so quiet, intimate and romantic, but tonight it was loud and busy. For a moment, her irritation flared again, until she saw the root of the transformation – two tables of impeccably dressed men, some of them dinging the bell at the top of the attractive scale.

In a split second, the vibe changed, as one by one they spotted her, fixed eyes, and she felt the adrenalin start to kick in. Her reaction to the attention was instant – she threw back her shoulders, worked those hips, adopted a catwalk strut, while all the time acting completely oblivious.

By the time she reached the table with Cammy – who was looking decidedly hot tonight – and her mum and dad, the buzz of the entrance has almost dissipated her earlier fury. A break? Ken didn't mean that. He loved her. It was just some stupid knee-jerk reaction to the photo. Note to self – must be more careful about location of photos. A second thought struck her – he'd obviously been looking at her Facebook page. He wasn't on social media at all, so he must just have been checking out her latest posts. That wasn't the actions of a man who wanted a break.

That realisation was enough to get her back on an even keel. Telling Bernadette was the right thing to do. She had never been surer of anything. In the meantime, she just had to get through this dinner.

By the time the main course came, that was proving tougher than she anticipated. Cammy was in a weird mood – edgy and distracted. While her mother... urgh, she really had to have a word with her. Dad was totally monopolising her attention and it was really starting to get annoying. Much as she'd never admit it, she actually preferred it when he was away two weeks out of the month, because then she had Mum all to herself. Now they just talked about their plans to travel and bloody golf. They hadn't shown a moment of interest in her all night. Pathetic. And all that stuff about going away for New Year? Not if she could help it. This was going to be her first Hogmanay with Ken and she wanted her parents to share it.

To make it worse, she couldn't even use her favourite Cristal to take the edge off because she wanted to be able to drive later. This was no time to get hammered. One glass, that was all she could have. Maximum. Bummer.

The only way to get through it was to amuse herself with a few photos. Her with Cammy. Her with Mum. Her with Dad. Her with some French footballers that were dining there too.

It took a good fifteen minutes to work her way around them all, but it was hardly a hardship. Four of them asked for her number. One of them had been particularly keen, Jean Pascal something-or-other. If she was single, she totally would. And if Ken could see her now he would soon shut up about taking a bloody break.

Back at the table, she was out of options for passing the time. All she wanted to do was get the bill, get out of there, and then head over to Ken's house, knock at the door, reveal all. She'd even made up some lie about wanting to go to the gym to set up an alibi. Then Cammy tried to get her to order dessert. Why would he even think she'd want to join him in the pudding club? Did she look like a Bernadette? Someone who would let herself go and sail off on a sea of carbs? And why was he being so insistent about it? It was only a bloody meringue.

This was so tiresome and she needed it to be over, needed to be out of there and was about to call it a night, when Cammy stuck his fingers right in the pudding, fished something out... What the hell was he doing? What was going on?

Why was he sliding off his chair. Had he dropped something? Taken ill? Oh, hopefully not because then they'd need to wait for an ambulance and they'd never bloody get out of here. No, he wasn't falling. He was on one knee. And now he was looking at her, all misty-eyed.

A moment of realisation dawned.

He was holding a ring. Her eyes fixed on it. It was the most unremarkable ring she'd ever seen. Nothing to it. A band. A tiny stone. Seriously, was that it?

The rabble of noise in the restaurant seemed to drop, as people started to stare and she felt her face begin to burn. This was, like, so mortifying.

For a split second, her gaze shifted to her mum, who was, as far as her latest round of Botox would allow, bloody beaming with glee too – but there was no surprise there. She knew! She absolutely knew Cammy was planning this and she didn't even give her a warning? He was speaking, but all she caught was the last line...

'Lila Anderson, will you marry me?'

Was this a joke? One of those prank videos that would go viral on Facebook?

It had to be, because otherwise he meant it, he really was down there asking her to spend the rest of her life with him.

She couldn't think. Couldn't process. Couldn't speak.

Marry him? She didn't even want to stay with him. Sure, they'd had a good time but this was never a 'forever' deal.

The stares were burning into her skin now. The irony. Her whole life, she'd adored being the centre of attention, and now she would give her last pair of Louboutins to be anywhere but here.

This was a nightmare.

For a split second she saw a different image – Ken, on one knee, asking her to marry him. That's what her future held, not this.

'No... I can't... I...' There were no more words. Instead, she grabbed her bag, jumped to her feet and rushed to the door. No catwalk swagger this time. Just a heart-thudding charge, as fast as she could go in those heels, while every bit of her seared with embarrassment at the fact that every person in the restaurant was watching her with astonishment.

Outside, another moment of panic. Keys. She fumbled in her clutch and pulled them out, beeping the car open.

'Lila!' Her mum's voice. Traitor. Last person she wanted to speak to. Why hadn't she told her Cammy was going to do this? She could have been prepared, cancelled dinner, spoken to him.

Horns blared as a lifetime of practice in heels allowed her to break into a run across the road, with no attention whatsoever to the cars coming along the street. Thankfully she made it, opened the door, jumped in, pushed on the ignition button and she was out of the space, in another cacophony of horns, in seconds. No doubt there would be a CCTV camera covering this street and she'd get a visit from the police next week, but right now she didn't care. She wanted, *needed*, to be out of there. She put her foot down, and negotiated the grid of Glasgow's one-way system, left, lights, left again, lights, lights, more bloody lights, left, and then she was at the end of Great Western Road, heading towards the West End, stopping every few hundred metres for more hugely irritating lights.

Her stomach was revolving like the inside of a tumble dryer. This was too much. As she sat drumming her fingers on the steering wheel at another set of lights, halfway to her destination, her phone buzzed. Cammy. She declined. It buzzed again. Her mum. She declined. She didn't want to speak to anyone. That wasn't true. There was only one person she wanted to speak to.

Another set of lights. Drumming her fingers again. An image in her head. Cammy. Looking so thrilled, so gorgeous, so hopeful that she would say yes. For a moment she thought she was going to have to open the door and vomit on the Corsa full of young guys, music pounding, that had just pulled up next to her.

Cammy wanted to marry her. Her first ever proposal. Someone actually wanted to spend the rest of his life with her and she'd just crushed him. That must have been horrendous for him. She felt a brief moment of sympathy and then shook it off. He should never have ambushed her like that. If he'd actually spoken to her he'd have realised that she wasn't in that place.

She clenched her veneers tight shut. It wasn't her fault he was the wrong guy. He shouldn't have done it. He'd get over it. Cammy was just another man trying to make her dance to his tune.

No more.

From now on, Lila was in charge of the soundtrack and it was going to play out very differently. Cammy wasn't going to call the shots. Neither was Ken.

She wasn't her mother – she wasn't going to spend half her life waiting for the man she loved to walk in the door, missing him, her happiness determined by whether or not he was with her. It was that existence, that childhood experience, that had given her the strength and tenacity to wait for Ken all these years – but she wasn't going to be the one who waited another two decades to have her man by her side.

She wanted Ken now.

More lights. This time they turned to green almost instantly – definitely a sign that this was meant to be – and she roared through, turned right, went along the all-too familiar street and stopped, turned, looked...

His house. There were lights on, so he was home. His car was in the driveway, next to the Fiat. Another car sat on the road outside. Visitors to Ken's house? Or one of the neighbours?

It didn't matter.

Her phone rang again.

Cammy. Decline.

Priorities.

She checked her face in the driver's mirror, then emptied her clutch, grabbed her face powder, dampened down any shine, reapplied lipstick, touched up her hair, applied some hairspray. A quick squirt of Opium, Ken's favourite, and she was done.

Phone rang again. Cammy. Decline. Bloody hell, could he not take a hint?

She shoved it in the glove compartment, prepared, for the first time in living memory, to go anywhere without the device that meant more to her than just about anything else on earth.

She opened the door, slid out, and took a moment to steel herself for this. She could do it. He would thank her. It was going to be a moment of pain, then that would be it. Bernadette would realise the truth, know that Ken was no longer in love with her, see that it was a lost cause, and she would walk away, go find someone else, someone who was more her type. They could have matching bloody Fiats in the driveway.

She started walking. Confidence. Hair done, lipstick on, face the world. What did she have to lose? Nothing. Her job was undoubtedly gone. Ken was talking about calling it off because he was too much of a nice guy to make the move. Didn't he see that this was only making it worse for Bernadette in the long run? She was wasting her life in a loveless marriage. Lila was about to do her a favour, and sure, it would sting, but she'd probably even thank her later.

It was time.

Apart from her lunchtime quickie, today had been horrendous. Now was her chance to change that and make this one of the best days of her life.

Bravery and conviction surging through her, all regret, fear and anxiety dissipated as she prepared herself to ring the doorbell.

This was her moment.

Her finger was almost on the bell, when she heard footsteps from inside the house, coming towards her. She couldn't tell if it was a man or a woman. She needed it to be Bernadette, because if Ken answered there was always the possibility that he would thwart her plan.

Not that she'd let that happen. One way or another, she was going to speak to Bernadette, even supposing she had to shout through the letter box.

More footsteps. More than one person?

The tumble dryer started in her stomach again.

She froze, the bell still not pressed, as the footsteps stopped right at the other side of the door. The sound of a doorknob being turned. The door opened.

Lila felt like the ground was moving beneath her feet as she came face to face with her rival.

'Can I help you?' Bernadette asked.

'You're Kenneth Manson's wife,' she said. It wasn't a question. She'd seen her once in the hospital and she'd just spent half the afternoon watching her and her car boot pal lugging bags in and out of the house. She was still wearing the same clothes. Jeans. Boots. A shapeless black jumper. One of those waterfall cardigans that women used to cover the fact that they ate a pudding the night before. Even now, on a Friday night, she didn't have on a scrap of make-up.

Bernadette nodded. 'I am. Sorry, who are you?'

For the first time, Lila noticed a young guy standing behind Bernadette, obviously her son, given that there was an unmissable likeness. Next to him was a woman, tall, dark hair, around her own age, and for a moment Lila was thrown. Ken's eyes, his mouth. This must be Nina.

Oh, fuck, it was the whole family at once. There was a momentary urge to flee, but it was quickly overtaken by the realisation that this was actually a positive thing. Better that everyone found out at the same time – that it was all out in the open and everyone knew exactly where they stood.

Wasn't that what she'd wanted for seven long years? She inhaled, pulled back her shoulders, tried to project a confidence that she didn't quite feel, but as always, she wasn't going to let any fear or weakness show.

'I'm Lila Anderson.'

Blank looks.

'I know this will probably come as a shock…'

More blank looks. They genuinely had no idea who she was.

'… I'm Ken's girlfriend.'

10 p.m. – Midnight

29

Caro

'What's happening now? WHAT'S HAPPENING!' The words were the same as before, but this time Caro could hear that Todd was hyperventilating on the other end of the phone. However, no matter how hard she tried to make her vocal chords work, they were resisting all commands.

Holy shit.

Lila had bolted. One minute the boyfriend was down on one knee, and she was looking at him with what Caro could tell, even from this distance, was horror, and the next thing she got up and flew out of the restaurant. Her mother then jumped up and ran after her, while the boyfriend – that poor, poor guy – slid back up on to his seat and stared after them, jaw dropped, his expression one of almost tangible confusion and devastation. Ouch. That had to hurt.

There was a delayed reaction in the rest of the room, roughly half of the diners just stared at the door, and the other half did that thing people do in the face of someone else's complete mortification, where they tried to act like absolutely nothing had happened and went back to chatting, eating, perusing menus. Thankfully, the woman at the next table but one had taken that approach and was no longer frowning in her direction for using her phone in a high class establishment.

The mother was back in now, face aghast, hand over mouth, as she made her way back to the table.

'If you don't answer I'm calling the police, I swear.'

Todd. She'd forgotten about him. Putting the phone back to her mouth, she tried the vocal chords again.

'Oh the poor, poor guy. The boyfriend – who by the way, looks really sweet and is incredibly handsome – proposed to her, she said no, she made a run for it, the mother chased her, but now she's back without her and they're all sitting there looking like they've been hit by a bus. If that's my sister, she's completely bonkers.'

'Shut up!' he said, chiding her for joking. 'Tell me what really happened. Has she said yes yet? Why haven't I heard a round of applause?'

'Because I wasn't joking. The boyfriend proposed, she said no, she made a run for it,' she repeated.

There was a moment of silence as he processed this. 'I can't tell you how much I hope you're related to this lot because I need this kind of drama in my life. I love them already. It's like having your own *Lifetime* mini-series.'

'Todd!'

'Sorry. I mean, my heart's breaking for him, obviously!' he prattled, making it perfectly clear his heart wasn't broken in the least. Obviously.

Her eyes still hadn't left the other table. The boyfriend was sitting, looking utterly dazed, shaking his head every time Lila's mother spoke to him. She had her hand on his arm, but it didn't seem to be helping at all.

A man, Caro was sure he was the manager, had gone over to talk to him now, hand on shoulder, as if he knew him. They conversed for a few moments, before he headed off, back towards the kitchen area.

Seconds later, the boyfriend called the waiter over.

'Oh, crap, I think he's asking for the bill,' she hissed to Todd.

'Then you have to go over now. Right now!'

'I can't! That poor guy has just had his heart broken! I can't appear at the table, and accost his dining companion, and accuse him of being my father. There's only so much crap one table should have to deal with in one night.'

'Do you think it's him?' Todd asked.

Caro sighed. 'I have no idea. He's still got his back to me.'

'Look, you have to go over now. You won't have another chance at this.' Todd countered. 'If it's not him, you can just make some breezy claim of mistaken identity.'

'And if it is him?' Caro pressed.

'Then at least it'll take some of the heat off the poor bugger that just got jilted. You have to do it. You've got nothing to lose,' he said, repeating her thought from earlier.

He was right – but knowing that and acting on it were two separate things. Besides, after all the anxiety, she wasn't actually sure her legs would support her at the moment.

'I fricking hate it when you're right,' she groaned. 'Okay, I need to hang up – only five per cent battery now.'

'Don't hang up! Don't you dare hang…!'

She hung up.

Right then. This was it. Pushing herself up to a standing position, like a baby giraffe trying out its legs for the first time, she stood for a second, checking that she could carry her own weight.

She succeeded. Just.

With a cheesy smile to Mrs Stern Face at the next table but one, she made her way down the two steps to the lower area. There were two choices, go right, then walk up the aisle that led directly to the door. Or walk straight ahead, pivot right, and go past the row of diners sitting along the window, practically skimming the Anderson family's table. She chose the latter.

One Next sexy suede boot in front of the other. Left. Right. Past the French team, all of whom were surely having their conversations drowned out by the rave-thudding beat of her heart.

Left. Right.

Now a 90-degree right turn, walking parallel to the window. Past one table, then another. There were only ten feet separating them now, and she had direct eyeline on his side profile now. If this wasn't her father, then he was a twin, separated by birth. Or a clone. His hair was longer now, there was a bit of a designer stubble thing going on, but there was absolutely no doubt that if her dad committed a murder and this bloke was in a line-up, he would be packing for a long stretch at Her Majesty's pleasure.

The boyfriend and the mother were deep in conversation, but he was sitting back, unengaged, drinking from a champagne glass. That's when she knew. She'd seen that posture so many times over the years, that separation, the demeanour that reflected a lack of interest, a man that wasn't concerned with the lives of the people that were sharing his oxygen.

She stopped in front of them. As if he sensed her presence, he glanced up and their eyes locked.

It was him. No doubt at all. Daddy dearest. For a second, she wondered if he'd try to pretend he didn't know her, maybe make a run for it, but he did the last thing she expected. He closed his eyes, as if to block out the fact that she was there.

The mum and the boyfriend became aware of her and broke off from their conversation.

'Sorry to intrude...' she said, heart hammering. Hang on, why the hell was she apologising? At least he'd opened his eyes again. 'I'm...' She stopped, looked at him. The spineless, cheating, deserting fucker. She wanted to see him squirm, to make him as uncomfortable as he could possibly be. She tipped her head to one side, eyes challenging, hostile. 'Actually, would you like to introduce me?' she said, with a cold calm that in no way reflected what she was feeling inside.

There was a pause. Longer. Uncomfortable. Two sets of eyes staring at her, one staring straight ahead as if she didn't exist.

'You're Caro,' said a calm, clipped voice.

Caro's head spun to face the speaker. Lila's mum. 'You know?'

Her reply was delivered with an air of... what... resignation? Weariness? 'Yes, I know.'

'I don't,' said the boyfriend, clearly baffled, but staring at her, like he recognised her but couldn't quite place her.

'Please sit,' Louise said.

Now Caro's first instinct was to run. Actually, that wasn't true. Much as she didn't approve of violence, her first instinct was to slap her father as hard as humanly possible across the back of the head, and strut out of here, the way Lila had come in, dignity and class intact. She knew now. It was him. He was a lying, cheating prick. Did she really need to know anything else? Did she really need to sit down and give him an opportunity to explain or salvage his conscience?

All her apprehension had dissipated, replaced with a potent mix of confusion, curiosity, fury and feet that were hurting in new boots.

She sat down.

The gutless wonder finally spoke. 'Cammy, this is my other daughter, Caro.'

'But... but I thought Lila was an only child?'

Caro felt for him. Poor guy. Just when he thought that getting jilted was the most shocking thing that could happen to him tonight, he discovers his girlfriend has a secret sister.

'I'm sorry about... I saw what happened,' Caro said, momentarily suspending her rage to express sympathy. 'But trust me, if she's inherited this guy's talent for lies and deceit, you probably had a lucky escape.' She didn't mean it to sound as harsh as it did, but she felt she had to stress the point for his sake.

The burning sense of indignant rage kicked back in as she turned to Jack. 'At least you're acknowledging me as your daughter. I should be thrilled. I wasn't sure you'd remember,' Caro bit, through gritted teeth, disproving her lifelong theory that she didn't have much of a temper.

'You have every right to be angry,' Jack conceded.

'I know,' Caro countered. 'I'm just struggling to decide what to be most angry about. The fact that you must have lied to Mum for all those years? Or that you walked away from me and never looked back? That you left Mum when she needed you?' She felt Louise flinch at that one – it still seemed so unreal to her that Louise actually knew – but she went on... 'The fact that you care so little for us that you never write, never call? Or that you clearly chose another family? Or how about just the fact that you had another family at all?'

'You don't understand...'

'You're damn right I don't. Explain it to me,' she challenged, eyes blazing.

'And me,' Cammy added.

Caro noticed Louise press a button on her phone, and Lila's face popped up on screen, only for it to flick off again. She obviously wasn't answering. Wow. Even now, when it was pure chaos, Louise was still only thinking about Lila. No wonder her half-sister had a gargantuan sense of carefree entitlement.

'I was married when I met Louise,' Jack said, to Cammy.

'No,' Caro snapped. 'You don't get to explain it to him first. Explain it to me. You at least owe me that.'

Jack sighed, the way he'd done a million times in her childhood. This was so weird. He was the man she'd grown up calling 'Dad', but he was like a distant, more polished version, with a side-twist of disinterest and disdain. 'You're right. I do. I was married to your mum when I met Louise,' he said, repeating himself. 'Louise and I wanted to be together, but I loved your mum too. You were a baby, only a few months old. I didn't want to leave her, to leave you.'

This was actually happening. Her most outlandish speculations were coming to fruition. Her dad had another family. Holy. Fuck.

'So I'd spend a week or two in Glasgow every month...'

'Living with her?' she gestured to Louise. She knew she was being obnoxious, and that was entirely out of character, but anger on behalf of her mother was controlling her side of the conversation, and, whatever way it was dressed up, Louise was the 'other woman'.

'Yes, living with Louise...' he continued, 'and then a week or two in Aberdeen, and the rest of the time visiting sites. Always on the road. Then Louise fell pregnant with Lila and suddenly I had two women, two children... So I carried on splitting my time between them. Somewhere along the line, that pattern became the normality, and living with two families did too.'

Caro turned to Louise. 'And you were okay with this?' she asked, unable to fathom that any woman would accept an arrangement like this.

She shook her head. 'When I met him, he told me his relationship with your mum was over, that they'd split and he just stayed at your home in Aberdeen because he wanted to spend time with you.'

'So he lied to you too?'

She saw Cammy's head swivel to face Louise as they waited for an answer. 'He did. I found out later. Your dad had a heart scare – one of many he's had over the years – and your mum turned up at the hospital. That's when I realised they were still married.'

'So you met my mum?'

Louise shook her head. 'Not really. When I realised who she was, I made some excuse that I worked for the hospital and I was in checking the room and then I got out of there. I was crushed.'

'And yet, you forgave him?'

Louise nodded. 'In a way, the thought of losing him proved to me how much I loved him.'

It took a moment for Caro to process Louise's words. That was top-level delusion and gullibility right there. She couldn't shirk the suspicion that he'd played on the whole 'heart scare' stuff to emotionally manipulate these women. He didn't seem to be worried about his bloody heart now and if ever there was a chest-clutching shock, tonight had to be it.

'And in another way, I respected that he wanted to be in your life too,' Louise went on.

'I think that was the last thing on his mind...' Caro snapped, unable to control herself. 'He couldn't have been less interested in me.' She didn't care if it made her sound childish and petulant. This was home truths time.

Jack tried to interject. 'Caro, that's not true, I...'

Caro shut him right down. 'Don't you dare try to rewrite history, D—' She broke off, unable to address him as 'Dad'. He wasn't a father. He was nothing. 'You know, I honestly think all we were to you was somewhere to live when you were in Aberdeen. Did you ever love Mum? Ever care?'

'He did, Caro,' Louise stepped back in, and Caro realised that she was trying to play the peacemaker. She felt a stab of pain in her gut. Just like her mum had always done. Made excuses for him. Sanded off the edges of his failings. Minimised his disregard for his daughter. At first glance, it didn't seem that her mum and Louise were similar, but perhaps they had some things – as well as a husband – in common after all. So it would seem her dad had a type.

Leave. Stay. Leave. Stay. Caro was so furious that she was fighting with herself over what to do next. She knew all she needed to know. She'd got the truth that she'd come for. Sticking around was achieving nothing, and if she didn't go soon she was going to do something that would necessitate a call to Todd for that bail money.

She looked at the man who had contributed his sperm. 'Does your other daughter know?' It didn't seem right to call her Lila. Too intrusive. Too familiar. Like she knew her, instead of just sharing fifty per cent of their DNA and a Facebook habit. She couldn't foresee a time when she'd ever refer to her as her sister.

'No,' Jack admitted.

'So you've been lying to her too.'

'Look, it's not that simple. It's...'

Caro put her hand up. 'Do me a favour. If you knew me like most guys know their daughters, you'd know that I don't have a temper, I'm not prone to drama and I've never been violent in my life. But I swear if you say one more word, or try to make one more excuse for everything you've done, I won't be responsible for my actions. So don't speak. Don't breathe. Don't even look in my direction.'

'Caro, for God's sake...'

Caro kicked his chair so hard, it stunned him into silence, and attracted the attention of just about everybody at the nearby tables. They were certainly getting entertainment with their meals tonight. And bugger, her foot hurt.

Caro ignored his stunned expression and addressed Louise. 'You said when you met, you thought he was separated, but then you found out he wasn't.'

Louise nodded, embarrassed. 'When he recovered, he confessed everything...' Her gaze went to him and a look passed between them. Love? Forgiveness? Caro wanted to throw up. '… I decided I had two choices. Walk away. Or accept that he chose me and live the rest of our lives together, just being happy. It took me a while, but I chose *him*.'

Caro wanted to shake her. How could she? What kind of person accepts that kind of betrayal?

'So are you married?'

For the first time, Louise's face clouded. 'We had a ceremony on a beach in Bali when Lila was a little girl. That was good enough for us.'

So he wasn't technically a bigamist, and therefore he couldn't be jailed. Another wave of disappointment.

'And you knew he was coming home to us for all those years afterwards?'

'Caro, don't…' Jack tried to interject again and she shot him a death stare.

'Don't. Speak. Yet. Just. Don't.'

'I knew,' Louise admitted. 'But I made a choice to wait – and it took a long time, but it was worth it to me. He always promised that when he retired he'd move to Glasgow full time, and he did.'

Caro had to swallow the urge to vomit. So it wasn't even her mum's illness that had driven him away. He'd had it planned for years. Or maybe he just told Louise that, and he was hedging his bets the whole time. She wanted to kill him.

But first she had one question for him. 'So Louise

knew all about us. Did Mum know about your cosy little set-up down here?' Please say yes. Somehow it would make her feel better if Yvonne hadn't been the only person in this messed up triangle who didn't know what was going on, even if she'd chosen not to share it with her daughter.

'No.' Of course she didn't.

'You're a fucking coward,' Caro spat, making Louise jump to his defence again.

'Caro, please, it was complicated…'

'Did you know my mum is ill?' she spat, then watched Louise recoil.

'No, I didn't.'

Caro could see she was telling the truth because for the first time, there was an edge of uncertainty on her face. That had rattled her.

'Caro, don't…' Jack pleaded again.

'I said shut up!' she bit back, before resuming her conversation with Louise. 'My mum has early onset dementia. She was fifty years old when it started. It led to her being knocked down by a lorry. Right now she's in a hospital bed, where she's lain, in a coma, for months. She'll die soon.'

For the first time, her dad's expression changed to something that looked like genuine concern. 'Caro, I'm sorry…'

'You're not,' she shut him down, before resuming the conversation with Louise. 'That spineless prick that you chose walked away from her when she first got sick and never looked back. Changed his number. Broke off all contact. I'm sorry. You seem like a nice person, but he didn't choose you. You were just the better option because my mum couldn't do anything for him anymore. The minute she got sick, he came to you. That should tell you everything you need to know.'

Louise reeled like she'd been slapped, and it took her a moment to recover before she looked at him searchingly. 'Jack?'

A buzzing in her clutch distracted Caro and acted almost like an alarm, calling time on this whole scene. She'd heard enough. There was nothing to gain by prolonging the confrontation. She knew the truth, and while it hadn't exactly set her free, she could at least close the lid on the box.

'You know, Jack,' she said, as she stood up. He'd never been a dad to her and he certainly didn't deserve the title any more. 'I'm going to leave you to explain it all.' She turned back to Louise. 'Why though? Why did you let him treat you like that? Why did you share him?'

Louise hesitated, then said sadly. 'Because I love him. And when it came to a choice of having him some of the time or none of the time, I chose to take what happiness I could get.'

Caro felt the air leave her lungs as the urge to fight left her. What was the point?

'I can see you're as much of a victim in this as my mum, but now that you know the truth, I can promise you that any excuse he makes for himself is a lie, because what he did was indefensible. If you choose to believe him, you're a fool. And you,' she stared down the man she used to call her father, 'you are a duplicitous prick, who was never worthy of my mum. Or me. I hope you rot in hell.'

With that, Caro stood up, and pointed her new boots and rapidly bruising toes in the direction of the door.

It was only when the cold air hit her, did she realise her eyes were stinging. She blinked back the tears. She would not cry one tear over that man. Instead, she leaned back against the wall, closed her eyes, waiting for her cardiovascular system to kick in and allow her to breathe again. The buzzing started in her bag again and she ignored it. It would be Todd, hysterical and demanding an update. She couldn't trust herself to speak right now.

'The shop. You were in my shop today.'

Caro opened her eyes to see Cammy standing in front of her. She'd barely registered that he'd just sat through all of that, on top of his own nightmare night. Poor guy. Now, he wasn't angry, or accusing, he just seemed... concerned. Maybe curious. She cleared her throat, hoping the blockage would shift enough for her to speak.

'I was. I'm sorry about that. I was trying to meet Lila, to… actually I don't even know what I was trying to do. I suspected she was my sister and I thought if I saw her I'd know.'

'I think you would have known straight away,' he said. 'There's a definite resemblance.'

Caro laughed, and she hoped it didn't come out as bitter. 'Thank you, but I think I can safely say that I look nothing like Lila at all.'

Cammy was shaking his head as he looked at her, eyes full of sadness. 'When she doesn't have any make-up on, first thing in the morning, and her hair is tussled and wavy… I promise, there's a resemblance. I didn't spot it on the shop's camera footage, but I see it now.'

The buzzing started again and this time, Caro decided to answer it quickly, then get him off the phone.

'Todd, I…'

'Caro, it's Charge Nurse Sandra, on your mum's ward.'

Caro had heard the expression about blood running cold, but she'd never actually experienced it until that moment.

'I'm so sorry, but your mum's taken a turn for the worse. I think you should come in.'

No. No. No. This couldn't be happening. Not now. Not tonight. She looked at her watch and saw that it was 10.30 p.m. The last train was gone.

'But I'm in Glasgow. I'm going to have to wait for the first train. Will she make it through the night? Will she...'

'Caro, I don't know that she will. I'm so sorry.'

'Noooooooooo.' Caro's cry was guttural, seeped in pain. 'I'll get there as soon as I can. Somehow. I'll... I'll... I'll get a taxi. I'll be there. Please keep her alive just a few hours longer. Please,' she begged.

She hung up and immediately scanned the street.

'Are you OK?'

Fuck, she'd forgotten he was even there. 'I'm sorry, but I can't talk now. My mum... That was the hospital.' To her absolute mortification she felt tears start to flow down her face. 'I need to get back to Aberdeen right now.'

'I'll take you,' he said, instantly, making her stop and search his face for clues as to whether he was as crazy as that offer would suggest. 'I heard what you said. I'm cheaper than a taxi. I'll take you,' he repeated.

Caro tried to stem the tears with the palms of her hands. 'Are you sure? What about Lila? Don't you want to go find her?'

'No,' he said quite simply. 'I think I just got dumped, so it's fairly safe to say I don't have plans.' His expression suddenly changed. 'Fuck, I don't have a car either. Hang on.'

He dashed back inside the restaurant, then was back in seconds, brandishing a set of car keys. He pressed a button and the orange lights on a swanky big Range Rover across the street flashed on and off.

'Whose car is that?'

'Jack's.' Cammy hesitated. 'Is that going to be a problem?'

In her panic-stricken state, she started to ponder the question and then immediately came to a profound conclusion. Fuck it. Right now, she cared way too much about making it to the hospital to worry about how she got there.

'Nope, no problem. Thank you so much,' she said, as the two of them started running, Caro with a slight limp, across the road.

This was insane. Nuts. She'd come down here to find her sister and less than twenty four hours later that sister's jilted boyfriend was driving her home in her father's car.

As she jumped into the passenger seat, she sent a silent wish out into the messed up universe. *Hang on, Mum, please... just hang on until I get there.*

30

Cammy

Ten-forty. It had taken less than ten minutes for them to get out of the city centre and on to the motorway. Cammy mapped the journey out in his head. Stirling. Perth. Dundee. Aberdeen. If they were lucky and didn't hit any hold-ups, they should make it in a little over three hours.

Lucky.

Again, not an adjective that applied to him or the lady sitting next to him right now. The only consolation was that it seemed pathetic to mope about Lila when this woman, Caro, was dealing with so much more, and doing it with dignity and amazing strength.

His phone buzzed, but he ignored it.

'I hope you don't mind, but I just need to make a quick call,' she said, her voice tight, panicked, as she plugged her phone into the iPhone charging cradle on the dashboard. 'Sorry, battery is almost dead,' she explained as she dialled, putting the phone on speaker because the cable was too short for it to reach her ear.

Cammy heard a male voice answer before the first ring was even out. 'WHAT THE HELL HAPPENED?' he said, making Cammy flinch. Jesus, he sounded wound up and decidedly unhappy.

However, his reaction didn't seem to faze Caro, who spoke quickly and calmly. 'Todd, forget all that. The hospital called. Mum isn't great and they want me to come in.'

'Oh, God. Right. I'll come get you, it'll be quicker than waiting for the first train. I'll leave right now.'

'No, it's okay. I'm already on the way home.'

'How?'

'Lila's... er...' She glanced at Cammy and he sussed immediately that she didn't know how to refer to him.

'Ex,' he said, filling in the blank.

'Lila's *ex* is giving me a lift. In my dad's car.'

'Holy shit, how much did I miss?' the guy gasped, then immediately caught himself. 'Sorry! None of that matters a toss. Oh honey, I'm so sorry.'

'Me too,' she replied and Cammy heard the words catch on her grief as she said them. Her boyfriend (or was it husband?) sounded like he really cared, so at least she had someone at the other end to support her. He'd have done the same for Lila. It was both strange and sad that he was already thinking of her in the past tense.

His phone buzzed again. It went unanswered.

'I'll go straight there now and be with her. How long do you think you'll be?'

Caro looked at her watch. 'About three hours. But Todd, call me if… you know.'

'I will, m'darling. I love you.'

'Thanks, Todd. I love you too.'

She disconnected her phone and put her head back against the headrest, eyes squeezed shut as if she was trying really hard not to cry. After a moment or two, she opened them, more composed now.

Cammy felt such a rush of sympathy, it took him by surprise. Taking on other people's problems and woes wasn't his thing. Until now. Perhaps it was a diversion from his own debacle. Maybe it was just an instinctive human reaction. Or maybe it was just the fact that he was in awe that she was dealing with all this on her own, yet she was still holding it together. Whatever the reason, he felt an urge in his gut to help.

'Listen, I'm a bit useless at dealing with emotional stuff…'

'Me too,' she blurted, attempting to smile, despite the red-rimmed eyes and the exhausted pallor.

'I'm really sorry about your mum, though. And your dad. Jesus, that was a shocker – although, in hindsight, so much makes sense now.'

'In what way?' she asked.

'Och, just all stupid stuff. None of it matters. If you want to put your seat back and get some sleep, or just close your eyes and ignore me until we get to Aberdeen, I promise I won't be offended.'

She shook her head. 'I couldn't sleep, and if I just sit here, the time will drag by, so to be honest, I'd rather talk stupid stuff with you,' she said, before tagging on, 'No offence! Sorry, I've just realised how that sounded.'

'You're fine,' he laughed. 'I'm actually well known for my skill in talking absolute bollocks, so you're in good hands.'

That made her smile again. There was a natural lull in the conversation. 'Do you mind if I just give the hotel a call?' She asked.

'Of course not.'

She pressed redial on a number on her phone's call list. 'Good evening, this is the Hilton, Glasgow, how can I help you?'

Caro explained that she had a room, but wouldn't make it back tonight because she'd been called home on a family emergency. She asked them to collect her things and store them for her, then told them to charge the credit card they had on file. Only after the call was finished did she resume the conversation.

'So...' she began, 'what did you mean about things making sense?'

He thought about it for a moment. 'I guess there was just always something off about his relationship with Lila.'

That seemed to surprise her. 'But on her social media pages she was always going on about how wonderful he was and how much she loved him. I thought they were really close.'

Cammy kept his eyes on the road as he answered. 'There was a lot of stuff on Lila's Facebook that wasn't quite what it seemed. Sometimes I wondered if I was living with someone completely different. The stuff that went up there was the airbrushed version of her life, where everything was wonderful. Don't get me wrong – most of the time it was. But it didn't tell the whole truth. I always figured she needed to do it to fill a hole somewhere. Weird that I'm only realising that now....'

'Thought you were no good at the emotional stuff?' she said. 'That seems pretty perceptive to me.'

'Maybe I have hidden depths,' he joked. 'Or maybe, my pal Val, who is a kind of surrogate aunt, and one of the smartest people I know, told me that once and it stuck with me.'

'Sounds pretty smart to me,' Caro agreed.

'Yep. For what it's worth, Val and my other surrogate aunt, Josie, also told me not to propose to Lila because apparently she's completely wrong for me. I guess I should have listened. My bad.'

'Are you dreading telling them?'

'Nope. I'm focussing on the fact that after the first hundred or so "I told you so's", it'll make them so happy. Every cloud...'

His phone buzzed for the tenth time since they had got in the car.

'Is that who keeps texting you?' she asked.

'Yes,' he smiled. 'They'll be going out of their minds with nosiness. Josie threatened to storm the restaurant and smuggle me out earlier.'

'Look at all the fun you'd have missed,' Caro said, with sadness more than sarcasm.

Cammy nodded, before going back and picking up the other strand of the conversation. 'But anyway, her dad...' He thought about the best way to put it. 'I thought she always seemed like she was trying to get his attention. His approval, even. He never gave it. I've only known them for six months, and they don't seem close at all. In fact, I think there's a bit of her that resents the fact that he's hijacked her mum. Lila never actually said as much, but she did go on about how she and her mum spent all their time together before he moved back full time and now her mum is pretty much with her dad twenty-four seven. I think it bugged her.'

'I can see how that would be the case. It's weird, I've got such mixed feelings about her. I hope that's okay to say, given, you know... you were her boyfriend until half an hour ago.'

'It's fine. Really,' Cammy replied, surprised to realise that he meant it. A few hours ago, he was contemplating spending his life with her, yet now he knew with absolute certainty that it was over. And he was… fine. It was beyond surreal. Maybe he was in shock and would experience some kind of delayed reaction later, but he very much doubted it. Right now it felt like this was the first time he'd been thinking clearly in months.

Caro went on, 'I think in a lot of ways I was jealous. It seemed like she had everything… the carefree life, the loving parents, the brilliant job, the glamorous existence, the boyfriend…'

'Did you say incredibly handsome and smart boyfriend?' he asked, hoping it was okay to joke with her when she was right in the middle of such a terrible time.

'I did indeed,' she agreed. 'And humble. Very humble.'

'You're so right. Carry on.'

'Part of me, the part that was convinced she was my sister, was really envious that she seemed to skip through life having a blast, while I was dealing with my mum and all the crap caused by my dad leaving. It sounds pathetic now, but it just didn't seem fair.'

'No one's life is that perfect,' Cammy said, flicking on cruise control and letting the car take over now that the traffic had almost disappeared and it was pretty much a straight road past Stirling and on to Perth. 'I think she just became really good at putting on an act.

Certainly fooled me. I thought we were really happy and she wanted the same things I want. Eh, *wanted*,' he corrected himself.

She picked up on it. 'Maybe you shouldn't give up. Maybe she just got a shock, and bolted because she felt like she was put on the spot.'

'Trust me, Lila isn't the type of person to bolt when she's centre stage. She's more likely to take a bow and demand a standing ovation. If she loved me at all, she'd have said yes, and lapped up the congratulations and good wishes. The whole thing would have been on Facebook, Twitter, Instagram and Snapchat by now and she'd be fielding calls from shops offering her discounts on wedding dresses.'

Despite the harsh words, he hoped he didn't sound bitter, because he genuinely didn't feel it. It was beyond strange. There was no anger, no disbelief, no regret... just an overwhelming feeling that it wasn't right. Wouldn't have worked. Why the hell hadn't he had this feeling this morning and then he'd have had time to call the whole thing off?

'I was in love with someone else.' It was out before he even realised that he'd said it, and in his peripheral vision he could see that she was staring at him now, eyes wide with surprise. 'I think Lila wasn't the only one trying to fill a hole in her life. I think maybe I was too. Shit. Sorry. You're the first person I've admitted that to.' Oddly, it felt good to say it and what the hell, he had about two hundred miles to travel and then he'd never see this girl again.

'Another girlfriend? Don't tell me you were being unfaithful too. Oh for God's sake can no one just stick with one person and...' Her fury took him aback.

'No, no, no!' he blustered. 'I wasn't unfaithful, I was talking about someone I knew a long time before I met Lila.'

'Thank God, because otherwise I was getting out and hitching a lift on the next truck that passed this way. And when that happens on *Criminal Minds*, the female always ends up dead in a ditch.'

He laughed, thinking this was surreal. One of the worst nights of both their lives and they were still having moments of levity. He didn't understand it but he was going with it because otherwise it was going to be a long drive to Aberdeen.

'This is surreal,' she said, plucking the word right out of his mind.

'That's exactly what I was just thinking,' he agreed, realising the fact that they were both thinking the same thing at the same time made it even more surreal.

'So who were you in love with?' she went on.

The words almost got stuck in Cammy's throat. 'Her name is Mel. I worked with her for ten years, when she owned the shop that I own now. I loved her from the day I met her, but she was married. A few years later, she split from her husband, and I told her how I felt. There was something between us for about a minute; until she found out I'd been seeing her best mate. Her married best mate. Who was also her sister-in-law. Please don't try to jump out of the car. It was a long time ago. I've learned my lesson and, in my defence, it wasn't me who was being unfaithful.'

'I've got one hand on the door handle,' Caro replied, but her expression said she wasn't serious. 'Go on.'

'That's pretty much it. I blew it. Mel wanted nothing to do with me, so I upped and left and went to LA, Mel met someone else, married him and they're really happy, living abroad. Oh, and in this world of imperfect lives, they're the only ones living in a little bubble of perfection. Did I sound bitter there?'

'A little,' she said, holding her thumb and index finger about an inch apart, in front of her tear-stained face.

'Thought so. Probably because I am. I can't help myself,' he said, with a rueful grin. 'Anyway, in L.A., I thought for a moment that I had fallen in love with my best friend, Stacey. She's lovely, but that didn't come to anything. Then I came back about six months ago and the rest is history...'

'That's how long you've known Lila?' she asked, surprised. 'It's just, with the engagement, I figured you two had been together a long time.'

'Nope, it was a bit of a spontaneous thing. I thought Lila really wanted to get married so I decided to make it happen. And also she just seemed so happy and gorgeous, and the complete opposite of Mel in so many ways... not that Mel wasn't happy and gorgeous because she was! But Mel hated being the centre of attention, she was all about heart and friends and she was the most content and truly decent person I've ever met. Maybe I just thought Lila was so larger than life that she would block Mel out of my head.'

'And did she?'

'No. She's all I've thought about all day today, even when I was picking up the ring, planning the dinner, choosing a suit... all day. It's not because I want her back, because that ship has sailed, it's just because I think I knew that was how I should be feeling about Lila. Val and Josie knew it too. That's why they didn't want me to marry Lila. Well, that and the fact that they thought she was a "vain, self-centred, humourless, cold pain in the arse who never thought about anyone but herself". That's a direct quote from Josie. I argued every time anyone criticised her because I was sure I was in love with her but I guess the fact that I'm not destroyed that she said "no" proves something.'

'Maybe you'll have a delayed reaction.'

'I don't think so. I think I just feel... relief. See, this is why I began this conversation with an admission that I'm bollocks at emotional stuff.'

'You're getting no argument from me. You really are abysmal,' she said, making him smile again. 'Why do you think she didn't say "yes"?' she asked.

He shrugged. 'I have no idea. Maybe she knew it wasn't right too. Maybe she didn't love me to start with. She said she did, but we've already ascertained that she's great at creating illusions. The strange thing is, she'd cooled off in the last few weeks and I thought it was because she wanted me to make a commitment. I obviously had that all completely wrong too. I shouldn't be allowed to make any relationship decisions or assumptions without the presence of a professional.'

That thought should sting, shouldn't it? Yet, it didn't. Josie and Val would have a field day with all this stuff. They'd be analysing him until the end of time.

Her phone rang then, halting the baring of his soul, and she answered it immediately, again she flicked it on to speaker because the device was still in the charging cradle.

'Babe, I'm here, and...' The guy's voice again. What was his name? Tom?

'Todd, is she...' She stopped, and Cammy could see she was unable to say it.

'No, no, she's still with us, but the nurses think...' He broke off.

'She doesn't have long?' Caro finished the sentence.

'I don't think so, sweetheart.'

Caro's features crumpled and, instinctively, Cammy put his hand on hers. Anyone else would have done the same. Just a human gesture, one person trying to comfort another.

'Ask her to hold on for me, Todd. Tell her I'm coming. Tell her to wait. Please. She'll hear you.'

'I will, Caro. I'll tell her.'

She disconnected again, then didn't say anything for several miles. When she did the sorrow was almost tangible. 'I knew this was going to happen. Sometimes I actually hoped it would happen soon because it was no way for her to live, so I should be prepared for this, yet I'm not.'

Cammy searched for the right thing to say. 'I don't think anyone ever could be. Are you okay?' Stupid question. Of course she wasn't.

She paused until more words came. 'She would hate living like that,' Caro went on. 'She was funny and loved a party and was so full of life... so much more so when my dad was home. In a way I understand what Lila has been feeling, because I grew up with that too. I do think Mum loved me, but there was no doubt that her sun only rose to full height when he was home. She worshipped him. And when he was gone it was like the temperature dropped a few notches, like nothing else was quite enough. Of course, I didn't realise it at the time.'

'I find that whole scenario – the two families thing – impossible to get my head around,' Cammy admitted.

'Me too, in a way, but in other ways, not so much. He was never much of a dad to me. I think that's why it hurt so much that I thought he and Lila were really close. It makes me a terrible person but I'm glad that wasn't true. I think that would have been too tough to handle and would have ended up costing me a fortune in therapy. At least he was an equal-opportunities inadequate lying scumbag.'

'And it hasn't put you off relationships,' he said, looking for the silver lining. 'Your husband seems like a really nice guy and he sounds like he really cares about you.'

'I'm not... Oh, you mean Todd?'

'The guy you were speaking to.'

A smile. 'Todd's my cousin. More like a brother really. We grew up together and he loves mum just as much as me. We stick together, have done since we were kids. He's very happily engaged to a Canadian hairdresser called Jared. Madly in love. Gives me hope.'

'I could probably do with some of that. Ouch – how pathetic did that sound?'

'That was right up at the top level of "pathetic",' she concurred. 'Are you still hoping things will work out with Lila?'

A faint smile. 'No. Not to sound clichéd, but I can already see that she's done me a favour. Whatever her reasons, whatever is going on, I think it's probably worked out the way that it should have.'

His voice tailed off into comfortable silence, leaving her to stare out of the window, watching the Dundee landscape go by.

Cammy reckoned they were about halfway now. It was almost midnight, he'd had barely any sleep last night, then today had been the most stressful day in memory, he'd been driving for an hour and a half, his life was in tatters, and... shit... he'd just realised that he'd have to move out of Lila's flat, so he was now homeless too. Not up there with the more successful days of his life, but nothing was broken, nothing irreplaceable had been lost, this wasn't going to leave him in a dark room for months waiting for the pain to subside.

It was unexpected, but even if he prodded his heart for signs of pain, he'd only be able to register a faint ache, and only then because he was a bit mortified that he'd got it so wrong.

The ring of Caro's phone shattered the easy, comfortable silence.

'Caro...'

Todd again, and this time there was something in his voice, an extra layer of sadness. Caro heard it too.

'Is she gone?' she asked fearfully.

'No, but the nurses think it's only a matter of minutes. I don't think you're going to make it, sweetheart,' he said, his tone thick with care and compassion. 'What shall I do?'

'Are you next to her bed?' He could see her face had drained of colour and her eyes were brimming with tears.

'Of course,' he answered.

'Then put me on loudspeaker.'

They heard a click, then a change in the acoustics. When Todd spoke again, he sounded fainter, further away and there was an audible, steady slow beep in the background.

'Okay my love, the phone is next to her ear. She can hear you,' he told her.

A few seconds passed before she spoke. Cammy wasn't sure what to do. Pull over and respect the moment, or carry on driving, hoping that he could get her there? He put his foot down. If there was even a slim chance, he wasn't giving up.

'Mum, it's Caro. I'm so sorry I'm not there. I told you to hang on and wait until I got back and now I'm not going to get to you in time...' A sad laugh. 'I'm thinking maybe you did that deliberately. You never did like to make a fuss. I'm so sad I'm not there with you though, Mum. My whole life you've been there for me and I want you to know I'm so grateful. I love you Mum. I love you so much and I know how much you loved me. I know, Mum.' Her voice broke and, once again, Cammy put his hand on hers and she squeezed it, before carrying on. 'Every time I think of you, I'll see you smiling, in the garden. That's how I'll remember you. Todd's with you now, Mum, and he's going to stay with you until I get there. If you can hang on, please wait for me, but if you can't... Know I love you. And

Mum, I just saw Dad… he wanted me to tell you that he loves you too. He's sorry he's not there with you. He really is, Mum. He loved you so much and he wanted me to tell you that he always will. So Mum…'

She didn't get any further.

The faint, regular beeping sound in the background turned to one long steady tone.

'Caro, she's gone,' Todd said, choking on the words. 'I'm so sorry. She's gone.'

'I know,' she whispered. 'I'll be there soon. Stay with her?'

'You don't have to ask. I'll be here,' Todd promised.

There was a layby a few yards ahead, and Cammy swerved straight into it, pushing the brake pedal at the same time. He pulled to a stop, leaned over and wrapped her in his arms and let her sob, just for a few moments, until her shoulders stopped shaking and she sat up.

'Thank you,' she said. 'That doesn't seem anywhere even close to adequate for what you've done for me tonight, but I want you to know I'm so grateful. I'll never forget how kind you've been.'

Cammy's only thought was admiration for her strength and selflessness. 'I'm glad I was here.' It was an odd thing to say, but it was so true. A few hours ago, he didn't know this woman at all, and yet now he couldn't bear the thought of her having to deal with this in a stranger's taxi or in the cold, lonely carriage of a train. 'Let's get you home,' he said, gently, releasing her.

He put the car into gear, pulled out of the layby, and drove, his hand still on hers. It stayed there for the next hundred miles, as Caro talked about her mum and Cammy listened, glad he was there for her. There was nowhere else he would rather be.

31

Bernadette

Bernadette was sure she'd heard wrong.

'Sorry, dear – you're what?'

'I'm Ken's girlfriend.'

'Ken who?' Bernadette had a horrible feeling that she was on one of those game shows where everyone was shouting the answer but she was the hapless contestant whose mind had just gone completely blank.

'This has to be a wind-up,' Stuart said, taking the words right out of her mouth.

One of those prank hidden camera shows, maybe? Dear Lord, not tonight. Not when she was almost out of the damned door and freedom was so, so close.

Well, she wasn't going to get caught on one of those cameras being rude to a stranger. If the girl was deranged and deluded, then she wasn't going to turn her back and refuse to help. Nor was she going to let a girl in a barely there, strappy dress die of hypothermia on her doorstep. For God's sake, had she never heard of a coat?

Her professional training kicked in and she stepped back from the door, forcing Stuart and an absolutely dumbstruck Nina to edge backwards too. This hall had never been so crowded. 'Come in before frostbite sets in.'

The woman – probably about the same age as Nina – looked at her warily.

Bernadette's detachment, undoubtedly the result of thirty years dealing with chaos and unexpected shocks in A & E, continued to take charge of proceedings. 'I'm not going to bite. Clearly there's a reason you're here and it's not going to help if you faint from the cold before you can share it with us, is it?'

That did it. Shivering, the blonde visitor took two steps into the hall, allowing Bernadette to take one of Kenneth's cardigans off the coat hooks behind the door and wrap it around her shoulders. The woman – what did she say her name was? – didn't resist.

'Right, I'm less worried about you collapsing now. Tell me again why you're…'

'Lila?'

Kenneth's voice came from behind her, in the kitchen doorway, sounding about as shocked as she'd ever heard him.

'What the hell are you doing here?'

Oh he didn't sound pleased. Was it wrong that there was something comforting in the fact that she wouldn't be the one who would have to deal with him like this anymore?

'Dad, this woman claims she's your girlfriend. I'm sure there's a really good reason for this and I can't wait to hear it.' Kenneth's fury might just be matched by the quieter, but every bit as forceful anger in Nina's voice.

Bernadette snuck a glance at the incongruous sight before her, still shivering, despite the heat of the Fair Isle cardigan her mother had bought Kenneth for Christmas two years ago. He had moaned that the one she'd bought him the year before had brought his neck out in a rash, and when she'd heard this, she bought him another one exactly the same. In hindsight, Bernadette could see that this was her mother making a mischievous point, but at the time she'd thought it was just a coincidence.

Anyway, back to the new arrival. Fair play to her, she wasn't shrinking back from Kenneth's outrage. And my word, she was beautiful. Absolutely stunning. Like one of those pageant queens that want to save the world and cure disease and famine in a bikini.

Kenneth didn't answer Nina's question, instead directing his words squarely at... at... Lila. Yep, that was her name. Lila.

'What the hell are you thinking? Why? Why would you come here?'

Rage. Disbelief. Exasperation. Irritation. Frustration. It was all there in every vowel and consonant.

'Because I can't let her do this to you anymore. Ken, I know you didn't want me to do this, but it's time you put yourself first. You can't keep putting their happiness before your own.'

Bernadette was fairly sure that she, Nina, and Stuart were now sporting absolutely identical expressions of astonishment.

Then, the strangest thing. She heard laughter. Belly-aching, contagious, absolutely uncontrollable laughter. It took a moment for her to realise that it was coming from her and everyone's gaze of disbelief was now focussed in her direction.

'Oh come on – him put our happiness first,' she spluttered through the giggles, as she wiped away tears of mirth. It must be the stress of the day. It had all bottled up and now it was coming out as pure hysteria. This was why people laughed at funerals. Same thing.

'Mum, I think…'

Bernadette was folded over now, holding on to her sides. She put her hand up. 'No, no I'm fine. Let Lila speak. I can't wait…' she dissolved into giggles again.

'Jesus Christ, Bernadette!' Kenneth raged.

That set her off again.

'I think we're going to have to have her sedated,' Stuart said.

Bernadette's hand flew up again. 'No, no, I'm fine.' She said again, clearing her throat. 'All good. Under control.'

The others eyed her sceptically, but she held it together. This was outrageous. Unbelievable.

'Let Lila speak,' she repeated, meeting the other woman's horrified stare. That was almost enough to set her off again, but she managed to summon every ounce of discipline she possessed to keep a straight face.

Kenneth took the opportunity to have another rant. 'I'm not standing here, listening to…'

'Shut up, Kenneth!' Again Bernadette heard the sound, then realised a split second later that it had come from her. Well, well, well. It had taken thirty years but she had finally found the balls to shut him down. Somewhere inside her, her ego was doing a celebratory conga. 'You're his girlfriend,' Bernadette said, like a police officer repeating the facts to a witness. 'For how long?'

'Bernadette!'

'Kenneth, shut up. The lady is speaking. Go on dear.'

Lila paused, as if this wasn't playing out the way she expected and she was unsure as to how to proceed.

Eventually, she found her voice, and – all credit to her, Bernadette thought – there was still an edge of courage and defiance in there.

'Seven years.'

'Holy fuck.' Nina this time. 'You've been shagging my dad for seven years?'

'It's not just shagging. I've *loved* him for seven years. He loves me too.'

'For Christ's sake.' That was Kenneth.

'And he wants to be with me, but he didn't think you could cope on your own, so he's stayed with you, all these years, sacrificing his own happiness. I can't let him do it anymore. We want to be together.'

She was welling up now and Bernadette felt a twinge of sympathy for her, swiftly followed by an avalanche of rage at Kenneth.

'You bastard,' she said, swearing in front of the kids for the first time in her life. If they were scarred by it, she'd arrange the therapy. 'All these years you were shagging this poor woman and feeding her a whole lot of lies?'

'He never lied to me!' Lila protested.

'Oh. love, you have no idea.'

'Ken, tell them!' Lila wailed.

Bernadette could see that she was getting upset now. Kenneth had really done a number on her, yet Bernadette didn't quite understand it. Her husband's mistress – for she absolutely believed her – was young, and stunning, and clearly adored him, yet he'd stayed with her all these years in a loveless marriage. Why? Did it really all come down to the fact that he enjoyed the control so much that he wouldn't let it go?

'Yep, tell us, Dad,' Nina prompted, her gaze deadly.

It was no use – he stood there, stony-faced, refusing to be drawn in to it.

'Tell them you love me,' Lila demanded, and Bernadette had a flashback to when the kids were small and throwing a tantrum in the supermarket because they weren't getting what they wanted.

'For Christ's sake, Lila, of course I don't love you. That's not what this ever was. It was danger, a bit of excitement. Did you really think I was going to divorce my wife and show up at hospital dinners with a young blonde, looking like the poster boy for a midlife bloody crisis? I'd have been a bloody laughing stock.'

That was Bernadette's answer right there. It was vanity. While some might think that having a beautiful young trophy wife was an ego boost, Kenneth wasn't cut from that cloth. His mother, the old crone, hadn't believed in divorce and she'd drummed into him the importance of reputation and perception. Thus, he ate in the right restaurants. Courted the right alliances. There was absolutely no way that he would allow his career, his reputation or his standing in the community to be tainted by a scandalous affair or by people pointing fingers and perceiving him as a silly old fool with a hot bit of stuff on his arm. This was all about him. His vanity. His pride. His narcissism.

She had never hated him more.

Her thoughts were halted by a whimper from Lila, who was staring at him, eyes blazing, enraged by his words.

'You don't mean that! Is that why you like me to tell you what underwear I'm wearing every day? Is that why you fucked me at the hotel this afternoon? Is that why you let me suck your dick on your desk before surgery?'

'Eeeeeew!' Stuart and Nina reacted in perfect sync.

Bernadette realised it was time to intervene.

'Lila!' she exclaimed, loud enough to shock her to her senses. As soon as she was mute, Bernadette continued, using years of training in de-escalation and handling hysteria. 'I can see he's hurt you, and trust me I know what he's capable of, so here's what I'm going to do.'

Lila was looking at her now, and Bernadette could see she was close to unravelling. Poor woman. If anyone did this to her Nina she'd have their balls for it.

'I'm going to tell you where all this stands right now and then I'm going to leave you to it.'

Lila's face was shadowed by wariness.

'I haven't loved him for longer than I can remember. He's an arrogant, controlling, vile specimen of a man... sorry kids, but it's true... And I wouldn't wish him on anyone. Every night since my children here were small, I've gone to bed and prayed he wouldn't be there when I woke up. He always was. He could have left me at any point. Nina and Stuart have been out of the house for a long time, ten years in Nina's case, and yet, still Kenneth is here. That should tell you something about his intentions. As for me, I've finally had enough. I told him tonight I was leaving him and I am. When I walk out of that door it will be for the last time, and I'm never, ever, coming back because he's a despicable human being. What you decide to do with that information is up to you. I can't think why any woman would want him because, trust me, what you see is not what you get. It sounds like he's been mistreating you and lying to you for years, and I promise you that will continue. He cares nothing about anyone but himself. He won't give you a shred of tenderness or care. And it'll be no time at all until you're lying there, same way as I have, praying that you were with anyone but him. That said, if you ignore everything I've told you, and pursue him anyway, then hell mend you, you were warned. The moment I walk out of here will be one of the happiest of my life. And by the way, when I told him tonight that I was leaving, he begged me – absolutely begged me – to stay with him. I've been with the man for thirty years and I know every bit of him. If you're arrogant enough to think you can change him, then...' She looked at Lila, looked at Kenneth, '... then you two deserve each other. I've got nothing else to say. Goodnight. Kenneth, you lying, cheating bastard. Have a good life.'

With that, Bernadette Manson strutted out of her old life, with her children behind her and her dignity, self-esteem and sheer bloody zest for life restored.

And as she'd promised herself every time she'd thought about this moment, she didn't look back.

32

Lila

'You bitch.'

Lila stared at him, horrified, stunned into silence.

'You absolute bitch,' he repeated, just in case she hadn't quite caught him the first time.

An unstoppable wave of nausea rose from her twisted gut, and she buckled over and vomited right there on his hall carpet.

If she thought his sneer couldn't be any more venomous, she was wrong.

'What the fuck…?'

His clenched fists told her that he was fighting to control his temper, as he turned on his heel and stormed back into the room behind him. Lila followed him and when she got there she saw that it was the kitchen and

Ken, her Ken, the love of her life, was now pacing up and down.

He rounded on her. 'What the fuck were you thinking?'

Lila was on a different wavelength altogether. There was no way his boot of a wife was telling the truth. No way. Was there?

'You begged her to stay? She was leaving you and you begged her to stay?'

'Of course I did. Didn't you hear everything I just said?'

'You couldn't have meant that.'

Full-scale, epic level self-preservation and denial kicked in. She'd heard. Of course she had. But those weren't the words of her Ken. Her Ken loved her. He wanted to be with her. Surely he'd just been saying all that to placate his daughter and son, to try to salvage his relationship with them by convincing them that he really wanted to stay with their mother. Well, it didn't work. She was gone. Finally, his wife had got the message. And now he was going to fold Lila into his arms, tell her that he hadn't meant any of it, that he loved her, that of course he wanted to be with her, and that now their time had finally come. This was it. A tiny white flag of triumph raised itself above the parapet...

'Of course I bloody meant it.'

It wasn't triumph. It was surrender. Game over. Battle lost.

All her life, her mother had waited for a man and she'd got him. Lila was so sure that the same would happen to her. He'd be worth the wait. The end would justify the means. What was meant to be would be.

Until it wasn't.

However, she had to check one more time that she wasn't getting the fairy tale ending she'd been dreaming of since the first time he kissed her. 'You don't love me? Because I can forget everything you said out there. I know you were just trying to save face. This could be our time Ken. We could be together, share our lives, make love every day, build a new future together. This is the chance to have everything we've ever talked about…'

'*You've* talked about!'

'No! Don't you dare say this was all me. You were every bit as desperate to be with me as I was with you!' Even as she said it she knew, somewhere deep inside, that it wasn't true. How many times over the years had he called it off. How many times had it been her who'd engineered a 'chance' meeting to rekindle their relationship. The reality of everything that had happened today was sinking in, seeping into her pores, and the nausea was back. She forced it down. There was no way she was giving into it a second time. 'You didn't answer my question,' she said, like a puppy, waiting to be kicked again. 'You don't love me?'

He stopped pacing, ran his fingers through his hair, his exasperation bubbling like lava in a volcano that was just about to blow. 'Of course I don't fucking love you,' he said through gritted teeth.

Lila knew then, actually believed it. He didn't. It was over. She'd wasted seven years of her life on a man for whom she'd always been just a shag.

How could she have been so stupid? She retreated out of the kitchen, taking several steps before she felt able to turn her back on him. In every sense.

Stepping over the pool of vomit on the hall carpet, she paused, before a fit of petulance compelled her to drop his cardigan on top of it, and followed the path taken by Bernadette only minutes before.

By the time she got to the car, the shaking had started.

What had she done? She'd lost Ken. She'd lost Cammy. She was on the verge of losing her job. She'd lost everything. Everything!

Why hadn't this worked out for her? It was so tragically unfair. Hadn't she done everything he wanted, moulded herself into his perfect woman and still he didn't want her? How could that be? How could he live with that... that... *frump* for all these years and then not choose to be with Lila?

None of this made sense. She wanted to scream. And then she wanted to go back in there and persuade him to change his mind, but she wouldn't. If he didn't appreciate her worth, that was his problem. She wasn't going to beg. He'd regret it tomorrow. He'd wake up and grasp what he'd done and he'd want her back, she knew it.

But in the meantime...

She realised, to her complete devastation, that she didn't know where to go. She couldn't go back to the flat because she couldn't face Cammy. How could Cammy have done this to her? How could he have been so deluded that he actually thought she might say yes? Hadn't he noticed that she'd been off with him for weeks, that whatever they had was fizzling out? What a fool. No, the flat was definitely out.

She couldn't go to her mum and dad's house either, because no doubt she'd be interrupting them and lately she'd been feeling decidedly unwelcome when she landed on them without warning. Besides, they were probably furious with her for running out of the restaurant and then rejecting at least a dozen calls from her mum. And she was still absolutely seething with them for failing to warn her about Cammy's plan to propose. Traitors.

She had nowhere to go. She pressed the ignition button and started driving, heading back into the city. The first building she saw was the Hilton, where she'd changed earlier, a place of familiarity. It was all she needed.

She veered off the motorway, onto the street that took her up the ramp to reception, then stopped, grabbed her handbag, laptop, phone, and her ever-ready toiletries, before she jumped out and handed the keys to the concierge to park the car.

The doorman gave her a smile of recognition. She was a regular here. Everyone knew her, at least by sight, so she was always treated with the respect she deserved. Even the receptionist went out of his way for her.

'I'd like a room for tonight please?'

He checked the screen. 'I'm afraid we're full...'

She was a split second away from going full-scale diva-strop, when he quickly remedied the situation.

'... But we've just had a phone call from a guest to say they've been called away and asking us to check her out, so if you don't mind waiting...' he checked his watch, 'maybe half an hour, we'll get the room turned around and ready for you. Perhaps you could have a drink in the bar?'

She'd heard worse ideas. Picking up her phone, her laptop case and her bag, she crossed the lobby, aware as always that she was gathering admiring glances from at least half of the guests enjoying a late night chat or drink. Not an attractive one among them.

In the bar, she ordered a glass of champagne, then parked herself at a corner table and opened her laptop. She was immediately assaulted by a succession of high-pitched pings, and watched, uncomprehending, as the notifications flashed up on her Facebook and Twitter accounts.

What the hell was going on?

She ran her eye down the list.

'Lila, is that you in this clip?'

'Damn, she whipped his ass.'

'That has to be @LoveLila – would recognise those tits anywhere.'

'OMG, his face though!!!!!'

What the…? She clicked through to the post they were referring to and her heart felt like it had actually stopped.

The setting, even on the still frame at the beginning of the video, was instantly recognisable. Grilled.

There was Cammy. Her mum. Her dad. Her.

With a shaking finger, she pressed play.

Whoever had taken the footage had obviously been nearby, perhaps at the next table, and had been mighty swift when Cammy got down on one knee, because there he was, holding that pathetic ring up, all bloody misty eyes and hopeful.

Her toes curled so tight her Louboutins began to pinch.

'Lila, I love you – and I want to love you every day of our lives…' Oh, crap, there was sound too. This was a nightmare. A nightmare. The most humiliating moment of her life and it was caught on film.

She watched as the Lila on the video looked at the ring, at him, back at the ring, then him, clearly in shock.

'Lila, will you marry me?' he said.

The nausea threatened to rise once again. The horror. The sheer mortification. How could she not have known he was planning that?

'No... I can't... I...' Lila-on-video didn't finish the sentence. Instead, she grabbed her bag, jumped to her feet and rushed to the door.

This was awful. For years her life had been played out on social media and she'd relished every like, share, and comment, but not this. This was her worst moment, out there for the whole world to see. She wanted to die. She actually wanted to die. Until she played it again and realised that, embarrassment aside, she looked pretty hot. Scrap that, she looked sensational. That dress was definitely the right choice, and when she'd ran out of the restaurant, the back view... well, those endless squats at the gym had definitely paid off.

It might be a moment of mortification but at least she looked incredible. If she didn't get a free Cavalli dress out of this she'd be furious.

So anyway, silver lining, she was gorgeous.

The figure below the video drew her attention then, and she realised that there was another silver lining.

One hundred and six thousand views and increasing

by the second. Holy shit. One hundred and six thousand people had watched her video. One hundred and six thousand! Now, one hundred and seven thousand. And climbing rapidly.

'*Elle est magnifique.*'

'*Man, I so would.*'

'*Mignonette!*'

'*Well, fuck me sideways (that is actually a request – call me).*'

'*J'aurais eu le sexe avec elle toute la nuit.*'

Lila wasn't one hundred per cent sure of the literal translations of the French comments but she got the gist. They loved her. Thought she was gorgeous. Wanted to make love to her. She felt her breasts swell and butterflies of sheer glee push every negative emotion out of the way. A bolt of realisation. The name of the person who had posted the clip was French. Jean Pascal. She quickly googled him. Twenty-seven years old. French team captain. Single. Gorgeous. Played for Paris St Germain. National hero. He was a modern day, Gallic equivalent of David Beckham and as soon as she saw his face she recognised him. He was the most gorgeous of them, the one she'd spoken to first, when she asked him to take a selfie with her. No wonder the thing had gone viral. He had over half a million followers, and many of them, it seemed, now adored her.

One hundred and eight thousand views now.

This was unbelievable! Incredible.

The champagne arrived and she knocked half of it back in one go.

More pings, and this time she saw that her Facebook personal messages were in treble figures, as were the DMs on her Twitter feed.

She scrolled through them, and saw that – be still her heart – there were messages from at least half a dozen newspapers, magazines, and media blogs, and the video had only been up for an hour and a half. Hang on, one of them was saying that he was... he was... she had to stop herself from punching the air. A producer on *This Morning*! He wanted to talk to her. Aaaaaaaaaagh, she was going to be on a sofa with Holly and Phil!

She scrolled down some more, when another name caught her eye.

Jean Pascal.

With a shaking Shellac nail, she opened it.

Je te veux. Nous devrions parler, non?

She quickly plugged the sentence into Google translate.

I want you. We should talk, no?

Oh yes. Oh yes, yes, yes.

Ken Manson could piss right off. Clearly she didn't need him.

Being the wife of an eminent heart surgeon had been her dream for so long. But you know what topped that?

Being the wife of an international football star, especially one who looked like Jean Pascal.

She clicked reply, then typed in the phrase she'd just acquired courtesy of Google translate.

Ne fais que parler?

Only talk?

A minute past midnight

33

Just a person. Lying on a bed. In a hospital room. Breathing.

There was no time to say goodbye. No time for regrets or recriminations. No time to wait until the loved ones had gathered by the bed to bid them farewell.

They didn't know that somewhere out there a heart had just been crushed by the weight of broken promises. Or that someone else sighed with relief as they walked away from the past. Or that someone's plans for a new life had turned to dust. Or that a very unexpected love was pulling two hearts together.

They didn't know that the person they loved most in the world wouldn't make it in time. Maybe wouldn't make it at all.

They didn't know that a love had died, that when it came right down to it, the only love that mattered was the one that endured, that stuck, that was meant to be.

Just a person. Lying on a bed. In a hospital room. Breathing.

Just a heart beating.

And then it stopped.

Yvonne Anderson, Caro's mum, was gone with the words of her daughter echoing across the void...

Know I love you.

Nine Days Later –
New Year's Eve

Epilogue – Part 1

Caro and Cammy

'How do I look?' Todd asked, jutting his jaw forward and putting his hands on the hips of his sharp suit, in a superhero pose.

Caro descended into giggles. 'Clark Kent right after he realised he was gay and got a great wardrobe,' she replied.

'My work here is done,' Jared said, laughing.

She needed this. At first, she'd thought it was a terrible idea, returning to the city her dad lived in, so soon after her mum had passed. There was still perhaps a one per cent chance that her recent trauma would cause a psychological break that would set her off on a violent hunt for him, ending only when she'd tracked him down again, and removed his heart with her bare hands. Or perhaps that thought was only there because she, Todd and Jared had got through most of the last week and a half by binge-watching four seasons of *Criminal Minds*. That could plant seriously twisted seeds in a person's psyche. Now, though, she was glad she came.

Besides, coming here had killed two birds with one stone. No, that wasn't another *Criminal Minds* reference. It had given them a change of scenery and she'd been able to pick up the stuff that the Hilton had kept in storage for her.

'So I'll go on down to meet him. I'll only be half an hour or so, then we can go for dinner.'

'No problem. Just give us a shout when you're ready. We'll be here,' Todd replied, hugging her.

'You always are,' she murmured, gratefully. He'd been incredible over the last week. Strong. Steady. Always ready to laugh or cry, whatever the moment required. She knew how lucky she was to have Todd and Jared in her life.

The lift down to the lobby seemed to take an age, or maybe it was just that she was keen to get there and thank the other guy who'd been great this week. Since he'd dropped her at the hospital, making sure Todd met them at the door, Cammy had called her every day, just checking in, asking how she was. She appreciated it. Lila was a crazy woman to have walked away from a guy like that.

As soon as the lift doors opened, she spotted him.

Cammy stood up to greet her, arms outstretched and she realised she was ridiculously pleased to see him.

'Hey, you made it,' he said.

'Hey, you have a top on,' she retorted. Teasing him about all those topless photos Lila used to post had become one of the mainstays of their conversations.

'Wow. Bitchy. Sarcastic. I love her already.'

Caro's head swivelled to the two ladies sitting across the coffee table from where Cammy had been perched.

Now he was sighing, but Caro could see it came from a place of affection. 'Caro, this is Josie...' he gestured to a woman in perhaps her sixties, with a shock of grey, spiky hair, dressed in a black polo neck sweater, black tailored trousers and high leather boots with a steel-spiked heel. She looked ferocious. 'And this is Val.' Val was younger than Josie, her blonde hair piled high on her head in an elaborate beehive affair, her make-up perfect, her grin wide and welcoming. Cammy went on, 'I'm sorry, they made me bring them. I had no choice. You've no idea what they're like.'

For a moment Caro wondered if she should feel disappointed that they weren't going to get a chance to speak on their own, but the two faces beaming at her from the chairs batted that thought right out of the park. As did the easy atmosphere and obvious love between them. In some ways it reminded her of Todd's relationship with her mum. Funny. Cheeky. All about love. Caro immediately felt herself relax.

'It's good to meet you,' she said, hugging each of them in turn. 'Cammy told me all about you both.'

Josie cackled. 'Did he say anything about getting a restraining order in the same sentence?'

Caro was chuckling now too. 'He said he tried but it wouldn't work, because you have no fear of the authorities.'

They were still laughing when a waiter came over to take a new drinks order. She asked for a gin and tonic. It wasn't up there with, say, going on a search to find herself or taking a world cruise, but it was just one of the little things she'd found herself embracing. There had been major things too. She'd decided to sell her house. She was going to take a sabbatical from work, and do a bit of travelling. She'd come to this hotel. She'd bought some new clothes. Okay, it was a smart suit for her mum's funeral, but in past days, she'd just have gone with the old trusty one she'd had for years. But no. Caro had decided that after years of looking after her mum, of living the same life, doing the same things every day, it was time to start living. Really living.

These women seemed like they knew a thing or two about that. For ten minutes or so, they chatted, their conversations easy, full of warmth and fun, invariably teasing Cammy in that way that made it obvious just how much they loved him.

Caro loved every moment of it.

'Right, so I have to ask...' Josie blurted.

'Here we go,' Cammy interjected. 'Don't say I didn't warn you.'

Caro took a deep breath, then exhaled, aping an athlete warming up for a challenge. 'Okay, I'm ready. Shoot.'

'Have you heard from your dad? Or that daft cow of a wife? Or that feckless tart that this one tried to propose to?' Josie asked.

The answers should hurt. Really hurt. Yet even as she prepared to deliver them, Caro felt no pain. It didn't matter. If she'd learned anything in the last week, it was that the lies, and the past and the people who didn't love her didn't matter. All that mattered was the future, and the people she brought into her life from this point onwards.

'He called, once, the day after I got back. I didn't tell him Mum had died. Didn't want to give him any kind of closure in case there was even a tiny bit of guilt in his messed-up mind. Anyway, he wasn't calling to say sorry, or to ask how I was. He was calling because his wife, his other wife asked him to...'

'She stayed with him?' Val gasped, incredulous. 'I'd have had my Don's balls off and his stuff in a skip.'

'She stayed with him,' Caro confirmed. 'She actually came on the phone and asked me to promise that I wouldn't contact Lila and tell her the truth about him.

Said his heart wasn't up to it. After all that he's done, she's still pandering to him, defending him, still allowing him to live a lie.'

'What did you say?' Josie this time.

Caro shrugged. 'I said he'd been using his heart condition to manipulate her and my mum for years. Then I said he could rot in hell.'

'Good girl,' Josie responded.

'It wasn't my best work,' Caro said, with a rueful smile.

'Are you going to tell her?' Cammy asked.

Caro shook her head. 'No. What would be the point? It's not my story to tell. They made it quite clear that she wouldn't appreciate knowing that she had a half-sister, sharing her space in her dad's life, and that they wanted to preserve their family unit. I'm not one for dropping bombs into people's lives so I'm going to leave them to it. It's up to them. I hope if you see her that you won't tell her either.'

Josie and Val gave her a look that wasn't entirely convincing, but Cammy nodded.

'I agree. No point in messing up her life...'

'Oh for the love of God, what are you like?' Josie reprimanded him.

He put his hands up in a surrender position. 'Look, I admit I was a first-class idiot, but come on; Lila isn't exactly going to welcome Caro with open arms is she? She'd hate it. It would cause chaos with her parents, and let's be honest, they're all she's got. Caro doesn't need the carnage that Lila would bring either. I agree with her – best leave them all to it.'

Caro nodded. They'd discussed this on the phone so none of it came as a surprise.

Cammy clearly decided it was time to change the subject.

'Anyway, enough of all that. So Caro, we were thinking...'

*

Cammy was trying not to let Josie's glare of irritation sidetrack him. He knew she thought he was sticking up for Lila and sparing her heartache by not telling her, but it wasn't that simple. His biggest motivation for agreeing with Caro was that it would prevent any more heartache for the woman sitting next to him, holding her own against the Glasgow inquisition by Josie and Val. Lila would want nothing to do with Caro, he knew that for sure. She was cut from the same cloth as her dad. Caro, meanwhile, was completely different, and she'd lost enough. Her dad. Her mum. Her life as she knew it. He wanted only good things for her, no more heartache. It was beyond strange. He'd known her for a handful of days, and yet he felt like he'd known her forever, got her, understood her. It wasn't like his relationship with Lila. This was more like the bond he had with Josie, with Val, with… Mel. He waited for the stab of longing that always consumed him when he thought about her. It didn't come.

'So anyway, we were thinking…' he said, switching from the topic of Lila to better things. 'You know I've moved in with Val until I find somewhere to live…?'

Caro nodded. He'd told her that he'd picked up all his stuff on the way back from Aberdeen.

'Well, we're having a party tonight to bring in the New Year and we'd like you to come.'

Caro's face broke into a huge smile, then immediately flicked to what looked like disappointment. 'Thank you so much, but I'm here with my cousin and his boyfriend and I couldn't leave them.'

'Of course you can't!' Val agreed. 'They're invited too!'

'Really? Because I'm sure they'd love…' She was cut off by the sight of the two gorgeous men alighting from the lift and walking towards them.

Val and Josie's eyes immediately followed in the same direction.

'Val, the one on the left is yours, I'll take the one on the right. He looks like he could lead a conga.'

Caro was laughing now, properly belly laughing, and Cammy realised immediately it was contagious. He also knew he wanted to watch her laughing for the longest time. No, it didn't make sense. And perhaps it would never come to anything more than great friends, but he was all in to find out.

Caro introduced her cousin Todd, and Jared, and they exchanged handshakes and hugs.

'Thanks for taking care of her last week,' Todd said to Cammy.

'I was happy to do it,' he replied, and the two of them shared a glance, a smile, a moment of mutual gratitude.

'Right, that's enough of the mushy stuff,' Val interrupted. 'Gents, you can either stay here tonight in a very civilised bar with all these very civilised people doing very civilised things, or you can come to my house, drink way too much, eat great food and let Josie teach you how to do the slosh. It'll scar you for life but it'll be worth it.'

'I'm so up for that,' Todd beamed.

'Hell yes,' Jared agreed.

Cammy felt a rush of relief.

'Then I guess that's what we're doing. Caro?'

Instinctively, he held out his hand.

Instinctively, she took it.

'Let's go,' she said, and Cammy knew. This was it. This was what it should feel like.

He squeezed her hand and followed the two couples in front of him, Val and Jared, Josie and Todd, each pair with their arms linked as they crossed the foyer.

'You know that she wants him to go travelling with her,' Todd whispered to Josie.

'You know that he wants to go,' Josie replied, and they danced to the door to the soundtrack of her infectious cackle.

Epilogue – Part 2

Bernadette and Lila

'That woman has the best laugh I've ever heard,' Nina giggled as a group passed their table in the foyer of the hotel.

Bernadette couldn't reply as she was in mid-action.

'Mum, if you start with the "Wheels On The Bus", he'll never let you stop,' Nina warned. Bernadette was having too much fun to care.

This had been Stuart's idea, coming out to a hotel to bring in the new year, rather than celebrating it separately or having it at home. Sarah had invited them to spend it with her and Piers and their families, but Bernadette had gratefully declined. It was time to be with her children and grandchildren and start a new tradition for their family. They'd arranged for a babysitter to take the little ones up to their room at 9 p.m., leaving the adults to enjoy the party that was taking place in the ballroom. Nina and Gerry, and Gerry's parents, and his two brothers and their lovely wives, and Stuart and Connor, Bernadette and... Just Bernadette. She hadn't yet got used to not saying his name in the same sentence, but it was still a blessed relief every time it dawned that she no longer had to.

It was amazing how quickly a lifetime together could be unravelled. He'd already had his lawyers send her the contracts to buy out her share of the house, just as Nina had demanded. She was a smart cookie, her girl. At first Bernadette had resisted, bending to his protests that it would completely wipe him out financially, but she'd finally signed this morning and sent them back. He'd just have to deal with losing his savings. Maybe there was justice in that. She'd lost years of her life to their marriage, now he'd lost his wife, his money, and according to Marge, there were rumours swirling as to his relationship with Lila. That kind of gossip could damage a pillar of the community.

Retribution wasn't the reason Bernadette had forced him to give her what she was due. The deciding factor had been the cottage that was for sale, tucked away in a beautiful little cul-de-sac down by the river, roughly halfway between Sarah's home and Nina's, about ten minutes either way. She'd made an offer for it and it had been accepted. Her settlement would be enough to buy it and to have enough left over to enjoy life, to go on holiday, to have some new adventures. Sarah's husband Piers, had already persuaded her to join them on a Caribbean cruise over Easter. She couldn't wait.

The best thing about it was that she hadn't had to ask Kenneth's permission. All those years she'd been desperate to go on a cruise and he'd blocked her. No more.

She'd insisted that Nina invite him tonight so the kids could share the celebration with both parents, but he'd declined. Instead, he'd boarded a plane to New York, going a couple of days early for some big medical conference he'd been invited to. It was probably just as well. Stuart had told her that Kenneth was still apoplectic that he'd dropped medicine and was refusing to take his calls. He hadn't even had a chance to tell him about Connor. Bernadette had invited them to Sarah's for Christmas dinner and had a great night.

Kenneth had spent the day alone.

The man was a fool. Well, good luck to him. Bernadette could honestly say that she didn't feel anger, or resentment or hostility.

She just felt free.

Fifteenth chorus of 'Wheels on the Bus' over, she headed to the ladies room, and Nina joined her at the mirrors. 'I've never seen you look so great, Mum. You're glowing. Makes me really happy.' Bernadette knew she was right. Sarah had made her go to the hairdressers, have a couple of highlights added to her hair, tonight she had a bit of make-up on. But none of that was what really made the difference in how she looked. That was all down to happiness, pure and simple.

'Thanks, my darling. If I'd have known it was going to feel this good, I'd have done it years ago,' she said lightly.

'I wish you had,' Nina replied. 'I really do. I hate the thought of him lying to you all those y—'

Bernadette put her hand on her daughter's to stop her. 'It's all happened the way it was meant to. I don't want to be all Doris Day, but everything for a reason.'

'I know,' Nina agreed, laughing. 'I'm just glad they didn't get together. Having her as a step-mother would have been a total nightmare.'

The first part of that revelation came as a surprise to Bernadette. She'd assumed that after she'd left him, Lila would have moved straight in and she'd be sitting on the plane to New York with him right now.

'They didn't? How do you know that?'

Nina was grinning at her now, like she was the only one who had no idea what was going on. Not an unfamiliar situation, it would seem. 'Mum, it's been all over the Internet! Haven't you seen it? It's like, the biggest social media story of the year.'

'What is?'

Nina pulled out her phone. 'Look. There's Lila and that's…'

★

Jean Pascal ran his fingers down the curve of her back, then back up across her shoulder blades, along her neck, her chin, stopping at her mouth. She kissed his finger, took it in her mouth, enjoying his groan of pleasure.

This was the sexiest man she'd ever known. And what did it matter if he barely spoke English, and the only French words she knew were Chanel and Gaultier? This was a true meeting of minds. Since Christmas Eve, when he'd sent her a first class ticket to join him in Paris, until now, they'd only left the bed to eat in gorgeous restaurants, luxuriate in a spa, take walks in the park, where they were relentlessly pursued by paparazzi. Neither of them minded.

This was like a dream come true. Jean Pascal loved to share their relationship on social media, so every public moment, and some not-so-public moments had been caught on camera and caused a frenzy when they were posted.

The irony was, none of this would have happened if it weren't for Ken and Cammy. If Ken hadn't made her believe that he wanted to be with her, she'd have broken it off long ago. And then, when Cammy proposed, perhaps she'd have said yes, and there would have been no story, just a few hundred 'likes' on her Instagram page for a cute video and a few shots of an embarrassing ring.

She was destined for more than that. Jean Pascal's video of her rejecting Cammy now had over a million 'likes' and tens of thousands of shares. Overnight she'd become a celebrity. People knew her. Others wanted to know her. Jean Pascal had chased her until he knew her intimately.

She had called her boss, informed him that she wouldn't be coming down to head office for their meeting and told him he could shove his job. It might seem rash, but she was all about opportunity and this was one that she wasn't going to refuse. He told her the company would have no option but to pursue her for the expenses she had illegally charged to her credit card, but when she'd gone crying to her parents about it, her dad had offered to pay it. He might not have been the most loving father when she was growing up, but at least the money showed just how much he loved her now.

So. Job gone. Cammy gone. Ken gone. But she didn't care. That was her old life. This was her new one. Just her. Jean Pascal. And a camera lens.

Not that she was deluding herself. She'd done her research. She knew that Jean Pascal had a hideous reputation, and a long trail of womanising and broken relationships behind him. He was a serial playboy, who never settled with one woman for more than a couple of months. But Lila was pretty sure she could change that. And if she didn't?

That was fine by her. The break-up would cause a huge stir, hit the headlines, bring her even more followers. Jean Pascal might have brought the attention, but she was pretty sure she had what it took to keep it.

Screw Ken. Screw his wife. Screw them all.

'*Chérie*, show me sexy.' Lila glanced up to see Jean Pascal holding up his phone. She shook her hair, adopted her best pose, smouldered into the lens.

She had everything she needed right here.

Her life was perfect.

The whole world could see that.

Click.

Acknowledgements

With immense and heartfelt thanks to the incredible team at Aria. I'm so happy to have found my publishing home here.

A Letter from the Author

Dearest Reader,

Thank you so much for choosing to read my book – I hope you loved it.

The basis of all my books is friendship, so I hope that when you turn the last page of one of my novels, you feel like you've had a meeting with a friend, one that may be happy, or sad, or facing tough times, or laughing until their sides hurt.

Most of all, one that you want to keep in touch with.

So please join me on Facebook, Twitter, and pop over to my website www.sharilow.com.

And of course, I'd be hugely thankful if you'd leave a review or share your thoughts on social media – don't forget to tag me!

With love and thanks,

Shari x

About the Author

SHARI LOW is the No. 1 best-selling author of over 20 novels, including *A Life Without You*, *The Story Of Our Life*, *With Or Without You*, *Another Day In Winter* and her latest release, *This Is Me*. And because she likes to over-share toe-curling moments and hapless disasters, she is also the shameless mother behind a collection of parenthood memories called *Because Mummy Said So*.

Once upon a time she met a guy, got engaged after a week, and twenty-something years later she lives near Glasgow with her husband, a labradoodle, and two teenagers who think she's fairly embarrassing, except when they need a lift.